A GRATEFUL NATION

To Paige —
Thanks for your
support! Hope
you enjoy!
Best!
[signature]

A GRATEFUL NATION

A THRILLER

IVAN WEINBERG

CURTIS BROWN UNLIMITED
NEW YORK • 2015

This is for Marilyn, as is most everything I do.

PROLOGUE

A SEMI-HUMAN SHRIEK PIERCES the jungle air and a female Io snaps her head up from preening her four-week nestling. Her talons clamp tightly to a gnarled koa branch, and her severe raptor eyes dart into the distance, searching nearby trees for her mate, who has strayed out of sight hunting mice to feed the growing chick. Mother and baby are frozen instinctively, DNA taking control to prevent the loss of another in a species on the brink of extinction. Only the hawklike eyes move, glaring down through scarcely rustling leaves toward the source of the interruption.

Fifty feet below, a half-clothed man, sweaty body covered with grime, bolts from the shelter of giant camellias. Adrenalin surging, he hurls himself into the open. Aging face craggy and lined, he scans the surrounding forest for sanctuary. A prominent faded blue-green dragon tattoo covers one of his glistening shoulders.

Another penetrating scream echoes off through the trees as a larger man breaks from the undergrowth a hundred feet away, legs pumping as he closes the distance between them. The pursuer is bare-chested, his stringy silver hair tied back under a filthy red headband and an ugly jagged scar puckering his cheek above a graying beard. The afternoon sun glints off a serrated combat knife in one hand.

They thrash through the nearly impenetrable bush until Dragon dives into a thicket, crawling desperately, then hunkers down, a hand over his mouth to suppress his gasping. Scar pulls up fifteen feet away, listening. Even the insects are silent, motionless, frozen in time.

Abruptly, several quail skitter into the jungle and Scar lunges reflexively after the sound. Dragon watches him thrash away through the scrub, then emerges tentatively and limps back down the path. Stretching a nearly depleted arm over the lowest branch of a massive koa tree he agonizingly muscles himself up and stares, still gasping, after his tormentor, through a clump of epiphytes.

Within minutes Scar returns, combing the bush on either side of the trail. As he passes under the overhanging koa branch, Dragon drops, howling, out of the thick growth above, crushing a knee to Scar's head and driving him to the ground. The knife falls free, and Dragon is on it.

Scar rises unsteadily and circles, shaking his head, then lunges for the weapon. Dragon sidesteps and seizes the momentum, mounting all his strength to grip Scar's arm and wrench him around. The two are suddenly face to face, eyes locked.

In an instant Dragon thrusts the knife forward, but Scar's superior size and strength are too much. Powerfully clutching the smaller man's wrist, he torques radically. The heavy blade thunks to the jungle floor. In a single motion Scar snatches it up and drives it home.

Steel slashes flesh, and Dragon buckles to all fours, gushing blood from his nose and mouth, then collapses face down into the sticky crimson.

Chest heaving, Scar drops to his knees and struggles to roll the body over. For a long beat he squints through greasy strands into the lifeless face; two fingers press the carotid artery. Slowly he rises, glazed, then fills his lungs and explodes an interminable animal scream that proclaims his dominance.

Far above, the female Io's head once again jerks toward the sound. She stares unblinking for several seconds, then turns back to her nestling and resumes preening the fuzzy down as the ritual below, an encounter as old as the rainforest itself, concludes.

PART ONE

THE REASON

"The heart has reasons that reason does not understand."
–Jacques-Benigne Bossuet

CHAPTER ONE

GRABBING NOAH SHANE BY the jacket, the reeking gray-bearded giant yanked him around and crushed his larynx with a huge forearm. Noah couldn't yell, couldn't breathe. Panic propelled the fingers of his right hand that clutched reflexively at the monster's grease-stained army surplus overcoat as he choked. In a desperate last effort to summon help, Noah kicked out for the door of the padded hospital room just as the crazed homeless veteran jerked him backwards. He went to the floor like a rag doll, the back of his head hammering the asphalt tile, splitting his scalp. Through a swimming haze, Noah could dimly make out the grimy fist raised high above him, a toothless grin, a God-awful thick stench of mixed unidentifiable human fluids—then black.

* * *

"Department Five of the United States Court for the District of Hawaii, County of Hilo, is now in session. The Honorable Robert Asaki presiding."

A round baby face made the dark-skinned, black-haired bailiff look no more than twenty-one, but the heft of a Sumo wrestler lent credibility. As he ambled to his desk at the right of the bench, he nodded a greeting to a deputy seated in the back of the full courtroom. Next to the deputy sat a middle-aged man in a brown corduroy jacket. His gray-black hair tufted into curls around the ears, merging with sideburns that extended down his cheeks and morphed into a close-cropped salt and pepper beard. Softly lined, deep-set, Semitic eyes surveyed the courtroom through round-rimmed gold spectacles as he groped to follow the unfamiliar proceedings.

Judge Asaki thumbed through a stack of files, then returned to the case on top, opened the folder and perused it briefly.

"Call *United States v. Samson*," he instructed.

The deputy in the rear stood and turned to his charge.

"That's your cue, Doctor," he said, and stepped into the aisle, allowing the defendant to precede him to the well of the ancient courtroom that was nestled toward the rear of the second floor of Hilo's historic Federal Courthouse.

Designed by Henry Davis Whitfield and constructed in 1914, the imposing structure was originally planned in the Arts and Crafts tradition. As built, a colossal Tuscan colonnade spanned the entire façade, above which a green terra cotta roof cast the building much more in the Classical Revival character. It was impressive, particularly for the Islands. And the external stylings found their way into this white-walled courtroom, trimmed in elegant blond woods, mostly hard mango from the local rainforest. The wood motif was echoed in the ceiling two stories above, and in a narrow balcony railing that circled the perimeter. The furnishings were opulent, large chairs with deep-brown, woven upholstering. The counsel tables and bailiff's desk continued the mango theme.

Rotating slowly over the well of the court inside the bar, an old-style fan was impotent as to the internal climate, given the up-to-date air-conditioning system that was installed in 1978, but it preserved a Polynesian colonial essence that was trapped in the DNA of this community. One almost expected Judge Asaki to be fitted with a white wig.

"*United States v. Dr. David Samson*," the clerk announced.

An attractive woman in her mid-twenties stepped forward. Her complexion, the color of rich café au lait, was complemented by the tailored gray suit and navy scarf at her neck, all of which resonated perfectly with the decor. "That matter is ready, Your Honor," she said. "Federal Public Defender Stephanie Kauna-Luke appearing specially."

The judge glanced down at her, then returned to scrutinizing his file through the lower half of his bifocals. "Is Dr. Samson eligible for the services of the Public Defender, Ms. Kauna-Luke?"

"I don't believe he is, Your Honor, but I haven't interviewed him with representation in mind. Dr. Samson is a physician with the Department of Veterans Affairs here on the Island. He is not represented at this time, and in a case of this magnitude, we agreed to appear for him specially until he obtains counsel."

"I see." He turned his attention to the prosecutor's side of the counsel table. "Are we ready for arraignment?" he asked.

A man in his mid-fifties climbed slowly to his feet, buttoning the jacket of his white suit. He appeared healthy and vigorous, face tanned in stark contrast to his snow-white hair. This was the U.S. Attorney for the Big Island, Marvin Pitts. "The prosecution is ready to proceed, Your Honor."

"Dr. Samson is not," Kauna-Luke rejoined. "He has not yet retained counsel."

"What about that, Dr. Samson?" the Judge asked the defendant, who had just arrived in the well with the marshal at his side. "You will need an attorney. The court must move this matter forward."

"I have made a request for an attorney who practices in the States to come over here and represent me, Your Honor," Samson replied. The delivery was slow, measured despite his anxiety: the practiced pace of a psychiatrist. Judge Asaki had an immediate aversion to him, interpreting the composure as indifference, and there was something condescending in people who referred to the mainland as "the States."

"I'm hoping to hear from him this week," Samson said. "I wonder if I could have another thirty days to make the arrangements."

"This court cannot wait thirty days while you shop for an attorney, Doctor." The judge was stern. "Understand, you are accused of complicity in a murder. The charge against you will be homicide in the first degree and the court takes such allegations very seriously. Do you wish to be heard on the matter of continuing bail, Mr. Pitts?" Though he was not about to remand the doctor into custody, teeing this up for the prosecutor's hyperbolized screed on bail and the attendant potential for incarceration would underline that this was serious business.

"As the court will recall, the prosecution opposed bail when it was initially set, Your Honor. We were concerned with the seriousness of the charge and the potential for flight. The government's position has not changed. Our office is informed that Dr. Samson's psychiatric practice at the V.A. compound at Kupuna is ongoing, and that he is continuing to knowingly prescribe the very drugs that resulted in the brutal homicide of a combat veteran of many years' service. Now, if Dr. Samson is continuing to administer these dangerous drugs to veterans in his care—"

"Thank you, Mr. Pitts." The point had been made and Judge Asaki wanted to maintain a tight rein on attempts to grandstand, taking care not to prejudice further proceedings. Nor did he want the case tried in the press. He did not acknowledge the two reporters seated in the first row of the jury box, but he was acutely aware. "I appreciate your concerns, but Dr. Samson has not yet been arraigned, let alone tried and convicted, on the allegations the government is making. As to the nature of his ongoing medical practice, that is a matter for another forum. Whether the Medical Board has any interest in looking into it, I don't know, but it is beyond the jurisdiction of this court. The only issue of importance to me on the bail question is whether we can expect Dr. Samson to return for further proceedings. He has a clean record. The allegations arise from his medical practice, not from any acts of violence on his part. He will be continued on bail pending arraignment, which we are going to keep on a short leash. May we have a date in three weeks, Madam Clerk?"

"April twenty-third, Your Honor?"

"That will be the order." Judge Asaki slapped the folder shut with finality. He picked up another file, then looked up at the defendant severely.

"Dr. Samson. Know that if you do not have an attorney by your next court appearance, your bail will in fact be revoked, and you will be remanded into custody. Hopefully, that will motivate you. And I would remind you that there are plenty of capable criminal defense attorneys right here in the Islands."

Before the doctor could respond, the judge returned his attention to the file on the bench in front of him and said loudly, call "*U.S. v. Avola.*"

CHAPTER TWO

"How many fingers, counselor?"

No response. Lights were flickering, but Noah still hadn't quite arrived home.

"How many fingers?"

Noah pushed the meaty hand out of his face with a feeble motion.

"So, you decided to rejoin the ranks of the living," the grinning guard snickered.

Peering up through the mist, Noah whispered, "The hell happened?" One guard held him in front, the other gripped his arm firmly from the side, propping his still jelly like body in the chair.

"'Colonel' Maxwell apparently got a little exercised with your insubordination. Decided on a little discipline. I told you not to humor his big-time military notions. Fortunately for you, we heard you boot the door and came to check it out. He was screaming something about you being the VC."

Woody, the guard supervisor of the sixth-floor jail ward at the Psych Unit at Highland Hospital, called upon the full extent of his first-aid training as he peered into one eye, then the other. "You were lucky. He might have really fucked you up. You wanna go down to the ER?"

"Ummm?" A number of synapses were still misfiring.

"Shane!" Woody tried again. "Help me here! You wanna have the ER doc take a look at you?"

Noah rubbed the back of his throbbing head. "Nah," he murmured.

"Sure?"

Mustering as much wherewithal as he could, Noah tried to look the part. "I'll be okay." *He'd been put on his back worse than this more times than a quarterback could count. Seemed like he'd always had a sieve for an offensive line.* "Asshole," he mumbled.

Woody jumped on it. "Wait—who?" he grinned. Any little wedge between lawyer and client was a delight. "You're not talkin' about the 'Colonel'?" He saw that the raz was wasted on this one, at least for the moment, and turned to pontification. "You oughta know by now these homeless guys are all like that. Off their medication and they're nuts, violent. You wanna stay away from the bigger ones, or at least have some reinforcements along. I shouldn't'a let you talk me into leaving you in there alone."

"Yeah, well, you guys ever hear of, ah," *The hell was it? Couldn't find. . . words. Mmm yeah*—ah—law-thing. . . privilege? How do I get anything—from the guy—with you guys. . . ?" He tried to get up, but it was a little dicey. ". . . in another galaxy for Chrissakes—there was no way—"

"Another galaxy?" the other guard queried.

"N'er mind."

"You don't sound so good," Woody told him. "I'm still thinking maybe you oughta let a doc look you over. I'm gonna have to do an incident report, y'know. They'll kick my ass if I don't have a medic sign off."

"Just put down I'm seeing my own doc, okay?"

"Are you?"

"Maybe."

"So whaddya wanna do now, counselor?"

"Get into some other—line a work." Noah finally managed to stand, testing his rubbery legs.

"Right. So will you be needing to go another round with your 'client'?" he asked, smirking.

"Not my client for long," Noah snapped, the inhibitor neurons still out of service. "I don't need this kinda shit." He'd meant it to be under his breath but he still wasn't sure where his breath was. Even through the haze, he wished he had it back the instant he'd said it.

Now was clearly Woody's moment. "Whoa, whoooa," he pleaded in mock protest. "Everyone accused by evil shit-kicking cops is entitled to a lawyer. Isn't that the party line, counselor?"

All cops, including jail guards, loved seeing lawyers, especially public defenders, get sideways with their clients. These were the bad guys, for

God's sake. How young idealistic PDs could defend them with such fervor was a mystery of their universe. There was a dance that had to be two-stepped between PDs and cops, but sometimes it got nasty. Their truth was that PDs made a business out of questioning the integrity of solid, courageous warriors who were sometimes dying on the battlefield trying to protect the community, and they didn't appreciate it. Years of being cross-examined by state-appointed mouthpieces left scars. Noah knew the mindset, and he detested giving them the satisfaction of knowing he loathed his own client. The guards were trading amused glances, chuckling.

"Okay, okay," Noah said, sighing. "I admit you guys are a lot of laughs, but I gotta get home." Noah blinked a few times and shook his head, wincing with the resulting stab of pain somewhere in his occipital lobes. "I think I've had about all the fun I can stand for one day."

Woody could apparently stand some more. "What about the 'Colonel,' man? Aren't you gonna take him home with you? You're not gonna just leave that poor mistreated victim of police brutality here all by himself? All he needs is a little love, y'know?"

"Yeah. I'm sure he appreciates all the sincere concern." Noah was already feeling the bruises as he started unsteadily down the hall—his head, his throat—his ego.

CHAPTER THREE

EXCEPT FOR THE SOUND of squeaking Nikes and the occasional shout calling out a screen, the gym was surprisingly quiet. No conversation, no banter, all business.

Arms extended, the 6'5" high school forward stepped deftly in front of a driving Noah, sealing off the lane to the basket. Noah pulled up in frustration. For a split second, he considered the shot, then snapped the ball outside to Sandy Sutherland who hesitated at the three-point arc, bespectacled eyes locked on the rim. Noah faked right and cut left, trying to break free and get open for the return pass, but the ball didn't come. *Wait.* He looked back. *He isn't going to. . .*

"No!" Noah gasped.

Oblivious, Sandy launched it. For three agonizing seconds, Noah contemplated murder, torture, mayhem– then the trey ripped through the cords.

"Shiiit. . . " Noah snorted, shaking his head, then muttered, "Nice shot," as he fell back on defense.

The sizeable knot on the back of his head, a memento of his dance with the Colonel last Monday night, throbbed, but little by little, Noah had gotten his legs back under him until by the end of the week he was nearly full strength. No way he would miss the high-level B-ball pick-up game on Swett Sunday.

Sandy and Noah's addiction to the game dated back to first year at Hastings College of the Law, four blocks away. Noah, a standout high-school quarterback who had, through lack of commitment, managed to achieve back-up, never-was, status in the position at Stanford, was definitely gifted athletically. Round ball was always a second favorite, so not long after arriving at Hastings, he launched a search for a week-end basketball venue and found the high school jocks from the Fillmore, along with the occasional City College ringer, at "Swett Sunday," which was played at John Swett Junior High gym in the Western Addition of San Francisco. Noah had immediately become a regular.

"Shane" and "Sutherland" being cheek and jowl on the seating chart, Noah and Sandy were thrown together from their first day at Hastings. Not lacking for brash, Noah pulled Sandy's somewhat more timid chestnuts out of the fire more than a handful of times. The Socratic method, the *Paper Chase* question-and-answer teaching technique employed by most high-end law schools, terrorized students into an early decision on whether they were truly committed to a career in the legal pressure cooker. The survivors developed vital litigation skills; those who succumbed sold insurance or ended up in therapy. Often when Sandy found himself babbling in the spotlight, Noah would step up to bail him out. The two formed a study group and a close friendship from early on.

In time, Noah dragged Sandy out to Swett Sunday and, despite his questionable athleticism, made a shooter of him. Unfortunately, he'd created a monster. Sometimes Sandy was hot, sometimes not, but he always made up for his classroom tentativeness on the basketball floor, firing the long ball, driving Noah crazy. And so it went, through three years of law school and into the tyro stages of their legal careers which they were able to tolerate, still cheek and jowl at the Alameda County Public Defender's office across the Bay in Oakland, in no small measure due to the weekly distraction provided by Swett Sunday.

Today, Sandy was definitely smoking; everything he put up was going in. After being down four buckets in the five-on-five half-court duel to fifteen, the good guys closed the gap as Sandy relentlessly poured them in from downtown.

Sensing disaster, the forces of evil became more physical, hammering Sandy's slight 5'10" frame mercilessly, trying to throw him off his rhythm, and finally putting him on his bony butt. Noah, six feet and thick, rivulets of sweat trickling down through the dark furry mat on his chest, was working hard to protect his smoking shooter with an elbow here, a hip there.

Sandy dribbled the perimeter, looking for the opening. Noah set an outside screen as Sandy approached on the right wing. As the criminal guarding Sandy dropped a shoulder preparing to bust the pick, Noah faked and allowed the defensive man past him. Drooling to clobber Sandy before he could power up another trey, the defender threw up his hands and staggered momentarily as Noah released on the pick and roll. An instant before he was hammered, Sandy lobbed the pass around the opposing guard to the cutting Noah, who took it to the house. Game over.

"I don't know why you get so uptight," Sandy said as they wandered from the court, toweling off. "I couldn't miss out there."

"Gray hair. That's what you're giving me," Noah told him. "Dude, throwing those bombs up like that? Look at this." He grabbed a lock of his abundant, kinky blackish mane and held it out from his temple. "Jesus. I'm only twenty-eight, way too young to have these."

Sandy paused and inspected the strands. "My shooting's got nothing to do with your gray hair," he said as they descended the stairs to the sidewalk and walked up McAllister Street toward the car. "It's defending the guilty. That's your problem. And now that's not even enough. You're all into trying to keep the psychos out of Bedlam. That's worse. A guy can get killed doin' that."

Noah's smile was engaging, even teeth contrasting with Mediterranean olive skin. "You got that right."

"If you'd be cool and not take all this shit home, your hair would be fine. So would your head, by the way."

"See, now that's your problem, Sandy. You don't take anything home."

"Oh, but I do," Sandy retorted. "And I'm gonna try to drink about a half dozen of 'em starting"—he glanced at his watch as they arrived at Noah's massive '78 Dodge sedan that he affectionately called 'Captain America'—"in exactly T minus fifteen minutes."

* * *

"Weren't the guards there while you were in with him?" Kate Waverly asked.

Kate and Noah sat on either side of a half-full pitcher that rested on an antediluvian wooden table, carved with the names of generations of

Hastings hopefuls. Sandy was in a corner, trying to take some easy beer money from a few semi-fried locals in a game of shuffleboard.

An ancient dive situated a few blocks from the law school, the Oarhouse was populated partly by law students and partly by hoodlums and halfwits from the surrounding Tenderloin District. Along with a battalion of other law students, Noah, Sandy, and Kate had made the Oarhouse their regular hangout, a daily refuge from professorial Nazis. Since they all still lived in the neighborhood, the beat went on as alumni.

Sunday night at the Oarhouse was dinner for Kate. She enjoyed the fried calamari, and invariably lined up a Caesar salad to go with it. The event was more of a weekly pilgrimage for Sandy, who tonight was already well on his way to a quota that was calculated to blur the horrors of the West Oakland courts and jails, to which he would return tomorrow. Noah just liked the feel of the place, old and venerable. It had character.

Kate had been the third musketeer in their study group, having transferred from USC Law her senior year, a refugee of a failed romance. She was bright, straightforward, and athletic, a combination of flavors that Noah immediately appreciated. Her shoulder-length wavy brown hair was often tousled, giving her an active, outwardly directed, non-self-possessed look. That may have been what prompted Noah's first impression that she was reasonably stable, a rare quality, to his thinking, among female law students. The gray-green eyes were deep set and engaging, and often flashed when she was roused in some way. The thing Noah loved most was her playful smile, which somehow projected a sense that she knew something she shouldn't. Their attraction was mutual, dangerous, and chronic, but strangely, apart from a handful of passionate moments that had misfired, sometimes embarrassingly, they had never been able to get a significant romance jump-started. Even so, neither had given up on something deeper; hope surviving for three years now, if not yet springing eternal. Meanwhile, they both remained free-lance combatants in the dating wars.

"We were in this tiny hospital room," Noah answered. "There was nowhere else to interview him, so I had to send them out. It was complicated enough getting him to open up without having the gestapo poring over every word."

"Well, I know, but some PDs have been pretty badly roughed up in the lockup. I'm never comfortable when I'm locked in a holding cell with no guards around. And there was a PD stabbed in the neck with a pencil by a Symbianese Liberation Army thug in the courthouse jail downtown. Remember? Why would you take chances like that?"

Noah had no immediate answer. He gazed into his beer, then looked up. "Know what?" he reflected, teeth starting to grind. "I really am getting pretty damned tired of the whole charade." There was clearly plenty of last Monday's ration of rage remaining to provide leftovers. "It's not just about getting popped." He frowned. "It's a total pain in the ass trying to communicate with humans who're content with living in alleys under cardboard boxes. I used to think it was all about poverty, maybe schizophrenia, but now I'm not so sure. The psychotics get hospitalized. The City builds shelters, and the State builds housing to cover the rest. Social services provides jobs at unskilled workshops. But my clients? I get 'em out and they keep coming on home to the cardboard boxes. What, in the hell, is with that?" He rolled his eyes and, shaking his head, he added, "And what am I thinking, still setting that kind of bogus type? Who was it said insanity is doing the same thing over and over and expecting a different result? Einstein? Mark Twain?" He scoffed, shaking his head some more. "So who's the real crazy in this same picture I keep painting?"

Kate could feel her anxiety building. She always found herself uneasy with his displeasure, like she was supposed to fix it somehow. But the job dissatisfaction diatribe was the worst. The fear was that he'd leave the PD's office, find something else that wouldn't include her. What was that about? Was it some kind of quasi co-dependence? They weren't in a relationship, currently. And now recently she'd sensed this growing discontent in him, but from what? Was it the office? Was it her? She tried to stick up for the job.

"But a lot of those guys don't have a choice." She knew he had a soft spot for clients who got the short end of the justice stick. It had worked before. "They don't have a pot or a window, and scrambled brains don't fix them up with many alternatives in the job market."

His head tilted. He inhaled, then exhaled long and hard. Definite exasperation. "Dammit. I know that, Kate. How many times have we been through this? I get the 'urban casualty' thing, but I kind of draw the line when they turn out to be monster psychos trying to lobotomize me, y'know? Give me a murderer, a petty thief, even a bona fide psychotic, I'll tell his story for him. But alkies and druggies and garden-variety depressives who just want to wallow in it and take me apart in the bargain? That's getting old." The invective paused, then concluded: "I guess I'm just not buying the bullshit lines anymore. There's gotta be something better."

She definitely didn't like the sound of that. "Well, I guess I just don't get why you insisted on the nut run," she said, crunching a calamari. He didn't respond. After an uncomfortably long silence, she said, "Okay, okay, okay. I agree. So they're a bunch of sickos," she heard herself say. God, what a wuss. Hadn't she just been carrying those guys' standards into battle, not two minutes ago? Didn't take much to completely turn her around. "Poor, but sick," she added. Right. Totally feeble.

Sandy slid onto the chair next to Kate and clunked his mug down on the table. Noah wasn't buying Kate's effort to smooth it over. "Yeah. Sure. I went with the nut run," he said. "But this whole PD nightmare was your idea in the first place."

"Wait, wait," she protested. She wanted to soothe his disillusionment, but this was becoming unfair. "Don't I ever get to live that down? The theory was that the three of us get jobs where we could stay together. We were all on board with that. We had no idea when we signed on about being charged with saving bad guys who don't care much about being saved."

Noah stared at her for a long beat, then softened. "And such a beautiful woman to be so cynical." His face bent into a sly smirk as he reached over to flick her hair. "You're not ending up like the rest of us whiners, having second thoughts about this noble profession, are you Ms. Waverly? And all this time I thought you loved protecting guys who let their libidos lead them astray." She was the calendar PD in Judge Renee Krousse's court. Krousse was the feared nemesis of males charged with violation of Penal Code 270, non-support of children they'd fathered and wanted to forget.

Kate shrugged defensively. "Nah," she said. "I'm still okay with the

270s. At least my clients are mostly sane," she said with a chuckle. "A little horny, maybe, but sane. Anyway, I'd rather be dealing with deadbeat dads than clients who think I'm a stalk of broccoli."

"Easy now, Lady. Broccoli isn't all that bad. Broccoli as a lawyer might serve them better than some of those Oakland legal hacks." Noah topped off their glasses, draining the pitcher. "Broccoli's better on its feet than some of those guys, no doubt," he said, snatching another cruncher from the calamari bowl. "Wait, does broccoli have feet?"

The usual crowd noise nearly drowned out the distant emanations of a one-lung juke box which was valiantly trying to pollute the environment with throbbing rap.

"I loved the felony trial staff," Noah mused. "But this involuntary commitment stuff." He shook his head. "And I actually asked for it. The choice was that or juvenile. Christ. Should have gone with juvenile."

"Juvenile?" Sandy said. "You think?"

"I thought the nut run was going to be all about complicated psych issues." Noah held up the pitcher in the direction of Stork, the Oarhouse's lanky middle-aged bartender who doubled as waiter during the rush. Stork waved, and Noah looked back at Kate. "Even picked up some books at a used book store, a textbook, the DSM-IV, and read up on what I thought I was getting into. Unfortunately, it turned out to have precious little to do with science."

"Ya'vol—Heir Doctor likez da zienze—" Sandy could always be counted on for a contribution totally from left field, depending on how far into the brew he was. With Sandy, beer was an art form. Years of chugging had honed the skill of consuming half a mug with one draw while, to the outward observer, it looked like a sip. There was something almost Houdini-esque about it. He always seemed to be wasted before anyone else, raising questions about his capacity. On the other hand, pitchers seemed to inexplicably disappear around him, making him an expensive date. He stroked an imaginary goatee. "Vell, Doktor?" he said, then, realizing the schtick was in the tank, he tried to repair it. "So how'd you get so into psychiatry?" he asked Noah. "Is it in your genes somewhere?"

Noah shook his head slowly, and grabbed another morsel. "If it were genes," he said, "it would have been geological engineering." He contemplated for a beat and said, "Hmmm. Come to think of it, I guess my mom did spend a fair amount of time on the couch, but all she got from fifteen years of therapy was that it was okay to reside at the exact center of the universe."

"Was she in analysis?" Kate asked.

"Beverly Hills therapy."

"What's that?"

"The New Age school. Treatment meticulously calculated to last exactly as long as it takes to put the shrink's kids through college." Noah leaned back in his chair. "I don't know. Maybe I went for this nut run thing just to diagnose my own neuroses."

"Obviously haven't had much success," Kate murmured. "Might wanna get a second opinion."

"Pfffft." Noah flipped a leggy tidbit of the greasy seafood in her direction.

"I'll take misdemeanor trials any day," Sandy said. "Don't gotta know shit. Besides, they're actually starting to be fun."

"Fun?" Noah shot him a look. "Dude, being in trial had you totally petrified last year."

"Y'know, you do enough of anything. Though I gotta say, steady diet of petty thefts and auto boosting is getting old."

"Tell me," Noah said. "So is a total parade of ambulatory schizoids self-medicating with forties of Colt 45."

"There you go again," Kate said. "Remind me what happened to 'they all have their stories to tell'?" If she couldn't talk him out of the bad vibes, she'd at least take a few shots as lieutenant on the exaggeration police.

Again Noah gazed at her, the smirk returning. She returned the stare, chewing absently, even a little defiantly. Finally he thrust out a lower lip and shrugged. "I did say that, didn't I. Tragically, I discovered they all have a story, but it's always the same one, about the romance of living on the street with mottled brains."

"Right." Sandy raised his mug, by now unsteadily. "Here's to mottled brains. Anything like sweet-breads? I hear mottled brains're good with garlic and basil. . ."

Noah looked at his watch. "God," he said. "It's after ten. I gotta get home. Check out my cases for tomorrow."

"Ah," Kate responded. "One of those responsible broccolis."

"Best kind." Noah pulled on his faded jean jacket, then grabbed Sandy's shoulder, gave it a shake, and looked at Kate. "Come on, bro," he said. "I'll walk you guys home."

"Nah, I'm okay," Sandy told him. "B'sides, I think I'm gonna go one more round at the slab." He nodded toward a couple of bearded denizens thrashing the pucks around noisily. "I need some lunch money for tomorrow."

"I'm okay too, Noah," Kate said. "I'm going to finish this beer and polish off these last couple of squid. See you in the morning at the usual place? I'm gonna have to run these calories off."

"Sure you're ok?" Noah lowered an eyebrow at Kate. "I don't like this neighborhood, especially this time of night."

She looked over toward a weaving Sandy. "This superhero here'll walk me home when he finishes his business venture."

Noah frowned. "So, call me if the X-Man's fully in the bag. I'll be up."

Kate cocked her head, then nodded with a hint of a smile. "Thanks," she said. "See you at seven a.m."

He turned to go. "Franklin and McAllister," he said.

CHAPTER FOUR

TEN MINUTES LATER, ALMOST exactly ten thirty, Noah unlocked the door to his "suite" at the Larkin Hotel, a fleabag in the Tenderloin, five blocks from the Oarhouse. As he felt for the light, relishing how great a bed was going to feel, his foot kicked a fat manila envelope just inside the door. Flipping the light switch, he scanned the package. There was nothing more than his name, no stamp, but a label that bore the identification of California Messenger Service.

The ad had originally described the room as a "studio" but Noah preferred to think of it as his garret, which it was, in the roughest sense. It was nestled up under the eaves of a run-down three-story brick building mid-block on Larkin between Eddy and O'Farrell in the heart of the Tenderloin. Out front, drunks, addicts, and the homeless wandered the sidewalks and prowled the alleys for the garbage/refuse that kept them alive. At dusk, the crack whores began touting their wares on the corner, waving and baying at passing cars, in skirts cut to please and skin-tight camisoles.

The Larkin had been home to Noah since his first year at Hastings almost five years ago. After graduation, he'd discovered that it had been a bit of a commute to the Public Defender's office in Oakland, but he liked the idea of the bay serving as a moat between the violence and insanity of his chosen employment and the trappings of his natural habitat. The Tenderloin wasn't the suburbs, but somehow crime was less cruel, more manipulative, than the hard-core violent fare in West Oakland.

There was a kind of rolling catharsis in coaxing Captain America out of the chaos of the East Bay at the end of a brutal day, and gliding across the Bay Bridge toward the comforting lights of San Francisco. Often he flashed on the image of an enormous drawbridge, somewhere mid-span, pulling up behind him. The Tenderloin was somehow civilized, ancient; it had a kind of pre-Earthquake derelict charm.

Noah's garret was crafted precisely to his specifications, less decorated than adapted. Sports memorabilia hung everywhere. Posters of the old quarterbacks, Johnny Unitas, Bob Waterfield, and Otto Graham, adorned the walls, hiding the chipping paint beneath. He was partial to quarterbacks. Their travails were metaphoric, a microcosm of the daily task of survival. They huddled their troops, made a plan, and executed around it. When the play was over, these guys assessed the damage but didn't judge the outcome. They just re-huddled and made another plan. And so it went. In time, things settled out, and a result emerged. It was process. Win or lose, the great quarterbacks were always left standing, stronger, wiser, and more skilled, when it was over. The battle was everything.

Hanging alongside the quarterbacks were photos of Branch Rickey with Jackie Robinson at Ebbetts Field, Bob Gibson at old Busch Stadium. Then there was a broken bat supposedly used by Duke Snyder in the the '55 series. These were the titans who had done it daily, for years, withstanding the test of time.

Noah had handpicked the furniture at St. Vincent de Paul, a threadbare settee and a somewhat discolored overstuffed chair. Not Architectural Digest, but long on comfort. A bureau and an old armoire housed his limited wardrobe. On top of a prehistoric desk, its roll-top wedged open, was a tarnished brass lamp with a green glass shade that illuminated his workspace. Marred and marked, a circular maple table stood in the middle of the room, serviced by two unmatched wooden chairs. Noah might have had enough left of his paycheck after current necessities to afford a bit more sumptuousness, but then there were the student loans and the one-sixth share of the Warrior tickets.

Crossing the room, Noah struggled with the envelope. Before he had it open, there was a knock at the door.

"Yeah?" he said, pulling at the sealed flap. Painful experience from his early days at the Larkin taught him never to open the door on the first knock. Drunks and crazies were hard to get out once they were in.

"It's me, Noah," a small voice replied.

Noah smiled, returned to the door, and opened it to a petite eight-year-old with blond ringlets beaming up at him. Maggie was the daughter of his downstairs neighbor, Lisa Sanders, an attractive Minnesota emigrant to San Francisco in her late twenties who had found herself stranded in the Bay Area in her late teens and in desperation had gone to turning tricks to survive. Food, lodging, and a growing crack habit required a good deal of enterprise to support. Somewhere along the way, she had become pregnant with Maggie and the child had become her obsession, her chance for redemption. Lisa kept the child perfect, innocent, with her hair in ringlets.

Shortly after he'd moved into the Larkin, Noah met Lisa, or perhaps more accurately, Lisa met Noah. He immediately bonded with her precocious youngster, and he and Lisa became pals, confidants even, though it was Lisa who did most of the confiding. She had tried at first to make things more intimate between them, but Noah was not up to a potential entanglement, which might ruin his bond with Maggie. Then there was this deep Talmudic resistance when it came to sex with a hooker.

As luck would have it, Child Protective Services took Maggie when she was seven and placed her in a foster home with a middle-aged couple, the Goldmans, who harbored six such urchins. Noah had been instrumental in getting Lisa into a rehab program, then into work-study, and finally into a job at Kragen Auto Parts on Van Ness. Later, he appeared with her at the hearing on the application to end Maggie's foster placement and, after a long ordeal, the homecoming had finally come to pass.

"What are you doing up, squirt?" Noah said. "It's after ten thirty."

"It's okay. Mom said I could stay up until you got home."

"What's she thinking? You got school tomorrow."

"I know, but she said I could ask you something."

Noah reached out and scrunched her nose between his fingers. "Ask me what?"

She pulled away, and then, crinkling her nose and bouncing on her toes, she almost squealed it: "We're having a party tomorrow night and you're invited!"

"On a Monday night?"

"Mom has to work weekends. It'll be early."

"What's it about?"

Still bouncing. "It's a 'welcome home Maggie' party."

"Wow. Who's coming?"

"I don't know. Some of Mom's friends at work. The Goldmans and all the kids. Sammy, Rita, Mark, and Alexander, and—and I don't know, everybody. Will you come?"

"Wouldn't miss it if you're going to be there."

"I'm the guest of honor."

"Course you are. You want a Coke?"

"Mom says I'm not allowed to have Coke after dinner. She says it keeps me up."

"And she's absolutely right. Here I am trying to contribute to your delinquency. Your mom want me to bring anything for the party?"

"I don't think so."

"What time you gonna start?"

"About six. We're having stuff to eat—and a big cake."

"Well, I can't get there that early. I have court tomorrow, then I've got to stop by the office. But I'll get there as soon as I can, okay?"

"Okay." She stared at him, then frowned. "Noah, do you like your job?"

He cocked his head. "Why do you ask?"

It was a grown-up look. "You seem a little tired—and nervous. Maybe it's cuz you always get home so late. Do you think you work too hard?"

He shook his head slowly, marveling at her maturity but lamenting how early kids had to grow up in the Tenderloin. "You're a pretty perceptive kid, squirt," he said. "I didn't think it was that obvious."

"Maybe you need a vacation."

"Maybe I was just thinking that myself." He abruptly looked at his watch. "Hey, you gotta get to bed." He took her by the hand and led her through the front door, down the dimly lit hall to the stairs, and then he squatted. "Now gimme a hug," he said.

She threw her arms around his neck. "See you tomorrow at six o'clock!"

"As early as I can," he said, squeezing her, then he walked her down several stairs and looked after her until she reached the door of her apartment next to the second landing. She made a quick turn to him in the silent semi-darkness and stuck out her tongue. He jammed a thumb in each ear, wiggled his fingers, and stuck out his own tongue, then motioned her to go inside. The door closed, and he returned to his room, found the message envelope on the table, opened it and read.

Dear Mr. Shane:

I am a psychiatrist serving in a Veterans Affairs medical facility in a remote area on the Big Island of Hawaii. I was recently arrested and am informed I will soon be charged with the murder of a patient of mine. I am innocent and for a number of reasons I am reluctant to trust my representation to any of the VA lawyers or any of the local attorneys in this area.

I obtained your name from Professor Graham Kennedy at Hastings Law School whom I have known for many years, and am informed that you are a specialist in criminal law who may have some knowledge of psychology. I would be grateful if you would consider representing me. I am told you can be admitted to the bar in Hawaii for purposes of this case. I am willing to pay your reasonable fees.

I enclose an airline ticket for your travel to Hawaii on the noon flight to Hilo, Friday, April 7th so that we can discuss my case. I have left the return flight open. I will be away seeing patients for the next several days but ask that you call and speak to my assistant, Sgt. Grayson Slade, to confirm. My phone is 808-671-0808.

If you cannot get away this weekend, we can reschedule if you are interested, but the court has ordered that I have a lawyer by my April 23rd court date.

We are somewhat short handed and cannot get down to Hilo to pick you up, but if you are willing to come, I will have a rental car waiting for you at the airport on Friday with directions to our hospital.

I look forward to meeting you.

Many thanks,
David Samson, M.D.

David Samson? Who the hell was David Samson? A doctor? A psychiatrist? Hilo, Hawaii? Why would that old bastard Kennedy have recommended him? What in God's name was going on here?

CHAPTER FIVE

KATE WAS DEFINITELY TROUBLED as she and Noah jogged up Franklin toward Pacific Heights. At seven-fifteen in early April, they were thankful that their sweats staved off the lingering morning bite. Kate's mind was a jumble of fantasies, none of them pleasant. Heads down, they powered up the last block before the turn onto Broadway, and she pondered the unrest Noah had displayed the night before, his apparent dissatisfaction with his life—the job part, at least. When they hit the level stretch and her stride evened out, Kate glanced over at him and brought it up again.

"So what were you saying last night, Noah? You're not really thinking about quitting?"

He didn't look at her. "I don't know. I haven't decided anything yet."

She'd been counting on a denial and his ambivalence hit her harder than she would have predicted. They were quiet for the next three blocks as it sank in. She felt close to tears. The silence. "Why don't you take a little time off and think it through?" she said. "You haven't had a vacation since we started."

"Funny, I was just thinking the same thing."

The gradual uphill toward Divisadero leveled out a bit after Franklin.

"What were you thinking?"

"Hawaii, maybe."

"Whoa, Hawaii? I was thinking Laguna Beach. What lottery did you win?"

"Yeah, lottery is about it. Out of nowhere I get this package last night from some VA psychiatrist on the Big Island asking me to defend him on a murder charge. He even sent me an airline ticket."

She tried to compute this, then she frowned and looked over, wondering if she'd heard it right.

"What?" she said.

They were both still puffing after the long uphill grind. "Yeah. . ." he panted. "Ticket from this doctor in Hawaii."

"Well when were you going to tell me? What if I hadn't asked. . . about vacations?" she said. "What murder? Who. . . is this guy?" She suddenly wondered about how upset she was about this. What made her think he was under some kind of duty to report such things the instant they materialized?

"No clue," he gasped between strides, "but besides the plane ticket. . . he rented me a. . . car. . . and. . . is providing the accommodations. Thought I might as well. . . check it out. Hawaii might be good. . . therapy."

"A doctor? Don't mean to minimize your international reputation. . . but don't they have. . . criminal lawyers in Hawaii?"

"Yeah. . . That's what I thought. But for some reason he doesn't. . . trust. . . the locals. Funny thing is. . . Graham Kennedy at Hastings. . . referred him. . . ."

"Kennedy? The Civ Pro ogre?"

"I'm assuming. . ."

"How does this guy. . . know Kennedy? And why would Kennedy send him to you. . . ? You weren't one of. . . his favorites."

"I'm gonna call. . . the guy and. . . Kennedy. . . but right now. . . you know as much as I do." They were silent for a block, and then he added, "I'm thinking. . . couldn't hurt to take a few days. . . go out there. . . might steam clean my brains. . . a little."

"When are you planning. . . ?"

"Friday. . ."

She stopped, gaped, still breathing hard. He took a few more strides, then looked back. "This Friday?" she puffed. "Kinda. . . short notice, no?"

"Yeah. . . my guess I'll be back Monday or Tuesday. Can't imagine this going anywhere. . . " They turned back uphill. ". . . but then you can't argue with. . . a Hawaiian getaway. . . price is definitely right."

As they turned downhill on Divisadero, pounded the three blocks to Union, then right to Franklin again and back uphill, she listened to Noah rasping through his doubts about whether he was ready for a private case, particularly a murder that might turn out to be high visibility. He confessed that he fantasized about what he would charge, and was thinking this guy must expect to pay a pretty hefty fee, but he wondered whether he could deliver value for the big bucks. Then he went back to why this doctor would call him in the first place.

This particular loop was about seven miles. Noah and Kate had been running together since law school, that is, when things were going well between them. They tried to get out three times a week, but there were times when they didn't run together for a month or two. Their first year at the PD, there was a six-month stretch that seemed endless when they went without speaking, never ran. It followed a night gone bad at Bodega Bay, a little fishing village on the Sonoma coast north of San Francisco. Things had gotten intimate on the beach, then crashed and burned with Noah in the midst of some kind of phobia about the relationship, or relationships in general. She'd been confused, but they'd never been able to discuss it. There was something about him that just couldn't seem to commit to long-term. Must have been some kind of hurt as a kid. He'd talked about his father leaving, his mother being into her own thing. Kate's own family had been pretty tight. What must it be like to be abandoned like he was?

She'd been so enraged after Bodega that it took all of six months to approach normal, if that was an appropriate description for their manic-depressive attachment. More than a few times over the years, she'd thought she was in love with him, but she invariably woke up with a start as to where all this was going, really. All she knew for sure was that she loved being around him.

As they neared Hayes and her apartment, Kate again felt the anxiety tighten her chest. She couldn't imagine Noah leaving the office. But why? What did she expect? It had to happen someday. He drove her crazy, but she couldn't imagine life without him. Seemed like Hawaii was definitely the first step in a major unraveling.

They slowed in front of her building, still breathing hard, and continued to walk as they both cooled down. The hell with it. She wasn't going to let this go by default. "How about we continue this discussion at the Oarhouse tonight?" she blurted. "Dinner, maybe?" Oh God. Too possessive? She groped for a way to diffuse it. "Maybe get Sandy into it? He might have some thoughts."

"Thanks," Noah said. "I would, but I've got a thing I've promised to go to. Downstairs neighbor."

"Not that hooker with the little girl?" Kate snapped. "Is she pulling on you again?" It was out before she could censor it. Noah had some kind of caretaker streak that came out with this precious little family. It made her blood boil. She'd always feared he was just naïve enough to mistake it for real feelings, and she didn't need this now on top of everything else.

Noah's look was irritation. "Come on Kate. It's not like that, and you know it."

So now he was defending her. "So what is it like?"

He studied her. "She's a good person who's had a tough go is all. And she's got a great kid who deserves a lot better than she's had. Protective Services separated them. They were lost without each other, and now they're. . ."

"Yeah, so you said—more than once."

"It's just a little celebration of Maggie's coming back home." His breathing had slowed, and he drew a sleeve across his forehead. "That's all."

Kate gazed up the façade of the century-old brick building toward the windows of her apartment on the second floor. "I've always had the feeling it might be more serious for her than for you," she said, intending to plumb the depths. She'd heard him talk about Maggie over the years, particularly the last year. She tried to believe that this child was the main interest, but didn't the mother come with the package? Kate flashed on the three of them as a little happy family and winced. When he didn't respond after a few moments, she met his eyes again. They flashed an intensity for a beat, then he softened.

"C'mon Katie." He smiled and reached over to pull her headband off. Her hair tumbled over her forehead.

She cocked her head slightly and surveyed him suspiciously from behind the tousles. She knew this wisecracking routine and often found it attractive, but somehow didn't want to encourage it. It wasn't really him, the him that she wanted anyway, especially in what she considered a serious situation.

"You know you'll always be the only girl for me," he said smirking, sustaining the disgusting charming banter.

Irked, she turned and started up the stairs. "You're not cute. You obviously don't know what you're getting into here."

He grabbed her hand and tugged gently, returning to the real Noah. "Hey, hey," he cajoled. "Gimme a pass on this one willya? Let's have that pizza at the Oarhouse Thursday night. I'm leaving Friday."

She felt herself giving in, but she said nothing.

"Okay?" he said finally. "I'll call Sandy." He tilted his head, then tugged her hand and whispered. "Okay?"

Suddenly she wished she hadn't suggested Sandy be there. "Okay," she said, matter-of-factly.

"Great," he said. "I'd say let's have lunch today, but I'm in court over at the hospital. No time to get down to Oakland Division and back by two o'clock." He shook the sweat out of his hair. "Seems like I hardly ever see you around the shop since I'm over at Highland."

She looked down at him from the first stair. "You seem to be managing pretty well," she said with a remnant of sullenness.

"How about tomorrow? Twelve fifteen? What time d'you think Krousse'll break for lunch?"

"I don't know. Maybe. Call me in the morning."

"Good." He pressed her hand, looking pleased with himself; then he turned abruptly and jogged off down Hayes.

A gnawing emptiness seeded in her gut as she gazed after him until he turned the corner out of sight.

CHAPTER SIX

"CALL THE CASE OF Edgar William Maxwell."

Judge Frank Harrigut was well passed seventy, and had been the judge in the Superior Court Commitment Department on the third floor of Highland Hospital's Unit II for the last twenty-eight. The judicial fire had long since gone out.

Noah stood. "That's ready, Your Honor."

Maxwell entered through a door at the rear of the windowless, converted conference room, led by two deputies and shackled at the wrists and ankles like Hannibal Lector. It was diminutive as courtrooms go, with a bench that was more of a large desk in front of which was an abbreviated well with two counsel tables, all done in the usual gray metal. At a smaller desk to the right of the judge an aging clerk studied the files on today's calendar. To the rear, the empty gallery consisted of two rows of three seats on either side of a central aisle.

Maxwell, still reeking, but now dressed in an orange jail jump-suit, shuffled absently to the counsel table where the guards sat him next to Noah. For the moment he was docile. At the other counsel table, County Counsel Rowena Simmons was reviewing her files. Middle aged, dowdy, and obstinate, Simmons had been a social worker in a prior life.

Judge Harrigut cleared his throat. "Mr. Shane, I understand there will be misdemeanor charges filed against Mr. Maxwell," — he looked down at the file — "couple petty thefts and a battery, and that it will be the position of your office that he is not competent to stand trial. Is that correct?"

"That is provisionally correct, Your Honor. I have — ah — interviewed Mr. Maxwell and feel based thereon that he should be evaluated by a court-appointed psychiatrist to address the issue of competency."

Harrigut turned to the DA. "Ms. Simmons?"

She rose. "Your Honor, though he may be somewhat eccentric, we believe that Mr. Maxwell is perfectly able to stand trial. It appears that he stole some items out of a supermarket, and attacked security when he was detained. We see no reason to delay the proceedings and squander county funds belaboring a professed psychiatric condition."

"Response, Mr. Shane?"

"I believe the Court can judge for itself by looking at Mr. Maxwell that he is not in possession of his faculties. Moreover, charges have not yet been filed and there is plenty of time to get professional insight into his condition. If it would be helpful, I would invite Your Honor to interview Mr. Maxwell."

"Thank you, Mr. Shane. Ms. Simmons, any objection?"

A cautious, "No, Your Honor."

"Mr. Maxwell, would you please stand?"

Nothing.

"Would you stand up Mr. Maxwell," the judge persisted.

Still nothing.

"Deputy, would you help Mr. Maxwell to his feet?"

The guard standing behind Maxwell put a hand on his shoulder, and one under his elbow, and jerked him up. Maxwell lurched forward awkwardly, then suddenly lunged over the counsel table, reaching toward the judge and bellowing.

"Bugs! Leeches! Don't let him touch me! He's covered with bugs! Stop him! Leeches!" He thrashed at the chains.

The earlier painful encounter never entered Noah's mind. On sheer reflex he grabbed Maxwell's massive arm with both hands, trying to pull him back into his chair as one deputy yanked his other side and the second guard grabbed for his neck. Despite the chains, Maxwell jerked all three men wildly, knocking the heavy counsel table onto its side. Noah pulled the arm tighter, but Maxwell ripped loose, thrusting an elbow into Noah's chest and driving him backwards into the first row of the gallery.

Neither Harrigut nor his ancient clerk flinched. They'd seen it all before. The judge calmly pressed the button under his desk, ringing the alarm in the sheriff's office next door. In an instant three more deputies were up and on their way.

Noah reeled from Maxwell's blow, but bounced back to grab the shoulder of his jump-suit as the monster continued to strain at his chains, shouting about "bugs and leeches." The deputies were still grappling with him when reinforcements bolted through the door and down the aisle into the well.

"Okay, okay, big guy," the original guard repeated as all six, including Noah, wrestled Maxwell back into his chair. "We won't let the bugs and leeches get you." Noah slowly released his grip as the five deputies leaned hard on Maxwell, pinning him as he screamed and writhed. His panic slowly subsided, and the volume decreased, then at last the yelling stopped.

Without dropping a beat, Harrigut continued in a bland monotone. "Yeeess, Mr. Shane. Perhaps there is reason to believe that there may be a competency issue here. A psychiatric evaluation will be ordered so that the court may be informed." He looked down at his list of physicians. "Is Dr. Melvin Cohen acceptable to both sides?"

"No—objection, Your Honor," Noah panted.

"The County Counsel does object, Your Honor." Simmons was also unphased. "The evidence will show that Mr. Maxwell was able to—"

"Spare us the rhetoric, Ms. Simmons," Harrigut interrupted. It was almost surreal, the proceedings continuing with the counsel table on its side, Noah's papers and files scattered on the floor, ostensibly unnoticed. "Dr. Cohen will tell us what we need to know. You'll have your chance to comment. The matter will be continued for 30 days. May eighth?" His head swiveled slightly to the right.

"May eighth, Your Honor," the reptilian clerk intoned.

"We will be in recess for five minutes," Harrigut said, and exited through the door behind the "bench."

Three of the five deputies "assisted" Maxwell to his feet and dragged him toward the door. As he passed Noah his eyes locked on, narrowed, and continued to follow Noah until the squad of guards yanked him through the door. Noah scoffed and turned back to the task at hand, shaking his head slowly as he gathered his files from the floor. *Jesus. What is the sense in all this?*

* * *

By the time they finished the commitment calendar, it was almost six o'clock. Before hitting the commute, Noah made his bi-weekly stop at Main Office to collect his mail. As he riffled through the detritus of ads and magazines, a hand squeezed his biceps, and he turned and flexed reflexively.

"Now those are some kinda guns," the warm, deep voice resonated. Noah turned to look into the grinning face of a middle-aged African-American man dressed in gray Armani pinstripe and a blue silk tie.

"Oh, hey Fill," Noah said. He went back to his mail.

"Y'doin' my brother? You seem a tad down."

"Yeah, maybe a little."

Fillmore Parks was Boalt Hall Law, former PD, who now had a successful criminal defense and personal injury trial practice. He was a serious and thoughtful lawyer and a persuasive advocate. A year and a half back, he and Noah had co-defended a case in which Noah had the indigent armed robbery defendant, and Fill had the brains of the operation, who could actually afford an attorney. Fill had been a welcome mentor, and Noah liked that success had not spoiled him. Still invested in the East Oakland neighborhood in which he had grown up, he nonetheless found time for the public interest stuff, civil rights and anti-discrimination cases, despite a busy schedule.

"What's the issue? Hot shot like you oughta be ridin' high. Brains, a job, some major successes on tough cases." He cocked his head and looked Noah up and down. "And all the broads say you're one fine looking Jewish mothafucker. So what's up with the long face?"

Noah couldn't help but smile. "Just another wonderful day at the office, I guess," he said.

"Those nut-cases getting to you?"

"Right. Not much meat, and then there's the fact that one of my maniacs tried to take me out—" Noah's hand unconsciously went to the residual knot on the back of his head. "Twice now."

Parks' concern was immediate and genuine. "No way. When?"

"Last week, then again in court today."

"You okay?"

"No bones broken, but I gotta say it brought home that this whole catastrophe is getting old. I mean, I guess I like the lawyering. There's some kind of order in it. You bust it, you can win. But Jesus—these fuckin' mush-mind nut cases. What's the point?"

"Yeah. Kinda went through that same blue period myself. Ended up hanging up my own shingle." Parks reached into his inside pocket and drew out a pair of Ray-Bans. "You oughta think about it."

Noah checked out the Ray-Bans, shook his head slowly, fantasizing as they had the desired effect. "I don't know, Fill. It's a big step. Where would the clients come from? I got bills to think about."

"Y'know? You hang on to that kinda talk, and you're looking down the time tunnel to retirement still raking in your cool 50K a year. Now I know you got more goin' for you than that. I been in those god-awful trenches with you."

It wouldn't have taken much to convince Noah just now. "Maybe," he said, shuffling through the handful of junk mail a final time. He pitched it into a nearby wastebasket and started for the lobby.

Fill didn't let it drop. "I'm serious, man. Things were a little slow at first, but the clients started comin' before long. I swear I never looked back. Gotta just grab your ass with both hands and leap."

Noah nodded. "Maybe," he repeated. "So what are you doin' in the office?"

"Just had a conference with Milner. We're co-defending another two eleven—not unlike that one you and I had." They reached the double glass front doors. "You up for a cool one? You step into my office over at Ramona's, I'll give you a little more career counseling."

Noah glanced at his watch. "Y'know, I would, but I got a function tonight. Gimme a rain check?"

Fill smiled broadly, exposing a perfectly matched set of teeth. "I bet you do," he drawled, "and I'm sure she is something to behold."

"In fact, she is," Noah agreed. "Eight years old and the cutest ringlets you ever saw."

"What's that about?" They ambled across the large second floor foyer, spurning the decrepit elevators in favor of the stairs.

"Neighbor's party. It's her little girl."

"Alright, man. I'm gonna give you a pass this time, but you do truly need to give the private sector some thought. These kinda funks don't usually get better. Can strangle your soul, know what I mean? Your psyche's tryin' to tell you something here."

They reached the Fallon Street door. "Well," Noah said, "if there was anyone I'd want lessons from about breaking into the private bar, it'd be you. When I get there, I'll definitely give you a call."

"You wanna be careful about breakin' into bars, young son," Fill chided as they stepped into the early evening chill. "PD takes a dim view of that kinda thing from its lawyers."

* * *

Grayson Slade was late fifties, ruddy, pockmarked, short, compact. He rode the desk in the outer office of the administration building at the Veteran's Affairs Medical Center at Kupuna, Hawaii. Mostly former military personnel, the VA medical staff often continued to go by prior rank designation, and so it was "Sgt." Slade. Outside, a warm up-island breeze rustled the broad-leaf palms and towering tree ferns as the late afternoon sun cast long shadows over the front porch. The squawks of tropical birds and mongooses laid down a persistent background din which Slade had long since ceased to hear.

Kupuna was a remote compound that occupied a clearing in the deep jungle twelve miles northeast of the peak of Mauna Kea. The encampment was small, consisting of only three buildings: barracks, supply, and administration, the last of which contained Dr. Samson's office. All of the hospital's patients lived "off the base." Kupuna was carried on the VA radar as a "hospital" but the only medical services provided there were psychiatric, and the occasional first-aid by Slade, who doubled as a medical orderly. Any serious medical problems were referred to the ER at Hilo Medical Center, the VA Hospital at Pearl Harbor, or Tripler Army Medical Center in Honolulu. Kupuna was manned by a compliment of two: Samson and Slade.

Slade covered the receiver and turned to peer over his shoulder through the open door into Samson's office. Samson, seated at his desk, nodded.

"Are you saying you'll be able to meet with Dr. Samson, Mr. Shane?" Slade asked.

"Yes, I plan to fly over Friday." Noah caught a touch of the jungle sounds in the background as he sat at his desk in the 'suite' nursing a day's-end beer. He had a mental image of himself immersed in the tropics within days.

"Excellent. Dr. Samson will be pleased. Would you like to speak to him?"

"Definitely."

"Stand by."

Slade turned and looked at Samson, who nodded again. Slade punched the hold button.

Samson pressed the line key. "Noah Shane," he greeted him warmly.

"Hello, Doctor."

"I'm so glad you got my letter and have decided to take me up on my offer."

"I haven't really decided anything yet. I was just wondering why you-"

"Yes, I'm sure you must be curious as to why I thought of retaining you, how I found you."

"In fact, I was."

"I'll explain everything when you're here, but for now, let's just say I wanted someone from the Mainland and, and since I know very few lawyers, I called my old friend Graham Kennedy, who I knew at UCLA, before he went up to Hastings."

"How did you come to know Professor Kennedy?"

"I did a fellowship in Law and Psychiatry at the medical school and the law school at UCLA. He was my professor for criminal law, and I was impressed."

"You went to medical school at UCLA?"

"No. A post-doc fellowship when I was an army doctor. In any event, Professor Kennedy and I stayed in touch off and on over the years, so I thought to get his recommendation in this instance."

"But why me? I'm a PD, only two years in. Gotta be any number of lawyers from California, or anywhere else for that matter, who can give you the representation you need. Maybe somebody from Hawaii? I'd think they'd know the local prosecutors, which could be a huge benefit."

"Fair questions, Noah — May I call you Noah?"

"Sure."

"There are implications in my case that deal with the Army Medical Command. I feel that the case is being contrived against me by someone in the system. Maybe in the military. Hawaii is steeped in military tradition, and I simply don't know what I'm getting into locally. I just can't trust anyone from here."

Jesus, wasn't this guy going to answer the question? "Okay, but that still doesn't answer, why me? Why not someone with a few gray hairs?"

"I have a bias that with professionals, sometimes younger is better than older. Haven't been around long enough to get jaded, burned out. If he's qualified, I'd go with the younger guy."

He wasn't going to answer. What the hell is the deal here? "All due respect, Dr. Samson, you're still not answering it. I get that you don't trust the bar over there, and though it might be questionable to put yourself in the hands of a short-timer on a murder case, I also get your thoughts about young lawyers and their passion, but you still haven't answered, why me?"

Samson didn't drop a beat. It was a bit brusque but definitely flowed. "*People v. Ruiz,* a high profile special circumstances murder case, your first case in the office by the way, dismissed on your motion. *People v. Hildebrandt,* armed robbery with great bodily injury and a prior. Acquittal despite finger print evidence at the scene. *People v. Marian,* assault with a deadly weapon, also with great bodily injury, a third strike case, also an acquittal."

Christ. What's going on here?

"*People v. Martinez,* defendant charged with importing large quantities of heroin for sale, maintaining a meth lab, resisting arrest. Priors stricken on motion, evidence of imports suppressed, pleaded to simple possession of meth for county time. In addition, you've worked for a number of months on the commitment calendar and purportedly have a good grasp of psych issues, which my case is all about. Shall I go on?"

"Where did you get all that?"

"I've done my homework. I think it'll be a good fit and Graham Kennedy agrees with me. He thinks you're ready. But listen, we can talk about all this when you're out here. Then, if you don't think you're up to it, you make your own decision."

"I — I guess it can't hurt to talk."

"Wonderful. Sgt. Slade is second in command here, and since there are only the two of us, he'll have to stay close while I'm in the field seeing patients Friday. That means we'll be unable to pick you up in Hilo, but I'll have the Thrifty rental desk hold a car for you. I'll leave directions to Kupuna with them. You'll be arriving about fourteen hundred hours?"

Noah glanced down at the ticket. "Uh, yeah. Two o'clock in the afternoon. About how long will it take to get to Kupuna from Hilo?" He rolled the cold beer bottle over his forehead, then held it to the lump on the back of his head.

"It's about an hour and a half drive. We're a pretty long way off the trail."

"Can you tell me a little more about the case? What was the nature of the homicide? Is it in federal or state court?"

"I understand your curiosity, Noah." Samson gazed out the window at the stand of banana palms twenty feet beyond the buildings. A mongoose jumped onto the porch, skittered to the open front door, raised up on its haunches and glanced in, then scampered off into the trees. "I don't want to get into the details at the moment, but I'm looking forward to discussing the whole thing with you in person."

"Can you at least tell me about the charges?"

"Nothing filed as yet. We understand that will happen any time."

"Will I be staying there with you?"

"Yes, at Kupuna. We have accommodations for you. It isn't a resort hotel, but we make do. It's pretty warm and wet out here, so all you'll need are jeans, a few T-shirts, and a windbreaker. We'll supply the rest. We don't wear shorts because the bugs can get pretty oppressive. Have you got hiking boots?"

"I do. Should I bring them?"

"That would be a good idea. Like I say, we're pretty remote. You'll be in some rugged spots."

"Are you free on bail?"

"I'm not in custody —" Samson paused and took a breath. "You know, I don't mean to sound mysterious, but I really don't want to say any more about the case on the phone. I'll see you Friday afternoon."

"Was there violence involved?"

"Death is often violent, Noah. Good-bye."

CHAPTER SEVEN

"Noah!" Maggie shrieked. "Mommy, Noah's here."

"Hey, squirt," Noah said, grinning. "How's my favorite girl? Am I the first to tell you 'Welcome home'?"

"Nooo. Everybody said that. It even says it on my cake. But we haven't had any cake yet. You're just in time." She grabbed his hand and pulled. "Come on in."

The small living room was crowded with a smatter of people drinking wine and eating sandwiches. It was almost nine o'clock, but the party was still in full swing. There were only five adults and five children, but nonetheless a crowd in a room that was only a little larger than Noah's. The Larkin had joined it with the smaller room next door and called it a one-bedroom apartment. Like Noah's "suite," there was no kitchen. Just a sink, a hotplate, and a small refrigerator.

Noah pulled the hand with the brightly wrapped package from behind his back as he put the bottle of wine on the "kitchen" counter. Maggie spied the gift immediately.

"For me?" she squealed.

"You don't get a homecoming every day, do you?"

"Can I open it? Can I open it?"

"Sure," Noah said. She was already ripping at the wrapping paper. Within seconds, she pulled out a yellow-orange T-shirt with SQUIRT emblazoned across the front in green rhinestones.

She pasted a mock frown, put a hand on her hip, and protested: "I'm not a squirt."

"Yes you are," he said. "You're my squirt. Always will be."

Then she giggled. "Thanks, Noah. Can I put it on?"

"That's what it's for," a voice told her from over Noah's shoulder. Noah turned and smiled. Lisa had soft, pale blue eyes, above high

Scandinavian cheekbones. Her hair was fixed the way he liked it, and she knew it: loose, low ponytail with the wispy tendrils falling onto both shoulders. Her ample breasts were prominent even beneath the long, baggy green sweatshirt. He flashed back to her hooker days, even though there was no remaining trace. She was pure Minnesota farm-girl now.

Lisa put her arms around his neck and pressed the baggy green against him. As she kissed him on the cheek, she whispered in his ear: "I'm glad you're here."

"Me too," he said, hugging her.

"I'm going back in the bedroom to show the kids," Maggie announced after wiggling into the shirt, and she scurried off.

Lisa stared after her then turned back to Noah and lowered one eyebrow in a serious sexy pose. "Without you none of this would have happened, you know."

"You've done great things, Lees. Both of you. This is your celebration as much as Maggie's. Lotta people wouldn't'a had the courage to do what you did."

"Pooh. You thirsty?"

She marched him to the refrigerator, opened it, grabbed a cold beer, and handed it to him. "I'm assuming the wine was for me?" she asked.

"Right," he said, twisting the beer cap.

"Good, c'mon." She led him to the others. "Noah, I think you know the Goldmans? April and Marv? Maggie's foster parents?"

April Goldman was a heavy woman, draped in a large, gaily-painted muu muu that said major mom even from a distance. Marv was thinner, balding with a graying beard, deeply etched laugh lines, and a denim jacket that was worn around the edges, the uniform of the math teacher at John Swett Junior High. He pumped Noah's hand.

"Sure," Noah said. "Nice to see you. You did a wonderful job with Maggie."

"Takes a village," Marv said, smiling.

"We hated to give her up," April said. "She's a pretty special child. We're grateful to be able to stay in her life."

"I'm the one who's grateful," Lisa told her. "Come on, Noah. I want you to meet the Jenkinses. Bob's my boss."

As the adults chatted, the kids shrieked and yelped, jumping on the bed. Noah filled Lisa in on his upcoming trip to Hawaii, repeating his refrain that it was just what he needed at the moment. She mused about how she got it, that she would love some kind of vacation too.

It was almost ten o'clock when Lisa went to the counter and picked up the cake, announcing that it was getting toward time to "end this thing. . . it's a school night." As she made her way back to the group, the front door suddenly banged open behind her, and a large African-American man strode in without knocking. Everything stopped, and heads turned toward the intruder. Dressed in jeans and a tight black, short-sleeved turtleneck that exposed a cut chest and bulging biceps, he was imposing, and obviously loaded.

Noah knew instantly that this was Turk Lorimer, Lisa's former pimp, whom he'd heard her describe, and whom he might actually have seen a time or two around the neighborhood. Noah was immediately concerned from across the room about the level of sobriety even behind the sunglasses. He glanced at Lisa, who appeared stricken.

Lorimer wore a toothy crooked smile as he wobbled for a few seconds before he spoke, his focus on Lisa.

"Hey, baby," he said finally. The voice was deep and hoarse, vintage Lou Rawls but with slurred words. "Jus' passin' by and saw you're havin' a party. Figured I musta not got my invitation."

Lisa willed herself to stay in control. "This is a party for Maggie, Turk," she stammered. "You have to go."

Noah said nothing. He knew he was going to have to do something; unfortunately, he didn't have a viable game plan yet. This guy had to go 6'4" maybe two-thirty.

"C'mon now, don' be like that." Lorimer smiled broadly. "I don' mean nobody no harm. Wouldn' wanna spoil y'git down."

The room remained tensely silent. Then Lisa spoke again, using all her effort to be calm. "This is no good, Turk. You don't know any of these people. You gotta leave."

Lorimer started forward toward Lisa. Noah jerked. *Not yet— He hasn't touched her yet.*

"Jus' one l'il drink. Thas' all." He looked around for the first time, then back at Lisa. "An' maybe I meet some casper-lookin' white folks. Tha's all," he said again, more softly with a smile. He put a hand that spelled ownage on Lisa's shoulder. *Now he's crossed the line.* Noah took a step forward. This guy would probably pitch him out the window, but there was no way. He was going to have to take a stab at it.

Suddenly a steady, clear, albeit high-pitched, voice came from the doorway to the bedroom. "You have to go," Maggie said. Her face was crimson, etched with anger, no fear. "This is my party and you weren't invited."

Lorimer snapped his head around. "Watch y'mouth," he growled. "Jus' cause you ain't grown don' mean you can dis' mah ass. Git over here. We gonna get a few things straight."

"Stay where you are, Maggie," Lisa instructed.

"It's not nice to break in on someone's party," Maggie said. Several little heads could be seen peeking from behind the bedroom door. The adults were rooted.

Lorimer's nostrils flared as he eyed Maggie like an aging male lion readying to swat a disruptive cub. "And it ain' nice for a l'il' girl to have such a smart mouth." He cast a severe look back at Lisa. "Not impressed with the way you raisin' this child, lady."

This was going downhill fast. Before Maggie could respond, Noah stepped in front of the pimp and said: "Turk Lorimer, isn't it? I'm Noah Shane. I live upstairs."

He squinted at Noah. The wheel was turning, but the little ball wouldn't drop. "How d'you know who I am?" he asked darkly. "I don' know you."

"Seems to me I've seen you around the neighborhood."

He frowned. "I don' remember you," he said.

"Listen," Noah started again. "We're all having a good time. Why don't you join us for a few minutes? All Lisa has is wine and beer, but let's pour you something. Lisa? How about a beer for Mr. Lorimer?" He had no idea where this was going, but he needed to buy some time to compute before things got really ugly.

Lisa didn't move. "Everything's fine," Noah said, still smiling at Lorimer. He walked to the refrigerator. "We were all about to go home anyway. But why don't we hang out for a few more minutes?" He nodded to the Goldmans and the Jenkinses as he popped the cap on a beer and handed it to Lorimer.

"What about my cake?" Maggie asked.

"We'll think about that in a bit, Sweetheart," Noah told her in a measured tone. "Why don't you play with your friends awhile longer, and the grownups will all have a drink." He picked up a wine bottle and began filling glasses. Lorimer took a swig of beer as the others tried to resume their conversations, glancing over every few seconds.

"Listen, Turk," Noah said. It had some volume to it, meant to call signals for the upcoming play. "These folks are going to have to take off. The kids have to be in school in the morning. But you and I'll have another drink."

He turned to April Goldman, trying to sound like another afternoon at soccer practice, working out the logistics. "April, why don't you take Maggie with you. Lees, go along with them and put Maggie to bed. I'll stop by the Goldmans' in the morning and pick her up for school. Oh, and take the cake with you. You all can have a piece before bed."

Maggie started to protest. "But I wanted to—"

Noah shot Maggie a look. "You heard me, young lady," he snapped. Lisa grabbed Maggie without looking for her jacket. Bob Jenkins picked up the cake, and they were all out the door within seconds.

"Wait a minute." Lorimer wasn't all that steady. "Where y'all think you're goin'?"

"I'm gonna have another beer, Turk," Noah said, fumbling in the fridge. "You in?" He nodded a pressured goodbye to Lisa and the others as he waved for them to get out. He cracked the beers and turned to Lorimer, who was just draining his last one. When he heard the sound of the throng moving down the stairs, Noah handed Lorimer a replacement.

"I told Lisa I'd lock up." *The moment of truth: could he get this behemoth out of the place without a beating, namely his own? Even if he couldn't, now that Lisa, Maggie and the others were safe he could sprint upstairs to the suite and call the Marines if he had to.* He opened the door and shuffled out. To his amazement, Lorimer followed him. *Yessss.* Noah pressed the lock and closed the door behind them. They walked over to the landing and Lorimer quavered, one hand on the rail.

"Fuckin' ho was mah bottom girl a long time." He belched. "Now she thinks she's offa the stroll. Ain't none a mah bitches get vacations. I look like some kinda corporation mothafucker? This shit's all got consequences."

"Know what you mean," Noah said. He stopped and faked a swig. He'd had enough before he knew there was going to be a crisis. Now he wanted his head as clear as possible for when this got out of hand.

"Damn bitches better toe up proper." The fire was out in Lorimer's eyes, but the rant was still warm. "You don' be rollin' deep on the Turk. Stay till the fuckin' show's over. Know what I'm sayin'?"

"Must be a tough business," Noah observed. He faked another swig and sighed a long sigh. "You ever think about pitching it in?"

Lorimer squinted up at Noah, groping for a name. "Me?" He took a long pull, shaking his head slowly. "Nahhh, I'm ownin' this end of the hood. I'm cash down here." He drained the bottle, then fumbled for the rail to steady himself. The empty bottle flopped loose and bounced down the stairs below, rattling into the lobby.

"Listen, Turk. I gotta be up early. I think I'm gonna turn in."

Lorimer stared at feet, weaving.

"So, uh—" Noah hoisted his two-thirds full beer to him, then tilted it up and pretended to drain it. "See you around, huh?" He started up the stairs and was almost halfway up the first flight when the bellow came.

"HEY!"

Ohhh shit. Noah had an overwhelming urge to sprint for it, but he stopped and turned. "Yeah?"

Lorimer's gaze was still fixed on the floor as he wavered, jaw flexing. Noah stood motionless. *He could no doubt outrun the guy in his present condition, but he'd have to unlock the door when he got to his place, which would give the monster a chance to catch up.* He was reaching in his pocket to ready his keys for the mad dash when the beast slurred: "You gonna drink the rest a' that beer?"

Noah looked at him, then down at the bottle. "Mmm—uh, yeah. Uh, no. It's yours." *So much for sleight of hand.* He came back down a few steps and extended the brew to Lorimer who lifted his head with great effort and took the bottle. Holding it up to Noah, he smiled the crooked smile.

* * *

An hour later Noah was awakened by a quiet knock.

"Yeah?"

Lisa's voice was almost a whisper. "It's me."

He hauled out and dragged some sweats over his shorts. Opening the door, he found her in a terrycloth bathrobe and red striped flannel pajamas. She held a bottle of brandy and two tumblers.

"Can I come in?" The gaze was smoldering.

Uh oh. Alarm bells blaring. *God, she looked luscious. Yes, no, yes, no, no, NO.* "Sure," he said, opening the door wider for her, then closing it and following her to the settee.

"Sorry to wake you. We got the kids put down at the Goldmans'. Maggie stayed over there but I came back."

"So I see."

"I always told you my door was open any time for late talk over brandy."

"Right."

"Tonight I thought, 'Well, I'm still waiting all this time for a late-night talk—so I decided to bring the invitation up here."

"Nice, but—"

"Come and sit?" She leaned and patted the settee next to her as the half-buttoned pajama-top parted, revealing deep cleavage between rounded, ivory breasts.

Scrumptious. "Maybe just a minute," he answered.

She poured both glasses, handed him one, took a sip, then turned to him, pulling one leg up under her and extending an arm on the back of the settee behind him.

"You were wonderful tonight," she said quietly.

"No big thing. My new best friend, the incredible hulk. We just wanted to have a beer together."

"You're always there for Maggie and me, Noah," she said. They both took another sip.

Maybe a light anesthesia might make dealing with this a bit easier.

"I can't imagine anything more I'd want in a man," she said.

"Whoa. Let's not get carried away," he said, chuckling. But she wasn't laughing.

He turned and looked at her. She returned his gaze, the little girl eyes oozing sincerity, the low ponytail now tumbling down on both sides, framing her face. As she breathed, her breasts slowly rose and fell, her stare darting from one of his eyes to the other.

God, now what?

Clearing his throat, he glanced down at his feet, as if they might offer some profound insight. He took another gulp of the brandy, then leaned his head back against the couch. Drawing her other knee up, Lisa snuggled against him, and he rested his cheek against her hair. It smelled fresh, feminine, and dangerous. He inhaled deeply, exhaled slowly.

"Mmmmmmmm," she purred.

The street noise three stories down played in dissonance with her soft breathing. *She was so warm, so soft—What was he doing?* He sat up, superego finally overtaking the testosterone.

"Uh, listen, Lisa. You're driving me crazy, and you know that, but we—well—It's only going to complicate things."

She swept the bottle up from the floor. As she refilled the glasses, she said, "I'm not asking for anything, Noah. I went over to the Goldmans' with Maggie, and we had some cake. I found myself thinking about how grateful I was for what you did tonight, how you make everything right. Then I suddenly had this image that I was lying beside you, wanting to hold you, make love to you. So I hurried home and came up here. I just want to be with you."

He looked at her. *Was it really that uncomplicated? He always knew she'd wanted this, and he'd always been tempted, but so far he'd always made the "right" decision. Tonight seemed different. The brandy? She was beautiful, like some of the girls he had known in college, eyes innocent, face fresh and clean, like her hair. So different from what she used to be. But what about Maggie? If he made a mess of this it would ruin everything.*

He started to speak, but she leaned forward and kissed him, her lips parted, her eyes closed, her warm, feminine breath surrounding him. Her skin was soft, supple, as he touched her shoulders. He took her in his arms, his lips gently brushing her neck, her cheek. A deep warmth numbed him as he gazed through half-mast eyes. The single lamp cast the room in muted earth tones. Stroking her hair, he breathed deeply, taking in her intoxicating essence. As their lovemaking grew more urgent, it occurred to him that he couldn't recall feeling more cared for. . .

CHAPTER EIGHT

THE YOUNG WOMAN'S VOICE squawked over the intercom: "I have Dr. David Samson for you, General Reeves."

Brigadier General Harley Reeves sat at the large gray-metal desk in his office on the fourth floor of what they lovingly called the "Pink Palace on the Hill," Tripler Army Medical Center, a vague reference to the Royal Hawaiian Hotel a couple of miles downhill where sunburned tourists squealed and bobbed in the surf at Waikiki. A tall, well-built man in his mid-sixties, Reeves was more John Wayne than George Clooney. Wavy silver streaked through thick brown hair that swept back and feathered over his ears. Reeves remained tan and athletic from daily workouts in the Tripler gym, frequent runs, hikes, and regular scuba trips. Maybe he would have preferred the front lines, but there were definite advantages to being "quartered safe out here," at least for now. He put down his pen, leaned back in his chair, and gazed out the window at the morning sun on the lush green hills behind the sprawling hospital complex.

Major General Harrison Forsythe had been the VA Chief of Psychiatry for almost twenty-six years when he died suddenly almost a year earlier from what was tentatively diagnosed as a stroke, though there was no history of embolic disorder. As Chief of the Department of Psychiatry at Tripler, Reeves had taken command of the entire complement of Veterans Affairs psychiatrists in Hawaii on an "interim" basis while Washington sought a replacement. Civilian psychiatrists like Dr. David Samson fell under his authority.

"Thanks, Margaret. I'll take it." Reeves punched the phone. "David," he said.

"Hello General," Samson responded. "You called?"

"Just checking in to see how you're holding up. What's happening?"

"Things aren't so good I'm afraid," Samson told him. "They've set my next hearing in three weeks, and they're threatening to put me in jail."

"You got a lawyer yet?" Reeves asked.

"I'm still trying to get one, but I don't have a final answer from him."

"Who is he?"

"Just someone from the States."

"Why don't you get someone from here? Like I told you, I'd be happy to have JAG send someone over."

"No thanks. I think I'll have someone soon."

"Perhaps just until you get someone?"

"I'll be okay."

"So is there anything I can do for you?" His voice was sincere, inviting confidence, trust.

"Why are they doing this, Harley?"

After a lengthy beat, Reeves blew a prolonged sigh, "We've been through all this."

"I know. But I still don't get it. I'm getting great results. Why should they be so concerned now?"

"It's Washington. They're an uptight utilization culture of bean counters who hover over the numbers. Congress comes down heavy, especially in an election year, and they're in constant fear of heads rolling. You were in the military long enough to know that. GSA has a super sharp pencil, and that stuff you're using isn't FDA approved at the dosages you're giving. It's as simple as that. Fact is, I've reviewed the literature, and I don't know of anyone else in the world who's reporting the doses you are. Besides, it's a lot of men you're dealing with. They see you as costing the government a fortune." He paused. "And you're not making me look any too good, either."

"The literature now," Samson said. "But it's a major breakthrough. I'm convinced of it, and I'm going to publish all of it as soon as I finish gathering the data on these informal trials. It'll be approved by the FDA soon enough. Psychotherapy is finally becoming a real option for these guys. You should be happy about that. We all should."

Reeves leaned toward the phone. "See, that's the problem, David. You keep talking like that. Justifying it so Washington figures they're not getting your attention. I've tried to go to bat for you, but they don't listen to me anymore."

"Yeah, but a murder charge? What sense does that make?"

"I guess they're saying they're serious."

"I didn't kill him. There have been deaths before."

"I hear that, but the guy who did this was a patient of yours on these megadoses of SSRIs. They're convinced that that's what caused the whole thing. They're frustrated because they've warned you again and again. The way they see it, it's a power struggle now. Even reassigning you to Tripler last year didn't change anything."

"Harley, you know how I feel about these patients."

"Right. And you're the only one those lunatics seem to be willing to work with. But the point is that you've been told, you've had your requisitions cut, and you keep using more and more of the damn stuff. They don't like that, David. And you know what? I don't either. I've told you, too. Why the hell don't you stop? You don't have to be the hero. Let the FDA catch up with you."

"But if I'm not doing it, no one is. How will the FDA get any baseline? I'm plotting the dosage curves, and the next step is formal clinical trials. Besides, you know as well as I do it's the only hope these guys have. We've tried everything else, and we're finally getting some promising cognitive and behavioral changes. It's early, I grant you, but this is going to happen."

"Clinical trials? Right. When they've shut the regimen down completely? What part of 'No way' don't you understand?"

Silence, then Reeves moved to the real purpose of the call. "So where are you getting the drugs? They cut you off over a month ago."

"That's something I'd rather not talk about."

"Why not?"

"I'm not going to talk about it."

"See, now Washington wouldn't be as concerned if they weren't paying for the drugs. But the problem is that even though they're not supplying the drugs, your expenses are up dramatically in the last month anyway. You're hiding the cost of this stuff somewhere, and I want to know where."

"I really don't want to get into that."

Reeves dialed up the volume. "You gotta stop all this, David. I can't get these guys to back off. I would if I could, but they're serious about this murder charge. What good are you going to be to your precious jungle vets if you're in Leavenworth?"

"They're not going to convict me of anything. I'm only treating patients."

"I don't know. That's not what they say. The literature is full of studies reporting the violent side effects of Prozac."

"This wasn't Prozac."

"Same thing. It's an SSRI. When you get into doses that are ten times the recommended clinical max, they're all going to be the same. And they say you knew all that, that you knew the violence was a well-documented adverse reaction, but you continued the treatment, and didn't stop even after the violence. If they can prove that—"

"The SSRIs didn't have anything to do with the death, Harley. You get guys with these kinds of histories together, and bad stuff happens sometimes. It happens at every institution that deals with seriously disturbed patients. It's part of the risk. But like I say, good things are happening, too. We have to bear in mind that a couple of these guys are already starting to really come around."

"Meaning what?"

"I told you a few months ago that we started to get some memory about combat events. Now we're actually starting to break through some of the pre-war amnesia. It's fuzzy so far, but we're definitely making progress. If I can unlock this stuff, I've got a chance to get many of these guys functional after thirty-five years. We owe them some of their lives back if there's any chance."

Reeves's thick eyebrows gathered over squinting eyes, then he abruptly responded: "You need to let this go, David. The most recent diagnosis for them was PTSD. Everyone has bought that but you."

"I'm not giving it up, Harley. I've got to make this happen if I can. Besides, FHS is a whole different animal from PTSD."

"FHS?"

"Fallen Hero Syndrome."

"Where the hell did that come from?"

"I've started writing it up. I had to call it something. Descriptive, isn't it?"

Reeves paused again, eyebrows still furrowed. "What kind of clarity are you getting in these pre-war memories?"

Long pause. "I'm not saying anymore," Samson said. "I've got way too much trouble already."

"I'm sorry you feel that way, David, but you're on a path to a lot more of the same. I've warned you so many times now. I don't think there's any more I can do."

"I'm sorry *you* feel *that* way, Harley. I could use some of the power that comes with your stars right now."

"Not gonna happen. I told you. I've already squandered all the political capital I can afford on your little project. But listen, I wish you luck." He straightened. The conversation was over. "I hope you'll come to your senses and stop all this before you do irreparable damage to your career. Hell, to your life."

"Goodbye, General."

Reeves said nothing but he punched the speakerphone angrily. When the line went dead, he dialed the intercom.

The response was immediate: "Helms."

"Marcus? Can you give me a moment?"

"Yes, sir. I'll be right in."

In less than a minute, Reeves's secretary buzzed.

"Captain Helms here to see you, sir."

"Send him in."

A tall, African-American uniformed officer in his early forties entered and closed the door behind him.

"Have a seat, Marcus." Reeves had composed himself. "I need your help on a sensitive matter." He opened a file.

"Certainly, sir. What did you have in mind?"

"I know we've discussed this before, but I need to say again how sensitive Q407 is. Essential that it's strictly confidential. No reports, no memos, no emails, no writings of any kind. Any disclosure could seriously threaten both of us. Understood?"

"Of course. Q407 has always been top secret. National security."

Reeves studied him. He knew Helms was a family man, and even in today's army a captain's bars meant a lot to a Black soldier. "Good. Now I want you to take care of some records for me."

"What records, Sir?"

"Some of the old medical records."

"But we addressed the pre-1980 Q407 medical records ten years ago in Washington, General. Even before you came out here. They're all long gone."

"I know, but there might be some earlier things emerging now that we'll need to anticipate. All of the recruiting files have to be lost, too."

"Wow. That's going back a long way."

"Can you handle it?"

"Of course, General. But there are a few things I don't understand."

Helms had been his exec in Washington, and it had taken Reeves forever to get him out to Tripler. When he had doubled up with the interim VA job, they finally gave him Helms as an additional adjutant to handle the extra load of VA administrative matters. Reeves knew he could trust him, but there were still things to which Helms shouldn't be privy. But the captain had to know the minimum, lest key pieces be unintentionally leaked.

"What don't you understand, Marcus?"

"I guess mainly the criminal prosecution. I mean, why doesn't Washington just get him out of there?"

"We tried that before you came aboard, but it was botched. We tried to deal with it through a VA disciplinary action connected to the drugs, but Samson demanded a due process hearing. Claimed he would have lost his medical license if the charges stuck."

"So what happened?"

"Things threatened to get out of hand. Too much visibility. We finally had to dismiss it. That was two years ago."

"Why dismiss it? He was using huge doses; he was told not to. That seems pretty straightforward. It's insubordination if nothing else, isn't it?"

"Any further proceedings would have blown the thing wide open. We couldn't have that. We could control the peer review process, but if Samson was canned, he'd pursue it further in civil court. He's not military personnel. His case would have opened up all the details. I don't have to tell you what that would mean. These guys were all distinguished combat soldiers. We were into a war in the Middle East that wasn't so popular in a lot of sectors to begin with. We couldn't have it come out that combat does this kind of thing to our heroes."

"But if he's charged with murder, won't it all come out at a trial anyway?"

"The lawyers don't think so. 'National Security' they say. They think they can keep the sensitive stuff out on motion. Worst case, even if some comes in, the testimony is taken behind closed doors, and transcripts can be sealed."

Neither spoke for a few moments; then finally Reeves said, "So are we together on this, Marcus?"

"Absolutely."

"Great. What's the timetable?"

"Well, I don't know. We're talking about a fair number of names. These records could be anywhere. Sixty days, maybe? Maybe more. I have to do it all myself."

"Damn. That's a long time," Reeves said. "Let's get started."

CHAPTER NINE

THE OARHOUSE WAS PACKED on Thursday nights, but then, the Oarhouse was packed every night.

Sandy poured himself another. "Why is it still such a big mystery? Kate said Kennedy put the guy onto you. Did you ever call him to find out what it's about?"

"I did," Noah said. "Kennedy's on sabbatical."

"Sabbatical?" Kate said. "Then how did the doctor get in touch with him?"

"They said he just left last week. Old goat's gone to Nepal. Must have talked to Samson before he left."

"What did Kennedy's office say about Samson?"

"Didn't know anything about him."

"So, Noah," Sandy said, nodding over to the shuffleboard corner. "Wanna give a couple of townies a lesson in humility?" Kate knew she shouldn't have invited him.

Noah shot her a glance. "Nah. You go ahead. I'm gonna nurse this one and get home. Gotta fly tomorrow."

As Sandy wandered off, Noah put down his beer, leaned in, and took Kate's hand in both of his. "Thanks for worrying about me, Katie," he said, his eyes locked on hers, emotionless. She searched for any sign of sincerity. Suddenly he looked down and snorted, and she hit him in the shoulder.

"Bastard," she said, swinging at him again as he ducked away. "You make me sick."

"Best thing for nausea is a little night air. How about I walk you home?"

"Now?"

"Now."

They stopped at the shuffleboard table on the way out.

Sandy paused in his dismantaling of a bearded challenger, took a slosh from his mug, and admonished Noah: "So when you get into some big Hawaiian trouble over there, lemme know. I'll come bail you out."

"Don't pack yet," Noah told him. "I'm not planning anything more than a little R and R."

Noah and Kate wound through the throng, then pushed through the polished, bronze-plated door and into the evening. Ten minutes later, they stopped in front of Kate's building at Hayes and Laguna.

Noah took both of her hands, looked down, then up with a half smile. "I know you're concerned, Katie," he said, " but don't be."

"I wish I had your confidence," she said. A group of revelers from the Hayes Street Grill sauntered down the block and passed them, negotiating their next stop. Kate waited until they were gone, then continued, "We all came over here together. Now it feels like you're getting ready to leave. It scares me." The night was crisper than usual for April. She looked up, beyond the city's radiating light into the night sky where the stars were barely visible, and shuddered.

Noah pulled her over to the concrete steps in front of her building. The lobby was dark behind the craftsman glass door seven steps above. He peeled off his windbreaker and threw it over her shoulders, then drew her down next to him on the second step where they sat, silently. The ever-present sound of traffic a block down on Laguna, punctuated by the occasional honking horn and screech of brakes, was white noise that didn't reach the consciousness of either. Illuminated apartment windows of the surrounding buildings were protected by curtains and shades that shielded the domestic scenes within from the world outside. Hayes Street was quiet, and so were they, both lost in thought.

Kate had struggled with her hormones all the way home, and decided for and against it three times, but now it just slipped out: "You wanna come up?" she said, pulling his jacket tighter around her.

He looked down at their feet, the sidewalk, groping for a response, smiled, and finally stage whispered, "Whoa, during the nighttime when it's all dark out and I turn into a vampire?"

"I was thinking about it."

He hesitated another beat, then said softly, more seriously, "You think that's a good idea, Katie? We're running over a year now on a perfect record."

Her mind went back to the night on the beach in Bodega Bay that had started so perfectly, then descended into disaster. She looked down Hayes toward the lights at the corner, wishing this were easier. "Maybe you're right," she said.

Noah stretched an arm around her, and she put her head on his shoulder. They were in dangerous territory here, and both knew it. Both were rehearsing the unspoken dialogue, rejecting the choices.

Finally it was Kate who said, "Maybe records are made to be broken. We're different people now."

"All grown up," he said.

Suddenly she sensed a rising urgency. It felt like some kind of window was closing. She wanted him closer, but for some reason he kept retreating. "I don't like all this, Noah," she said.

"All what?"

"It feels like everything's getting away."

"What is?"

"You are." She turned to him, and he looked over at her. She searched his eyes. "Our lives together. Our future." There. She'd said it.

His attention returned to the street in front of them. "What did you have in mind?" he asked.

She continued to focus on him. "I don't know. Don't you ever think about what we mean to each other?"

"Sure I do."

She waited. Nothing. "So?" she said.

"Well, I—I like being together. I think we'll be important to each other even if I don't stay in the office."

"For Christ's sake, Noah. What does that mean? 'Important to each other'? Do you see us ever really *being together*?"

"I don't know, but I like the way things are."

Something broke loose. "Dammit. Maybe you're content to have beers at the Oarhouse, runs in the morning, chats about the office, mixed in with the occasional disastrous beach fiasco." Now he turned to her, with a look of concern. "Maybe that works for you, but I'm not about to wake up at age forty, still running along behind you, never having had a real life."

He stared at her, then shook his head disconsolately. "I'm sorry, Katie. I just don't know. I love being with you. We share a lot. I love doing all the things we do together." He raised an eyebrow. "And I'm sorry about that melt down in Bodega. I was nuts." He pulled his arm away and hung his head. "Jesus. I don't know. Something is just bent in me. I don't know what it is, but maybe if it's something more permanent you want. . ." The half mast eyes were wider now, fixed on hers, apologetic. "Maybe I'm not your guy. I just can't seem to get comfortable with it."

"What do you mean? With me? Or with the idea of it?"

He reached out and brushed her cheek with the back of his hand. "No. God, no. If I were to be with anyone forever, have kids, have a home, it would be you." He frowned slightly and shook his head. "You have to know that Kate." His stare was questioning. "You know that don't you?" Another beat, then, "No, it's me. I just don't think I'd be good at it. I don't think I could pull it off."

She studied his face, glanced away, shook her head, and looked back at him. "Oh, Noah—" Her eyes reached out, trying so hard to engage, to connect. "Of course you'd be good at it. You're a caring, charming, wonderful man. You'd be a great father. I hear how you talk about that little girl downstairs. That isn't the problem."

"Then what?"

Her brain was churning. Finally she said, "You're right. There's something bent, something missing. I don't know what it is, when it happened, or why. But you just can't seem to commit, to me, to this job, to anything. There's an emptiness in you somewhere."

He didn't respond.

"I'd like to be the one to fill that emptiness. And I think I could, only you won't let me in." She looked away, her eyes welling up. "Why?" she breathed.

He turned from her, grimacing. "I don't know," he said. "It just seems like I'll screw it up in some way. That's all."

"What are you saying? You see lots of women."

"I don't know about lots, but there's nothing in it. It's like nothing really matters. It's easy. Fun even. But it's not like with you." He cocked his head, squinted, grunted softly, searching for the words, then suddenly he turned back to her and said it, quietly, "If I let you love me, you'll be hurt."

Kate couldn't respond. Was it true? It was true. And it was too late. She did love him. She probably had for years.

He was shaking his head slowly. "But I can't let you go, either," he added.

It was torture, and her face reflected it. The tears were tracking down both cheeks. She sniffled, searching her purse for a tissue. "I know it feels like that," she murmured. "But you'll never know unless you try." She looked up and sniffed again. "You'll never fix it unless you give it a chance."

He exhaled, blowing out through his lips. "Maybe," he said.

A siren wailed as an ambulance pulled around the corner at Laguna, half a block away, and sped down the other way on Hayes. They stared after it.

She turned abruptly and looked at him, searching for something, praying for some kind of change, some kind of resolution. Suddenly the longing overwhelmed her, and she reached up, took his face in both hands, and kissed him. He pulled her in and held her as they drifted with the warmth, the textures, the scents of each other. Then, as it passed, she started to speak but he put a finger to her lips.

"Don't say any more, Katie," he whispered. "I really can't give you a better answer. I wish I could." He looked vulnerable, almost fragile. Then he straightened, reached an arm around her shoulders again, and drew her to him. His tone was even when he said, "Let's work on breaking that record when I get back."

CHAPTER TEN

THE INSTANT THE DOOR of the 737 opened and Noah stepped out onto the boarding stairs, he was immersed in the thick fragrance of sweet tropical foliage. The airport was open on all four sides, and people in flowered shirts and flip-flops hurried to meet deplaning passengers. The day was partly overcast, the afternoon rain having just passed through. The Islands were a new experience and Noah was buoyant, feeling as if he'd arrived in some exotic haven. He wandered to the Thrifty counter to pick up the car Slade had left for him, a late-model Corolla.

"There were supposed to be directions," he said to the attendant.

"To where?" She had a pleasant smile; a soft white-orchid lei hung from her neck in sharp contrast to her dark skin, beautiful teeth.

"The VA Medical Center at Kupuna?"

"Never heard of it. VA Hospital? In Hilo?"

"Kupuna. They were going to leave directions for me. It's near Mauna Kea. The reservation was made by a Dr. Samson, or Sgt. Slade."

"Don't know anything about it. Let me check with my manager."

She disappeared into a small windowed office behind the counter where Noah watched her conversation with a heavy-set, middle-aged Hawaiian; then he looked down the sparsely populated court to the end, where banana palms rustled in the gentle breeze. His mind sifted again through the whole project. He had checked the Veterans Affairs website for medical treatment facilities in Hawaii and found the VA Hospital at Pearl, the Veterans Home outside Lahaina on Maui, and the Spark M. Matsunaga VA Medical Center adjacent to Tripler. Then there were outpatient facilities at Hilo, Kona, Kaui, Maui, and Guam. No Kupuna. He had checked the Hawaii Medical Board site. No David Samson. Not dispositive, but curious. Still, a weekend in Hawaii was pretty much what he needed, and no denying, a guy could get used to this. But now no directions to the hospital?

"Sorry, Mr. Shane. There actually was an envelope for you after all. I hadn't seen it." She handed it to him, again with the warm smile.

Noah smiled back. "Thanks." Maybe there was something to all this aloha business.

"*Mahalo*. Enjoy your stay."

As he followed the directions out Highway 19 to the north, through the outskirts of Hilo, and onto the hip of the monster volcano, Mauna Kea, Noah marveled at the lush overgrowth that became increasingly dense as the road wound higher. At the foot of the slope, the landscape was scattered, intermixing rolling fields of Macadamia trees, papaya orchards, and cultivated flowers with residential streets and homes, but now there were walls of foliage on both sides of the road. Fourteen miles out of Hilo, he found the almost invisible unmarked turnoff that was described in the directions as: ".8 miles north of the Hanalea Fruit Stand." He turned right.

Very soon the "road" coiled gently upward, where the jungle attacked with a vengeance. In places the enormous tree ferns linked overhead into a lacy tunnel, shutting out much of the sunlight. Noah checked the directions again, struggling with names that seemed to lack in consonants. *Kaapaulaaka: easy for you to say.* And there were no signs.

Although Mauna Kea was the highest point on the island, some 13,796 feet, it was a "shield" volcano, named for the rounded appearance of a warrior's shield, rather than an impressive peak. Somehow Noah had envisioned a giant cone jutting upward out of the sea and rising above mysterious clouds that would shroud its higher reaches, with steam billowing into the ionosphere like something out of *King Kong*. Surprisingly, when measured from the ocean floor, Mauna Kea was by far the largest mountain on earth. Yet, apart from the notion that he seemed to be tending gradually uphill, Noah had no awareness of the proximity of any mountain at all.

The volcano hadn't erupted in the last 3,000 years, a source of some reassurance to Noah as he drove up its massive flank, but having had a Jewish mother, he couldn't shut out the niggling apprehension that maybe this meant it was due. "*Dormant*," *the airline magazine had proclaimed. The hell does that mean?* He suddenly visualized a cataclysmic explosion pitching his Corolla miles out to sea, where a tsunami carried it all the way to Tokyo. *This was no place for a kid from Beverly Hills. He belonged down on the beach getting one of those famous Island tans, smelling of coconut oil and working on his surfing.*

Guiding the little car through several forks, Noah stayed left according to the instructions as the tropical vegetation all but swallowed the narrowing lane. Zero traffic, but occasionally he could see a small, non-descript structure nestled back into a makeshift driveway hacked out of the trees.

Everywhere was living color. Enormous white, pink, and mauve orchid blossoms of varying sizes and shapes peeked through the lush green growth, lending credence to the Big Island's designation of "Orchid Isle." Its east side was one of the wettest places on earth, over 200 inches of rain a year. Far above was the tundra: arctic terrain where one could snow ski almost year round, the source of the name Mauna Kea, white mountain. *Hard to believe. It was a sauna down here.*

Finally he came to the sign described in Slade's directions as marking the turn for Kupuna VA Medical Center. It read: "Access Road." *Road? Really? End of the asphalt and nothing beyond but rutted red clay and mud. All he'd need is a car coming the other way and he'd have to back all the way down to Hilo.* The notes said it was another 2.4 miles from there to the compound. Noah coaxed the Corolla onto the trail, having no trouble staying in the two tire furrows that were three or four inches deep. But the vehicle vibrated like a lawn mower and periodically lost traction. *Piece of shit Corolla! This was definitely four-wheel-drive country.*

After lurching ahead for a few minutes, Noah negotiated a gradual curve to the left. A shadow suddenly flickered in his peripheral vision. He glanced over to see a small gray animal dart from a tree onto the ground, stop momentarily to stare at him, then skitter back into the neighboring vines. He thought it was a squirrel until the tail and small pinched face identified it as a mongoose. As he braked to get a better look, the Corolla bounced violently and jerked right. There was a loud pop from the right front, then a rhythmic thumping as Noah battled the wheel, and the car jolted to a stop.

"Dammit!"

He got out and surveyed the deflated tire. Squinting back down the narrow mud track, he saw the large angular stone emerging from the muck. The sun was still high, the air warm and damp. Except for a slight rustle from the trees, it was absolutely still, as if the entire tropical environment were holding its collective breath. Then, as it seemed to accept him, the buzzing, chirping and squawks slowly resumed, increasing to a steady din. He glanced up ahead, then back the way he had come. There had been no sign of life, no structure, for some time. He was alone. *What the hell kind of hospital was this? Christ, this was totally the very center of nowhere.*

Wiping his already damp brow, he glanced at his watch. Almost three-thirty, and still maybe a couple of miles to Kupuna. Too far to walk. Besides, he'd probably need the car soon enough. The good news was there was no apparent damage to the rim or any other structural components. He opened the trunk and fumbled for the jack and spare.

Twenty minutes later, the sweat streamed down his face, over his neck, and under his shirt as he returned the damaged tire and jack to the trunk, but hung onto the tire iron to give a final tightening to the lug nuts before resuming the trip to Kapuna. He slammed the trunk lid, and the jungle noises again stopped abruptly. Silence, then a sudden loud rustle in the trees behind him to his right. Later he thought he might have heard a grunt or some kind of animal snarl, but he never saw what hit him.

Adrenalin pumped him into total panic as the grimy, bulging forearm ratcheted up, constricting his airway. As his vision started to fail, Noah summoned all his remaining strength, and on pure instinct twisted his body to the right and blasted the tire iron into his attacker's ribs. There was an explosive release of breath, and the grip slackened for an instant. Noah lunged free and spun.

His first thought was "Rambo," complete with ripped and glistening bare chest, fraying camouflage fatigue pants, long hair and headband. But with the facial wrinkles and sagging midsection, this version had to go sixty or better, graying and tattooed, but still weighing in at something north of two twenty. The face was grisly, eyes wild, a large jagged scar on the cheek. The grin revealed a couple of missing teeth.

Noah circled, arms extended, tire-iron now in his right hand, knees bent, trying to stay away from him. "What do you want?" he yelled. "I haven't got any money!"

"Fuckin' VC," the maniac muttered, thrusting a gnarly hand at Noah, who swatted it away with the iron.

Again he grabbed for Noah's arm, "Slimy motherfuckin' tunnel rats."

Noah desperately dodged away. "Wait, wait!" he shouted. "I'm not who you think!" The monster lunged forward and drove him to the ground with a cross-body block, Noah's hand striking the hard clay, sending a bolt of electricity up his arm. The tire iron bounced free. Noah gulped for air, his solar plexus nonfunctional. Jerking him to his feet by the front of his shirt, the lunatic grabbed Noah's throat with the other hand. Noah croaked breathlessly, arms flailing frantically. Suddenly there was a booming voice from somewhere.

"Great work, corporal! You got another one. Leave him alive. Headquarters needs to debrief the bastard before we dispatch him to Buddha." But the nightmare on steroids didn't flinch.

"Stand down, corporal! That's an order. There may be a medal in this for you, but you gotta follow orders!" Slowly the crushing hold on Noah's larynx relaxed, and he slid to the ground.

Noah sprawled on his back and squinted toward the voice to see a silhouette move forward out of the sun. Struggling for breath and control of his legs, he tried to stand but flopped back onto his butt.

"That will be all, corporal," the voice ordered in a strident but more measured tone. "Return to base. I'll meet you there." The hulk paused reluctantly, glancing back at the figure like a rebuked tiger.

"Return to base!" the shadow barked again.

Slowly the monster moved to the side of the road. When he reached the tree line, he looked back, delivering a brief ferocious scowl, then silently disappeared into the jungle.

A hand reached out to Noah.

"Sorry about that. You okay?" The man was shorter than Noah by six inches. "I'm going to bet you're Noah Shane."

Noah scrutinized him, baffled.

"Grayson Slade," he said, now extending a hand in a more formal greeting. "Sergeant, U.S. Army, retired."

"Sgt. Slade," Noah repeated numbly. "Who in the. . . Who was that. . . lunatic?"

"Cpl. Ferguson gets a little out of hand now and again. Hope he didn't hurt you."

"I don't know," Noah managed, looking over his extremities and surveying the wreckage. "Thought for a minute he'd killed me, but I guess I'll survive." He wiped his brow. "Glad you came along when you did."

"Me too." Slade motioned back down the road. "My pickup is right around the curve there. Are you drivable?"

"Yeah. Just a flat. I fixed it. But what was that all about?"

"Great. We're about a mile and a half from the hospital. Pull up there about fifty feet. The road widens a little, so I think I can squeeze past you, and then you can follow me." Slade started back to his truck.

Noah wasn't about to let it go. "Wait a minute," he said. "Who the hell was that guy?"

Slade kept walking. "I'm sure Dr. Samson will explain everything."

* * *

"So, how's the world's most beautiful public defender?" Marvin Pitts put a hand on Stephanie Kauna-Luke's shoulder as he overtook her walking north on Waianuenue Street, a block from the Island's courthouse. The gooey opening line was typical, about as subtle as a cheap hair piece.

"What is it, Marvin? I'm kinda rushed." She looked much different than she had in the courtroom, now in a brown and red leather jumpsuit over a Calvin Klein T-shirt and jeans, with a matching brown and red motorcycle helmet under her arm. Law school and an uptown government job had resulted in a sort of "ethnic schizophrenia." By day, Stephanie was well put together in almost every way for the courtroom and conference room. Though at first it had taken constant vigilance and superhuman will to bring her Hilo street-speak around into the more dignified delivery of a federal public defender, after a while the cloak of multiple personalities became more natural. But once she left the Federal Building, the persona reverted to the Island girl that was indelibly etched on her soul. In fact, the only present clue to her day job was the black alligator briefcase poking out of her backpack.

The harassment continued: "You're always 'kinda rushed', aren't you. As a U.S. Attorney and a defense lawyer, we could be so much more efficient if you'd dance a little." He leered at the surfer girl proportions still visible despite the leathers. "What about it, Steph?"

"Not much of a dancer, Marvin, especially with married men. You got something specific, or this just one of your fishing expeditions?"

She arrived at the parking lot and stopped, turned to him, her dark eyes now serious. Tall at 5'8", she was near his eye level, Marvin being a shade under six feet. He smiled, not easily dissuaded and quite used to failure in the female fantasy arena. He was more uncomfortable with the potential of success. It was mainly the trash-talk that churned his juices.

"I guess I'd rather be wrangling with a barracuda, but there are a few loose ends we need to tie up. We've got those three goons with the meth lab on calendar tomorrow. Asaki is going to want to set them for trial, and I'm going to push that they go as charged. We've had quite a number of these would-be entrepreneurs lately, and I think it's time we sent a message."

"Sounds just like you, Marvin: 'Let's see, what can I do to ruin a few more young lives'? How we gonna nail some no-prior UH freshmen to the wall. Put another notch in our over-heated prosecution guns? Make your day, no?"

"Come on, Steph. I was about to tell you that when I met with the Disposition Committee yesterday, a couple of my young sharp-shooters convinced me we ought to listen to you about a deal on these guys." He gave her an oily smile. "I might be a Great White, but I'm not without feelings."

She eyed him severely, and then her face softened into a smirk. "I'm gonna ask your wife about that." She turned to address the lock on her sleek Suzuki Katana 750, also brown and red. "What's the matter? Your trial calendar too jammed for bullshit narcotics cases?"

He chuckled. "Okay, so we do have some bigger cases to worry about. But our loss should be your gain. What do you want to do with those guys?"

She swung a leg over the big bike and bounced it forward, sweeping up the kickstand. "What I want is for all three of 'em to walk and we waive the apology, but I'm gonna give it a little more thought."

"So what's up with Samson?" Pitts re-directed to the subject he had wanted to discuss in the first place. "Did he get a lawyer yet?"

She looked at him, detached, as she donned her helmet, tucking strands of straight black hair into the sides. "You know? I really don't know. Our office doesn't represent him. He told me after his last appearance that maybe he had somebody from the mainland."

"You might let him know that we've got no room on this one. It's gotta go as charged. Our office is dead serious, and I get the feeling Asaki wants to get it cooking."

One eyebrow elevated as she cocked her head. "What's this all about, Marvin? Guy's a longtime doctor, history of good work for the VA, and the way I get it, he didn't kill anyone."

"Suffice it to say, there's a lot of pressure. He's one of those bigger cases I was talking about. If you're in touch with him, best to let him know he's got trouble, *nui nui.*"

"Right," she said, his efforts at speaking Hawaiian seeming somehow condescending. "So, why don't we talk deals before the nine o'clock calendar in the morning?"

"Better yet, why don't I meet you for coffee in the lounge at eight-fifteen?"

Snapping the helmet strap, she said, "Pass. Got some other files to get ready. Take a cold shower, Marvin. See you at eight-fifty." She turned the key, and the Suzuki surged to life, growling ferociously a couple of times as she torqued the handgrip. She left Pitts with a quick forced smile, then noisily powered down Waianuenue and banked around the corner.

CHAPTER ELEVEN

"DEPARTMENT OF VETERANS AFFAIRS, United States of America," was written in unassuming black block lettering on both doors of the 1998 gray Chevy pick-up. Mud caked the rims and undercarriage, since there was no motor pool and only the daily afternoon rain to wash it.

Slade pulled the pickup alongside the small administration building that required frequent attention to keep it from becoming overwhelmed by the jungle. It stood three feet above the muddy surface on stilts sunk deep into the lava bed below. The rain, often driven by seasonal hurricane-force winds with gusts up to 85 mph, passed beneath it and down the flank of the volcano. Slade set the brake and got out as the Corolla glided to a stop behind him.

Putting the car in park, Noah studied the bearded man standing on the porch. He wore a faded blue, green, and gold aloha shirt and light khakis. *Strange. This had to be Samson. What's he doing here? Hadn't he said he'd be "off in the field seeing patients?"* Behind the wire-rimmed glasses, the psychiatrist's soft gray eyes followed Noah intently as he grabbed his bag out of the back seat and made his way toward the building.

Noah stepped forward and extended a hand. "Dr. Samson, I presume."

The staring eyes studied Noah fully as a smile played at Samson's lips. He took Noah's hand warmly. "Guilty, at least on that count. Welcome to paradise. I appreciate your coming."

"Couldn't very well pass up a weekend in the tropics, though I barely survived your welcoming committee." Noah put his bag down and drew a hand across his moist brow. "Some maniac nearly killed me a few minutes ago."

Samson regarded Slade severely. "What happened?" he demanded.

"Ferguson," Slade said without looking at him as he picked up Noah's bag and started inside. "Think he may need his meds adjusted. Won't do much good, though. He never was much on compliance."

"What happened?" The doctor was more forceful this time.

"Shane had a flat tire." Slade tried again. "He was out of the car changing it when Ferguson jumped him."

Samson turned back to Noah, concerned. "Were you hurt?"

"Panicked, mostly. Who is he?"

"One of ours," Samson said. "Come inside. Would you like some coffee? A soft drink?"

"I'm fine," Noah answered. "But I'd sure like to know what the deal is with this guy Ferguson."

"Come inside," Samson repeated.

Noah mounted the steps and followed Samson through the front office and into the inner sanctum. Slade busied himself out front at his desk.

Though the sun outside was still high, the light in Samson's office was subdued. An auburn hue from downward-canted wooden window blinds cast a warm glow on the faded blue and ochre of an ancient oriental rug. Noah's eyes slowly adapted to the dimness. The room was cool and still.

Samson moved towards a distressed cherry-wood desk that was scattered with papers and periodicals. Surrounding it on three walls, bookshelves that reached almost to the ceiling were overflowing with eclectic titles of traditional fiction and classics, mingled with familiar nonfiction, psychiatric and psychopharmacological texts, as well as binders of case histories. Scanning the spines quickly, Noah could make out Emerson, Thoreau, Hemingway, and Fromm, alongside Harper Lee and Steinbeck and the obligatory Freudian texts. A government-issue ceiling light was not in use, spurned in favor of a floor lamp that stood near the desk and threw light directly onto the work surface. Two unmatched armchairs faced the desk; behind them, an aging overstuffed Queen-Anne chair and another floor lamp offered an inviting setting for long hours of reading. A few feet away, a classical guitar crafted of a dark wood was perched upright on a chrome floor stand. On the rear wall were the only two hangings in the room: matching framed prints with Japanese calligraphy etched in bold black strokes. The place was redolent of books and leather, and a hint of candle wax.

Samson motioned him to a chair. "Sit, sit," he said with mock Semitic impatience. Noah obliged, relaxing into one of the armchairs. Samson settled into the other, spurning the scarred leather judge's chair behind the desk. Noah sensed that he blended perfectly with his warren, like Bilbo Baggins huddling down before the fire in his Hobbit hole. The lines around Samson's eyes seemed to exude a combination of comfort, humor, and confidence, a curious blend for a man accused of murder. The effect on Noah of the whole Gestalt was immediate and intense: a profound calm, almost hypnotic, quite sedating in the wake of the afternoon's events. He was surprised at his conscious awareness of how much he already liked this man.

"I know you must be curious about this whole affair, Noah," Samson began, "and now maybe even more so about Corporal Ferguson." He stirred a cup of tea that still steamed on the desk in front of him.

Intrigued, Noah watched him in silence. The yellow rays from the lamp glinted off the rims of Samson's round, gold glasses. His face stood in relief from the gloom behind him, like a portrait in sepia.

Samson spoke again, still staring into his cup. "I've thought a great deal about this moment," he said, "how I would explain all this to you. You'll have to get the whole story, of course, but it's hard to know where to start."

Noah didn't see the problem. He had interviewed any number of potential clients. *Why not start at the beginning and go from there?* "I've certainly got a lot of questions," he said.

Samson didn't answer immediately. Nodding slowly, he said, "I imagined you would. There's so much to tell, but none of it will really make sense unless you understand what we do here. I decided that it would be best if I show you around a bit first; then our discussion will be more meaningful." He glanced at his watch. "We still have a few hours of daylight. Let's make use of it, then we can return here for evening mess and I'll fill you in on the rest. I'm eager to have your thoughts, but I'm afraid it's all somewhat complicated."

"Whatever you say, doctor," Noah said quietly. "I'm covered until

Tuesday, so I'll have to make some decisions by then. Meantime, I'm at your disposal."

Samson was puzzled. "Tuesday? This Tuesday?"

"Yeah, I figured that would give us enough time."

Samson reflected for a moment. "Of course," he said, rising with his cup and starting toward the door. "Why don't you go with Sgt. Slade? He'll show you your quarters while I wrap up a few things and get the jeep. I'll meet you out front in ten minutes."

* * *

"We call it the 'guest room,'" Slade told Noah. "I think you'll be comfortable here."

They were standing in a small, nondescript, but private room in the barracks. Furnishings were utilitarian: a cot, a small desk, and a wardrobe. A window guarded by more wooden blinds looked out onto a cozy grass atrium between the buildings, where tropical flowers grew in abundance.

"It's where the folks from Tripler and Washington stay when they're in for audits and such," Slade rambled as he showed Noah the inside of the wardrobe. "Never had any complaints. The bath and shower are just down the hall." He pointed. "Water's okay for showers, but don't drink it. It's from a local well. Probably potable, but we'll bring a bottle for you anyway. If you keep your door closed, you won't be bothered by the snakes and mongooses. The bugs are pretty impressive, but if you use the netting at night, they shouldn't be a problem."

"That's reassuring," Noah observed. He stashed his carry-on in the wardrobe to unpack later.

"So I guess that's it," Slade said at the door. "If you need anything, shout. My room's down past the bathroom. Dr. Samson lives across the way in what we call the 'Supply Building.' Only one locked room with supplies and pharmaceuticals. The rest is a living billet: kitchen, mess hall, Dr. Samson's quarters. Like I said, it's not the Hilton, but we do pretty well with the basics."

"Right, thanks."

"Dr. Samson will meet you out front in a few minutes," he said, and closed the door.

Noah went to the window and gazed out, then wandered outside into the atrium. A heavy fragrance from the many blossoms hung in the air. He stood taking it in as the invisible jungle choir chirped and squawked against the accompaniment of a rushing stream just beyond the Supply Building. It was staggering to think that yesterday he had been in court, arguing that some inveterate derelict living under an Oakland overpass, who had lost touch with why one removed one's pants for purposes of elimination, was not gravely disabled.

* * *

"This first encampment will be Khe Sanh Village. We have twelve patients living there. It's the closest to the hospital. A little under three miles."

Samson had to shout to be heard over the rattles, squeaks, and groans of the grime-covered 94 Jeep Wrangler as it bounced ever deeper into the rainforest, its wheels often spinning in the deep mud. Each time it faltered, Samson would feather the gas to urge it forward, and the old warhorse would reach back for a little more four-wheel muscle to grind it out of the mire. It had a ragged canvas top that Samson kept up against the constant threat of up-island rain.

"You don't have any patients that stay at the hospital?" Noah asked.

"No. They're all outpatients in that sense, I guess, unless you consider the entire area the 'hospital.' I suppose that would be reasonable because Veterans Affairs built the outbuildings, though sometimes I used to wonder why they did. Most of the patients have opted to live in the jungle until very recently. But they're all considered hospitalized for purposes of record-keeping and allotments."

"So they voluntarily come in to the compound for treatment?"

"Most do not. I treat them wherever I can find them. I'm hoping that will change soon."

"How so?"

"You'll see that these men all seem pretty lucid right now, even somewhat cooperative. Many do sleep inside with increasing regularity. As I say, that's actually a fairly recent development. Until about a year ago, we had trouble convincing them to use the barracks, collaborate in the preparation of meals, eat together, or engage in any real social behavior. They were pretty much loners."

"Why? What's wrong with them?"

"Well, to begin with, they're pathologically independent types, but that's not really the answer. They undoubtedly share a profound mental disorder. It's a matter of some controversy. Some say it's PTSD, but I doubt that."

Noah looked over at him. "PTSD? From what?"

"Combat."

CHAPTER TWELVE

THE JEEP PULLED UP in front of a long, run-down, one-story barracks, covered with graffiti, set up against Mauna Kea's relentlessly rising flank. Lush jungle vegetation surrounded, overarched, and sought to devour it. The building, constructed of heavy plywood and perched on stilts like those at Kupuna, was quite large, but appeared dwarfed by the enormous tree ferns. Though moderately trashed from many years of abuse, the setting against the huge natural backdrop gave Khe Sanh a picturesque quality, almost like the pueblos of the southwest etched into a gargantuan limestone cliff.

Before Noah and Samson were out of the vehicle, a tall, unsmiling, bowlegged man with shoulder-length gray hair, gray beard, and military-issue wire-rimmed glasses approached. He wore a tattered camouflage-fatigue shirt and jeans.

"Evening, Rat," Samson greeted him, stepping down from the jeep.

Rat nodded. "Doc. . ."

The eyes were deep blue and darted from Samson to the jeep, to the nearby bush and back to Samson, avoiding Noah. The voice was cigarette gravel.

"I want you to meet Noah Shane, a lawyer from the Mainland who's come over to help me with the criminal charges down in Hilo."

Rat glanced over. "Mr. Shane," he said, nodding again.

"Any of the guys around?" Samson asked.

"Nobody but me."

"Can we come in?"

"Suit yourself." Rat turned and walked back toward the barracks.

Noah eyed him. *No Jay Leno or Regis Philbin, but friendlier than the maniac on the road.*

Samson followed Rat up the steps with Noah trailing. They stepped through an institutional double-door into a large room that occupied the full width of the building, with two heavily marred wooden tables encircled by six chairs each. Noah was struck by the emptiness. *Wonder when the dwarves get back from the mine?* Toward the other end of the room was an open door and a kitchen beyond. To the right of the kitchen door was a threadbare upholstered settee and chair, with a cluster of several more wooden chairs.

Noah glanced back toward the other end of the building. Another doorway, symmetrical with the kitchen door opposite, opened into large sleeping quarters with a number of metal cots, some with mattresses, some without. Only one or two appeared to have been slept in. At the end of the building was a bathroom. Noah noted that the broken windows and graffiti motif was carried inside to complete the ambience.

Samson walked straight to the settee and sat down. "How you feeling, Rat?" he asked. "Any panic attacks this week?"

Rat fumbled in his shirt pocket and extracted a single, bent cigarette, shooting a fleeting glance at Noah. "Not so far," he said, lighting up.

"You're taking your capsules?"

"Every day." He exhaled a large cloud.

"Good. I'd like to spend an hour with you first of the week. That work?"

"Nothin' but time, doc. You name it." Rat chewed nervously at his long gray moustache with his lower teeth.

"What about Monday afternoon?"

"I'll be here. No appointments."

"Have you thought about going down into town, maybe stopping in at the store for a soda?"

Rat's stare paused on Samson for the first time. After a few seconds, he said, "I really haven't thought about it. Towns aren't good places. There aren't any good places."

"I think maybe you're ready to try it," Samson said softly.

Rat's eyes narrowed. "I don't," he said emphatically.

Samson's expression was unchanged as he remained fixed on Rat's eyes. After a few moments, he said, "Why don't we talk about it Monday." No response. "So, has Cpl. Ferguson been around?"

Rat's stare persisted, intense; then he brusquely looked away. "Haven't seen him," he said.

"He was down by the hospital a while ago," Samson told him. "Thought he might have been staying with you guys up here."

Rat looked up. "Haven't seen him," he repeated, a little more volume.

"I was wondering what your thoughts are on whether he had anything to do with Sauce being killed. There was some talk about that. You know anything?"

The response was instantaneous and firm, dialed up a bit more. "I don't know anything about it."

"I'm concerned that some of the guys aren't taking their meds. I think Cpl. Ferguson may be one of them. You know, I really have to have that information if I'm going to--"

Rat stood abruptly. "I *told* you I didn't know anything!" he barked. "Do I have to draw you some kinda picture?!" He was menacing now.

Noah looked over at Samson. Still calm, he was nodding, not meeting Rat's angry stare. Finally he looked into his eyes, his expression serious but non-threatening. "All right, Rat," Samson said quietly. "Maybe you'd talk a little more about that with me on Monday."

"Maybe I don't have time on Monday after all," he snapped. It wasn't quite as loud, but it was definite.

"I thought you said you were available," Samson said quietly.

"Things get large, and small."

Samson was still calm. "I understand. We don't have to get into that if it's not comfortable for you."

"It's plenty comfortable, God dammit!" Rat shouted, walking toward the kitchen. He looked back. "I fuckin' told you I don't know anything. Why aren't you getting that? The Captain understands all this."

"I get it," Samson replied. "Why don't we leave it there." After a few moments, he said, "Listen, Rat. Are you sure you're taking your capsules—morning and night?"

"I said I was taking 'em, didn't I?" Rat snapped back.

"Yes, you did. But you seem a little on edge to me. Not as relaxed as you were last week." Pause. "Would you agree with that?"

"I'm fine. I feel fine."

Samson stared at him. "Alright," he said. "So, the food delivery is coming in Monday morning. Anything I can have them bring you? Newspaper? Magazine? Some chocolate, maybe? Tobacco?"

"Nothin'," Rat rejoined, grinding his teeth and flexing his jaw muscles. He rose curtly. "I think I'm done here. Got things to do, y'know?"

Samson stood, and Noah followed suit. "Alright then," Samson said as he started toward the door. "Thanks, Rat. I'll see you Monday afternoon." No response.

"Nice meeting you, Rat," Noah said as they left. Still nothing. As they walked out, Noah glanced back over his shoulder and through the door. Rat was gone.

* * *

"So what did you think?" Samson asked Noah as they drove away from Khe Sanh Village.

"Bit volatile," Noah said. "Loose associations. Panic attacks. Seems withdrawn, some fear of getting involved in any outside contact may be indicative of delusions of persecution, paranoia. Ambulatory schizophrenia?"

Samson glanced over with a raised approving eyebrow. "Not bad," he said. "Under other circumstances I might agree with you, but here, I don't think so. This behavior is fairly typical of these guys. They've been strikingly improved lately, but this is what you get if they short their meds. Some are even worse, like Ferguson. It resembles schizophrenia in some ways, intermittent psychotic manifestations, delusions, fears, panic. Problem is, there don't seem to be any frank hallucinations. Or at least they're rare. Also looks like PTSD in some ways, but the history doesn't fit. These guys were all outstanding soldiers, decorated in combat. Multiple tours. Rat—he goes by his initials, Roger Allen Trumbull—was a Ranger scout. Advance reconnaissance. He saw a lot of major action."

"Combat where?" Noah asked, looking over at him.

"Vietnam. These are all Vietnam vets."

"My God. Vietnam vets still living in the jungle after forty years?"

"Still living in Vietnam, most of them. Or at least still living in the war." He checked his watch. "I want to stop by Kham Duc. They named the barracks after famous Vietnam battles. Kham Duc is a little further out, but I think we can get there before dark. So, Noah, sounds like you've got a pretty good knowledge of psychiatry. Tell me about what you've been doing in the PD's office."

"First I'd like to hear a little more about Ferguson. Does this killing you were talking about with Rat have anything to do with the charges against you?"

"It does, but we'll get into all that when we get back. Tell me about your job."

Noah explained the nut run, his undergraduate training in psychology, and the psych course he had taken at UC Extension to get ready for the assignment. By the time he had recounted a few case studies, they had bounced another couple of miles down the narrow mud road and farther into the rainforest. Ultimately Samson told him that Kham Duc was just up ahead.

Seconds later, the jeep burst into a grassy clearing some fifty yards wide with a stream running down the far side. The water bounded and played in among black lava rocks with grasses of various hues of green lining the edge. Orchids and other tropical flowers pressed in, each competing for the splashing torrent. At the other end of the clearing, the road meandered in front of a barracks similar to the one at Khe Sanh. This time, there was no one in sight.

"I hoped there'd be someone around, but it doesn't look like it," Samson said as he reined in the Wrangler next to the stream, some fifteen feet from the building. The forest was not as intimately interwoven with the structure as at Khe Sanh. Samson went up the steps with Noah following.

Inside, the layout was identical to the other, but there was only one table and no sitting area. The place looked largely unoccupied. A back exterior door in the common area was standing open.

"There are seven vets presumably living here, but like the others, they still spend a lot of time in the bush. This is where Cpl. Ferguson is assigned. I haven't seen him in several weeks, and after that episode with you, I'd hoped at least to get a line on him, if not the chance to talk to him. Maybe assess his meds. . ." Samson's attention was suddenly drawn to the floor. He walked over toward the back door.

"What is it?" Noah asked.

"Looks like blood," Samson said.

Noah went over next to him. There were two sizeable slicks of deep red fluid, still damp, and a trail of intermittent drops and footprint smears leading to the back door. Samson was already out the door and down the stairs. Noah followed him.

"What do you think happened?" he asked.

The trail of blood proceeded to the stairs and down. There were a couple more bloody footprints, and then the trail disappeared into the wild grass. A few feet beyond, the trees marked the edge of the rainforest.

"Hard to say. Whatever it was, it was only a few minutes ago. The blood hasn't coagulated yet. There were several of them. Some were walking in it. They might have seen us coming."

"Someone's hurt." Noah said. "You think we should go after them?"

"I would guess, whatever it is, it's not too serious, or they wouldn't all have been gone so quickly. We used to see this all the time. These guys would get into it with each other pretty often out here. Things got a lot better after we changed the meds last year, but it's complicated trying to titrate the dosages and keep them all compliant. Compliance is the biggest problem."

Noah peered off into the jungle behind the barracks. "You think they're still nearby?" he asked. "Seems like somebody might need some medical attention."

"They're reasonably self-sufficient, used to doctoring themselves. And besides, you'd never find them out there unless they wanted you to. They're all accomplished survivalists." Samson looked up at the sky, then turned back toward the building. "It's getting late. Why don't we go back and have something to eat."

They climbed into the jeep, and Samson cranked it around the clearing in the gathering twilight. As they bounced back down the rutted jungle trail, the night intensified until it seemed that the inky blackness was closing in on all sides. The jeep's headlights illuminated only a few yards in front, playing on the undergrowth ahead, casting eerie shadows as the forest enveloped them in a seemingly endless living channel. Noah marveled at the speed at which Samson negotiated the twists and turns.

After ten minutes, the lurching and rocking of the jeep had begun to take its toll on Noah, who had been up early that morning and, with the time change, was beginning to fade. He leaned back and gazed ahead as the trail entered a tight set of curves and Samson had to slow to about ten miles an hour. As they rounded the last one, the headlights suddenly blazed off the figure of a massive man, twenty feet dead ahead. The lined face was glistening, blotched with mud, grimacing, contorted, eyes wild. Naked from the waist up, the monster was heavily muscled, flowing shoulder-length gray hair confined by a headband.

"Jesus!" Noah yelled, reflexively grabbing for the dash as Samson cranked the wheel and slammed on the brakes. The jeep went into a counterclockwise slide, the headlights spun, and Noah saw the apparition place both hands on the fender, vault clear, then disappear into the jungle. Samson didn't stop, but applied power and turned into the centrifugal skid, fighting the wheel to straighten out the jeep. The engine whined in protest as the rear end fishtailed. Finally, the vehicle acceded to Samson's commands and continued down the road.

"What the hell was that?" Noah gasped.

"You didn't recognize him?" Samson spoke evenly, apparently unfazed.

"Recognize him?"

"Yeah. It was Ferguson."

"My God! What the hell is he doing out here in the middle of the night?"

"Well, to begin with, it's only about nine-thirty. But secondly, he lives here."

"Lives here?"

"Like I said, we provide them food and lodging, but they'd rather be out here. It's more familiar, more anonymous. Pathological loners like these guys need that."

"Damn—that was pretty radical." Noah's heart rate was only now beginning to dip below a hundred.

"I noticed a few of the vets off in the trees between here and Kham

Duc, just as it was getting dark. They're curious, probably about you. You didn't see them?"

"I didn't see anything. Why didn't you point them out?"

"I didn't want to alarm you. They can be pretty intimidating if you're not used to them."

"Yeah, I had the crash course on the way in."

Noah gazed over at Samson who was wrestling with the bouncing vehicle. *This guy is nails! How can an unassuming shrink be so calm about these homicidal maniacs lurking out here in the dark? What the hell is he, some kind of X-Man?*

"What are they still doing out here? Why didn't they get hospitalized back on the mainland after the war? How come they didn't go home?"

"There's a lot to tell, Noah. Like I said, we'll get to all that."

CHAPTER THIRTEEN

"LONG DAY, YES?" SAMSON said as he worked the corkscrew into a bottle of Central Coast white. "How about some Chardonnay?"

The mess hall stretched the full width of the Supply Building at the end closest to the Administration Building and was distinctly non-military. A faded oriental rug similar to the one in Samson's office lent some warmth. A large teak dining table, surrounded by eight teak chairs, was covered with a cream-colored tablecloth. The service was Navy issue, white with blue rims, anchor insignia. The stainless flatware was matching, for the most part. Clear taster's glasses served as stemware, also of Navy origin. Two large candles in dark wood candlesticks illuminated the table. On an adjacent teak sideboard, another pair of candles added additional light that flickered on a large, dark Constable-like oil painting of a British countryside. On the wall opposite, an antique mirror added depth to the room. Noah surveyed it all, nodding. *Very civilized.*

"Sure," Noah responded about the wine. "I'm pretty much a beer guy, but it's not a religious thing."

As Samson poured for both of them, Slade brought out a colorful salad, served it, then disappeared. Samson raised his glass. "Welcome to Kupuna," he offered.

Noah smiled, nodded, and raised his in return. "You've managed to make it pretty comfortable here, Doctor."

"We try," Samson responded. "I think it's important to maintain a level of civility when you deal in brutality. It allows for a little perspective."

"Brutality?"

"These men have been severely brutalized. I don't think there's any other way of putting it."

"What do you mean, 'brutalized'?"

"How else would you describe being subjected to the horrors of combat for years until you've seen enough carnage, committed enough carnage, that you can't function with another human being, can't live peacefully in a community? Then, rather than being treated for your condition, you're warehoused on heavy tranquilizers, away from family, friends, childhood home, imprisoned in a God forsaken jungle at the end of the earth?"

Noah nodded. "I see what you mean." He ate in uncomfortable silence, not feeling he had anything worthy to follow that. Samson didn't speak, either, dwelling inwardly.

At length, Noah went to something more neutral: "How long has Kupuna been here?"

"Since 1981, in one form or another," Samson told him. "Most of our patients were hospitalized at the Okinawa VA after the war ended. Then they were brought here. We had fifty-two here originally. Now there are only twenty-eight."

"What happened to the rest?"

"Dead. Mostly by violence of some form or another. They've been pretty healthy, physically at least."

"How long have you been here?"

"Only the last eight years. They all have a fair amount of longevity on me."

"How did they pick the guys to bring here?"

"They're a special breed. You like the salad?"

"Very nice."

"It was decided early on that these soldiers, the heavy hitters in their combat units, simply couldn't be re-socialized into mainstream society. Too violent."

"Did they try bringing any of them home?"

"Not to my understanding. But I have to say, for their part, these guys preferred to stay here in their present state of mind. They didn't want to go back, or even live in contact with civilians here in Hawaii."

"Why?"

"Have you heard the term 'Bush Vets'?"

"No."

"They're veterans, typically of combat, who have taken up residence in the wilderness. There's a contingent in the Pacific Northwest, Washington mostly. A few others in North Carolina, even some in the Philippines. For one reason or another, they just can't exist in a conventional social unit."

"So what about the Kupuna group? Are they Bush Vets?"

"They are, but a bit more violent variety. These guys were the toughest of the tough, thrived on combat. All decorated. They adapted to jungle warfare, lived that way for fifteen years, some of them. They simply haven't been able to readjust." He looked up from the salad. "But there's more to it than that. The men in this group aren't just angry combat veterans; they have a distinct mental illness. You saw it earlier."

Slade arrived with the main course, broiled Ono with steamed asparagus and potatoes au gratin.

"Ever had Ono?" Samson asked.

"Never."

"Are you a fish eater?"

"Sometimes."

"It's our local variety. Firm white fish. Very flavorful. No one prepares it like Grayson Slade." He refilled Noah's glass.

"Let's see," Slade mused as he picked up the salad plates. "Only been doing it fifteen years. Guess you can get good at anything by then."

"Looks great," Noah said.

As Slade returned to the kitchen, Noah and Samson ate in silence. The candles flickered; from outside came an occasional weird shriek followed by alien chatter. Noah had no idea what kind of animal made those noises. Insects buzzed. The night sounds of the jungle were markedly different from the constant daytime din.

"What do you think accounts for the pathology in the Kupuna group?" Noah asked.

"I really can't say. There are lots of unanswered questions. I was about to say that last year I stumbled onto some research indicating that some of the newer antidepressant drugs were being successfully used in very high doses to treat serious mood disorders. Are you familiar with the SSRIs? Selective Serotonin Reuptake Inhibitors?"

"Like Prozac? Zoloft? Sure."

"Those are the ones. We use something called YM992. It's been an experimental form until recently. Sort of a super med that has the usual reuptake inhibition, plus what they call 5-HT2A receptor antagonism on the firing activity of norepinephrine neurons." He looked at Noah. "You know what those are?"

"Hey, remember, I only had an extension class in psych."

"Okay. Well, the studies were reflecting that the normal dose, around forty milligrams a day, was being doubled and tripled with good results. So I decided to give it a try."

"What happened?" Noah asked.

"Nothing, at first. We were prescribing eighty milligrams for a while. Then we decided to take a flyer and go to a hundred. We worried a bit about toxicity with sustained usage, but it didn't prove to be a problem, so we kept increasing. Anyway, I became convinced we were starting to see a clearing of thought processes. It's difficult to measure, particularly with the patients living on their own in the bush, but subjectively it looked like the frequency of violent incidents began to fall. It seemed like the men were able to interact on a more socialized level. This was just about a year ago now. I've continued to increase the dosages, and the results have been dramatic."

"How do you mean, dramatic?"

"Well, the volatility has cooled down, to the point we've actually been able to get some of them into psychotherapy. For the first time, they're able to discuss recollections of combat. Some have even started sleeping inside, cooking in the kitchens and eating together. It's remarkable. Before, we could hardly keep this population from killing each other; now they're beginning to interact." He returned to the Ono. "But we still have a long way to go."

"Why? What's the problem?"

"There's a list. First, we haven't had a long enough track record to know whether we're just cooling off current emotional issues, or whether the effects will be profound and lasting. Second, the progress is slow. They continue to experience episodes of panic and paranoia. They still don't want to come out of the jungle and associate with normals, or go into town. What Rat said this afternoon is typical. They just don't feel like they're part of the people world. Afraid of what they might do.

"Then there's the fact that a hallmark of the syndrome has been loss of long-term memory. None of these patients has any memory before Vietnam. No family, no hometown, no high school, nothing. We wanted to see if we could jog some recollection, so we tried to cast about for some of their biographies. But here's the major mystery: we haven't been able to locate any records, medical or otherwise, army or civilian, relating to any of them."

Noah cocked his head and frowned. "No records?"

"Nothing." Samson took another bite of fish.

"How could that be?"

"It's the damnedest thing. But we've searched."

"You suspect some sort of wrongdoing?"

"I don't know. I guess the army could have gathered all the files together, because this population has been hospitalized in various places together for some time, then they just got misplaced. Not entirely unprecedented. I really don't know, but it makes the current medical management extremely difficult."

"Aren't at least some military medical records scanned? Computerized?"

"Often not, going back that far. But whatever had been on the computer relating to early histories was all missing, too. We've looked, believe me."

Noah frowned and shook his head as he reached for his wine-glass.

Samson brightened. "But just recently, over the last couple of months, there've been some glimpses of pre-combat recollections during therapy. A kid sister's face, a first car, a puppy. We've had early experience memories in four separate patients."

"How can you be sure what you're getting is real memory?"

"Well, of course, that's the question, isn't it. But four patients progressing at a more or less similar rate? Different memories, at about the same period of their growth and development? And there's often cathartic tears when they remember." He nodded. "No, I'm convinced we're onto something. Maybe it's all still there, buried deep, but still there. If we stay with it, and we can avoid side effects, I'm hoping we might be able to return them to some kind of life, for whatever time they have left."

They finished dinner in the flickering light, each deep in thought. Noah broke the silence. "So what about the murder charge?"

Samson frowned, sighed, set his fork down, adjusted his glasses, then finally looked up. "They want me out."

"Who does?"

"I don't know exactly. Someone in the VA or military chain of command."

"Why?"

He studied Noah. "I'm not sure. I know what they say, but that can't be what's really behind all this. They started by criticizing my utilization numbers. I know we're using large amounts of drug, but there's got to be more to it than that. They pushed to get my VA privileges revoked. And when that didn't work, they tried to take my medical license."

"What happened?"

"They took statements from several patients who actually said they knew what they were taking and that the medication was helping them. I guess the brass concluded there was informed consent."

"Did you have a lawyer?"

"I didn't think I really needed one. Not at that point at least. If it had come to a hearing, I guess I would have looked into it."

"How did it come out?"

"Well, the charges were dropped. They reassigned me to Tripler to watch me, proctoring they said, and brought in a replacement at Kupuna, but he couldn't work with the patients." Samson leaned back in his chair, wine-glass in hand. "The intensity of the violence increased again. After a month or so, they brought me back."

"When was that?"

"Last year."

"I'm amazed that any of these patients could get it together enough to give a coherent statement."

"So was I. I saw the statements, and they weren't all that coherent, but I guess they convinced the peer review investigation committee enough to deter them."

"What did the people at Tripler think about what was going on over here?"

"My boss is the Chief of Psychiatry over there. Guy by the name of General Harley Reeves. Old career army doc who paid his dues in Vietnam. He seemed to have a lot of interest in Kupuna. But he was the only one. He's tried to give me the impression that he's going to bat for me, but he's as against the therapy as they are, and I think he'd line up with them if it came down to it."

"'Them'?"

"Well, that's the thing. He keeps referring to some nameless, faceless cadre of people in Washington who he says are driving the witch-hunt. I have no idea who they are, but the attempts to cut back our funding, to remove me, it's all coming through Reeves's office. He says it's filtering down from the Pentagon."

"Do you believe him?"

"I don't know what to believe." Samson took a swallow of the Chardonnay. "I think he would do me in if he could."

"Why?"

Samson paused again, considering. "I guess I'm a thorn in his side. Is it really the utilization numbers for him? I don't know. These guys have strict budgets for resources they're using. Maybe he really thinks I'm making him look bad. The drugs are pretty expensive, and, truth be known, they're not FDA approved for what I'm using them for. A couple of months ago, they cut off our supply of SSRIs."

"Cut off the drugs?"

"Cold turkey."

"So what happened? They haven't stopped taking them?"

"No. That would have been disastrous."

"Where do you get them?"

Samson put his fork down and looked at Noah. "This is all subject to attorney-client privilege?"

"Of course."

"When Tripler canceled our order, I went over to Honolulu and got with a guy who deals in that sort of thing."

Noah put his own fork down, and stared. "You don't mean they're illegal?"

Samson said nothing.

"Wait, wait–" Noah said. "SSRIs? On the street?"

"Not exactly street market. My source is a couple of steps above that. Not an easy guy to get in touch with, I might add, for a VA doc, anyway."

"What are street dealers doing with SSRIs?"

"They don't deal with them routinely, but you'd be surprised. You can get pretty much anything you want if you know the right people."

"Aren't they prohibitively expensive coming in that way?"

"Not really. They don't mark this stuff up like they do the meth and crack. I've been able to bury the cost here and there in our budget. Then we've had some direct financial contributions from a California veteran's group to keep the program from going down the drain."

"Jesus." Noah reflected. They both sat in silence as Noah gazed into a flickering candle. Finally he asked, "So what about the criminal case?"

"About a month and a half ago, a sixty-two year old, historically violent patient was stabbed to death in the bush with an army-issue combat knife. Guy they called 'Sauce,' given name Martin Rodriquez, though as I say, we don't have any records that we could verify that with."

"And the murder charge?"

"It kind of dropped on me out of nowhere. After Sauce's death, the Hilo police came up here and arrested me. I had no idea what it was about, but they took me down there and the U.S. Attorney asked a lot of questions. They said they believed the high doses of antidepressants were the cause of the violence. Unclear where his information was coming from, but ever since, they've been saying they're going to charge me as an accessory to murder. There have been a handful of court sessions, but so far the judge has granted postponements for me to get a lawyer. He says he won't do it again."

Noah pushed back from the table. "Why after all this time would they seemingly care about a crazy old vet? I mean, you say these guys have been killing each other forever."

"I have no idea. Doesn't make any sense. Like you say, there've been countless incidents over the years. They're violent combat veterans living in the jungle. There's nothing new about it, or anything we can do about it, short of what we're doing." He paused. "Could it be about the drugs? How could it not? That war has been going on for some time now, but why would they care about a few thousand dollars a month in medicine? And the books don't even show that the VA is actually paying for them now."

"You say they haven't actually charged you? Then what's the status?"

"You'll forgive me, Noah, but I'm not the one to ask about all the legal ins and outs, so I set up a meeting for us with the Federal Public Defender who's been helping me. She said she'd be in the office until about noon tomorrow, and I thought it would be a good idea to meet with her. She understands the procedures, and she said she would explain things so you could understand. All right with you?"

"Sure."

"Good. So here's the plan. We get a taste of Sgt. Slade's coconut ice cream, home-made, first-class stuff. Then we get you some much-needed sleep. First thing tomorrow, we get down to Hilo and talk to the Public Defender."

As if on cue, Slade brought in two bowls of the signature dessert. A bottle of Opus One cognac and two glasses rounded out the tray.

"Great," Noah said. "But you were going to flesh out why you wanted me to be involved—I mean, instead of anyone else, someone locally here."

"Well, that's another long story. How about we pick up there tomorrow? After you've had a chance to digest all of this."

Samson poured a couple of fingers of the cognac for each of them. "This'll help you sleep. Sometimes visitors are surprised by the level of noise out here. Believe it or not, you might find it quieter in downtown San Francisco at midnight."

Noah's thoughts were becoming thick. Words came more slowly. The long day, the wine, and now the cognac, were definitely having their effect. "So what do you know about the murder itself?" he asked.

Samson lifted the snifter to his nose, took a savoring sip, then lowered it. "Not much other than it was a knifing. Sauce was a hero of the battle of Chou Lai. I don't know who killed him, but I suspect it was his best friend."

CHAPTER FOURTEEN

"DON'T GO TOO FAR, Noah!"

The four-year-old turned and looked back at his mother, framed in the rear door of the bungalow. Without speaking, he turned again and padded off over the enormous lawn toward the trees. Sanctuary. It was dark as he wandered in among them, but he pressed on. Stubby bare legs pumping, his little feet in brown sandals chugging the short steps, one after another.

Suddenly he was aware of someone ahead of him, just out of sight, moving farther into the forest. He looked back but could no longer see the grass, the house. The trees had closed in behind his shadow, enveloping him. He turned and doggedly pursued the adult figure.

The trees became gnarled, their leaves fleshy, branches covered with vines, as the forest turned steadily darker, damper, hotter. He looked up but could not see the sky, only the sinister, twisted branches. It was steamy now; he could hardly get a breath. Then he became aware of shrieks and screams emanating from the trees somewhere above, but he couldn't see from what. Ahead in the distance, he could still hear the footsteps.

He was conscious of something behind him. It was invisible, barely audible, at first. Breathing. Then it was closer. Stalking him. He turned slightly, but he didn't dare look at it. His legs moved faster, faster. He started to run. He glimpsed broad shoulders covered in khaki through the trees ahead of him; then he lost sight of them. He had to catch up, but the vision seemed to be getting farther and farther away.

Behind him, the beast thrashed through the jungle, its breathing intensifying, gaining on him. He ran as fast as he could, but there was no escape. Closer, closer. Now he could feel hot breath on his neck. Terror gripped him. He was helpless. "No! Stop! No!" But there was no escape. He looked imploringly ahead, stretching out a plump little hand to the only one who could save him. Desperately, he screamed for the gossamer, amorphous khaki figure as loudly as he could.

"DADDYYY!"

Noah awoke in a cold sweat, having no idea where he was. He squinted toward the window. At first, all he could see was bright green light. Then the trees in the atrium took shape and he remembered, little by little. Trembling, he looked at his watch. Seven-forty.

Still somewhat unsettled after a shower and shave, Noah sat down in the mess hall behind a glass of orange juice and a slice of papaya he found on the table and assumed was for him.

"Dr. Samson had to go out early to see patients," Slade told him as he brought in a pot of coffee and set it down. "He wanted you to go ahead and meet Ms. Kauna-Luke without him. Her office is in the Federal Building on Waianuenue Blvd. I'll show you a map."

"Kauna-Luke?"

"The public defender in Hilo. Didn't he mention her last night?"

"Oh, yeah," Noah said. "So I just go back the same way I came up here, right?"

"Right. Only this time, don't pick up any hitchhikers."

"I might not survive another one."

"Dinner at seven o'clock. We usually eat early out here. Work for you?"

"The way you cook, I'd never be late for dinner."

* * *

The first time Noah cruised down Waianuenue Avenue, he was so dazzled by the bright sunlight and the deep green splendor of the trees and lawns of downtown Hilo that he missed the Federal Building entirely. When he reached the beach, he reviewed the map and instructions Slade gave him, turned around, and backtracked.

It was eleven-fifteen by the time he got to the front door of the large, early twentieth-century structure. It being Saturday, a security guard let him in and directed him to the PD's office on the second floor. Peering through the locked glass front door, he could see no one inside. After knocking several times with no visible results, he was about to give it up when a woman's bronzed face, trailing long black hair, poked around a doorjamb down the hall followed by the whole package: abbreviated khaki shorts at the top of long brown legs and a dark blue tank top. There were no shoes, which Noah thought gave "law office casual" a whole new meaning. She opened the door.

"Can I help you?" she asked.

"Noah Shane. I'm here on behalf of Dr. David Samson." He took care not to say he was representing him.

"Yeah. He said he might be in this morning. I'm Stephanie Kauna-Luke. So where is he?"

"Got tied up with some patients. He wanted me to talk to you anyway. Okay with you?"

"Sure," she said, and smiled. "Come on in. Can I get you a soda? Coffee?"

"I'm fine." He followed her to her office, where she motioned him to a chair, then situated herself behind the desk and settled in with one leg tucked up under her. The room was rife with tropical plants: on the mahogany desk, the credenza, and several in pots on the floor. Books were stacked under a window that looked out over the front lawn to the park across Waianuenue Boulevard, where a gargantuan Banyan dominated. Several files lay open on the desk. On the wall opposite hung a large framed print of a lush island beach with powerful, roaring waves.

"So are you going to take his case?"

"I don't know yet. I wanted to get a feel for it. I'm a state public defender in California, out here on holiday, you might say. The closest I've been to federal court was when we all trooped down there on the day I was sworn in, but I've never made an appearance. So I guess that's the first thing."

"No worries. You'll find it virtually identical to what you're used to in state court. Particularly here. Pretty informal as the feds go. How long you been at it?"

"My third year. You?"

"Same. You tried any juries?"

"Something over thirty. Three homicides."

"Wow. You guys really move right along. That's one difference from federal court. You do any good?"

"Won a few, lost a lot. I was pretty compulsive at first, but pretty soon I discovered that by and large, cops aren't arresting innocent bystanders. Came as quite a shock to me."

Her laugh flowed easily, her smile radiant. Another perfect set of Hawaiian white teeth contrasted with her deeply tanned skin and black hair. "Yeah, I know what you mean." She nodded, her dark eyes engaging. "So listen, are you sure I can't get you anything?"

"Just some information. Have they charged Samson yet?"

"There's a complaint in the file, but so far they've held off filing and arraignment until he gets representation. The complaint says 'murder one by complicity and felony murder, knowingly prescribing illegal drugs with the intent to harm or reckless disregard.' I don't really know anything about the case. We haven't done any investigation, because he said he was hiring his own lawyer. Besides, he's not eligible for the PD anyway. He's an employee of the VA. Not indigent."

She was pretty sharp, in a number of ways. Noah wrenched his focus back to the case. "This whole thing seems a little far-fetched to me," he said. "Samson works with a violent patient population. One guy guts another one somewhere out in the jungle. One more in a long line of violent exchanges over a lot of years. What's that got to do with Samson? You see any justification for the charges?"

"Not really. But what I get from the U.S. Attorney is that it's not his office that's driving the boat. This is apparently coming from some kind of upstream pressure."

"Like who? What?"

"No clue. But it sounds like they're after Samson, and it's personal."

"What makes you say that?"

"As much as Pitts—the U.S. Attorney—spouts off in court about Samson and his use of improper drugs, he tells me it's really about the doc. He says somebody wants to bring him down, wants him out. Pitts says he doesn't know who it is. I think maybe he does. I've tried to get it out of him, but he's not talking. Anyway, somebody's got a thumb on the scales, that's for sure."

"Scales?"

She shook the long hair and made a face of mock disbelief. "What kin'a dumb *haole* are you? You got no scales a justice ovah da mainland, brudda?"

"Oh, justice. Nope. Not in Oakland."

Stephanie glanced out the window, then looked back at him. "So, now you know what I know. We just have to see how it plays out."

"Yeah."

"Anything else I can help with?"

Noah raised an eyebrow as he considered the offer. He glanced at his watch. "It's a beautiful town you've got," he said. "I'd spring for a latte if you'd show me where we could find us some."

She studied him, then smiled. "Why not? I'm about done here. Let's go."

They emerged into the sunlight, and she pointed out the various government buildings as they walked down Waianuenue. After picking up lattes-to-go at the obligatory local Starbucks, they continued toward the bay. As they neared Mamalahoa Highway, she showed him the marks on the buildings that represented high water in the 1960 tsunami. They wandered through the park and down the waterfront, then angled back toward the Federal Building. Stopping in front of the red and brown Suzuki, she grabbed her helmet and tilted her head, measuring him. "So, you a surfer?"

He gave her a sidelong stare. "Ah, no."

"We could fix that. You wanna go *he'e nalu*? It's a nice Saturday."

"Surfing? I don't know." He groped for an excuse that wouldn't admit he was no adrenalin junkie. "Uh, I've got no trunks with me."

"We could fix that. How about we go Honoli'i?"

"Honoli'i?"

"World-class beach a little north of here. Primo spot this side of the Island."

He was shaking his head. *Hell, there were easier ways for a Jewish guy to commit suicide.*

"It's insane," she said. "You'll love it."

"Uh, Stephanie, I'm really not a surfer. I mean, give me a ball, you know, a basketball, a football. A baseball maybe? And some kinda plot. Besides I've got no surfboard."

"You gotta lotta excuses, is what you got. I own plenty boards." They were already moving toward the door. "You walk down Waianuenue toward the water, back where we were? Pick one of those shops we passed and get yourself a pair of trunks. I meet you back here in half an hour. I gonna show you what you gotta know." She strapped on the helmet, swung a leg over the bike, and fired it up.

Noah looked at the motorcycle. "We going to the beach on this?" he asked. "Where do we put the surfboards?"

"I got 'an old green Subaru Outback." She wound the accelerator, and the machine growled. "Half hour." She grinned and blasted down Waianuenue, her long black mane swirling behind her.

* * *

Noah was right. He wasn't a surfer. But he had a patient teacher. The surf at Honoli'i had been mercifully flat, and a couple of times he'd actually gotten vertical before planting hard. He was definitely going to feel it tomorrow.

After a few hours in the crystal water, they sat under waving palms on a colorful flannel beach blanket. Behind them, a nameless stream emerged from the jungle, bringing a confluence of fresh water from fast-moving rapids uphill into the clear, briny surf. Just off the point beyond them, the big ones were breaking, and a few of the pros were doing their thing. Stephanie had brought a basket of mangos, bananas, and chips along with a six-pack. Noah watched the experts slide down the face of the monsters and shoot through the pipelines.

"Can you do that?" he asked her.

She squinted off toward the point. "Sometimes," she said. "Those guys are pals of mine. We surf together pretty often."

"I'm impressed," Noah said. He quaffed the beer.

"You do it since you're two, and pretty soon you got no trouble." She shook her wet hair and donned a pair of sunglasses, then cut a mango and handed him half. "Only thing you gotta worry about is the tiger sharks, but you keep your eyes open and mostly they don't bother you."

Noah's head snapped around. "There's sharks out there?"

"Lots."

"Where we were?"

"Lots."

He pondered for a moment. "Christ," he said. "Glad I didn't know that."

She raised an eyebrow. "They wouldn't be particularly interested in you." Reaching out, she gently squeezed his bicep. "Too much muscle. Not enough fat."

"That's a relief."

She leaned back on the blanket and slurped at her mango. "So, Noah. You gonna take the job?"

"A guy could sure get used to this," he said. "But I don't know. I gotta lot to do at home. I'm handling the involuntary commitments, and they really don't have anyone else who can step into that."

"You like the psych stuff?"

"I thought I would. I was figuring on some juicy insanity issues. Turns out it's all about homeless crazies trying to keep their freedom so they can sleep on the street and drink cheap wine."

"Maybe Samson's case would give you a chance to get into some of those juicy issues."

"Maybe. I'm only here since yesterday, but he seems to be an interesting guy. He's working with some very disturbed vets, guys who were heroes. Sounds like he's got some really good treatment going with them. You ever been up to Kupuna?"

"Never."

Noah sucked at a chunk of the succulent fruit. "Why do you think he doesn't want somebody local to represent him?"

"I never answered that for myself. He obviously doesn't trust anyone. There's something dark in the background, but I don't know what. He's no dummy. Obviously knows what he's doing."

"Seems odd that he'd want to bring someone from the mainland into the local federal court," Noah mused. "And a PD at that."

"Maybe he thinks you're something special." She raised her eyebrows, her full lips curling into a smirk. "And you might be. Anyway, it'd be fun to find out." The stare lingered, then she glanced away. "Besides," she continued, "you stay a couple of months and I'll have you surfing the point."

"With the sharks?"

CHAPTER FIFTEEN

"So—Ms. Kauna-Luke says the U.S. Attorney thinks the whole thing is coming from above?" Samson said.

A magnificent aroma once again filled the room as the sun faded outside. They sat in the mess hall, overwhelmed by yet another feast tastefully designed by Sgt. Slade. The main course was a succulent pork roast with a thick, pineapple-brandy glaze. Essence of thyme gave it a fresh sense of the outdoors. *Noah had just assumed that all Freudians were lanzmen. Now he wasn't so sure. The doctor certainly couldn't be accused of keeping a kosher table.* As before, the wine was vintage California: a Pinot Noir that glowed with the flavor of raspberries.

"Stephanie thinks it's more about you than the murder—and she also thinks there's something sinister going on."

"I wonder if it's just the Pentagon's problem with the numbers she's hearing about. According to Reeves, it turned into a power struggle. They're trying to teach me a lesson because I wouldn't just let these patients sink back into oblivion." His soft eyes narrowed as he held Noah's gaze. "You know what?" he said. "They're all heartless bastards."

Noah took a sip of the Pinot and went back to the roast. He still hadn't heard about why Samson had chosen him as his lawyer, but for the moment, he decided to let the doc address it in his own time.

They ate in silence, pondering, and then Samson abruptly laid down his fork and looked across the table. "Are you going to help me, Noah?"

This was the time. "Why me?" Noah asked. "Why not some local attorney who plays golf with the other side?"

Samson pressed on. "I just don't trust them. There's more to this than prescribing too much medicine. More than just trying to slap down some pain-in-the-neck VA psychiatrist who's out in the jungle playing missionary with some crazy vets. That's clear, but it's the amorphous quality of it that scares me. There's too much at stake." He took a deep breath and exhaled slowly. "And I'm not just talking about me. It's the whole project that's on the line here. The country owes these guys a shot at normalcy."

Yeah. So he had said. But was that all of it? Okay, it was important. So why wouldn't he bring in some big criminal defense name from San Francisco or L.A.? It didn't make sense. There was only one way to get at it. Tell him no. "You know? This is a beautiful place, no doubt. It's a compelling case. And I like you and what you're doing here."

"Then you'll do it?"

"I'm sorry, Doctor, but I don't think I can. The PD's office doesn't have anyone they can put in my slot. Everyone who's been trained has moved on to a heavy-duty job. There's no one to. . ."

"They'll find someone, Noah. It's only for a couple of months. I could even pay for you to commute a few times if you really had to get back there for something."

Noah frowned. *Commute? Why was this so important to him?* "They need someone every day. But there's more to it than that. I'm a third-year lawyer, an Oakland PD. Why would I come out here to defend a case that's all about military law, venued in federal court in Hawaii?"

"It would be good for you. The next step in your career. You're not going to stay in the PD's office forever."

Now there was a little edge to it. The germ of greed and ambition being peddled. What did Samson care about his career? What the hell was going on here? He was starting to feel defensive. "A career move? Come on. I don't see anything coming from this beyond an extended vacation in Hawaii and a whole lot of *tsuris*. Why me? And why would you care about my career?"

Samson sat up a little straighter, his eyebrows gathering along with the storm behind them. The voice was still controlled, ever the therapist. "I don't understand you, Noah. Don't you see how important this is? There are twenty-eight men out there who have lived in abject misery for forty years. You have a chance to help them, not just me. And you have the chance to make a real difference." His face grew more stern, his voice collecting volume, almost rebuking. "Why wouldn't you relish such an opportunity? How much of a sacrifice is it?"

"Sacrifice?" *Who did this guy think he was? Why was this suddenly his problem? He wasn't the one accused of murder.* "It's a worthy cause, I admit, but I'm not letting anyone down here. It's not as if I'm the only lawyer in the world who can handle this case. In fact, there are thousands of better choices. I don't know how you picked me, but what I do know is that you're somehow trying to make this my problem."

Samson locked on angrily, jaw tightened, grinding, and then his face softened and he looked down at the table. "You're right. Why would this make sense to you?" he said. "What do you care about any of it?" He paused and shook his head. "But it does make sense. And there *is* every reason for you to care about it."

"Why?" Noah demanded, still incredulous. "Why would I leave my own life and come all the way out to Hawaii to represent you in something that's way over my head? Give me one good reason."

Samson's eyes returned to Noah's in the flickering candlelight. Behind the wire-rimmed spectacles, the soft Semitic lines couldn't conceal a passionate intensity. Noah searched there for any hint of an answer. *Why him? What was he doing out here? How had he been selected?* He plumbed the depths of the eyes, of the man.

When the answer finally came, it was entirely matter-of-fact. "Because," Samson said, "I am your father."

PART TWO

BETRAYAL

"One should rather die than be betrayed. There is no deceit in death. It delivers precisely what it has promised. Betrayal, though—betrayal is the willful slaughter of hope." —Steven Deitz

CHAPTER SIXTEEN

"SORRY?" NOAH SAID.

Samson's affect was flat, his voice neutral, his eyes soft but serious. "It's true," he said simply.

Noah studied him in confused silence for any sign of explanation.

"I know this must be one the hardest statements you've ever been asked to accept. I've played this moment over and over in my mind all these years, and every time I've wondered how I would respond if I were sitting where you are now."

"What are you talking about?" Noah asked.

"I'm talking about you, Noah. You and me. It's time you knew about this—after all the years." He looked down at his hands and back up into Noah's doubting eyes. Then he began, again in the measured tone.

"It was when I was at UCLA doing that fellowship in Law and Psychiatry with the army that I met your mother. We got pretty close. After I went back to Japan, she found out she was pregnant with you. She didn't tell me until some time later."

Noah searched his face for some rationale. *Samson was talking, but there was nothing real in it. It clearly wasn't any kind of joke. The guy was totally straight. But it just couldn't be.* "My father is Neal Shane," he heard himself say, the words echoing someplace far away.

"I know that's what your mother told you, but it's not true. Neal Shane had been your mother's boyfriend before we got together."

What did that have to do with anything?

"Apparently, she told him you were his."

"Why would she do that?"

"You'll have to talk to her about that. What I know is that when I asked her to come with me, marry me, she refused. She didn't want to leave California. She didn't want to be an army doctor's wife. So I guess she went back to Shane when I left."

It simply wasn't possible. Noah was groping for something to grab hold of. His first thought was that the sheer coincidence of it was over the top. He somehow couldn't relate to the fact that he was out here, in the middle of the jungle, with this guy who was suddenly talking about being his father. It was like wandering into a bar in some foreign city and having the woman on the barstool next to you say she just happened to be your mother. Only slowly did it come to him that that was the whole answer. It was why Samson had lured him out here. To tell him this. But why?

In the midst of the chaotic thoughts, a wave of anxiety struck him, a bolus of adrenalin that grew from a niggling somewhere deep inside that there might be a kernel of truth in this. He had no idea why he thought that, but the possibility was somehow more frightening than the potential that it wasn't true, and Samson was round the bend. So many times after his father had left when he was three, he had fantasized that that man wasn't his father at all. After all, Shane never wrote, never visited. Noah dreamed many times that his real father was out there in the world somewhere and would come and find him, take him away. The dream had always surfaced when things had seemed impossible. Maybe at some level he'd known it all along. What he knew for sure was that at this moment, he was acutely uncomfortable with the whole thing.

He stood abruptly. "I don't know why you're telling me this," he said, turning to go. "But it makes no sense." He started to walk away with no idea where he was going.

"Noah," Samson said. He was regarding Noah with the analytical gaze of the clinician. "Just a minute." It was firm, professional. "I want you to come with me."

Noah turned. "Where?"

"To my office. I want to show you something."

"I don't think I want to see anything you have to show me right now."

Samson took hold of his upper arm. The grip was gentle, yet strong, definite. "Come with me," he said.

They crossed the atrium to Samson's office. When they arrived, Samson sat Noah in the large chair behind his desk. He went to a shelf and retrieved two large black leather volumes, brought them back to the desk, then went back for a third, which he set in front of Noah.

After turning on the desk lamp, he opened the first binder. Inside were numerous pages of yellowing medical documents, carefully encased in plastic protective covers.

"These are copies of your birth records. When your mother called to tell me you were my son, I had the same doubts that you have now. I hadn't seen her in three years, and—and I guess she felt I needed some documentation." He turned a page. "You see this lab report?"

Noah studied the UCLA Medical Center records.

"This is a routine neonatal blood screen. Do you see this symbol?" He pointed to a coded entry.

Still nothing from Noah, but he was squinting at the page covered with columns of numbers and letters.

"This is a test for PMD, phenylalanine monodecarboxylase. It's an enzyme, a blood factor for a rare genetic disorder found in Eastern European Ashkenazi Jews." Samson's voice had an unhurried, reassuring, cadence. "It's found in .013 cases out of a thousand. That's one in a million. And you are heterozygous for it. So am I." He looked at Noah, who now raised his face to him, shaking his head quizzically. "That means you carry the marker, but don't have the disease. It's a variant allele of the trait, that is, a variation of the gene locus that is much rarer than the marker alone. The likelihood of our both having this blood marker, and not being related, is exceedingly remote."

He carefully turned a couple of the ancient pages. "Then over here, it's clear from dates, size, length, fundal height, developmental parameters, that you were a term birth. That meant your mother and I were together at the time of conception. No one else was with her." Samson paused and looked at him. "There was no other explanation, Noah." He stopped.

Noah continued to scan the medical documents. It was almost thirty seconds before he began to nod slowly. After another twenty, he said, simply, "I see."

Samson turned a few more pages, and photographs began to replace the records. "Here's a picture your mother sent me of a pre-school play. You're the one with the cardboard crown." Noah was dumbstruck. He'd seen the same picture in his mother's album.

"Here are some newspaper clippings from the Santa Barbara papers that depict your high school football career at Ojai Prep. I loved following these. I actually subscribed to the Santa Barbara News-Press during those years." As Samson turned the pages, the highlights of Noah's life lept out at him, a cornucopia of familiar events. "Here's the total layout about your winning the CIF Championship in your junior and senior years. Oh, and here's a picture of you and your date at the Senior Prom at Ojai. Your mother sent that to me."

As the enormity of it began to sink in, Noah's anxiety was gradually replaced by anger. *All those years of thinking he was not important enough for his father to come and see him. He always felt like he was different from all the other kids whose dads coached Little League, showed up at open houses, came to the football games. There was something wrong with him that left him unloved. He always imagined everyone could see it. Was it possible that the father that never came wasn't even his father? And the one who was his father wasn't even in the picture?* As he pondered it, the first feeling was irritation, then annoyance, then a smoldering rage.

"These are some clippings of your football days at Stanford," Samson was continuing, becoming more animated. "I noticed that it wasn't quite the success that your quarterbacking at Ojai had been." He leafed through Noah's history, clearly relishing the catharsis of sharing secrets he had hidden for so long.

"This book is your career with the PD. I got a lot of case results from the office, some from the PD's Association. I had to tell them I was a journalist writing a story on PD development, that I needed all the records from your class." He laughed. "I got a lot of garbage about a bunch of other PDs I had no interest in. Of course, none of their achievements compared with yours. Most of the stuff about your courtroom exploits comes from the Oakland newspapers. You really got quite a bit of notoriety."

Noah was staring at him when the smoldering rage ignited into a conflagration. "You knew all that time that you were my father?" he hissed. Samson ceased the narrative. "And you sat here and pinned pictures into scrapbooks?" Noah went on, his head to one side, eyes small slits. "What were you thinking?" Then louder. "Why the hell didn't you let *me* in on the little secret?"

Samson stopped. "I would have, only—"

"Only what?" Noah demanded.

"Only—your mother asked me not to."

Noah stared, trying to make sense of this. "Asked you not to? Why would she ask a father not to see his son?"

"She said it wouldn't be good for you. It would be too disruptive after you had thought Shane was your father."

"And you bought that?"

"I really didn't have much choice."

"Why, for God's sake? Why didn't you have any choice in whether you could just come knock on the door?"

"She said she would get a court order."

"An order not to disrupt my life by having my father in it? I don't think so."

"She was very clear. She didn't want me to be involved. I thought there was more to it than just letting you think Shane was your father."

"Like what?"

"I don't know." He walked around the desk and sat in one of the patient's chairs. "Your mother is a very private woman in some ways. You'll have to ask her."

"I'll do that. So you just hid over here in the jungle keeping a scrapbook. That was your contribution to fatherhood?"

"No, I contributed financially to your support for several years until your mother remarried. And sent a number of checks for you after that."

"That was big of you."

"Noah—"

"A few checks. That ought to take care of it." His fist came down violently on the desk. "Jesus Christ!"

"Noah, let's talk about this rationally. I realize I haven't handled this as well as I could have. I want to make it right between us."

"Sure. Why don't you just write me another check? Make it a big one. That ought to cover it."

"You know, there was a lot going on over here, too. My patients needed me."

"Did they?"

"They were in a lot of pain."

"Now there's a novel excuse. A doctor with patients who are in pain." He slapped his forehead. "Why didn't I think of that? Some do have kids, though. And actually spend some time with them. Or so I hear."

"It wasn't that easy. I couldn't exactly bring you to Japan, or here, when you were young, but I couldn't leave, either. No one else could work with these men."

"You know what?" Noah shouted. "That's a bunch of shit and you know it. You made your own choice."

"Noah—"

"We all make choices." He stood and stared at Samson, his jaw grinding. "So here's one I'm making—I'm out of here." He stormed for the door.

Samson rose. "Wait, Noah." he called after him. "Wait, I want you to understand—"

Five minutes later, Samson stood on the porch of the Kapuna compound, the same place from where he had watched Noah's arrival. Silently, he stared into the darkness as Noah threw his bag in the trunk of the Corolla, got in, slammed the door, fired up the engine and cranked the car around. The wheels spun in the damp, muddy loam before they gained sufficient traction for the nondescript white rental to lurch forward and fishtail noisily down the narrow jungle trail. Samson slowly shook his head as he watched the taillights disappear into the night.

CHAPTER SEVENTEEN

THE LIVING ROOM WAS Beverly Hills opulent. Bona fide new money right out of *Architectural Digest*, the kitsch section: candy-striped upholstery, glass and chrome coffee table with numerous never-cracked picture tomes, a couple of indecipherable Calder prints on the walls, and a life-sized carousel horse in the corner.

Naomi Wheeler tilted her head and frowned slightly as she surveyed the scene, then called to her Latina house servant: "Dora, will you bring in the liquor cart? The guests will arrive about seven o'clock and I think we'll have drinks in here before dinner."

She enjoyed the rustling of her white silk dressing gown as she went to the piano, an antiqued silver baby grand. Lifting the bench seat, she withdrew a handful of unused sheet music. After paging through a few selections, she singled out the Rachmaninoff and opened it. Jagged black gashes, impossible runs of thirty-second and sixty-fourth notes, slashed across the page like the seismic tracing of a 9.0 temblor. She found a particularly dramatic passage and was propping it conspicuously on the music rack when the front door chimes echoed through the marble mausoleum.

"Get that, will you, Dora?" she called. Dora knew to always answer the front door, but there was a certain sense of power that bubbled up in Naomi each time she shouted the instruction. Her father would have been so proud.

After a few moments, Naomi heard low voices from the foyer. She was still busying herself about the non-essentials when she looked up to see the figure standing in the entryway. For a moment she was nonplussed, almost annoyed, then she recognized him.

"Noah! Darling! What on earth? Why didn't you call?"

"Hello, mother."

At fifty-three, Naomi Wheeler would still have been quite attractive were it not for the rather severe makeup and hair. The fact that everything was a bit overdone was mostly the result of an aggressive hairdresser and cosmetic consultant who had to earn his keep. He had tried to defeat the hint of facial puffiness with expensive oils and unguents that might well have served their purpose, had it not been for the chronic high level of alcohol consumption. Naomi was dark, like Noah, and her hair would have been curly like his had she not paid heavily to straighten out the DNA. The long, enhanced lashes were calculated to achieve a touch of Cher: sexy but open, honest despite all the secrets. Unfortunately, the years were unyielding; the total effect was more hardened and less vivacious. She rustled to Noah, trailing silk, and offered up a cheek.

"You bad boy," she chided, and the vocalization had a practiced, throaty quality. "How long has it been since you've been home?"

"Home? I never lived in this house, mother. Let's see, I think there were two more husbands since your casa was my casa." A cynical smile and some edge did not belie that it was also a statement of fact. "San Francisco is my home."

"Now you know that Frank Junior and I have always felt that this is your home." She was referring to husband number three, purchaser of the present residence and owner of a plumbing company founded and funded by Frank Senior. "We'd love it if you'd spend more time with us." She pulled him to the couch and they both sat.

"Oh Noah. I'm having a wonderful party tonight. You have to stay." The enthusiasm bubbled. "The Martins, the Silberbergs. You know the Silberbergs, don't you? Their son was Josh—wasn't it?—and Dr. Swazey and his wife. I want them to see my Stanford lawyer all grown up. You will stay, won't you?"

"Hastings."

She regarded him absently, the eager smile arrested mid-gush. "What?" she said.

"Hastings. I went to law school at Hastings. Stanford was undergraduate."

She frowned slightly, and her tone became a little more serious. "How long *are* you staying?"

"I have to talk to you, Mother. Right now. I need some information."

She seemed distracted. "Information? Well, certainly. But today is an awful day." She glanced at her watch. "Oh my, it's almost eleven-thirty. I have to get down to Rodeo. I need a table decoration. I haven't even thought about the flowers."

"The flowers will keep. I've just come from Hawaii, where I spent a couple of days with a Dr. David Samson, a VA psychiatrist." He paused for the reaction, which came instantaneously as his mother's eyes widened and she drew an involuntary breath.

Half smiling, she frowned an attempt at confused. "Am I supposed to know this Dr. Samson?"

"Yes, I imagine you are. He claims to be my father. That would be something you might know about."

"Your father?!" The explosive laugh was forced. "That's preposterous," she said.

"My reaction exactly. But he was actually pretty convincing."

Noah studied her face. Not a hint of the internal turmoil, but he knew her, and knew she was groping, mind racing, her Galvanic Skin Response off the chart had she been wired.

Finally, she looked up at him and pasted an impassive expression, backing up, starting again. "Who is this man?" she asked.

Seconds went by as he stared, then dropped his gaze to the floor, smiling faintly and shaking his head. When his focus returned to her, the smile had disappeared. "I think you know, mother," he said. "He had some old medical records of my birth. He said you sent them. He showed me a scrapbook of my life, from Ojai Prep through Stanford football, when I passed the bar, the PD's office. I don't think there's any mistake, unless he's some kind of major psychopath." He lowered his head level to hers and locked on. "I think you'd better explain this," he said slowly. "I have a right to know."

Their gaze remained fixed for several seconds. Noah was determined that she would speak next. She took a deep breath, exhaled resignation, and in the expectant silence that followed, she did not meet his eyes. Her time-honored defenses were beginning to crack, the thick fortifications of denial starting to fail. She blinked several times, and a tear broke

free, trickled down her cheek. This was where he was supposed to well
up with sympathy, to back off, maybe even to comfort her, but he was
surprised to find himself devoid of compassion. The dominant sense
was exasperation, moving quickly toward outrage. They sat in silence for
what seemed like minutes as she examined the taupe texture of the Luxe
Collection carpet at her feet. Distant sounds emanated from the back of
the house as Dora busied herself with the evening meal.

At last, Naomi took another deep breath and straightened. "Let's go
for a walk on the beach," she said with only the slightest hint of a tremor
in her voice. "Dora has some fresh coffee in the kitchen. I'll be back
down in a few minutes."

* * *

Occasional gusts from a cool inland breeze swirled loose sand into
mini-storms that peppered their faces. Slogging toward the breakers, they
intermittently turned their backs on the annoying assaults.

The fifteen-minute drive from Beverly Hills had passed in stony
silence. Noah parked his mother's Mercedes in a half-empty public lot
adjacent to the beach they had frequented when he was a youngster.
Venice lay just south of Santa Monica on the California coast that
bordered the vast sprawl of Los Angeles. It was a funky gathering spot
where all manner of humanity sought a daily dose of "negative ions." The
visionary creation of wealthy tobacco tycoon, Abbott Kinney, Venice was
to be a conglomeration of canals, gambling casinos, and an impressive
colonnade, Kinney's attempt to capture the glory of the Italian prototype.
An ambitious undertaking born of the optimism of the early twentieth
century, Venice Beach had long since fallen into disrepair and was now
inhabited by a gaudy array of extroverted, low-rent misfits.

The seashore was empty this late April morning except for an old
beachcomber, pants rolled up, sorting for shells through the detritus at
the top of the tide line. Two mongrels romped nearby, gnawing on each
other in blissful oblivion.

Naomi pulled up the collar of her tan windbreaker and suggested they
walk up to the boardwalk. In a couple of weeks, crowds of musclebound

and voluptuous paraders, boom-box skaters, and sidewalk artists would jam the promenade. For now, they were still holed up wherever such eccentrics go on cool, gray days.

Noah and his mother fell into a slow stride, sauntering past the run down shops and deserted vendors. Noah was still resolved to letting her find her own rhythm, and finally, she began.

"You have to remember, Noah, it was different in our family."

He waited.

"My father was a hard man, an angry man. He worked all his life catering to other people. He was from a different time, a different planet."

The image came to him of the grandfather he had only seen a handful of times. Morris Yezerski had died when Noah was six. A butcher, born and raised in the South of Poland, he had seemed like a giant, with his wild coils of black hair, bushy eyebrows, piercing eyes, and huge gnarled hands. Noah imagined him surrounded by his knives, his cleavers, that he must have used to slaughter silent and defenseless animals, like the illustrations out of a Grimm's fairy tale. He always remembered the hands. And there was this coldness about him, under which lurked a terrifying power that was totally mysterious to a small boy.

"We had nothing growing up." Noah couldn't see the eyes behind her sunglasses, but he could hear the tears in her voice. She went on, haltingly. "You know that your Bubbi died after Aunt Rachel was born, when I was seven. My father knew nothing about raising children, nothing about life in this country." She adjusted her scarf against the wind. "Nothing about life anywhere, for that matter."

He'd heard it before, but maybe this time she'd get to the heart of it, to the part where his father, whoever that was, walked out on him.

"Oh, God. It was all so humiliating. I had to wear a little schtetl apron and pinafore until I was twelve. Did I ever tell you that?" She glanced over at him as they strolled, searching for some sign of empathy. Nothing.

"As a teenager, I was never allowed out past nine. I had to go to shul every Saturday. Rachel and I sat over on the women's side with the second-class citizens while your grandfather danced and carried on like a—a, I don't know, a—some kind of refugee. Hassidism was all he cared about. The only thing he knew."

"No one cared what I thought. I didn't have a brain. I was a girl, for God's sake, a bitter disappointment. He didn't care about how I did in school. I'd marry some local loser and drown in that Polish cesspool. All he cared was that I didn't embarrass him." She inhaled deeply, struggling for control. "Jesus—" she murmured. "As if he was never goddamn embarrassing to me."

As they walked on, the painful memories spilled. It had stopped being an explanation. She was off into a reality she had long ago expended Herculean effort to bury.

"I always told you I was from 'Baltimore.' Just Baltimore. I never mentioned the old East Baltimore neighborhood, did I? I was afraid some day you'd go and find it. I tried to give it a little decency, a little respectability." She scoffed. "What a joke." Her volume dialed up a notch. "Thank God, Noah. Just thank God you haven't had to know what it is to grow up poor in a desolate Jewish ghetto like that. No mother. Working nights and weekends washing dishes in a hole-in-the-wall deli over on Corn Beef Row. I had to do it all myself." She slowed, looking over at him, stopped, and straightened.

"There was only one person—Miriam Tzaddik, my fourth grade teacher. I think she was the one adult I ever talked to, the only one who ever cared about me, who understood. Why she came back to Baltimore always baffled me. She had actually made it out.

"Well, I made it too. I got the grades, got into UCLA, and got out. I mortgaged my soul on student loans, but I got as far away from that little slice of hell as I could. And I never looked back. I was going to be a teacher like Miriam."

Silence.

Noah waited. *Get to it. What about Samson? What about Shane? Spare me the anguish, the insufferable self-pity. Now would come all the sighs, the goddamn day of sighs.*

She sighed heavily. "Maybe it would have been different if I'd had a mother. You know? Someone to help me with these things. Aunt Rachel was married and living in Detroit. She had her own life." Naomi stopped, gazed out to sea under the blanket of overcast. Noah stopped with her. "She and I never really got along, anyway," she said.

She drew a Kleenex from the pocket of her windbreaker and dabbed under her sunglasses, then started off down the boardwalk again.

"I thought David was the one." *Finally!* "An army psychiatrist, back from Vietnam, serving a fellowship at UCLA, the Neuropsychiatric Institute. I was a senior, just starting my credential work, my internship for my teaching degree." She walked over to one of the numerous benches that lined the boardwalk. Noah followed. They sat and looked in different directions, and then the purgative pilgrimage continued.

"I'd never met anyone so smart as David. And I loved his music." She drifted, remembering. "He played classical guitar." She smiled at some unarticulated recollection. "God, he was handsome," she whispered, then suddenly looked over at Noah, measuring the resemblance.

"We talked about getting married. I was so excited. We started with dates, wedding plans, and I wanted to talk about where we were going to live, where he would practice, and I would teach. It was then that he told me he wanted to stay in the army. Go back to Japan and treat crazy soldiers." She shook her head. "The army," she said with a snort. "Can you imagine?"

Noah flashed on the vets at Kupuna.

"I mean, there we were at UCLA. So close to Beverly Hills—the Mecca of psychiatrists—that if you threw a rock, you'd hit three. But he was going to give his best years to the army. And he wanted me to come with him? Throw it all away?"

"What did he want to do in the army?"

"That's what I said. Something about some men who had battle fatigue."

"So what did you tell him?"

"I told him I couldn't believe it. I told him that I thought he was wonderful, but I wasn't going to spend the rest of my life on some army base in Japan. Did my damnedest to change his mind."

"What happened?"

"Awful." She grimaced. "He said he loved me but told me there was no way I could convince him that what he was doing wasn't a really big deal, a huge earth-shaking issue." She reflected again, then shrugged. "I guess I just wasn't enough."

"What happened?"

"Well, he went back to Japan," she said matter-of-factly, paused a beat, then added in a near whisper: ". . .and I found out I was pregnant."

"Did you tell him?"

"No."

"Why not?"

She hesitated. "By then, I was involved with your father again." She shook her head. "I mean, you know—with Neal. We'd been going together a couple of years before I met David. Then when David left, we got back together. He asked me to marry him, and—"

"And what?"

"Well, I mean, under the circumstances—"

"You let Neal Shane think I was his."

"Well, you could have been his, only. . ."

"Only I wasn't. And you knew that all the time." He barked, incredulous. *It had had to be something like this.*

"Neal was settled. He had his engineering degree. He had already started at Bechtel. He had some ambition, for God's sake. I wasn't going to—"

"Why did you even tell Samson about me?"

"I don't know, I—"

"What did you have to gain?"

"I—"

"What happened?" he demanded.

"Calm down, Noah. We can get through this."

"Get through it?" he shot back. "This was my life you were playing with. What the hell were you thinking?"

She fixed on him defiantly, her jaw grinding, then she stood, turned her back abruptly, and walked off down the boardwalk.

No, damn it! No way she was going to walk away this time. That was her answer to everything. He bounded after her.

An instant before he caught up, she turned. It was all too familiar. He recognized the unspoken question on her face: did he want to talk or not? And the second part was: if he did, he would be civil, by God. He looked down the beach, took a deep breath, and let it out slowly, resisting, resenting, jaw tensing. She walked over to another of the benches just off the walkway and again sat, looking up at him with a self-satisfied silent invitation that said, "Okay then. Try to behave."

Fucking humiliating, but what were the options? He had to get the whole story. He sat, and she began again.

"Neal and I started to quarrel constantly. He always had to control me, be in charge. It made me furious. When things got bad, he'd say he wanted to leave but that he couldn't—because of you." She sneered, eyes narrowed. "I told him not to do me any favors. 'Go ahead—leave,' I said." She paused, then: "He could be so hateful. I don't know, one time I got so angry, it just slipped out."

"You told him I wasn't his."

"He went crazy. That's when he left. You were about three."

"That explains a lot," Noah said. "The total lack of interest in me. So why did you tell Samson?"

"I called David. I mean, he had some responsibility for your support, didn't he? I had nothing. Jesus. . ." She held out a hand, palm up, persuading. "I was a still an intern teacher in Santa Monica making peanuts. I had to pay back my student loans. What was I going to do? Win the lottery? I wasn't about to quit."

"Quit what?"

"The credentials program. I was going to take my masters," she said. "That was the one thing in the world I wanted. I was going to be a teacher." She searched his eyes, and then it broke and she scoffed again. "It seems so stupid now. But I really wanted to work with little kids, lost kids like I was. Maybe help them find the way out." She looked at her hands, musing, then back at him. "I don't mean back in Baltimore. God, no. Not there. Maybe out here somewhere." A beat. "I'd come so far. Neal had refused to pay anything. It was the only way, my last chance to stay in school."

"What did Samson say?"

"He didn't believe me at first. That's when I sent him the birth records. I guess there was some kind of rare blood thing. Did he tell you about that? Anyway, I said since you thought Neal was your father, it wouldn't be good if we suddenly changed that."

"What a great idea. What did he say?"

"He said he'd go along with it. And he sent money for you—until I remarried."

"Did you ever ask him to be involved in my life?"

No answer.

"He said you told him he couldn't see me. Did you?"

She was looking down into her lap.

So there it was. It was clear. Unbelievable. He leaned over, inches from her, eyes narrowed, veins tight on his neck. "You did, didn't you?" he growled.

Still nothing.

"DIDN'T YOU?"

A couple passing by stared, gave them a wide berth. She turned to him, confronting him now, addressing him in a low, measured tone. "You can't talk to me like this, Noah. I'm your mother. You didn't live through all of this. I know it's hard for you, but you have to get that I did the best I could—"

Bull-shit. Total bull-shit. He struggled for control. "See, I actually did live through all of this," he said, dialing down the volume with great effort. Then: "Did you tell him he couldn't be in my life?" he repeated.

"I asked him for support—"

"You told my father he couldn't see me, didn't you."

The air crackled between them, and then she exploded. "Yes, dammit, I wasn't going to have it! Your grandfather was an old-fashioned European Jew. A small-town Polish butcher. Do you know what it is to people like us to have such a disgrace in the family?"

He stared, speechless, shaking his head. Finally he stammered: "A 'disgrace—' I was a 'disgrace.' My existence—a 'disgrace.'" The pain contorted his face into a grimace. "I could understand you wanting to spare my feelings. Not wanting me to know I'm a fucking fatherless bastard. But a 'disgrace'? What kind of a mother sees her child as a disgrace?" He looked away, not wanting to see her, not wanting to hear any more.

"You have no idea what you're talking about," she said. "I gave up everything for you. My teaching, my future, everything."

His head snapped back around. "What do you mean?"

"I couldn't make it work. There just wasn't enough. Those aid and loan offices weren't kind to women in those days. Women didn't need bank money. They could just get married. Live off someone else." Her lips curled into a sardonic smile. "In the end, I guess they proved they were right. Ironic, isn't it? By shutting women down, making them get married to survive, they prove that's what happens, that they didn't need the money in the first place." She gazed into the distance as she reflected on the enormity of it. "Christ—"

Then she straightened. "Anyway, I had no choice. We lived in this hovel in Hawthorne with two other families until I couldn't stand it anymore. No way I was going to allow my baby to experience what I had gone through. I was going to give you a place to be proud of, a place to bring friends home to."

"You can't be serious. . ."

"Yes, okay, it was for me, too." Now it was her volume that flared. "I worked hard to drag myself out of the gutter! I deserved better. So I quit school and married someone who could care for us. . ." Gathering momentum, glaring bullets. "Someone who had the wherewithal to send you to a good school so you could make something of yourself, so you wouldn't have to be ashamed all your life." She stopped. All the years. All the times she had to make it up, hiding it from the teachers, the doctors, all the applications, the other mothers. Pasting it all together, again and again, always the fear of his coming across a medical record, someone who knew her back then. She knew it would come to this someday. But she never saw this coming. His loser father, out of nowhere, turns him against her? By God she'd been right. There'd been no choices. Jaw clenching, nostrils flaring, she hissed: "So who the hell are you to judge me?"

He stared into the green eyes with the bottle-brushed, Cher, spiderweb lashes, now fluttering with rage.

"And that's why you hid my life from me?"

"I wasn't about to let anyone know," she retorted. "I was only trying to protect you."

He stood, towering over her. "The hell you were! You never thought of anyone but yourself!" He started to walk away.

"Fine," she yelled after him. "Leave." She waved a dismissive hand. "You're just like all the rest."

He faced her one last time, seething. His head canted to the side as he glared askance, eyes asking the still-unanswered questions as she glowered back. So much unsaid, but nothing more to say, he turned with finality and strode off down the boardwalk.

CHAPTER EIGHTEEN

THE LONG SHADOWS OF early morning, coupled with the absolute silence, cast an eerie pall over the Khe Sanh encampment. Not a sound from the birds, the animals, the insects, all of which had converted on adrenalin to shallow breathing, straining to hear, but not be heard.

Ferguson crouched below the window line, eyes glazed, chest heaving, listening, the nine-inch combat knife protruding from his waistband. He knew the enemy was in there, even though he couldn't hear him. He could smell him. This was one of *them*. The evil ones. He had known their intentions for a long time. They would kill him. They had no choice. Their mission was to terminate the last one that could frustrate their master plan. They were all the same. Since the beginning of the world. And they always would be. His eyes darted back over his shoulder, then forward again. He would prevent it, at all costs. He was the only one who could. He was the last. The whole of the universe depended on him.

Deftly, noiselessly, he trotted in a crouch along the front of the barracks toward the main door, which stood ajar, long since warped from the relentless moisture. Reaching the door, he thrust it open and, hardly slowing, threw in a grenade-sized stone, which rumbled across the floor. Then he sprinted around the end of the building to the back, expecting to intercept the barrack's sole occupant rushing out the back door.

Alone inside, Rat leaned against the front wall. Years of repetition had steeled his nerves and galvanized him for such encounters. His fears of the civilized world and of interacting rationally with other human beings were now far away, out of mind. This was what he knew best. He recognized the confrontation for the deadly struggle it was, yet he welcomed the relief from the constant background anxiety and intermittent episodes of panic.

Without reacting, he watched the grenade-stone rumble along the floor to a stop, and then he instantly took a position next to the door. When he heard Ferguson sprint toward the end of the building, he darted out the front and ran, hunkered down, toward the opposite end. Sensing Ferguson had stopped, he too stopped, waiting.

Ferguson listened for movement inside the barracks. Hearing nothing after several seconds, he burst through the back door.

When Ferguson moved, Rat bolted. He knew he was no match for the larger man hand to hand, and talking it out was not an option. Rat had seen the predatory behavior before, but this was the first time it was directed at him. Others had tried him, but things had changed. Everything seemed different now, since Doc came up with the new meds. Problem was, Ferguson never took them. Said he didn't like being brain-dead; that it was poison, that they were trying to poison his brain so he wouldn't be able to fight. Whatever it was, Rat knew the insanity would pass; it always did. But for now, he'd have to find a way to survive, to disappear. He jogged quickly toward the end of the building. With Ferguson inside, he would sprint the twenty yards to the jungle and safety, until the next time.

Rat heard nothing until he rounded the corner of the barracks. He emerged into the small clearing in back, and there, not ten feet in front of him, stood Ferguson, breathing hard, nostrils flared, face twisted into a sadistic grin. The knife was in his right hand. The two graying men faced each other, then circled.

Ferguson lunged, and Rat feinted to the right, toward the back door, then sprinted left toward the jungle. Ferguson went for the inside move but, despite his size, was still quick enough to recover. Leaping forward, he tackled Rat and clamped a massive arm around his neck. Scissoring both legs around him, Ferguson drove the knife home, like a Black Widow delivering a lethal bite to a squirming moth. Rat took several final gasping breaths, then succumbed.

They lay like that for a number of seconds, one chest heaving, one still. Finally, Ferguson released the limp body, stood slowly, closed his eyes, and screamed, a piercing shriek that echoed through the forest.

Devoid of sense or reason, the scene was sheer testosterone-mediated power. The alpha male stalking his prey, his consciousness obliterated by an exquisite adrenalin high.

This would show them. Once again they would know. He may be the last, but he was to be reckoned with.

A hundred yards up the hill behind Khe Sanh, three pairs of eyes gazed down, bearing witness to the archetypal image: submission in the face of dominance. The observers recoiled one by one in silence, backing farther into the trees.

Presently, a bird called, then another, then here and there a mongoose grumbled, an insect buzzed. The crescendo continued until the jungle symphony that had been suspended for an almost imperceptible interval in the fullness of time resumed.

* * *

A few beach stragglers walked briskly along the breezy sidewalks as the lunch hour approached. Noah strode in total distraction from the boardwalk onto Windward Boulevard, and into the heart of old Venice. His thoughts were an array of unorganized snapshots, colored in the reds and purples of rage, unbidden images of the last chaotic days.

A week ago, life seemed to be proceeding in a sensible direction, perhaps a bit unsettled, but so what. He only needed a new direction. That was all, a little fresh air. Now, behind him, as far as he could see, there was nothing but emptiness, lies that laid waste to all he had understood to be his youth, his history. His past was a fucking fraud that washed over everything and cast the future in chaos, as dingy and gray as the decaying buildings of this decomposing beach town. Like his life, the place was populated by narcissistic, self-possessed bottom-feeders. All of it devoid of meaning.

His mother was the complete self-absorbed neurotic. And his father— who the fuck was that? The man who, he thought, for twenty-eight years, six months, and nine days had given him life but who long since ceased to concede he existed? Or the one who, it turns out, supplied the DNA and wandered off into oblivion. A goddam psychiatrist, for chrissakes, taking instruction in parenting from a woman who was using her only kid to leverage her various love interests. What a fucking joke.

The crushing blind-side block came out of nowhere.

"Hey, asshole!" A meaty hand grabbed Noah's arm and squeezed painfully, yanking him back to reality. "Watch where the fuck you're going!"

Noah looked up blankly at the obese refugee from World Championship Wrestling, complete with bleach-blond Mohawk and ugly tattooed biceps that bulged from a faded sleeveless jean jacket.

For an instant, irrational fury boiled up. Noah jerked his arm free and turned to face the giant. Then, gradually, self-preservation overtook self-pity. "Uh, sorry—" he murmured. "Didn't see you."

"Right. Didn't see *me*," the behemoth spat, looking at Noah like he couldn't decide whether to yank out his heart or his liver. He scanned the small audience that had gathered, then tossed Noah backward like a deep-sea fisherman throwing back a puny mackerel. "So get your head out of your ass. You might see better." As he stalked off, he leveled another elbow into Noah's already aching ribs.

Staring after him vacantly, Noah slowly realized just how close he had come to being another Venice statistic. As his consciousness returned by increments, he steadied himself against the front of a trashy dive adorned in washed-out green stucco. A pink neon martini glass with a bright green olive nearly filled a single window that was covered with peeling, tinted cellophane. How could he resist the strains of Merle Haggard that mingled with the rancid fumes of beer-soaked sawdust? Once inside, it took Noah only a few seconds to adjust to the gloom, and then he wandered over and slid onto a chrome barstool.

"What'll it be?" The voice came from somewhere in the smoky darkness. On a TV at the far end of the bar, Oprah was interviewing the wife of a NASCAR driver.

"Tequila," Noah said. "Corona back."

The bartender returned swiftly with the order and slipped the tab into a glass set on his edge of the bar.

By the time Noah had bolted down the third tequila, sucked the lime, and sloshed the Corona, the edge was starting to soften.

"Looks serious." It was the deep rumble of slightly wet gravel, and it came from Noah's right. He peered in the direction of the voice but could only make out a hazy silhouette several stools down. The place was otherwise empty.

Returning his attention to his personal space, Noah muttered, "Just thirsty."

"That kinda thirst can do in your liver," the voice rasped. "I oughta know." Silence for half a minute as Noah nursed his beer; then the voice growled again. "Hank, bring this suicide bomber another shot, willya? Cirrhosis loves company."

As the bartender set the shot in front of him, Noah was ambivalent at best about the unsolicited benefactor, any kind of social interaction likely to bring on nausea just now. He finally sighed, picked up the glass, raised it toward the apparition, and downed its contents. As the acidy warmth spread through his upper GI tract, Noah returned to the lime, and finally the Corona, actually beginning to enjoy the pleasant sensation.

"Does the job, no?" the phantom voice intoned. "Course, that's the problem, isn't it."

Silence.

"Y'don't look like a regular. Get some bad news, did'ya?"

Noah didn't answer.

"Sumpn' throw you a curve?"

As the alcohol seeped into small cerebral arterioles, doors were unlocked behind which lay more resentment. *What did he need with this barfly? It was none of his goddamn business.*

"A big unit special," he muttered.

"Know what you mean," the voice went on. "Life can get to you. What was it? A woman? Family?"

Who was this guy, the local therapist?

"You're in the ballpark."

"Get dumped?"

God dammit. Enough already. Noah turned in the direction of his tormentor, prepared to put an end to the conversation. He stared into the darkness, still seeing nothing but an indistinct shape backlit by the TV. Then he softened, exhaling. "What're you drinking?" he asked.

"Doesn't matter."

Beat. "Hank," Noah instructed. "Bring my friend another of whatever he's got going, will you?" Hank moved briskly, clearly basking in the exchange of kindnesses. He mixed a tall vodka and grapefruit, put it on the bar, and rang up the increment on Noah's tab.

The shadow nodded. "Thanks," he said.

In the background, Oprah chirped something about assaulting another NASCAR wife.

"Martin Van Buren Donohue," said the barfly.

Noah frowned. "What?"

"Name's Martin Van Buren Donohue. But they call me Jack, for obvious reasons."

"Obvious reasons?"

"It started as 'One Eyed Jack' but now it's just Jack to most people." The silhouette leaned forward into the glare of the flickering TV screen. Noah could make out a heavy-set, wizened man, probably mid to late sixties, with bushy, disheveled white hair and wire-rimmed aviator's glasses. The left side of his face was badly burned, his cheek, eye, and forehead gathered into an ugly pucker of heavy scarring. Tilting his glasses up, he opened his eyes widely so Noah could get the full impact of the jagged tissue and the grayed, opaque left cornea.

Jeezuz. Noah tried not to react visibly.

"Napalm," Jack said. "Battle of Hue, February 3, 1968, 0430 hours. Tet Offensive. Haven't seen a thing through that damn eye since."

"I'm sorry," Noah said.

"You get used to it. Caught a load of shrapnel in the leg, too. Land mine." He reached down with both hands and lifted his left leg, which was encased in an ancient chrome brace with cracking leather straps that bunched up the material of his faded jeans. "Took half the meat off my quad. 'Bout all of it off the calf."

Noah noticed the two aluminum crutches leaning against the bar to Jack's right. The old man squirmed, settling himself back onto his stool.

"I get how you feel, though. I've had a few problems with the ladies m'self," he said and chuckled, his face broadening into a good-natured grin that exposed yellowed teeth, some missing altogether. Turning back to Noah, he said, "So, you ready for another round?"

CHAPTER NINETEEN

"HAVE YOU TOLD ME everything about these dreams you can remember?" Samson was writing furiously, trying to record the images for comparison with future reports in order to see if there was some evolution, some linear development. It would be critical for the clinical study.

"I think so, but it's not really like a dream, Doc. I can't explain it. I do see it at night a lot. But I see it during the day, too. And it's like there's more different stuff now. I like it. Seems like it's real."

Samson continued his scribbling in the thick manila folder that bore the name *Wiley Matson* in bold black lettering on its tab. Matson, who was known as "Coyote Man," or just "Coyote," was seated in one of the two visitors' chairs in front of the desk. Samson was seated in the other. This was one of the therapy sessions that took place in the office rather than the field. Formerly rare, they were becoming more and more common with the advent of the megadoses of YM992. Samson was trying to draw out all the specifics he could about the vivid images the men were now reporting.

Admittedly similar to symptoms that had been described to him countless times over his career, these were different in some important respects. Their circumstances and content did not seem delusional, convincing Samson they were not hallucinations. They were not accompanied by fear, anxiety, or other negative emotions. In fact, they were invariably welcomed by the patient. Coyote was typical, reportedly experiencing them during sleep and as waking reveries. Although it would have been impossible to plot it in the field, at least so far, the frequency of these manifestations seemed proportional to the amount and duration of usage of YM992.

"How often are you aware of these images?" Samson asked. "When you're awake, I mean."

"I don't know. Seems like almost every day now." Coyote, a trim Black man in his early sixties, was powerfully built. At six feet, he didn't have an ounce of fat on him. His face was lined but, unlike most of the others, he shaved regularly. When the monthly delivery brought laundered clothing, Levis, shirts, underwear, and socks to the barracks, Coyote would squirrel away more than his share. He always seemed clean, virtually civilized. Looking perpetually amused, he wore a slight smile that broadened when he was pleased or titillated.

"Can you remember anything else about what you saw?"

Coyote drifted, gazing out the window behind Samson. "Like I said. It's places, people—" he mused. The smile broadened. "There was a woman. Seems like the face is familiar, but I mostly can't focus on it for a long time. There's a house, on a street with a broad sidewalk. Little kids." He looked at Samson. "I think it's real, Doc. Maybe stuff I couldn't remember before."

"Can you make it go away?"

"I don't know. Never really tried. Don't really want to."

"Did you have a vision today?"

"Not yet, but I did last night." He looked at the doctor and chuckled. "You'll love this. I was playin' football. Man, I hope that's true. Prob'ly made that part up."

"You were playing football? Where? With friends?"

"Like I was playin' in a stadium somewhere. Big crowd. I was a running back, I think."

"How long do the images last?"

"I don't know. Just kind of glimpses. I wish they were longer."

Samson finished writing, looked up, and stared at him. Something happening, that was certain. "So is that everything you remember so far?"

Coyote thought about it. "Well, that's all the sort-of scenes I can remember. I guess there're some more details."

"Okay, would you sit down in the outer office like we did before and see if you can write down as much of those details as you can remember?"

"Alright. You think these are actual memories, Doc? Things that happened to me?"

"I don't know, Wiley," Samson responded. "I hope so, don't you?"

The smile spread across his face again. "Yes, sir, I do."

"How are your meds holding out?"

"Think I'm fine for another couple weeks."

Samson rose. "Well, you'll be in next week. We can check your supply then."

"Right." Coyote stood, too, and started toward the door. Samson put a hand on his shoulder as he moved into the outer office.

"Sgt. Slade," Samson said. "Get Coyote his binder and a pen, will you? He's going to make some more notes. Then please come on inside."

Slade's expression was troubled, but his tone was composed as he sorted through a file drawer and handed Coyote a thin black binder. "There are some gentlemen out front waiting to speak to you, Dr. Samson. I told them you were with a patient." Samson glanced out the front window to see the white Hilo Police Department cruiser.

A few minutes later, Slade stepped into Samson's office and closed the door. "What can I do?" he asked anxiously.

"Any luck in trying to turn up some pre-enlistment recruiting records?"

"No, I mean about the police. They have a warrant. It's clearly about Rat."

"The records. Anything about any of our guys?"

Slade didn't hide his irritation, but he answered anyway. "Nothing. Like I told you, Army Record Depot in St. Louis has come up dry for all of them. I've got feelers out at the Recruiting Center in Schenectady, at Tripler. Even checking KIA and MIA records. You know how long these things take. But what do you want me to do about those guys out front? Shall I get a lawyer? Do you want someone from JAG in Honolulu, at least temporarily?"

Samson returned to his desk, still focused on the records. "I can't imagine why all these guys have a blank trail," he said. "It doesn't make any sense." He spoke as he scribbled in Coyote's chart. "Okay, let's stay with it. If we can come up with some histories we can match to their memories, we'll have some serious documentation."

"Don't you think you need some representation? This thing could really get sticky now. They're going to try to implicate you in this second killing. They may not let you out on bail again."

Turning to face him, Samson nodded patiently. "Thanks for your concern, Grayson. I'll talk to that public defender, Ms. Kauna-Luke."

"But, do you want me to—"

"Just send them in, will you?"

* * *

"Wiley Matson? Yes, that's one. Wiley Matson. And Francis Hicks was another we discussed, and Robert Sylvan Johnson, Victor Rosenfeld, Diego Martinez, Hank Sylva. There were fifty-two in all. I gave you the list last week. Do you have the list, Ms. Hilliard?"

Captain Marcus Helms stood across the counter from Holly Hilliard, the middle-aged records officer at Tripler who had been thus entrenched for more than twenty years. A bespectacled, crinkled-face smoker, she scratched absently at her blond hair, dark at the roots, as she stonewalled all demands.

Helms hated the glacially slow and inefficient VA administrators worse than the terrorists. A bunch of brain dead nine-to-fivers; at least the terrorists were committed to something. With these clerks, there was never any urgency, no matter what the emergency. Get some military personnel in here to kick some bureaucratic butt and things would start cracking. Perish the thought you would express any annoyance, lest these sloth-like desk jockeys take offense and actually reverse time, like in the *"Twilight Zone."* About to jump the counter and rip out her larynx, he couldn't contain his harsh tone and audible sighs.

"Yesss, Captain Helms," she hissed. "I have the list. We've obtained the records from St. Louis and Schenectady, and we've requested the rest. As I told you before several times, if you could just be patient, all this takes time."

"This is high priority, Ms. Hilliard. I don't have time, and I have no more patience."

"I don't know what to tell you, Captain." She shrugged. "We're doing the best we can."

"Are you really?" Helms held her gaze, then looked down and shook his head. "Alright," he said. "Just give me what you have." He grabbed the most recent stack and headed toward the door. "And stay on it, dammit. I want to be closely informed." Holly gave him a mock salute, then protruded her lower lip and blew her regulation-length bangs into the breeze.

Helms shook his head again as he waited for the elevator to five, thinking for the thousandth time that if they had idiots like Holly over at NSA, we'd all soon be pissing toward Mecca. He gave his secretary a rigid nod as he passed her work station, then stepped briskly into his office and settled behind his desk.

Thumbing quickly through several of the files, Helms perused the photographs of young, handsome, recruit-aged men. What caught his attention first was that they were all college students. His gaze came to rest on a light-skinned African-American who looked younger than his stated twenty-one years, innocent, with close-cropped wooly hair, a square jaw, and an attractive smile.

Helms scanned the recruiting profile, his lips moving as he murmured: "Matson, Wiley. Princeton University. Class of 1969. Currently a junior. Student body secretary. Dean's list in political economics both sophomore and junior years." Helms' eyebrows elevated as he nodded slowly. "Starting running back, varsity football. Residence: 1844 Rice Ave., York, PA. Father: bank manager. Mother: nurse. Three siblings." Impressive, though Matson was not unlike the others. Helms was so absorbed in the file that the phone rang three times before he picked it up.

"General Reeves for you, sir," the civilian secretary announced.

"Thank you, put him through." The deep voice came on the line.

"Marcus?"

"Yes, General?"

"I'm just going through the schedule. Are we meeting with the committee chairs Thursday, or a week from Thursday?"

"It's this Thursday, sir."

"This Thursday? I've got a brown bag meeting of the psych staff on my calendar. Aren't I talking to that group about Klonopin this Thursday?"

"No sir. That was canceled."

"Canceled? Did you tell Margaret about it? We don't have that change up here."

"I did, sir. There should be a memo."

There was a pause, then: "So, Marcus. Where do we stand with the Q407 thing?"

"Funny you should ask, General. I'm just looking at those records now."

"*Looking* at the records?" Reeves snapped, bolting upright. "You mean you have them here? I didn't tell you to *look* at them. I said they should be lost!"

"I can't really trust anyone to do this, sir," Helms told him. "This has all the potential to devolve into a hopeless bureaucratic mess. If I ask someone in Washington to do it, Lord knows what will happen, or when, or how we could ever verify that it did. So I instructed them to deliver the records here."

"I appreciate your concern, Captain, but no one should view those records but me. Have you read any of them?"

Helms knew when to keep his mouth shut. "No, sir. I'm just checking names and serial numbers."

"Have you seen the background profiles on any of these men?"

"No, sir. Should I be looking at that?"

He was either very good, or a moron, Reeves thought. If he had the actual records, some trends were bound to be apparent. He had to put a stop to this and find out what Helms knew.

"Don't do anything, Marcus. I'll be right down."

Minutes later, Reeves sat across the desk from Helms. Two stacks of records loomed between them.

"You haven't been through any of these, Marcus?" Reeves asked, the usual amiable tranquility missing. His brows were gathered, his gaze fixed on Helms, probing, demanding.

"No, sir. I'm just verifying identification, that's all. As you can see, the name and serial number is on the outside of the jacket. Occasionally I need a separation date which is on the ID printout inside the cover. Is there a problem?"

Reeves wasn't so sure. His expression remained severe. "No problem, Marcus. As you know, Dr. Samson is being arrested as we speak, and this thing will probably heat up. It is critical that you are able to maintain a position of plausible deniability. I don't want anyone to have any information beyond what's absolutely necessary. That's all. I want this matter to end. Immediately."

"I understand, General."

"Henceforth, all records will be delivered to me personally—unopened. Understood?"

Helms was careful to not even reflect curiosity. He raised his eyebrows and nodded. "Understood, General."

Reeves relaxed slightly and smiled. "Atta boy," he said.

Helms showed no reaction to the slur, though it was not the first time, and every time it came it cut through to where he lived, where he'd been raised, who he was. Years of army discipline had steeled him, but not numbed him. He smiled stiffly as Reeves picked up one of the stacks, showing no emotion.

"I'll bring the rest, sir," Helms offered.

"No need, Marcus. I'll send Margaret down for them. Are there any others besides what we have here?"

"This is all we've got for now. Like I said, the search is ongoing."

"Just let me know the minute anything arrives. Be sure the seals are not broken. Am I clear?"

"Perfectly, sir."

Staring after his superior officer as the door swung shut behind him, Helms shook his head slowly.

"Crystal—" he muttered through clenched teeth.

CHAPTER TWENTY

"HERE WE ARE," JACK slurred in a rasping stage whisper.

After several stabs, his key found the lock, and the door creaked open. Reaching in, he groped for the switch, and a second later a dim light came on over the landing above. Jack stared up the long, dingy flight that dated to the turn of the last century. Raising his good eyebrow, he exhaled loudly, lips flapping. Then, summoning his remaining strength, he straightened, leaned forward on his aluminum sticks, and embarked on the monumental ordeal for what seemed like the hundred-thousandth time.

Jack had called this second-floor flat home for the last twenty-six years. Its front door was tucked unobtrusively between the garbage enclosure of a Chinese restaurant and the grange box of a T-shirt shop in an alley a block and a half down Windward from The Pit, the hardcore Venice dive where Jack and Noah had been drinking all day.

It was almost 11:00 p.m., and Noah was ripped. "The fuck are we?" he murmured as he stumbled up the stairs holding onto the back of Jack's coat, steadying himself behind the guy on the crutches.

Arriving at the landing, Jack opened the door and stepped inside. Noah lurched through the darkened room, following Jack's lead, head against his back like one of the Marx Brothers. Noah's foot caught a wrinkle in the rug, and the elephant train pitched forward. Jamming both crutches in front of him, Jack caught himself before they both went down.

"Alright me boy," Jack said. "Y'could be arrested for walkin' like that." He turned and put a hand under Noah's arm and dragged him, half hopping, half limping, the few steps to the couch. Noah fell face down.

"Lissen," Noah muttered through a tequila haze. "I-I gotta take a nap. I'll be ready t'go inna minute."

"Right, counselor," Jack agreed. "You just take a little nap." He propped himself on a crutch and pulled Noah's leg onto the couch, then crossed the room and switched on an old-fashioned floor lamp, illuminating the flat with soft light that emphasized deep and glowing browns in the aged dark wood trim, in the "antique" furniture, and even in the Laotian rice-paper wall hangings. Grimacing red and black Chinese ceremonial masks and a Mexican serape, which covered the couch where Noah was sprawled, added splashes of color.

Nestled into an alcove was the abbreviated kitchen. Apart from a few coffee cups and a dish or two from yesterday's unscheduled meals, it was reasonably tidy. A dining room table, one side stacked high with journals and magazines, was positioned close enough for one on crutches to manage service. The other side of the table was clear, usable for meals.

On the adjacent wall, two tall windows were framed by heavy dark drapes layered with gossamer curtains. When drawn, the drapes protected against the oppressive glare and heat of the late-afternoon western exposure. Between them, two antique wooden chairs, upholstered in well-worn burgundy velvet, faced one another. Nearby, a box of tissues sat on a small, leather-inlaid, scalloped table. A multicolored-glass-shaded floor lamp in the Tiffany tradition completed the grouping.

Next to the front door was a wooden sideboard cluttered with photos of military units intermingled with shots of bare-chested soldiers standing next to oriental natives, primitive huts, and heavy ordnance, all of a bygone era. To the left was Jack's desk, covered with journals and papers. Several photos of an attractive woman and a young man in uniform competed for space with a personal computer and monitor. Above, an M-16 rifle was mounted on a gun rack, above a red velvet medallion that bore several service ribbons and medals, including a Silver Star and a Purple Heart. Next to the medallion, a cluster of framed prints of brightly colored tropical birds, along with a few of the local species, stared down placidly, offering stark contrast to the juxtaposed memorabilia of war.

On the floor was an ancient, threadbare, brown Persian rug that had no doubt once conveyed the active imagination of its weaver, but the patterns had long since faded. A short hall next to the front door led to a nondescript bedroom and a small, well-maintained bath, both sparsely furnished to allow comfortable passage for one on crutches.

Jack retrieved a blanket from under the couch, flopped it over Noah —
who was, by now, snoring sonorously — and switched off the light.

"Sleep well, Boyo," he muttered, then thumped down the familiar
hall in the dark with a syncopation sounding like Long John Silver.

* * *

"A leading proponent of the dignity of the combat soldier, and
a stalwart in the fight to return him to a useful post-war life, General
Harley Reeves has been an inspiration to us all."

The Marine colonel stood erect behind the dais, addressing the
multitude of Tripler physicians and other military royalty dressed in
tuxedoes and formal dress uniforms who sat at tables that crowded
the perimeter of the dance floor in the ballroom of the Pearl Harbor
Officers Club. It was the annual White Coat Ball, a self-congratulatory
celebration by the military and VA medical personnel stationed in the
Pacific. Military doctors received a fraction of the income of their civilian
counterparts, but there were other benefits.

The colonel droned on, then mercifully came to the peroration: "And
therefore, to offer this evening's toast, I want to introduce a man who
has dedicated his life to, and distinguished himself in, caring for the
medical needs of the United States serviceman. Our Chief of Psychiatry
at Tripler, General Harley Reeves, was raised in a military family, and
graduated West Point at a disgustingly young age." He looked over at a
smiling Reeves. "He aspired to be a line officer, but after service of an
initial tour, he returned to medical school at Johns Hopkins, then served
a residency in psychiatry at Emory University in Atlanta. With the advent
of the Vietnam conflict, he was sent to the front, where he developed an
outstanding reputation in research and patient care. He has published
extensively on treatment of battle-related affective disorders and other
psychiatric conditions afflicting combat soldiers. But you already knew
all that. So without further ado" — he held out a welcoming arm — "I give
you General Harley Reeves."

Bathed in applause, a graying Reeves, immaculate in his formal army
blues, leaned over and kissed the stunning middle-aged brunette on his

left, then stepped to the podium as she beamed after him.

He settled himself and looked out over the crowd, smiling, nodding, and waving to a familiar face here and there, before he began.

"As the incoming president of the Association of American Military Medical Personnel, Pacific Division, I want to extend a warm welcome to you all to our annual event. I am delighted to see that we have some members here tonight from beyond the Hawaiian Islands.

"Tonight," he said, his demeanor more serious now, "I offer a toast to the finest combat apparatus ever devised to serve America on the battlefield." He paused. "Of course, we all know of the M109 155mm Self-Propelled Howitzer, the Vektor M8 81mm mortar, the 37mm Thumper grenade launcher, and the M18 Anti-personnel Claymore Mine." Clearly no one did, but they got the point: no hospital soldier he. "But by far and away, the most resourceful, the most cunning, the most devastating war machine ever produced, is the American fighting man and woman." Applause and whistles. "It is they who are our heroes." More applause.

"Our combat troops surpass any in history, including the conquering armies of the Roman Empire, the Macedonian Empire, and Alexander the Great. Right here, right now, our own combat troops are at the pinnacle of that timeless evolution. And it is our privilege, our honor, as the medical support for those men and women, to keep them fit and fighting to protect and defend the values of freedom, and the sanctity of a democratic way of life, the only way of life which resonates with our human nature." Again, thundering applause.

"Now, in our department, the Department of Psychiatry, the challenge has been particularly daunting in recent years. Why? Because a creeping cancer spawned by a permissive society has threatened to emasculate our fighting men, to rob them of the courage that is their hallmark. That cancer is one that we in psychiatry have to deal with every day. A product of the last century, in World War I we called it "shell shock." In World War II, it was renamed "battle fatigue." In the Vietnam conflict, we labeled it PTSD, Post-traumatic Stress Disorder. It has been characterized by many in our profession as an illness, one which disables our combat personnel. But these labels do not constitute disease. They are an effort to pathologize fear, to rationalize cowardice. And as such, they are an insult to the heroic soldiers who have given their lives in all the many theaters of all the terrible wars to protect our homeland."

He looked from face to face. "There is nothing new about fear of battle. It is a natural response. Why wouldn't any of us be afraid? If soldiers were not afraid, then we would begin to think in terms of pathology." Heads were nodding. "So fear is not a disease. And thus we do not deal with fear by cloaking it in medical jargon and complex diagnoses, then excusing soldiers from executing their duty because they say they are terrified. We do not serve our young people by shipping them home and caring for them in Veterans Affairs Medical Centers for the remainder of their unproductive lives as disabled veterans, infected by PTSD, paying them to be immobilized. No.

"What, then, is the solution?" he challenged. "I'll tell you. Rather than support the weakness of our soldiers, we align ourselves with their strength. We accept that fear is a central feature of war, and always has been. We instruct our warriors to listen to that fear. It is God's way of telling them to be vigilant. But we train them that, once recognized, they do not have to act upon it. As human beings, we have choices. The response is called "fight *or* flight." Our collective choice throughout our history, from Washington to Patton to McCain, is to fight." The applause were scattered at first, but rippled into glowing support. Reeves's expression remained serious as he waited for the response to subside.

"And like those great heroes, each of our soldiers can stand and fight, *if,* they are prepared. If we teach our fine young men and women their jobs so well. If we train them to react with strength in the face of adversity. If we rehearse it, and practice it, over and over, what happens? Our natural response to the fear of battle will be to act on our strength, not on our weakness. We will not embrace the dread of battle, but rather our inborn courage." The large crowd applauded and cheered, loving both the patriotic message, and being included in its reverberation.

Reeves looked around the room at his admirers, then softened his voice again. "Therefore, let all of us in this room understand the profound importance of what we have been called to do. Ours is truly a duty that is central to the survival of our country, isn't it. One might even say it is a holy mission."

He raised his glass, half full of champagne. "And so, ladies and gentlemen, I give you a toast—" He paused, and when the entire throng was standing, glasses raised back to him, he proclaimed: "To the American fighting soldier with the love, the admiration, and the thanks, of a grateful nation."

* * *

Half an hour later, Reeves stood next to his female companion at a buffet table, mashing chopped liver onto a sliver of rye toast, when he was approached from behind by Marcus Helms.

"Great speech tonight, General," the captain said, nodding. "Very inspiring."

Reeves turned. "Oh, thanks, Marcus." He stretched an arm around his date and drew her forward. "Vicky, I think you've met my adjutant, Captain Marcus Helms. You remember Vicky Wilson, don't you, Marcus?"

Helms most certainly did. He had met her any number of times, always on the arm of the General. The thrice-divorced, never-to-remarry Reeves had a number of love interests, but whenever he needed someone respectable at functions such as these, it was always the high-born, highly educated, and formerly very married army brat, Ms. Vicky Wilson.

"Of course, Ms. Wilson," Helms said. "Nice to see you again."

"Always a pleasure, Captain." Vicky smiled, balancing some caviar on a toast square poised for consumption.

Reeves turned to her. "Vicky," he said, "I wonder if you'd fix me up a plate of these delicious hors d'oeuvres. You know what I like. I just need a minute with Captain Helms."

"Sure," Vicky shrugged.

"Thanks." The general put a hand under Helms' elbow. "Marcus, let's step outside and get a dose of that tropical breeze."

They walked out the French doors onto a large balcony with a breathtaking view of the harbor. The moon glittered off the water, over the WWII Arizona Memorial, out to the Hawaiian horizon beyond. The sun was just disappearing, a few stars visible against the pink and gray afterglow. Reeves took a sip of champagne and raised his glass to the panorama.

"Paradise, eh?" he said.

"Indeed, sir."

Reeves walked over and leaned against the thick balcony railing, staring into the distance. Behind him stood the distinctly Spanish-styled Wheeler Airfield Officer's Club, with its pseudo-adobe appearance, colonnade structure, and red tile roof. Gazing into the distance, he breathed deeply, then pointed off toward the water. "The Jap planes came up the valley straight toward us."

Helms' grimace at yet another racial slur was virtually unnoticeable.

"It was about five-thirty in the morning." Reeves looked back at the building. "All the pilots were sitting inside, in there at the coffee shop, having breakfast, preparing for the day. They say that music was playing over the radio, and just kept on playing. The whole thing was almost over by the time the state of emergency was broadcast on the commercial air." He nodded slowly, as if he were hearing it. "And then they started playing church hymns."

Helms regarded him and nodded. The general knew his military history, but he hadn't brought him out here for a lesson on the Pearl Harbor attack.

"The ak-ak gunners knew, though. Not long after the Nips arrived, the anti-aircraft emplacements opened up over there, and on the hill over there." He indicated points on the perimeter of the base. He studied them one by one, then scoffed. "They say there was a five-inch anti-aircraft shell, one of our own actually, that came screaming up the valley and hit a house right up there in Dowsett Highlands. Blew it to pieces. Killed a family inside." Frowning in disbelief, he looked at Helms. "Our own fucking shell." Then he snorted: "We were so totally unprepared." After another sip of champagne, Reeves shook his head slowly.

"Despite the fact that Europe was at war, the Far East was at war, Japan had taken over China and had designs on the rest of the Pacific, we were still asleep at the wheel. That's what I was talking about inside."

"Understood." Helms rubbed the back of his neck. He didn't know where this was going, but he thought it best to just listen and let the General spell it out.

"See that island down there?" Reeves leveled a finger at the harbor. "Right there."

"I see it."

"That's Ford Island. All the battlewagons were tied up down there," he mused. "Utah, Arizona. Everything was in flames. It was an inferno. A minelayer called Ogallala had been torpedoed and was lolling on its side next to the island when a Japanese plane came in low carrying another torpedo and dropped it towards her. The damn torpedo skidded up over the Ogallala's flank and plowed up onto the lawn of the Officers Club, the propeller still running," he chortled. "Right down there." He nodded at a small lawn about fifty feet downhill from where they were standing.

"Course, all the pilots and everybody in the club had come out here by then to see what the hell was going on. Man—" Reeves continued to chuckle. "I bet they scattered when they saw that thing sitting there grinning at them like a crocodile showing its teeth."

He took a long sip from his champagne flute. "See, Marcus?" he said. "That's what we've got to avoid."

"What's that, sir?"

"Being unprepared."

"Yes, sir?"

He turned to face Helms. "That's why I'm going over to the Big Island to take charge of Kupuna now that Samson's in custody. We need to see how big a problem we're facing here. A little damage control might be in order. Better to know now, before we get blindsided, right?"

Helms was unsure of exactly what Reeves had in mind. He knew that Q407 was an old project of the general's that had become troublesome from time to time, but he'd never really understood the thrust of it. "You're going to get involved in the treatment of those patients yourself, General?"

"I am, Marcus. I'm going to brush up on my old psychotherapy skills and see if I can't help out. Somebody's got to fill in over there, and I didn't see anyone else on the list we could spare."

"So, how can I help, sir?"

"You can nail down those pre-recruitment files. Stack them in my office as they come in. And stand by for further orders. Like I said, be sure the seals aren't broken."

"Certainly sir."

The moment drifted, then the general took another sip. "You're such a help to me, Marcus. And this is sensitive stuff. Critical times. I know you can keep things stable here while I'm gone."

"Of course I can sir. You can depend on it."

Reeves smiled at him. "I know I can."

CHAPTER TWENTY-ONE

"Alright, boyo. Can't sleep all day. Lots to do. Folks to see."

The 10:00 a.m. sun streamed in through the lace curtains as Jack stood in front of a plate of scrambled eggs and toast he'd set on the table next to a cup of coffee, all emitting tantalizing aromas that wafted across to the couch where Noah lay like a corpse.

One eye opened, then the other. "Ohhhh God, no, please," Noah protested. He looked up suddenly. *Where the—?* When he saw Jack, it all came back. *What in God's name had he been thinking? Everything he'd told this guy. His fucking life story. Now what?*

"Come on now," Jack nagged. "I got the One-Eyed Jack breakfast special here."

By the time Noah was on his second cup of coffee and third piece of toast, he was beginning to navigate towards semi-cognition. He was even aware that things looked decidedly better than yesterday at this time. Then again, how could they look worse?

Noah glanced around the flat as he chewed. "So, Jack," he said. "I never would have imagined you in a place like this. I confess I had you a little more down and out. The place looks like some kind of veterans' nerve center."

"I'm probably just as down and out as you thought. Sort of homeless with a home."

"What happens here? All these journals and books and stuff. Looks like—what?" He picked up a journal with his free hand while the other held the cup to his lips. "'*Psychology of the Combat Veteran.*' And here's '*The Compendium of Veteran's Benefits.*' What is all this?"

"Guess you might say I do some informal VA counseling."

Noah shook his head. "What is it about vets?" he said. "They're everywhere I go these days. Like I told you, a lotta my clients up north are vets. Just spent the weekend with a bunch of crazy vets in Hawaii. Now you. Not that you're crazy."

"Don't judge to quickly, Boyo." The semi-toothless grin was endearing, avuncular.

Noah's gaze lingered on him. He liked this old guy. There was something surprisingly solid about him. He took his coffee over to the desk where the war medals had caught his eye. "Looks like a Silver Star," he said. "What's this about?"

Jack glanced over, then demurred. "Yeah," he said. "Me and some friends crawled out of a firefight. Saved our necks, and some brass thought we were heroes. We didn't argue. So how about some more coffee? Seems to be doing you some good."

"I'm okay for the moment," Noah told him as he admired the decoration. "But you must have done more than crawl out of a hot spot."

"Nah. Listen, I gotta get over to the hospital this morning, and I've got an appointment after that. But how about we have a little walk later?"

"I'd like to, but I really gotta get home, back to work. Some clean clothes would be helpful, though."

Jack nodded. "So why don't you call and get a flight for tomorrow morning. We'll hang out a little after I see my guys."

"I guess, but it sounds like you've got a lot to do. I don't want to—"

"Hey, no trouble. It's kind of what I do."

"What's that?"

"Work with people like you."

"I'm not a vet."

"Not of a declared war. But you got your own battles. Hey, we're all vets of something. What'd you call it? *Sumis?*"

Noah looked at him quizzically.

"You know, 'trouble,' you said. *Sumis?*"

"*Tsuris*. Did I say something about that?"

"Right. So we'll talk a little more about your *tsuris*."

* * *

After Jack left for the VA Hospital, Noah prepared to get a cab back to Beverly Hills to pick up his rental car. Even with three cups of coffee taking his blood pressure to new heights, the alcoholic haze had not entirely lifted. He had located his jacket and keys and started for the door, when his eyes again fell on the M-16 and the medal medallion that hung below it. He ran a hand over the Purple Heart and the ribbon pinned next to it, under which was a small certificate card.

Who really was this guy? Clearly not just an old drunk, blown up all those years ago and living on a VA pension, like he'd have you believe. But there he was, drinking in the middle of the morning at a grimy Venice dive. What kind of life was that? He was obviously educated, knowledgeable about psychology, even though he didn't sound like it at first. Noah had found himself confiding comfortably, no doubt partially anesthetized by the tequila. But still, the guy had a way about him.

Adjacent to the Purple Heart was a Southeast Asia War Zone Bar, and next to that a Vietnam War Zone Bar, both identified by small certificates.

Jack had asked Noah about his childhood, and where he went to school. Noah had gone on, uncharacteristically, about his high school football career and how, as a highly recruited quarterback, he'd never really lived up to his potential at Stanford. He'd told him how he'd joined a fraternity and drunk a lot of beer and later found himself a reluctant law student. Having no other plans or ambitions, he'd taken the LSATs with some fraternity brothers as a lark, done well enough, and ended up at Hastings for reasons unknown. He described how the law had come easy to him, but had never really inspired him. Nothing had.

In the position of prominence hung the Silver Star.

As the afternoon had worn on into evening, he told Jack about Kate and Sandy and their decision to all go to the Alameda County PDs office together. He described how exciting it was at first, trying several murder cases in his first two years; how he'd keenly anticipated the Involuntary Commitment duty but had become disillusioned with the drudgery of the homeless misfits, many of whom were vets. No shock, no insult. Jack had just been interested in Noah's story.

Noah's finger caressed the ribbon's red field with the white band down the middle and the superimposed blue stripe. Below hung the silver five-pointed star.

They'd ordered hamburgers as Jack continued to gently prod, supporting, sympathizing. Why did this guy care? What possible interest could he have? And yet there he was, and the more he listened, the more Noah revealed. About learning only a few days ago that Samson was his father and that Neal Shane wasn't; about his mother having concealed his origins for her own selfish reasons; and about Samson working with the bush vets and the serious accusations against him. After the burgers, brandy was the truth serum of choice as they lounged in the dilapidated naugahyde booth at the rear of The Pit. Noah's memory of the late evening was dim, but remnants of his catharsis remained. His intense feelings of loss, reluctantly uncovering the fear of the chaos that lay beneath the denial, and the anger that was bubbling up into a cauldron of rage.

As he straightened the medal, Noah felt something crinkle behind the dark-burgundy velvet medallion on which the medals were pinned.

There had been tears. He had sat in that hole-in-the-wall bar, weeping like a lost child to a complete stranger. Christ—

Noah carefully turned the medallion over to find a yellowing certificate fixed to the reverse side:

DEPARTMENT OF THE ARMY
SILVER STAR AWARD
CERTIFICATE OF COMMENDATION

SERGEANT MARTIN VAN BUREN DONOHUE
has been awarded the Silver Star for distinguishing
himself through heroic service in military operations
against an armed enemy in that on February 3, 1968
at the Battle of Hue, in the Republic of Vietnam, he
did, at great personal risk, enter a known mine field
for the purpose of finding an escape route for his rifle
squad which was pinned down by enemy fire. After
the explosion of a land mine resulting in a mortal
wound to the recipient he continued his efforts and,
exercising exceptional valor in an ensuing firefight,
successfully led his squad to safety.

Noah restored the medallion to its original position and reflected. *This was no homeless drunk. But why had he played down the story behind his medal? He'd heard that many who have been decorated react in that way. Suddenly Noah had a spasm of patriotism, while regretting that most of the vets of Jack's generation were cheated out of the American Dream.*

* * *

"Beautiful, isn't it?" Jack said, more an observation than a question. The afternoon sun was dropping into the Pacific as he and Noah ambled along the boardwalk on Venice Beach, the second time in as many days that Noah had been out there.

"It is," Noah said. "But are you comfortable on those things? We could just sit if you want."

Jack stopped, turned to Noah, and scowled. "I been on *these things* upwards of forty years, Boyo. A lot longer than you been on *those things.*" He nodded toward Noah's legs. "So don't be doin' me any favors."

Noah smiled. "What'd you do at the hospital this morning?"

Jack didn't answer for a moment, thumping down the boardwalk. He glanced out at the water. "Thirty-eight-year-old Afghanistan vet in the psych unit," he said. "Cops picked him up in the park last night. He was half naked, screaming. Kinda down today."

"Sounds like some of my homeless clients."

"Could turn out that way if something doesn't happen for him damn quick," Jack said.

"Why's that?"

"Wife left him, took the boy."

Noah frowned. "What happened?"

"The usual. Guy's a little buggy since he came back from drag. Drinks too much. Been through a few jobs. Guess she got fed up when he lost the last one."

"Doesn't he have family?" Noah asked.

Jack glanced over and shot him a grin. "No more than you do, I reckon."

Noah's head snapped up. Seeing Jack's face, he scoffed and nodded. "Guess you got a point."

"He's pretty raw today," Jack said. "Says he's thinkin' about pitching it in."

"Jesus. You think he's serious?"

"About suicide? Absolutely."

"So what can you do?"

"Try to make sure he doesn't. Get him thinking a little more toward his future. He's a solid guy underneath. A plumber. Got potential."

"Does the VA pay you to work with these guys?"

"Nobody pays me."

"So why do you do it?"

"Needs to be done."

Jack stopped, gazing at a colorful bush fifteen feet from the boardwalk. "Mmmmmmm, *Archilochus colubris.*"

Noah was baffled. "What?"

"Ruby-throated hummingbird. Never seen one around here."

Noah peered toward the little bush covered with flowers. A tiny bird with a red head flitted from one bloom to another.

"Watch now," Jack pointed with a jerk of his head, "he can fly backwards." The bird darted back and forth. "See that delicate little black band on the crown. That's how you tell it's a *colubris.*"

"You study birds?"

"You might say," Jack muttered, as he clunked down the path again.

Noah recalled the prints of various species on the wall near the desk, next to the medals. "What's the attraction?" he asked, hurrying to catch up.

"Guess with all the chaos," Jack told him, "it's good to be reassured now and then."

"Reassured?"

"That God really knew what he was doing."

CHAPTER TWENTY-TWO

REEVES WAS SEATED BEHIND the desk in the office of the Supervising Lieutenant of the East Hawaii Detention Facility on the grounds of the police headquarters in Hilo when Samson was brought in wearing an orange prisoner's jump-suit. In view of his military rank, Reeves's request for special privacy in which to visit the prisoner had been approved.

"I'll be right outside," the guard told Reeves as he removed Samson's cuffs. "If you need anything, shout." He sat Samson in the chair across the desk that was calculated to place the Supervising Lieutenant's visitors at a level significantly lower than his. The guard left the fishbowl room that was surrounded on three sides by glass, closed the door and took up a position just outside.

"Hello, David," Reeves said, smiling.

Samson nodded. "Harley," he said. Samson's expression had initially been one of surprise when he saw Reeves sitting behind the desk, followed by indifference. He was seething, but he wasn't about to give Reeves the satisfaction of saying he'd told him so.

"Been a while since we sat down together," Reeves said. The attitude was triumph.

Samson didn't respond. He stretched and rubbed his wrists and hands to encourage the circulation.

"I just wanted to stop in for a little briefing on my way up to Kupuna," Reeves told him.

Now Samson was interested. "What do you mean?" he asked.

"With you in here," Reeves circled a finger indicating the lock-up, "somebody has to run the hospital on the hill. I figured it might just as well be me."

"Why would you want to leave Tripler? I thought you'd send someone. I thought maybe Clemens from Inpatient Psychopharm? Even Helms could cover until I get back."

"I thought it best that I take over myself. I'm sure you can figure it out. I can put an end to this foolishness with the SSRIs once and for all. Put those poor wretches back on some heavy tranqs so they can live out their miserable lives in peace."

Samson struggled to keep his chest from heaving visibly. "You can't do that," he said.

"I can, and I will." Reeves was still smiling.

"You'll never get away with it. When I get out of here, I'll reinstate the regimen and we'll get back to where we were."

"Don't think that's going to happen, David."

"They have nothing on me, and you know it."

"You just don't get it, do you?"

"Get what?"

"I think there'll be a conviction, at least for manslaughter. But even if there isn't, my folks in the Pentagon intend to remove you based upon the deaths and the prosecution. You'll lose your appointment with the VA and most likely your medical license. Whatever happens, you won't see Kupuna again."

Samson stared at him. "You can't do it."

"Why not?"

"Because I intend to bring all this to the attention of the press at the trial."

"I don't think so. We have a gag order, the trial is closed, and the transcript will be sealed. You can say what you want after you're convicted. There's no evidence of anything."

Samson's face drained of color as he considered the enormity of the situation, the utter helplessness. Suddenly he bolted to his feet and lunged toward Reeves, then stopped abruptly and looked around at the guard, who had lept up and started forward.

Reeves hadn't flinched. "I wouldn't do anything stupid, David," he said.

The door banged open. "Everything alright?" the deputy asked.

"Fine, Officer," Reeves said. "But I think we're finished here."

Samson was recuffed. As the guard led him from the room, he glared back and whispered, "You bastard."

* * *

They sat in the two "therapy" chairs under the windows, nursing brandy from tumblers.

"It's almost always about something letting 'em down," Jack said. "You gotta start with the pain. Let 'em take you where they will." He took a sip of the brandy and considered. "Most of 'em are stuck. Can't make the pain stop, so they start to self-medicate."

"I've seen plenty of that up in the Bay Area," Noah interjected.

"Bet you have," Jack mused. "I wasn't much different. But when I found out I had something to offer, that made all the difference. We're pretty much wired to be social animals, y'know? My philosophy is that we're programmed to want to be more tomorrow than we were today, and when we give somebody else a leg up to make that happen, well—that's when we see we're runnin' on all eight, gives us a feeling of value, know what I mean?"

"Whoooa. Where'd all that come from, your years in a Buddhist monastery?"

"Kinda," Jack said. "Venice style. I was down for the count after I got back. One eye, one leg, out on the street. But I was lucky. Master Kim found me."

"Master Kim?"

"Jung Hak Kim. Ran the Kuk Sool Wan studio over on Pacific Avenue. You heard of it?"

"No."

"Korean marshal arts." He chuckled. "Imagine how I felt waking up in that alley wasted, seeing Master Kim standing over me. Thought we'd been overrun by VC. So he takes me home. I didn't know what he saw in me, but he was the one showed me I had something to give—if I had the guts to try."

"What happened to him?"

"He's dead now. He was in his eighties when he did my extreme makeover. Lived almost another ten years. Sharp to the end. Don't think he ever ate a piece of red meat. Fish, tofu—" he grimaced, "other unmentionables."

"With your background, the vets must really respond to you," Noah said.

"Everyone responds to listening. It's a human thing. Master Kim taught me that forgiveness is the key. You don't motivate people by beating on 'em, runnin' 'em down."

"Yeah?"

"I read somewhere that Thurgood Marshall said something like, 'People are people.'" He groped for the words. "'Strike them and they cry out, cut them and they bleed, but treat them with respect and decency, and they flourish and grow.' That's what I'm talking about."

The muffled street noises seeped through the window cracks as they returned to their brandy.

"A guy can get pumped to defend his family, his kids—his mother, for God's sake. He'll train, fight, die, 'cause he knows why. Problem with Nam was it was set up by a bunch of old men, but it was the young guys sent over to do the dying. No reason, no threat. Those kids thought they were goin' off to kick some ass in another goddamn football game."

Noah was captivated. War was an experience entirely missing from his own life.

"But then they saw the mutilated arms, legs, faces, like I did. Scared them senseless, literally. That's PTSD. It haunts you. Day and night, when you're working, eating, dreaming, making love to a woman. The gift that keeps on giving."

Jack went to the brandy again. "You don't fix it by calling 'em cowards. Hell, you never really fix it, but you can give them their life back if you forgive the fear, the rage, the hatred. That's what Master Kim said. Get 'em to forgive themselves." He nodded toward the photograph of the young marine on the desk.

"Tried to tell my grandson over there." He sighed, rubbing the stubble on his chin. "They never listen at that age. Too much testosterone pumping. Gotta live it." He dropped his gaze into the depths of the warm, auburn liquid. "He's in Afghanistan now. No reason, no threat, nothin' to defend. Most all of 'em will come back in a bag or be doomed to a psych ward."

Noah broke another long silence when he asked: "What about the booze?"

"Yeah," Jack answered. "Turns out alcohol's one of the best medications for PTSD. My drug of choice. Was for most of the others, too. Dawned on me one night doing some Tokay with a bunch of the guys in the park. Now I do my trolling at the Pit and a dozen other places in Venice where adult beverages are served. The beach, the alleys. You'd be surprised."

* * *

Wrapped in a towel, Noah strolled into the living room, his face covered with shaving cream, razor in hand. Jack had been at the computer since dawn.

Noah held up the razor. "This thing is dangerous," he said. "You got something at least reasonably sharp before I'm total hamburger?"

Jack was still totally absorbed in the internet. "Drawer to the right of the sink."

Ten minutes later, Noah emerged dressed in yesterday's jeans, a clean flannel shirt he'd borrowed from Jack, and his Reeboks, carrying the duffel he'd retrieved from the rental car.

"Guess I better get going," he said. "Flight's at ten-forty."

"LAX or Burbank?" Jack didn't look up.

"LAX."

"You checked in?"

"Yeah, online, yesterday."

"You'll be okay," Jack told him. "Takes twenty minutes from here."

"What're you searching?" Noah asked.

"Archives. I've done a lot of combing through the military and VA data-bases over the years."

"Data-bases?" Noah came over to the monitor.

"I was Googling your dad, and when I couldn't find anything, I thought of that General you mentioned. Reeves. Thought I'd check him out. Turns out he used to be a guru in the PTSD, battle fatigue arena. Seems he did clinical research during Vietnam, then reported it in an obscure military medical journal."

"What kind of research?" Noah asked.

"Depression, apparently," Jack told him. "Studying the effect of an antidepressant, something called Fuerontin, on combat casualties. Says the medication was a precursor to the present-day tricyclic group, acted on something called the amygdaloid body."

"What's that?"

"Beats me. But Reeves's article said that at high doses over long periods, it apparently caused 'hostility, aggression, and sometimes violence,' instead of calming effects, relieving depression. They called it a 'paradoxical response.'" He looked up at Noah. "Hey, didn't you say these guys at the place your father works were pretty violent?"

"Yeah," Noah said. "Let me see that." He bent down in front of the monitor, reading out loud: "'Promising antidepressant effects.' 'Further study necessary to minimize paradoxical response.' Seems like Reeves was all over this stuff. Maybe that's why he's so uptight about these megadoses Samson is giving his patients? YM992, I think he said it was. Could Reeves be right? That Samson is causing more violence with the drug? That it really did cause the murder?"

Jack was still reading. "Wait. This is interesting. 'There appeared to be a long-lasting mobilizing effect—which, though accompanied by hostility, did not impair cognitive functioning. Energy levels were heightened, fatigue and dysphoria were diminished. In many cases patients could be returned to combat assignments on maintenance doses despite intermittent aggressive behavior.'"

Noah shook his head, somewhat confused. "So? What are you thinking?"

Jack looked at him. "Sounds like Reeves may have stumbled onto some kind of cure for battle fatigue. So what became of it all? Why haven't we heard of it? This would be a pretty big deal."

"Yeah. I don't know. I wonder if Samson knows about all this old work. He didn't say anything about it to me. What's the date on it?"

"Says 1973."

"Wow. Forty years. Is there anything else?"

"Let me see." He went back to the Google home page and brought the search forward again, scouring for other branches on the General Harley Reeves tree, or anything to do with Fuerontin. Meanwhile, Noah picked up his boarding pass and bag, then returned to the computer.

"Anything?"

"Nope, but I'll keep trying. Let's print what I got so far." Jack handed the page to Noah. "Here," he said. "Gimme your email. I'll do some further checking, see what I can come up with."

Noah scribbled the address. "What's yours?" he asked.

"Oneye@hotmail."

"Figures," Noah said. He folded the page, deposited it in his duffel, and put a hand on Jack's shoulder. "I'm grateful, Jack. More than you know. I was pretty fucked up the other day when I ran into you."

"With good reason," Jack said, collecting his crutches. Noah started toward the door as Jack thumped alongside. "You been dealt a bummer of a hand, Boyo. But don't let it take you out of the game, and don't blame the other players."

"I guess," Noah said. "Takes a frickin' saint to see it that way, though."

"You'll get some perspective in time." Jack opened the door. "And don't be too harsh on your folks. Sounds like your old man's doing some great work. A lot more hero than I was. I'm guessing they both got a bummer of a hand themselves at some point—like those nuts at Kupuna. "Not our job to judge." Jack squeezed Noah's bicep. "But if we're lucky, we might have somethin' to give."

Noah leaned forward and hugged the old man. "Thanks for everything," he said.

Jack blustered a bit. "Keep your head down out there, Boyo. But don't miss the good stuff. And let me hear from you."

"I promise."

Noah hiked the duffel over his shoulder and descended the stairs thinking that, though he didn't have a plan, he may have just received something a lot more valuable.

CHAPTER TWENTY-THREE

LYING FLAT ON HIS back, David Samson clenched his eyelids and pressed the back of his head into the pillowless cot in his eight-by-eight cell. He was waging war to shut out the relentless banter of the druggies, alkies, and cons, which echoed up and down the block against a background of throbbing rap, and he was losing.

Samson was now four days into his stay at the East Hawaii Detention Facility, whose twenty cells and two "tanks" housed federal, state, and county prisoners awaiting arraignment. After his meeting with Reeves, he suffered through two days of restrained fury, which ultimately gave way to resignation. How could this be happening? He'd done nothing but treat a bunch of Bush Vets. If they wanted to argue about dosages and side effects, fine, but murder?

He had no idea what time it was. There were no clocks, no windows. Based on feedings, he figured it now had to be late morning. As the vacant hours passed at a glacial pace, he obsessed about Noah, having failed him for so long. All those years he had longed to just pick up the phone and call, introduce himself. A handful of times he'd actually had the receiver in hand. But how could he just come out of nowhere after all the silence, all the time of letting him think someone else was his father. Maybe he should have done it long ago, when Noah was younger. But then, should he really have brought a son into the horror of all this?

Now Samson fantasized the two of them confronting the adversity of the case, pulling together through the hard times, standing shoulder to shoulder against injustice.

Right, he scoffed, then allowed himself to slide down into the depression, back to the first decision that had changed his life. Vietnam. It had terrified him, and yet, in some strange way that was probably why he did it. Somewhere back then, he knew deep down that it was time for a major crisis, even if it was one of his own making. It would help him grow up, wouldn't it? Find his way? Serving as a combat psychiatrist certainly qualified. And it actually had worked. Little by little, almost imperceptably, in the midst of it all, he had begun to forge a self.

It had happened in the MASH tents, he supposed, as he looked back at it, as he was utterly absorbed in the young GIs, kids who were all just as terrified as he. He guessed it had been their need for him that had saved him, that he had had a way to help. He was someone important in the midst of their terror, which ironically had eradicated, or at least moderated, his own. But their terror had been of war, of death, of mutilation. His had been of something quieter, more desperate, more internal.

In time he had found that his role in the war was a Hobson's choice. Treat them, relieve their pain, and they would be returned to the front, to the source of their terror. Was this medicine? Saving lives, preserving sanity, for what? So often in those early days, he agonized about his participation in it. But then, how could he turn his back on them? So his confusion lived on, and so did the co-dependent symbiosis. He would have done anything to relieve their pain, so he did. He brought them healing, at least temporarily; and they brought him meaning, at least temporarily.

His thoughts went to Okinawa after the war, how peaceful it was. Like a mausoleum planted in cherry blossoms, life punctuated with walks in the country, stark contrast to five years of gore, but still the endless parade of horribly maimed combat vets. He thought he had been able to give something to most of them, some hope, but his contribution could never compare to theirs. Then news of the bush vets reached him. The war was over, but for them, the torture continued. And thus, for him. He hated himself for all of it, the insanity, the enormity of the task. He had tried to alleviate it, but what could he do. . . really? God, there were some things he would regret to the end. But it had been a worthwhile life overall, hadn't it?

He had dreamed for years of the reunion with Noah. But how could he not have predicted Noah's response? Wouldn't he have had the same reaction? Now his lack of control over any of it made him anxious, intermittently panicky. Flickers of anhedonic doom began to play at the corners of his consciousness. His sleep was fitful, his dreams amorphous, troubled, working over it again and again with the same outcome. He knew the signs. He'd treated it countless times.

Grayson Slade had been in to see him several times, describing his struggles with Reeves taking over Kupuna, trying to convince Samson to agree to a lawyer. Slade had actually been his only friend and confidant. A former supply sergeant, he seemed to have the knack they all had to make the impossible happen. But now, Slade did not look good. He wasn't sleeping either. He wasn't thinking clearly. Samson was concerned. There was no way Slade could manage indefinitely, but what were the options?

So far, no bail. He'd left a couple of messages for Noah, both unreturned. It was Thursday, or was it? Hadn't he been arrested Monday? Then the charges must have been filed. Arraignment was set for next Monday.

He let his mind go blank, gazing at the ceiling, exerting enormous effort to focus on a remote beach with warm, caressing sun on his shoulders. Over the sound of the fantasized surf, he became aware of a presence at the door, then a key in the lock. He didn't stir.

"Got a visitor, doc," the portly Hawaiian guard told him. Thinking it must be Slade come to push the lawyer thing again, Samson elected to ignore it, preferring to indulge the darkness of his melancholy.

"Doc!" The deputy kicked the end of the cot. These guys weren't long on patience. He knew from experience with MPs that their training was to escalate, immediately, so they'd never find themselves one down in the relentless power struggle they perceived as the most basic law of the jungle. The old line, if your only tool was a hammer, you'd see a world of nails, wouldn't you?

"I said, you need to come down to the visitor's room!" It was a kind of slow staccato.

Samson reached over to a small metal stool and fumbled for his glasses. He stood without speaking, then slowly shuffled out into the corridor in loose-fitting sneakers with no laces, following behind the guard and down the hall.

Stephanie Kauna-Luke wore a tan, pin-striped pant-suit which made her dark skin look even darker. The jet-black hair flowed around her shoulders and hid her face as she sat, writing, when Samson was brought in. She didn't look up until he was seated across the visiting table.

"Hello, Dr. Samson," she smiled.

"Ms. Kauna-Luke," he nodded, managing a minimal smile.

"Sorry I didn't look in earlier. I had no call from you and thought you were represented. But Mr. Slade told me Noah went back to the Mainland, so he asked me to stop by."

Samson's eyes were soft, his tone measured. "I suppose he would," he said. Despite the quagmire of disturbing thoughts that had plagued him moments before, he was nonetheless still able to achieve the unruffled, calm visage that was the hallmark of his trade.

"I was disappointed that Noah didn't stay," Stephanie said. "I was hoping he might take the case, be around for awhile."

Samson studied her thoughtfully. "Me too. Did he tell you he was considering staying?"

"He said he was thinking about it. But he had concerns about his job back home." She flashed a grin. "We did some surfing on Sunday. He could've been a star with a couple more private lessons."

"Indeed?" Samson nodded, eyebrows raised. So there was something. Might this be a way to entice him back? "I wonder if there's any hope of getting him to reconsider."

She frowned suddenly. "I never understood why you called Noah in the first place. A Mainland public defender? From California?"

The eye contact didn't waver; he paused, weighing the alternatives, but only briefly. "Because he's my son."

She stared at him, searching his face for any sign of this being some kind of joke. "Your son?" she said at length. "I didn't know."

"Neither did he. That was why he left so abruptly."

She still seemed nonplussed.

"You mean—"

"It's a long story, counselor, one I think Noah should tell you, if he wishes." He paused, then returned to the business at hand. "But perhaps you might call him and discuss the case. See if he might be willing to come back and talk about it. I've left some messages, but he hasn't called."

Samson drew a deep breath and sighed. He looked back at Stephanie, then said quietly, "Please call him for me, won't you?"

"I'll think about it."

"The arraignment is Monday. Will you appear with me if Noah won't?"

She gathered her papers and closed her brief-case. "Well, you're not financially eligible for the office, but let's see what I can do with Noah." She stood and extended her hand. "We'll make something happen one way or another."

"Thank you, Ms. Kauna-Luke," Samson said. "You're very kind."

CHAPTER TWENTY-FOUR

"Do you remember the therapy, Wiley?" Reeves asked. Quiet but firm, and insistent. "That's what I want to know. Do you remember the psychotherapy work you did at Cam Ranh?"

Coyote's head rested on a clean white pillow at the head of an army cot covered with a brown, army-issue blanket that served as a makeshift psychiatric couch. They were alone in Samson's office. His eyes closed, Coyote drifted comfortably in a light hypnotic trance, supplemented by an injection of a cocktail of thiopental sodium, scopolamine, and nearly pure ethanol, all minimal dosages. Reeves had given just enough to disinhibit while the pateint was under, to allow exploration of current memory, but not deep enough to enter a regressive level that would expose what had to remain buried at all costs. The precise cocktail had been worked out with great effort to maximize hypnotizability and effects of post-hypnotic suggestion.

"I remember," Coyote responded robotically.

Reeves leaned forward intently. "Do you remember the room?"

There was a long pause, then: "the room."

"Yes, Wiley, the room. Can you see the place where you did the therapy? Think. I know it was a long time ago. What color are the walls?"

"Green," Coyote said without hesitation.

Reeves's eyebrows elevated as he drew a breath, and then he forced himself to relax. "That's right, Wiley," he said. "They're green. What's on the walls?"

No response.

"What is on the walls, Wiley?"

"Ummm— pictures."

"Pictures?"

"No—"

"What is it, Wiley?"

"Some kind of writing—Chinese writing. Long Chinese writing."

Reeves straightened. So it was true. They were getting dangerously close. It had to be the damned SSRIs. "Now listen carefully, Wiley. Do you remember who the therapist was? Who it was who helped you?"

Long pause.

"Can you recall, Wiley? Visualize it."

Coyote's face reflected the frustration. "Can't—"

"You don't remember?"

"Can't—"

"That's okay, Wiley, that's fine."

The patient became restless, breathing more rapidly. The muscles in his left cheek twitched slightly. "He—told me not to—"

"Not to what, Wiley?"

"Not to—not to remember," he murmured in slow monotone.

Reeves smiled. So the post-hypnotic suggestion was holding. He didn't want to undermine it further. "That's right, Wiley. He told you not to remember, and you don't remember, do you?"

"Don't remember—"

It was a temporary relief, but still worrisome. There could be no doubt that Matson, a.k.a. Coyote, was in that room right now, remembering the therapy. Could it be long before he remembered damaging content if he continued to take enough goddamn SSRIs to kill a horse? And what next? He would clearly remember who was involved.

Unacceptable. This project was worth everything they had sacrificed for it, and dammit, it would have succeeded if they could have seen it through. But they all got cold feet. Too many desk jockeys with political ambitions, quivering about public opinion. Lord. They were on the verge of something cataclysmic, something timeless. Strongest warriors in the history of the world. They could have won the damned conflict, and a hundred others, had they pressed on. It would have been over long before the whole fucking army slunk out of Saigon in disgrace. Ho Chi Minh City. . . Jesus.

His attention returned to Coyote. It had occurred to him many times to just take these guys out and eliminate the problem. Call it some kind of war between the maniacs caused by the drugs, Samson's harebrained treatment. But, had he ever been serious about that solution, the time was now long gone. Too many people knew about this compound now, particularly since Samson was being prosecuted. He had hoped for more containment, handle it through an administrative action, the Medical Board. But now there was no way. Whatever they tried, after a while, the smoke and flames would rise. It had to be stopped at all costs. Anything wide-scale would bring the whole mess down around him. He'd have *60 Minutes* crews on his doorstep in a heartbeat.

And what about the others? Had they remembered yet? They might be further along than Matson. It was the fucking drugs. He had to put a stop to the drugs. But where were they? He hadn't been able to find any cache at the compound. These guys lived out in the bush and he didn't relish the idea of going out there to scout around for their supply. Whatever they had left, he had to come up with it. But how? This could go on for months.

"Alright Wiley," Reeves said. "That's enough for today. I'm very pleased with your progress. You're doing extremely well. Now when I count to three and clap my hands, you're going to wake up refreshed and feeling wonderful, alright? Okay, now, one, two, three—" As he clapped his hands, Coyote's eyes opened almost simultaneously. He slowly gathered himself, stretching the muscles of his upper torso; then he looked up to see Reeves smiling at him.

"Well, soldier," Reeves said. "How are you feeling?"

Coyote turned to focus on the general, reassembling reality. "Umm— kind of refreshed." He echoed the general's word.

"Alright, now I want to see you again on Friday, you understand?"

"Yes, General."

"Good. So tell me—Do you have any more of the drugs Dr. Samson gave you?"

"Some."

"Are you taking them?"

"Yes, sir."

Reeves's face became stern. "This is very important, Wiley," he said. "I want you to stop taking them, and bring me what you have left on Friday. Will you do that?"

Coyote canted his head and frowned. "I don't know, General. Dr. Samson told me it was really important to take them. That I shouldn't miss a dose. Besides, I am remembering things that—"

Reeves was rigid, his tone stern. "I know he said that, Matson, but—" Then he caught himself and softened. "Yes, I know he said that, but we've discovered that these drugs could be dangerous. It's critical that you stop them immediately and bring the rest to me. Tell the others as well. You will see them before I do. Do you understand my order?"

"I hear you, General." Coyote's frown deepened as he stared at Reeves, searching. The general started to feel uncomfortable.

"Good," Reeves said abruptly. He helped Coyote to his feet and led him toward the door. "Now, I'll see you Friday. Ten-thirty."

"Yes, sir."

Reeves closed the door behind him, reflected a moment, then returned to the desk. He picked up the phone and dialed. A deep, familiar voice answered.

"Helms."

"Hello, Marcus."

"Afternoon, General."

"Fill me in."

"I was able to put off the M and M conference and the annual budget meeting, hopefully until you get back. But we can't stall for too long. Are you still projecting two weeks to a month?"

"Hard to say right now. I've got a long way to go over here."

"There's a lot of speculation about why you had to take over this duty personally. Chief of staff called me about the budget figures, then went off on me about the whole thing. Wanted to know what you planned on doing about your administrative duties. He says he doesn't get why this quote:–'damn VA stuff'—is so important that your military responsibilities have to suffer."

"Tell him there's no one else who can deal with this situation, and we don't want it to become a crisis. I worked with guys like this in Nam, he knows that. I'm the only one who can handle this. I just don't trust anyone else."

"I'll tell him," Helms said.

"Let me know if there's a problem. I'll call him. So have any more records come in?"

"They found records for three more of the men. Two sets arrived already. I put them in your office."

"Good work, Marcus. I knew I could count on you. Anything else pressing?"

"The Federal Prosecutor in Hilo called. Guy named Pitts. They're discussing the possible charges against Samson and they want to talk to you about the medicine."

"Yeah, Marvin Pitts, the U.S. Attorney. I spoke to him a while ago. What do they want now?"

"I didn't get exactly what he was saying. Sounds like he wants to understand the brain chemistry a little better. He's concerned about how he can prove that the drugs caused the murders. I told him he'd have to talk to you. I emailed you his number."

"I'll call him. And keep me posted on those records, Marcus."

"Will do, General."

Reeves checked his email and dialed the private number. Pitts picked up on the first ring.

"This is General Harley Reeves, Mr. Pitts. My adjutant said you called."

"Yes. Thanks, General. We're working on the Samson case. My boss in Washington is insisting that it be filed, but I told him it seemed that the causation was pretty thin. You know, hooking the killings to Samson's conduct? He said to talk to you about it."

"We discussed this before, Mr. Pitts. I told you then that there are a wealth of studies that demonstrate the danger of violence in patients who take selective serotonin reuptake inhibitors. This reaction is very well-documented. Didn't I send you some of those journal articles?"

"You did, General, but it's one thing to say that a drug has side effects that cause a small number of patients to become violent. It's quite another to say that the doctor who prescribes it is an accomplice to murder if his patient happens to kill someone. See the difference?"

Reeves's voice grew louder. "I'm not an idiot, counselor. This doctor has been prescribing megadoses of SSRIs. The danger of aggressive behavior goes up exponentially, and this fact was not lost on Dr. Samson. He knew that long before he had the first death, but continued to use the megadoses until he had another tragedy. It was totally predictable."

"I get that. But how do we prove that it was the SSRIs? There have been deaths before. This is a pretty brutal patient population. It's not like we're dealing with a Buddhist retreat out there, General."

Reeves held his fire. "It's absolutely reckless to keep giving those drugs. He's obviously doing it for his own reasons."

"All that may be very interesting in Psychiatric Grand Rounds. In fact, it may well be below the medical standard of care. Might be a civil case for malpractice, or even disciplinary action for unprofessional conduct, but I'm not tracking on it standing up in a criminal prosecution."

"It will—" Reeves fired back. "And I want you to pursue it."

Pitts was quiet. "Uh huh," he said finally. "I'll check again with Washington. See what they want to do."

"You do that, sir, and I'm confident they'll back me up once they understand the medical science."

"I assume that I can tell Justice that you're willing to testify as an expert witness on the issue of causation?"

Reeves stopped and considered being cross-examined on the details, then told him: "I'm Dr. Samson's superior officer. I don't think my testimony as an expert would be appropriate. I would certainly testify to the facts surrounding his insubordination. Disobeying direct orders. But opinions—"

"I see. Again, that might get him demoted, but murder? I have my doubts. I'd hate to get this one all teed up and lose it, know what I mean? It's an election year, and we've had some tough verdicts over the last few outings."

"Damn it, Pitts! Washington wants this case prosecuted, and so do I. We can't be bothered with your political problems. Besides, DOJ has your back on this."

"Wonderful, but I don't see how that helps me at the polls."

This jerk had no respect for the military. Who the hell did he think he was? Reeves's blood was boiling. But he forced himself to rein in. He really didn't care if Samson ever got convicted, did he. He just needed the case charged and tried, which would then get the guy off his compound and out of Hawaii. He just needed everything at Kupuna back to normal ASAP and this whole fucking business buried. No percentage in blowing it just to bring this small-time hack up short.

"I'll find you a damned expert," Reeves said. "There've been any number of civil suits against the manufacturers. I think there's a woman at Johns Hopkins who's written a lot on the subject. Likely she's testified, too."

"Many thanks, General. Nice to know you've got the DOJ's best interests at heart." Pitts hung up and Reeves slammed down the receiver. He was going to have to jump-start this whole damn mess sooner than he'd thought.

CHAPTER TWENTY-FIVE

IT WAS A SHADE past six-thirty when Noah trudged up the two flights to his "suite" at the Larkin. Exhausted, he banged the door open, pulled the strap off his shoulder, and dropped the tan leather briefcase on the table. He had been back two days, and the steady flow of LPS commitment hearings had yet to let up. All routine, and all resulted in detention orders of one kind or another, over the protests of the detainees. But then, his job wasn't to keep the homeless crazies on the street so much as to monitor their detention and make sure the government accounted for them. The cheapest approach for the system would be to let them sleep in cardboard boxes, but that became a health problem that would bubble up politically every six months or so when the rats abounded and the bouquet of human habitation invaded the surrounding residential neighborhoods.

An aimless evolution of bureaucratic machinations, rather than any considered legislative process, had settled on intermittent commitments to Bedlam as how the social structure dealt with its castaways, and Noah's job was to reconcile the proceedings with the Constitution. This particular evening, as he left Highland, it seemed that he was actually hearing the stories again, for the first time in a long time. One thing for sure, the way these commitment hearings backed up, there was no way he was going to be able to bounce back and forth from Oakland to Hawaii.

He hit the button that dialed his voicemail on his way to the fridge for the cold Bud he'd been thinking about for the last two hours.

The mechanical female voice announced that the call had come in at 5:26 p.m., then: "Noah—Aloha." The voice of the Islands snapped his head around. "Stephanie here, coming to you from Hawaii-Nei. You surprised to hear me, no?"

Noah's face melted into a broad smile as he pulled a chair from under the table and straddled it. He twisted the top off the beer and ran the icy brown bottle over his forehead.

"So here's the deal, dude. You gotta give your father a break." Short pause as Noah's eyebrows arched. "Yeah, your father. He's a good man, Noah. They got another death at Kupuna, and he's been arrested. They're holding him without bail, and I went up to see if he needed anything. He's not indigent, so I don't think our office can represent him, but we might be able to appear for him temporarily. He pretty much told me about the case. Anyway, he needs you. Many ways, Noah, but mostly right now you're the only one he trusts to represent him. So you call me, okay? (808) 521-6330." In his mind's eye, Noah could see the dazzling smile, the rich Kona mocha skin. "Hope you're good."

For only an instant the anger with Samson rose again; then it lifted just as quickly, and he glanced at his watch. It was about three-thirty in Hilo. He picked up the phone and dialed.

"Federal Public Defender," preached the officious, sing-song voice of bureaucracy.

"Stephanie Kauna-Luke?"

"She would be in court. You want to leave word?"

"What time do you expect her back?"

"Hard to say. If she comes straight back, maybe four-thirty, five-o'clock. If she goes to the jail or has meetings, hard to predict."

"Tell her Noah Shane returned her call. She has the number."

"Is there any message?"

Noah sat in silence. The knee-jerk response was "No message." But just before he said it, something seized him, and he applied the brakes. He was amazed to find that his mind was vacant. No pros, no cons. Vacant. He ran the cool bottle over his forehead again.

"Hello—do you want to leave a message?"

He heard himself say: "Yeah. Tell her I'll be in Hilo Monday."

CHAPTER TWENTY-SIX

AT EIGHT-THIRTY THE FOLLOWING morning, Noah barged into the office of his supervisor, Roger Moreland, and told him he needed some time off. Moreland, who ran the special units at the PD's office, including sex crimes, domestic violence, and the nut run, did not take it well. A light-skinned African-American with freckles and short red hair, he appeared much younger than his forty-two years. Moreland's habit of frowning and not making eye contact while listening always made Noah think that somehow he had it wrong, which made conversation difficult. Noah's hopes that this would go down smoothly were crash landing.

"No chance, Shane," was the reflex response. "No one knows the Highland backlog but you, and I haven't got anyone else I can plug in."

Noah knew the even-handed approach was his only hope. Getting this guy sideways was not going to bring a happy ending. "I can understand that it might cause some coverage problems, Roger. But this is a circumstance I really can't avoid."

"What might that be?" The ever-present frown was deepening.

"A family emergency."

"How long did you have in mind being gone?"

"I really don't know."

"Uh huh—" Moreland snatched a fleeting glance at him, then looked away again. "Well, see, that's a problem, too, because I really can't run a department giving my people open-ended leaves of absence. It gets hard to make up the duty rosters when you have no idea who's going to show up and who isn't. Know what I mean?"

"I have sixty days of vacation backlogged."

"That may be, but you have to have my approval to take it, for the very reasons we're talking about."

"You know, I just need some time," Noah said, upping the stakes toward loggerheads. "Sorry, but there's nothing I can do about it."

"Are you giving me notice?"

Noah was surprised even as the words came out. "Hope not, but if it comes to that—"

"Let's not go there yet," Moreland backed off. "I take my orders from Chuck Tolliver on these things. Let me talk to him."

Noah knew that talking to the top guy wasn't going to be much help. He had a good relationship with the Alameda County Public Defender, but Tolliver, a great litigator, wasn't deep on creative management solutions.

"You want me to speak to him?" Noah suggested.

"No, best if I do it."

"What's the timetable?"

"Jesus. First we're off to points unknown, until God knows when, and now we're in a damn hurry about it. What did you have in mind?"

"Well, I really need to leave within the week, but—"

"Let's see," Moreland said, sarcasm still his main stock in trade, "I've got three trials back to back, and my department audit is due end of the month. Suppose I let you know day after tomorrow—that work for you?"

"That'd be great." *I'm taking some fucking time off, Roger, for a fucking good reason, from a fucking government job that is fucking boring—that work for you? He wished he'd said that.*

* * *

It was nearly seven o'clock by the time Noah got home to check messages, drop his bag, and grab a quick shower. The plan was to meet Kate and Sandy for a beer, then a popcorn dinner with entertainment at the Opera Plaza Cinema over on Van Ness. He timed his quick change at ten minutes flat and was taking three stairs at a time on the way out when he passed Lisa coming up, obviously dragging after her long day.

"Hey," he said, pausing. "You're kinda late."

Her haggard look brightened when she saw him.

"Matter of fact, I am. Got an inventory going on at the store."

"Where's Maggie?"

"The Goldmans are about to drop her. We're gonna freshen up and go get some Chinese. Want to come?"

"Sounds great, but I'm gonna catch a movie with friends and I'm running late. Sorry, better goose it." He started past her.

She put a hand on his arm. "Noah—"

He paused and looked back.

"I—I've been meaning to tell you something." A beat. "My dad's sick. I'm going to take Maggie and go back to Minnesota for awhile."

"No way. Is it serious?"

"Pancreatic cancer. That's always pretty serious, isn't it?"

"I'm sorry, Lees."

"It's one of those things you just gotta deal with, I guess."

"How long will you be gone?"

"Well, it all depends. I don't really know. My mom died three years ago, and he doesn't have anyone with him. I'm actually thinking about putting Maggie in school back there and staying a while."

"Wow, so you're thinking about through the fall."

"Looks like it. You're going to be gone for a while too, aren't you?"

"Yeah, I gotta do this defense in Hawaii. Are you looking forward to going home?"

She scrunched up her nose. "Jesus, I don't know. My dad yelled at me for three solid years as a teenager, then forbid me to leave, said I was sure to come to no good out here. I didn't want to go back until I had something going for me." She grinned. "A rich lawyer husband or something."

"Yeah, well, you're making more money than some lawyers in the neighborhood. Doesn't that count for something?"

She picked some imaginary lint from his shoulder. "I guess it really wasn't him, I just didn't want to leave when things were starting to turn around," she said. "Maggie was so sad when I told her."

"What'd she say?"

"Oh, you know. She's a trooper. She gets that we gotta do this."

He shook his head. "I'm gonna miss you guys for sure. When do you go?"

"I've given notice. We're out end of the week."

The front door of the Larkin banged, and Maggie was suddenly on the stairs. She slowed and plodded when she saw them, and by the time she reached them, her lip was quivering, and the tears were starting to well. "Did Mom tell you?" she asked in a small voice.

"Hey, squirt," Noah said, scooping her up. "It won't be forever."

"I don't want to go, Noah," she gushed.

He put her down and sat on a stair next to her to her. "I know. I don't want you to," he said. "But your mom needs you, and her dad needs her. That's how things work sometimes."

"And I need you. Doesn't that matter?"

"Of course it does. I need you, too. We'll all be back together before you know it. You'll see." *Perhaps it was all lies, but he had to say it. He had to believe it. It wasn't going to be the same without this little person around.*

"Who am I going to tell my secrets to, Noah?" she said, sniveling. "Nobody knows the things I tell you."

"And you can still tell me. We'll email."

"Do you know how far it is from Hilo, Hawaii to St. Paul, Minnesota?"

"I don't."

"It's 3,912 miles, and that's a long way."

He nodded. "It sure is."

Lisa saw him look at his watch. "We gotta get going," she said. "We're gonna get some dinner; then we got a lot of packing to do. Will you help me?" she asked Maggie, who started to sob, her shoulders jerking. Noah picked her up, and she calmed a bit, resting her head on his shoulder.

"You gonna put things in storage?" he asked Lisa.

"Nothing to store really. What we're not taking goes to the Salvation Army." *Not the sign of a speedy return.*

"When do you leave?"

"Six o'clock flight Saturday morning. Cab at four-thirty."

"I'll get up and see you off," Noah told her.

"At four-thirty?" Maggie asked. Her eyes were crimson, her nose a river.

"I'll be there." He bent down to her. "Big hug and a kiss, squirt," he said. "One I can remember till I see you again in a few months." He looked into her brave little face and forced a smile.

No matter what Maggie had said, she knew the chances were slim; she knew that a major part of her life was ending. Although he had no idea what lay ahead for him, despite her tears, he knew this child was a good deal more confident about her future than he was about his. Tomorrow morning, or the day after, she'd get up, get dressed, and get on with it. It was a toughness she'd learned the hard way. She'd grown up with a single mom who had worked nights and was high most of the time, but a mom who loved her more than life. Then she was wrenched away from Lisa and farmed out to a foster family, absorbing a wild kaleidoscope of new ways and new faces. And when she'd finally gotten home again, this major upheaval. She could have been broken, seen life as one crushing blow after another, but she stayed positive, strong. What was it? The unconditional love that Lisa had had for her? Or were some people just born with a heftier supply of guts than others? Survivors? It broke his heart that she'd had to learn so young. When most kids were thinking only of themselves, Maggie had to take care of her mother, who wasn't as strong as she was. The kid wasn't like most adults. She didn't hang back, protect herself. She flung herself into everything. Noah envied that. And yet, while living to the fullest no doubt supplied a lot of joyous energy, the fall was pretty far now that things were coming apart.

Casting off the lies and embracing the only reality that mattered, Maggie put her arms around his neck and whispered in his ear. "I'll never forget you, Noah. I'll always love you."

So many changes. He wondered as he held her where the people close to him would land when it was all over.

CHAPTER TWENTY-SEVEN

On Sunday morning, Noah packed his briefcase, and pulled together the necessities for his return to the Islands. He was working on a second cup of coffee with Bob Marley throbbing softly in the background when the phone rang.

"Hey, Boyo," Jack said. "I've got some more stuff on Reeves and his studies."

"More abstracts?"

"Affirmative. Two, to be exact. I never get the full articles. I think there were more people involved in those studies than just Reeves. It'd be easier to track these things if I had more names, but he was the lead investigator, and only his name is on the abstracts. Anyway, they apparently stopped the experiments abruptly after post-mortems started turning up possible damage to that 'amygdaloid body' we were talking about."

"Interesting," Noah responded. "Back then, they didn't have the imaging techniques we have now."

"Right, so they only got smart after the fact," Jack agreed. "The other abstract dealt with some concerns about hyper-aggressive side effects. Looks like they tried to reverse them, but—"

"You mean these guys were permanently violent after taking the battle fatigue drugs?" Noah's interest was perked.

"All it says is there were some side effects that they were working on reversing, and they didn't have much luck. Looks like the work was coming out of the army hospital at Cam Ranh Bay."

"Where's that?"

"Central Vietnam. Major deepwater port. I had a pal who was an orderly there. Was working at the VA Hospital in San Diego last time I talked to him. I tried to get hold of him, see if I could get some info, but I found out he died two years ago."

"Jack, maybe these studies have something to do with the bush vets at Kupuna."

"Whoa, Boyo. All we know for sure is that Reeves, your dad's boss, led the team, and that's worth looking into. If I was guessing, I'd wonder whether Reeves might have gotten a little over-anxious before the clinical trials were done and unwrapped the package before Christmas."

"Meaning?"

"Meaning he went public with the drug before they could figure out whether the bad effects could be reversed."

"Dammit, Jack. I think there may be a link."

"I hear you. But you got a criminal prosecution to attend to. Let's take it one step at a time. When do you leave?"

"Couple of days. Email me those abstracts, will you?'

"Will do."

"I'm grateful, Jack. I'll call you from over there."

"Keep your head down, Boyo. And good luck."

* * *

Noah met Kate for dinner at Gang Yuk Lee, a favorite of theirs on Golden Gate, near the outskirts of the Tenderloin. After a walk through the warmth of early June back to her place on Hayes, they once again sat on the steps out front, her head on his shoulder.

Throughout the evening, there had been a foreboding that came with the unknown. Noah reported that Tolliver had denied his request for paid vacation, or even a leave of absence. Moreland had told Noah that since he couldn't say how long he would be away, there were no guarantees. If there was a job when he came back, he could have it.

As they sat there, watching the evening, they exchanged the usual promises about writing, emailing, phone calls, and a renewal of the relationship when he got back. The silences grew longer. Finally Noah stood, saying it was almost eleven o'clock and he had an early start. She gazed up at him.

"So, you wanna come up for a minute?"

He smiled and held up his hands like a picture frame. "Now, where have I seen this before? Let me think—oh, yeah. Wasn't it the last time I was leaving for Hawaii? I said something about a perfect record?"

She raised an eyebrow. "And someone said records were made to be broken. Was that me?" They shared a smile, then hers morphed into a longing look and she extended a hand for him to help her up. As he drew her to her feet, her arms encircled his neck. He stretched both arms around her waist and pulled her to him, kissing her gently. His breathing deepened, his tongue explored hers, and in that moment Noah found himself transported. He had always tried to protect her from this part of himself.

He could feel the muscles of her thigh tighten forcefully as she wrapped a leg around his, the intensity rising in him as she opened herself to him. He imagined he could feel her warmth against his own thigh through several layers of clothing. Standing there in front of her stairs, both were oblivious, of the night, of the traffic passing a few feet away, of the city around them, of all but each other. The kiss became more urgent as he crushed her to his chest, and she moaned.

When her breath returned, it was coming rapidly. "I think that record is in serious jeopardy," she panted, and jerked herself from his grasp. She backed up a step and they held a long stare, his lips curling into a smile. She glanced down briefly, and when she looked back at him, she was wearing the knowing smile he loved. As he turned and started up the stairs, she bolted past him, yanking him up behind her.

Later, as he lay alone at the suite, unable to sleep, still redolent with her fragrance, he was consumed by a sensuous glow that was new to him. He chuckled as his thoughts kept returning to how athletic she was. He had always known she was a jock, but God, she was strong! *What had the difference been tonight? For three years they'd studied together, run together, gotten drunk together, laughed together—but both times things had gotten physical before, they had ended up in disaster.*

She was obviously right. It had to be about commitment. He was no shrink, but it wasn't lost on him that a guy who was abandoned by his father, literally, and his mother, emotionally, was going to have some problems with commitment. Maybe a shrink would help, some kind of shock therapy?

The amazing thing was that she hung in there with him. What did she see in him? She dated other guys. Incredible she hadn't found someone. What could she possibly see in him? She talked about how his major cases would look on his resume. It came to him that no one else took such an interest in him. His accomplishments seemed to have more meaning when she was around.

Tonight had been sensational. No analyzing. No talking it through. Was it the murkiness of their future that had driven it? Something to remember, maybe? Some kind of sexual anchor? She'd seemed so comfortable. Whatever, the old foreboding had been gone, and just now he couldn't remember having stronger feelings about a woman.

CHAPTER TWENTY-EIGHT

STEPHANIE WAS WAITING FOR Noah at the Hilo airport in the brown and red leathers, helmet in hand. For some reason, probably the overwhelming ambience of the Islands that hit him when he stepped onto the tarmac, the leathers hadn't tipped him that she was on the Suzuki while there was still time to jump into a cab. It wasn't until they got to the parking lot that it finally dawned on him. He never had any idea how utterly miserable one could be, perched on the back of a howling, steroid-horsepower, rocket at seventy-five mph with his bag on his lap. He almost pitched ass-over-shoulders every time she blasted off from a stop. *It was clear that he was going to have to gin up his own transportation. This tandem thing wasn't going to work.*

They stopped at Stephanie's "condo" to drop his bag on their way to the jail to see Samson. Before he ever got inside, delight number two of the day, the growling and snarling, got his attention as they mounted the stairs.

"That's only Kane," Stephanie told him. "Don't worry about him."

"Kane?"

"Yeah. Mondo Kane. He's my boy."

"Boy? Who's his father, 'Hulk'?"

"He's just a sweet bull mastiff who takes care o' me and the homestead. You gonna love him."

"Right," was all Noah could say as he steeled himself. The snarling continued, and Noah thought he would have a coronary before she opened the door. In a nanosecond Kane was through it. He had to go one-fifty if he was a pound.

Noah held his ground and his hand went out reflexively, index finger extended and twirling, like Crocodile Dundee.

"Hello Kane. . ." he said, in a deep rolling voice. Kane stopped, sniffed, and for a moment Noah's heart stopped; then the monster's tail began to wave, and they were friends for life — mostly. Noah sensed the warm welcome and leaned down. He'd never had a dog, but had always loved them, and they him. Suddenly Kane was in his face, licking and whimpering, and Noah reluctantly went with it as his blood pressure descended from the red zone.

Stephanie smiled from the sidelines. "You gotta be somethin' special," she said. "Kane is one great judge o' character. He doesn't let many guys through the front door, let alone make out with 'em on the first date."

"I think we've arrived at an arrangement," Noah said. "Just keep me on his good side," he said, rubbing the neck of the beast.

"So come on in," Stephanie said as she strode into the flat. Noah followed, and Kane brought up the rear, nose uncomfortably close behind.

Whoa. What a place. Not entirely unlike his own suite at the Larkin, laid out with every item of memorabilia from her passion. Only he was into sports, and she was clearly into guys. He thought at first that the boards, the trophies, the pictures on the walls were recognition of her surfing prowess. Not really.

"So, what's this trophy over here?"

"That's for winning the Masters Competition at Sunset Beach. You know, Oahu."

"Wow, you *are* something. I knew you were a surfer, but I had no idea."

"No, man. Not me. Meka wins it for me. He rips for sure. Got the greatest cutback on the beach. See, here's Meka." She pointed to a picture of a dark brown Adonis in sunglasses with a blazing smile, standing next to an upright surfboard.

"Nice," Noah agreed. Kane was at his right hand licking, a significantly better position than directly behind him.

"And this, this is Kale." She turned to Noah with a smile. "Means 'strong and manly.'" She looked back at the photo. "We're standin' in front of the break at Makaha. You can't tell how big those sets are in the picture, but that's the big time, no doubt."

"What's this over here?" Noah pointed to an enormous set of teeth with a photo of a guy with a long board, wavy dark hair, and huge muscles.

"That's Olokahani. Surfs the biggest mothahs on the Island. And he's the strongest guy I know. He killed that Mako shark and gave me the teeth. Can you believe it?" She looked at him. Noah's eyebrows were hovering around his hairline. "Me neither," she went on, not waiting for the reply, "but I saw it happen."

"Okay, I get it." Noah scoffed. *He'd heard enough about the local stars.*

"You don' wanna hear 'bout Olokahani?"

"Not really. You want to hear about my girlfriends?"

"Matter a fact, I do. You got somethin' steady goin'?"

"Matter a fact I do." Noah said without thinking. "Or, I think I do."

She stopped the tour and looked at him. "And who might that be?"

"She's a PD. We went to law school together."

"Wow, got some history. Sounds serious."

"I guess."

"You seem to got a thing for lady lawyers," Stephanie said, and laughed.

"I do?"

"Well, you stayin' here with me, no?"

He studied her, trying to read her intentions. "Yeah, well. Thanks for the offer. You got a really great place here, but I don't think—"

"Come on, Noah. Let's not get too uptight about this. You need a place to stay in Hilo, I got one. We're going to be working on the case together, and you need a base of operations, I got one. Not mandatory you have bedroom privileges." She looked at him with a provocative smirk. "We take one thing at a time."

While he overanalyzed, she moved on again, before he could respond.

"Come on. Lemme show you the rest of the place."

Its theme a cross between college-girl and island paradise, the flat stretched across the top floor of a two-story wood-frame structure on Lehua Street, in a residential area just north of the center of town. It was built around the turn of the last century, according to Stephanie. Totally indoor/outdoor with a surrounding tropical balcony, it offered a view of Mauna Kea at the back, and the deep azure of the Pacific two blocks away out front. In the middle of the rich green lawn, watered twice a day by the oceanic squalls, stood a tall coconut palm.

The large living room had hardwood floors. Here and there, bright-colored Hawaiian area rugs divided it into various groupings: eating, reading, a game table with two chairs and a chess board. The wall coverings were woven grass, the furniture mostly rattan. Stephanie's bedroom came equipped with an enormous king-size bed with a canopy of palm fronds.

At her desk in the office was a full computer set-up, opposite a black leather couch with a hide-a-bed, just the thing for a visiting lawyer from the mainland. The bed was rolled out and adorned with colorful sheets and pillow cases. *Obvious preparations for a visitor. Nothing presumptuous here.*

Her kitchen was utilitarian and hung with every kind of pot, pan, and implement imaginable. *Another room in which Stephanie clearly knew what she was doing.*

"No locks," he said. "A little different from the Tenderloin."

"Tenderloin?"

"Yeah. Very picturesque part of San Francisco where I live. You ever been to San Francisco?"

"Nah. Farthest I been is Kauai."

"You should come see the City. You'd love it."

"Why?"

"We got great restaurants, bars, parks, beautiful buildings, lotta history. But we do lock the doors."

"No need here. Kane watches out for things. I usually leave him out during the day and he makes sure everything's okay. Besides, Leilani and Sid live downstairs. Nobody bothers me."

"Married couple?"

"Sort of. Couple of middle-aged guys."

No TV. She must subscribe to some other kind of entertainment, but he didn't ask.

"So what you think, Hotshot?" Stephanie posed when the tour was over. "You could be comfy here?"

"Most definitely. You've got a great place, Stephanie."

"You wanna come share it a while?"

He squinted into the afternoon sun, his eyes roaming out to the seductive sea. Then there was a wet nose in his hand, and he heard himself say, "Why not? Let's give it a try."

"Good deal," she said. "Now let's go see your defendant daddy."

"Daddy—" *He'd pondered the reunion with Samson many times in the days before he got there. How would he greet him? How would they get along after the blowup? And what the hell would he call him? A lot of possibilities came to mind, but "Daddy" wasn't one of them.*

CHAPTER TWENTY-NINE

"YOU CAN CALL ME anything you want," Samson told him. "I want you to be comfortable with all this. How would you feel about 'David,' until we get things sorted out?"

A jail visiting room wasn't unfamiliar to Noah, but he wouldn't have chosen this as the place for a reunion with a father who had been absent for twenty-eight years. Still, the event had been pretty mind-blowing, all things considered. Calling him "David,"—although Noah still wasn't used to it—had a way of making things easier. Kind of mind-bending. A Father. A Psychiatrist. A Murderer—?

Samson had been beaming when he was brought into the visiting room. Stephanie had made excuses and wandered up to her office, giving them time to sort things out. Samson walked to Noah, eyes drinking him in. Still smiling, he extended a hand.

"I'm sorry about that bombshell I dropped on you, Noah. I realized it was going to be difficult, but not giving you a little more room to absorb it was insensitive."

Noah took the hand, returning the smile, though somewhat tentatively. "I can't imagine there's any easy way to come out of hiding after twenty-eight years, is there? I don't know. You're the expert."

"There are no experts when it comes to that kind of thing. We do the best we can. Although I guess I could have put it in writing first and let you get used to it on your own time. I'd thought about it so many times. I just wanted to be with you when I told you. See how you reacted. It was selfish. I know that now."

Noah was uncomfortable with dwelling on it. He moved to the visiting table, took out his legal tablet, and sat down. "So, shall we talk about the case?"

Samson took the chair across from him. "Let's do that," he agreed, but then he said, "I want you to know how badly I feel about all those years of silence. It seemed to make sense at the time, but now it seems unforgivable."

Noah's look was doubtful. *Did they really want to get back into all this? Maybe. He'd chosen to get involved in the case. They did have to build a rapport, some honesty that wouldn't materialize if they just camped out on the tip of the proverbial iceberg. Pretty cold and precarious up there.*

"Why did you do it?"

"I guess I didn't know what way to do it. As this legal thing got more serious, I got concerned about it. I thought of you, and that it might provide an opportunity for us to get to know one another. My thought was that working together on a common goal might diffuse some of the intensity. It was mostly about getting to know you, but I truly do have confidence in your abilities as a lawyer."

Noah could feel the anger building again, but he contained it. "You know, I might be able to accept all that from a neurotic mother, but you're a psychiatrist. Your deal is fixing this kind of stuff in other people. You have to have heard a million times from patients how it feels to be abandoned by parents. What that does to people. You must've medicated them, hospitalized them, buried them. I would have expected more from you."

Samson was nodding. "I have to confess to some pretty troublesome neuroses of my own," he said. "If you haven't been through it, you can't know the horrors of the effects of war on young GIs. When you're saddled with trying to heal those gaping wounds, it's pretty onerous." He looked at Noah apologetically. "I'm not trying to excuse my not being there. I'm just trying to fit it into some kind of perspective. Anyway, it's not like pulling some shrapnel out of a leg wound, dousing it with antibiotic, taping it up, and sending the kid on his way. These tortures go on. The wounds may never heal. So I guess I became obsessed with my inadequacies. Trying to get back some kind of post-war life to these guys."

"Yeah. That's important, for sure." Noah couldn't work up the sympathy for the vets in this instance, and he found himself a little guilty about it.

"It wasn't until recently that I began to realize how totally one-dimensional I'd been about my work, what kind of tunnel vision I had to my own life, cheating the people around me, all for this kind of an obsession. I'd never seen my son. But then, I haven't seen my brother or my parents in twenty-five years, either. That's pretty nuts."

Here was a concept Noah hadn't considered. *Who were those people? He had grandparents, an uncle, and his family? Were they all still alive? Did he look like them? How strange would it be to be introduced to one's biological family at damn near middle age? This was all too complicated.*

"There's a lot to talk about," Noah said. "Why don't we just work through your case? Maybe we get to some of it in the process."

Samson smiled with the acceptance of a practiced psychiatrist. An ordinary father could never be that understanding. "Fair enough," he said.

"It's all about your complicity, your knowledge that SSRIs caused violence, and your continuing to prescribe them. So we need to attack on the ground floor, that is, the first assumption that you knew they would, or were, increasing the violence in predisposed patients."

"Not only did I not know they were increasing the violence in the Fallen Heroes, I don't think they were. I don't think that's the best research any longer. In fact, the whole point is that in the large doses I was giving, we were finding that we were getting less violent tendencies and increased ability to plan and organize."

"But the rap on the drug was increased homicide and suicide with its users."

"Sure, but that was in the very early days. There were subsequent incarnations of medicine that corrected a lot of that, and besides, it varies wildly with the patient. We were treating a population here that had a very specific disorder we were trying to attack, a disorder marked by violence already. The evidence we had was that the drug was decreasing that part of the picture."

"Who else knows about that other than you?"

Samson thought for a moment. "Slade does. Why?"

"Even though you tell the story pretty well, I'm reluctant to put you on the stand and give the prosecution a crack at trying to twist the way you were looking at it, get you to admit you knew about the earlier side effects, punch up your unwillingness to make the patients more comfortable and take chances with them killing each other."

"But they were less likely—"

"We know that. But bad things happen on cross-examination. Things take on a life of their own. Would Slade be persuasive?"

"He's not scientifically trained, but he knows his stuff."

"I'll talk to him. Who else?"

"Reeves knew. But he's a snake. He's going to be the prosecution's star witness. We stay away from him. But I think I have to testify. I need to get this whole conspiracy public. Without some bright lights on all this, they can pretty much do what they want with me, and with the men at Kupuna. Reeves is up there right now. Running the compound."

"Wait. Reeves? At Kupuna?"

"Reeves."

"He's a general, isn't he?"

"Yes, but he's also a psychiatrist. And he's worked a lot with these kinds of patients over the years. He says he's going to take the men off the SSRIs and warehouse them. He's going to wipe out all the progress I've made."

"That's exactly the kind of talk that makes me wary of letting you take the stand. Do you hear that you're saying you have a personal stake in the treatment? That there is some kind of competition with Reeves that would prompt you to risk murder? And why would Reeves go up there himself?"

"He does have a personal interest. He somehow takes this all very personally."

"Why?" Noah didn't get it.

"I don't know. He thinks his butt is on the line with Washington. Something."

Noah pondered it. "We're going to need to check into that. But you're right. You probably will have to testify. What do we know about who did the killings? What is the evidence that both were committed by the same man?"

"Unclear. It might have been the same man, some kind of paradoxical effect, a violent idiosyncratic response to the drug maybe, or even a failure to take them altogether. But a possible single adverse reaction was no reason in my mind to stop the medicine for everyone else, not without proof it was dangerous."

"Now, see. There you go again. That's what's going to make you vulnerable on cross. Can't you hear that you're saying you really did entertain the notion that the drug was making one of the patients into a killer, and you continued with the regimen anyway?"

"But there was so much to be gained."

"No good. You weren't sacrificing one patient, letting them kill each other, for 'scientific gain.'"

"Of course I wasn't!"

"We know that. But you've got to be careful how you say it. You have to underline your suspicion that one isolated rogue was responsible for the killings, and it had nothing to do with the drug. You told me you suspected the first murder, Sauce, was committed by his best friend. Who would that be?"

"Ferguson. That's why I was asking Rat about him. You saw he was pretty unstable. We've always had problems with him around compliance."

"I should try to talk to him, too."

"You should stay away from him," Samson snapped. "He's a dangerous guy. He doesn't really communicate in any meaningful way, and sometimes he demonstrates frank psychosis."

"But if we can demonstrate he's violent, dangerous, then he's a likely suspect without any reference to the drugs. You testify that was your thinking, and that's a head start on reasonable doubt."

"Noah, you need to stay away from him. Promise me you won't do anything crazy."

"Okay, okay. We'll start with Slade and some of the others."

"Not good enough. Can't you get an investigator or someone to contact him?"

"We don't really have an extensive staff working for us, as it turns out."

"At least promise me you won't try to find him without talking to me first. I can give you some ideas about how to go about it, keep from riling him up."

Noah studied him. *He liked the concern.* "Yeah, okay," he said. "I'll talk to you first. Now, we'll need an expert witness. Who do you know who has impeccable credentials as a researcher on the SSRIs, maybe written extensively about them?"

"Two come to mind. Dr. Edith Anderson at Johns Hopkins and Dr. Martin Fells at Texas. Both are psychopharmocologists with special expertise in the brain chemistry of SSRIs. Both have written and testified about them. I'd think that Fells would be the better choice. He's been clear in his journal articles that although the early generations of Fluoxetine—Prozac—were thought by some to cause violence, it hadn't been demonstrated in the subsequent generation drugs of Zoloft, Paxil, or Lexepro, let alone the more recent experimental versions like YM992. I think his words were 'Absolutely no evidence of that.' I found it impressive."

"I'm never comfortable with the old 'absolutely no evidence' mantra. The prosecution is going to get testimony about certainty. Certainty that there are such violent side effects. They'll say all bets are off at the high doses you were using. The studies haven't been done. We need certainty on our side. Not just a lack of evidence."

"Unfortunately, science doesn't work that way," Samson observed.

"Right. But juries do. We gotta paint a picture of certainty so the jury feels warm and fuzzy with a conclusion of acquittal. If we don't, the prosecution will, and you won't like the result."

Samson nodded.

"Alright. I've got to jam through all the patient records, research the medicine. I'll call Slade and get up to Kupuna to talk to him and some of the others one on one. We may want to get some of the other patients on the witness list, let the jury see first hand what kind of progress you were making."

"Well, don't expect miracles. These guys have been in the jungle for thirty years."

"I'll bear that in mind. Anyway, that'll get us going. We'll talk more in a few days."

"Impressive start," Samson said, nodding.

"I'm going to get with Stephanie and pound out a game plan. We have a trial setting conference on Wednesday. She's going to move my admission to the Federal Bar *pro haec vice*, and we'll need some breathing room before trial to get our expert on board and to get up to Kupuna to do some investigation."

"What were you thinking in terms of time?"

"I was hoping for a trial date maybe ninety days downstream."

"Ninety days! I've got to be in jail that long?"

"Most likely. Asaki has been pretty clear he's not going to look kindly on bail."

"Lord. What are you going to do about your job? You were worried that you had to get back because they didn't have anyone to replace you."

"Yeah, well—they decided to chance that. There isn't any guarantee of a job to go back to."

Samson's look was serious, concerned. "How do you feel about that?"

"I'll work something out."

"I'm grateful, Noah. I'll make all this right. Do you need money?"

"Not for the moment. I'll be staying with Stephanie, and my plastic isn't maxed out yet. The important thing is that this case doesn't go off before we're ready."

* * *

"What do counsel have in mind about a trial date?"

Judge Asaki had seemed a bit abrupt, actually dismissive, on the several matters he had called on his setting calendar before *U.S. v. Samson*. Then he'd galloped through Stephanie's motion to admit Noah to the Federal Bar. She had wanted to milk the usual ceremony, welcoming the outside lawyer to the local court, but that had been a definite swing-and-a-miss with Asaki this morning. It was Noah's first experience with him, and his impatience was not a good sign.

"The defense requests a trial date in ninety days, Your Honor." Noah spoke up first, trying to set the bar so he wouldn't have to battle back after the prosecution requested day after tomorrow.

"Ninety days, Mr. Shane? Your client is in custody."

"I'm aware of that, but time is waived and we have preparation to complete. This is a complicated case with significant medical issues, expert witnesses." The defendant has a Constitutional right to a speedy trial, within seventy days of filing of charges in federal court, but Noah was willing to forego that requirement by "waiving time" to get the trial date out ninety days.

"Your client should have thought about that before dallying about for the last several months. We're going to select the first available trial date after the required thirty days."

With this guy carrying his standard, the U.S. Attorney didn't even need to get into it.

"April twenty-sixth, Madame Clerk?"

"Your Honor, that's thirty days exactly. That will not give us sufficient time to—"

"Alright, I have a little leeway. Does May first work for you, Mr. Pitts?"

"Perfect, Your Honor."

"That will be the order. Call the next case."

"Ah, one other matter, Your Honor?" Pitts interjected. *Uh oh. Even Noah knew that the U.S. Attorney himself wouldn't personally handle a trial setting conference, even in Hilo. There had to be some underlying sinister motive. Here it comes.*

"The prosecution would move the Court to exclude witnesses and the press from all further proceedings and from the trial on grounds of National Security."

National Security? Noah's head jerked around.

"This is a high-profile case, and there are issues which might get into Top Secret, protected areas."

"What kind of matters would those be, Mr. Pitts," Asaki quieried.

"That's the problem, Your Honor. I'm not at liberty to say. In fact, I'm not certain I understand the full implications myself. All I can say is the issue is of paramount importance—"

"Your Honor," Noah interrupted. "If we can't know the nature of the concern, we can't meet the motion and speak to it intelligently. This is not only irregular, but the defense is unalterably opposed to any kind of gag order, or any effort by the prosecution to keep the trial of these trumped-up charges from being public. I am not surprised that they are ashamed of their position, but my client has a constitutional right to a public trial—"

"Alright, Mr. Shane," Asaki cut him off. "Let's not get carried away. I agree there isn't enough in your application at this time to permit me to evaluate the necessity, Mr. Pitts. We will take this up at the time of trial. Anything further?"

"No, Your Honor," Pitts said.

"No, Your Honor," Noah echoed.

"Next case, Madame Clerk?"

CHAPTER THIRTY

"So I GOT HOLD of another old friend," Jack said.

Noah was in his room at Stephanie's, with medical records stacked high on his desk, and the computer flashing as he clacked in his script for Samson's direct examination. Only a week left until trial. Outside the heat still hung heavily in the moisture-laden tropical air as early evening closed in.

"James Fiddler. He was a psych nurse at Cam Ranh. Guy's with the AVAPL now in Washington. I asked him about Reeves. Told him we're interested in what was going on with the research."

"AVAPL?"

"Association of VA Psychologist Leaders. He'd heard of the studies we're talking about. 'Experiments,' he called them. Kinda why I thought Reeves might have jumped the gun. Anyway, they were kept under wraps with super tight security. James said that at one point there was a lot of excitement, then suddenly everything stopped. No explanation."

"What happened to the subjects?" Noah asked.

"That's the funny thing, Boyo. They were expecting to see these guys at Cam Ranh in the psych ward when the studies ended. They'd talked about treatment, made elaborate preparations, but none of them ever showed up. Fiddler asked a few questions, but the response everywhere was that no one had ever heard of the project. End of story. No clue what happened."

"How many patients were there?"

"Fiddler said he understood there had been upwards of eighty-five at one point, but there were probably more. They just seemed to vanish."

"So what are you saying, that—?"

"Yeah. Maybe these *are* your bush vets out there."

Yesss! "Wasn't lost on me," Noah said. "I'm going up to Kupuna tomorrow. Reeves personally took over the compound after Samson was arrested. I'll look into it."

"Whaaat? A general running a backwater jungle compound? That's pretty damn strange."

"His story is that he knows these guys and can handle their therapy better than anyone else, now that David is in custody."

"I guess that fits, but I don't like it. I say you oughta be watchin' your back. You sure it's a good idea going up there?"

"Reeves is back at Tripler for a couple of days for some kind of audit, so the timing's right."

"Got a nasty smell to it, Boyo, like going up to make powwow with the Apaches without having their peace-loving chief along. Don't you think you might want to take some cavalry with you?"

"Not if I'm going to find out anything that will shed some light on David's case. I have to do it quietly, and I have to do it right now. Trial starts next week. I don't see any other way."

"Be in touch, will you?"

"Count on it."

When Noah thought of Jack, a geode came to mind, a stone that looked like an ordinary old rock on the outside: tough, rugged, mutilated. But cut it open, and you find the most intricate, colorful, and beautiful crystalline structures imaginable.

* * *

Like every night recently, Noah and Stephanie were up late slaving over direct and cross examination, studying the evidence, preparing the exhibits. Lots of Kona coffee and hard work, but Noah had come to enjoy it more than he had anticipated. Stephanie was definitely a smart lady and a gifted lawyer. David's records of the Kupuna patients had been tough slogging, but they were thankfully quite thorough. He had kept meticulous charts on how twenty-four men reacted to the drugs. The remaining four were hit and miss, and the biggest gaps were in Ferguson's file. But they would be able to show that David had been totally scientific about his whole approach, not reckless, not willful, not dangerous.

The other main percipient witness was Grayson Slade. Noah had talked to him briefly on the phone a couple of times, but Slade had seemed completely distracted, different somehow. The rather composed staff sergeant Noah had met weeks ago now seemed totally intense, refusing to get into any details on the phone. He said Noah should come up to the compound to discuss his testimony. He was pretty busy, but he would fit Noah in. He probably was busy without David up there, trying to pick up after Reeves, but still, he would have thought Slade would be more cooperative. With Reeves over at Tripler, Noah would have Slade to himself, and as many of the patients as he could get to.

By twelve-thirty a.m. Stephanie said she'd had it and went off to bed. Noah was still working on the computer in the remaining heat of the evening, stripped to his sweat-pants, no shirt, trying to construct the cross of the prosecution psychopharmacologist. In a telephone conversation earlier that afternoon, he had gotten some tips from Martin Fells and was working them into the act. He was engrossed in a particularly troublesome area, trying to make some complicated molecular structures understandable to a lay jury, when he heard the voice.

"Noah?" It was breathy, sexy, and definitely from the bedroom.

"What."

"Are you still working?"

"Still working."

Long pause. "You gonna go to bed soon?"

He glanced at his watch. "Soon," he said, riveted on the monitor.

Longer pause. "Noah?"

"Yeah?"

"Will you come talk to me a minute?"

"What's up?"

"Come see me."

See me? He knew she slept naked. He was getting sensations in all the right places. "Something wrong?"

"Maybe."

He was about finished anyway. He shut down the computer and poked his head around the doorjamb of her bedroom. "S'up?" he said.

The night-stand lamp cast an earth-tone glow. She was propped up in the canopy bed like a dying queen readied for an audience with the cabinet by her maids in waiting. Her long black hair cascaded over the pillows fluffed behind her, and her book lay open on the bed. Nearby, Kane lounged sleepily, his head down. *It looked like she had worked on the image for half an hour, and she probably had.* She patted the bed next to her and beckoned. "Come sit."

Jesus. He moved into the door frame where she could see all of him.

"Mmmmmm," she cooed. "You one pretty man."

"Now, Stephanie. We discussed this."

"What, Noah? I just want to talk. You're going up that mountain tomorrow. I'm worried about you."

"Okay, thanks. I'm going to turn in."

"Noah." She smiled. "Don't. Come sit with me. I won't touch you—if you don't want me to."

"Well, it's not that I don't, but—"

"Just come sit." She patted the bed again.

He sauntered over, watching her all the way, as Kane lifted his massive head, sniffed, then thumped his tail, smiling as only a Mastiff can. Stephanie put a hand on the behemoth, and he rested his head again as Noah sat next to her.

She was stunning, no doubt.

In the dim light, her skin tones blended with the beiges of the walls and the tans of the palm fronds overhead, her hair framing her round face; her almond eyes were soft, her full lips in a slight pout.

"So, what is it?" he said.

"Those guys up there are dangerous," she began the lecture. "You gotta be careful. There's two murders we know about, maybe more."

"So, you want to send Olokahani with me?"

She smiled broadly, showing him glistening white teeth. "Might be a good idea."

"I'll be okay."

"I'm serious, Noah. I wish you weren't going."

Silence, then she reached over and put a hand on his leg, staring at his abs. "What if you don't come back? What if they kill you? Then this is our last night together."

"Stephanie—" he said, quasi-exasperated, as he ran a hand through his hair. *He stifled a chuckle, loving the totally transparent gambit.* "What *could it hurt? It's just you and me, our last night on earth —* "

"S'matta you, anyway? This all about that gorgeous movie star, Kate, you chained to?"

Now he did chuckle. "It's just I don't want to complicate things. You and I have a case to try together."

"Maybe you don't like me, don't think I'm sexy."

"Come on, Stephanie. You are one amazing woman. It's just that I don't know —" He watched her hand crawl up his leg, eyeing it as if it were a tarantula.

"So why don't you just lie here with me a teeny bit."

This was total torture. How long was a guy supposed to battle? "Just for a minute," he sighed, and stretched out beside her. *Probably a big mistake.*

Kane, who had been comfortably snoozing in the place of honor, immediately beat a retreat, crawling under the bed. *Obvious Pavlovian behavior. How many repetitions it had taken the dog to learn that?*

They lay together in the semi-darkness for a few minutes under the palm canopy. Finally she whispered, "Noah."

"Yes."

"We joke, but I worry about you up there."

"I'll be fine."

"All the same —"

She rolled over toward him, up onto an elbow, gazing down into his eyes, her dark, full face beautiful in the muted light. Raising her hand, she brushed at his hair, and her lips parted expectantly. He stared into her eyes. There was no more protest left in him.

She leaned down and kissed him, her weight descending on him. He could feel the softness of her breasts against his chest, in counterpoint to the powerful upper body honed by years of surfing. Then she laid her head on his shoulder, letting her index finger trace the contour of his triceps as her breathing deepened, warm against his ear. He kissed her neck and she moaned, and then he rolled over on top of her, kissing her again, more aggressively this time. Island essence filled every one of his senses as they drifted and rolled amidst the sound of crashing breakers two blocks away.

CHAPTER THIRTY-ONE

"BEEN RUNNING MY ASS off. Tryin' to stay on top of everything. Managing the place. Taking fucking meds to the patients—course they're scattered everywhere again. Tryin' to figure out the effects of this cockamamie 'therapy' Reeves is conducting. Then I gotta report to Dr. Samson. It's all fucking killing me."

Slade was wound up tight, spraying angry verbs and colorful adjectives like nine millimeter rounds. After talking to him on the phone, Noah knew there was something different. Now it was clear. He remembered Slade as neatly dressed, well-groomed, and well-spoken. He was now unkempt, unshaven, dressed in jungle fatigues like the patients. He looked like he hadn't slept in days. His speech was not only accelerated, but laced with obscenities. Occasionally he would stumble and struggle for a word, stuttering to maintain the flow. Noah had an uneasy feeling about his eyes. Intermittently they were glazed, wild.

It was mid-afternoon as the jeep bounced along the trail while Slade continued his rant. Noah pondered the dramatic change but chalked it up to the heavy workload. He winced as Slade jammed the gas pedal to the floor. Noah's kidneys ached as the old jeep jerked in and out of the ruts and holes in four-wheel drive. *Christ, this guy might be bent on killing himself, but best he doesn't take anyone down with him.*

"Your father's a great man. He's brilliant, a brilliant psychiatrist—but he also cares about his patients, which is a lot more than I can say for Reeves. Dr. Samson has devoted his life to bringing these guys back from the prison of insanity they've been locked in for thirty years."

"Prison of insanity?"

"Fuck, yes—and every last one of 'em was a war hero. Heavily decorated guys—all Special Forces guys—These motherfuckers were afraid of nothing. Hear me? Nothing!"

"Right."

"We got some celebrities. Wiley Matson received the Silver Star. Nathan Platz has a Bronze."

"For what?"

"Coyote led a Special Ops team into the jungle, thirty miles up the Mekong River, to recover the black box of a high level reconnaissance aircraft. You know, those U2 planes? The VC had it. We'd have been in a pickle if they got that box to anyone who could decipher it. Those things contain intelligence about air defense, cryptography, communications, that kind of stuff. So they get into this firefight with a whole VC company. Coyote loses half his team, then busts out of there with the black box, running through the entire VC position like Marshawn Lynch through the 49ers. Got hit three times, but he made it home with the box."

"And Platz?"

"Platz took a team into a temporary jungle POW detention facility guarded like Fort Knox. Local intelligence tipped us we'd lost guys in there in the past three months from starvation, exhaustion, and torture. There were about a hundred still alive. Nate and his team blast in, automatic weapons blazing, bust our guys out, take them down a jungle road and across a river under a blanket of cover-fire to freedom, then blow the bridge behind them. Only lost seven guys."

"Jesus. Who's got the screen rights?"

"Fuckin' A!" Slade shouted. "But now they've all got this psychotic-like condition Doc calls Fallen Hero Syndrome."

"I know about that."

Slade apparently didn't hear him, because he powered on. "It looks something like schizophrenia, but acts a little different. They're violent, and sociopathic, which are actually pretty desirable traits in a war hero. Paranoid delusions leading to what Doc called 'increased threat perception', and over-responses with this massive force. They got no ability to get behind someone else's eyeballs and understand what they're feeling. Know what I'm saying? Makes for a pretty challenging patient population, bunch of those guys living together."

"I bet. You seem to really understand this stuff. A sergeant and a professor, huh?"

Slade laughed explosively. "Nah. Just workin' with the Doc all these years, writing up the reports. Kinda learn or die. This compound was a pretty dangerous place. Constant beefs before we got here. The shrink that ran the place tried to take weapons away, but these guys were clever. They concocted major armaments out of anything. That was actually part of their special ops training. There were killings, burning of huts—"nests"— they called them, and the prior chief numb-nut even claimed there was cannibalism, weird sex practices, and ritualized human sacrifice."

"Jesus."

"When we first came, Doc was beaten up a bunch of times, some so bad he was hospitalized. I even got my ass kicked. But Doc always came back. No one else would come near this duty. Impossible treatment, no chance of success, most dangerous patients on the planet. I gotta hand it to him."

"Well, you stayed, too," Noah observed.

This stopped him for a few moments. "Like I said, there was no one else. And we were making something good happen for 'em." He paused another few seconds. "Except for one."

"What do you mean?"

"Ferguson," Slade shouted over the growling motor. "No matter what Doc or I tried, we never could get that SOB to take his meds. Most of them relished the idea of going back to some kind of real life. But Ferguson? It was like he enjoyed the craziness, the raw power of it."

* * *

The only light in the flat came from the monitor screen as the advancing shadows settled around Jack, who was totally absorbed in page after page of PDF documents of ancient military medical reports dating back to Vietnam, Korea, and even beyond. Malaria, dysentery, jungle rot, Agent Orange. He scanned more closely when his word finder came up with any reference to "battle fatigue," "Fuerontin," or the real jackpot: "Reeves."

The coffee to Jack's left had long since gone cold. Every now and then he scratched a note on the pad to his right. He'd been at it for a couple of hours when there was a knock at the front door.

"Yeah?" he shouted, without taking his eyes from the display.

"Mr. Donohue?"

"Yeah."

"Edison."

"Edison, who?"

"Southern California Edison. Gotta read the meter."

Still absorbed by the archives, Jack mechanically grabbed for his crutches and dragged himself out of his chair. "Just a minute," he shouted as he started for the stairs. Arriving at the bottom, he twisted the bolt and opened the door. Instantaneously there were two men through it and on him, taking him to the floor.

"Hey!" was all he managed as one held his hands and the other slapped a swatch of duct tape over his mouth, then covered his head with a black hood and cinched it tight. With military precision, the man holding Jack's hands cuffed him with plastic restraints, then strapped his braced legs at the ankles. Within less than a minute, they had him in the trunk of the black Lincoln Towncar that had been backed into the alley. Silently, the car retraced its route down the narrow passage, then sped out onto Windward Blvd.

* * *

Slade and Noah arrived at Khe Sanh and walked around the building, then into the deserted barracks.

"They were living here when I visited last month," Noah said.

"Right," the accelerated delivery continued. "But after Reeves came, they started to retreat into the nests again. Prick's been trying to convince them to stop taking their meds. I keep telling them Doc would want them to take 'em, that they worked too long at this to give it up." He shot a look at Noah. "They don't like Reeves much, so I think they're taking the meds. At least I keep passing them out. But they're all living out in the bush and it's a bitch to run 'em down. Reeves won't go out there. I think he's afraid of 'em. If he's not, he should be. Anyway, I always stop in at Khe Sanh just to see if anyone's back. So far, nothing."

"So where are we going?" Noah asked.

"There's a nest about a half mile from here. Coyote and Garcia. I'm going to drop off some meds."

"Do we walk from here?"

"Nah. We can drive a little further."

They got back in the jeep, and Slade fired it up. He ground it into gear, then pulled back onto the trail, resuming his diatribe.

"Some years back Doc wanted to look into the cause of FHS, but it wasn't until recently, with the SSRI drugs, that he thought it made any sense to pursue it."

"FHS?"

"Fallen Hero Syndrome."

"Oh—yeah."

"Like I said, before Doc came here, they were pretty much just warehousing these guys. No real point in coming up with causes unless they were looking into treatment. So Doc tries to get their histories from Washington. You know, their early service days, recruiting documents, service medical histories, even pre-service medical and social histories. See if he could find a common thread."

"What happened?"

"Surprise, surprise. No records. All missing. I mean nothin'. Even the recruiting records were gone. Like these guys just dropped outta the sky. But when we start to debrief 'em as the SSRIs started taking effect, they start to provide a few pieces here and there. Doc starts to see a common story. I mean, it's amazing. Seems like they were all pretty bright and probably physically superior in high school and college. Many of 'em talk about being athletes."

"How can you evaluate intelligence out here?"

"Basic vocabulary, mostly. Underlying level of articulation, fund of knowledge. We suspected most were college grads. Course we couldn't prove that without the records, but lots of 'em actually described memories of competitive athletics. Then on the dark side, don't seem to be any memories of criminal conduct or prosecutions. Again, hard to say without any real histories. We're flying blind, but it seems like there were no violent tendencies before their service in Vietnam. If they'd been rounded up by the recruiters in prisons, or on the docks, you know, in the tough neighborhoods, you'd figure we'd be seeing glimpses of it, but we're not."

"Amazing."

"Yeah, we knew we had a bunch of Rambo types from Vietnam on our hands, but some of the memories when they started to cool down have been major. A few of 'em—"he raised his fingers, ticking them off—"Coyote, Winkler, Frasier, Platz, started to mention some weird medical treatment they'd received during their early days in Vietnam."

"Where? What facility?"

Slade frowned. "No clue!" he shouted over the roar of the engine as he kicked the jeep out of a deep mud hole.

"Could it have been Cam Ranh Bay Army Hospital?"

"Why there?"

"I've done a little research through the Vietnam archives. I was interested in anything I could find on Reeves, but that old stuff is pretty well-buried. Turned out there were a handful of abstracts about some clinical trials Reeves did on a drug called Fuerontin, which was supposed to cure battle fatigue."

Slade's head snapped around. "Reeves did the work?"

"Yeah, he was working on getting guys suffering from battle fatigue depression back to their units faster. Looks like he may have pushed it out into the field a little early. Anyway, the trials suddenly stopped, and no one has heard of it since. Contacts with staff who were around at the time indicate that the whole thing was buried and the subjects disappeared. The experiments were done at Cam Ranh Bay. I thought it might have had something to do with these guys at Kupuna."

Slade's intense eyes locked on Noah. "Do you have the abstracts with you?"

"I don't. But I'd be glad to fax you copies when I get back."

"Is there any way you can get them faxed here now?"

"Maybe. Let me make a call when we get back."

"Before Reeves came to Tripler from Washington and took over as our Chief, a part-time research assistant who helped out with our meds, guy named Rafael Bustamente, navy E-13, went to Honolulu to search for the records I was telling you about."

"Yeah."

"He called from over there and said he'd found a few odds and ends of interest. On his way back to Kupuna, his car went off the road, down a cliff, into a huge rift valley on the volcano. There was no briefcase or papers or anything found with the body. Doc and I always suspected something. Hilo PD and the VA investigated, called it accidental death, but we thought different."

"Who do you think is trying to bury Samson?" Noah asked.

"Reeves told Doc it was coming from Washington."

"Yeah, that's what David told me, too."

At a point where the narrow trail widened, Slade pulled the jeep off the road and told Noah they would have to go the rest of the way on foot. Slade rummaged in the back, grabbing a couple of boxes containing a two-week ration of SSRIs for two patients, a few magazines, and a couple cartons of cigarettes. He stuffed them in his backpack and started into the jungle, beating the growth back with a machete. Before long, they emerged from the dense thicket onto a narrow trail.

The path led along a rapidly flowing creek only a few feet wide that splashed down over several waterfalls, kicking up a fine refreshing mist that refracted beams from the early afternoon sun into mini-rainbows.

Arriving at a narrow lava ledge after they scrambled up a slippery face adjacent to one of the waterfalls, Slade pointed to an overgrowth of tropical shrubs partially hidden behind an outcropping of igneous rocks.

"Through here," he said.

"Where?"

"There's a tunnel. Just follow me." Slade dropped to his knees, pushed the broad leaves and ferns aside, and disappeared with Noah right behind him.

It got darker and darker as they crawled among the vines, deeper into the undergrowth. Noah was becoming increasingly uncomfortable, his amorphous jungle dream coming back to him. Still, he pressed on. The passage twisted and turned as Slade increased the distance between them, and finally was out of sight.

As the opening narrowed, Noah struggled to keep up, his tension mounting. *It was important to get these guys' stories, okay, but getting eaten alive? How could they live in this hell hole? Probably used to tunnels, but living in here like snakes— Snakes? Oh Jesus.*

He tried to move faster, but the tight confines made it impossible. Though not normally claustraphobic, Noah felt the tunnel closing in on him. There was a vague sense that the tightly-woven plants were actually moving, writhing slowly around him. Rising panic washed over him. He was breathing hard, soaked with sweat. *He had to get out.*

He stopped, heart pounding, and wiped his eyes. Peering into the gloom ahead, he could see only a few yards before the light was extinguished altogether. He squeezed around to look behind him. Total darkness. The hum of the jungle had ceased. The only sounds were the faint rushing of the stream somewhere off to his left, and his panting. He thought of backing out, trying to find his way back to the jeep. There was a tingling on his forearm, and he looked down to see an inch-long, black beetle crawling toward his elbow. He jerked, smacked it away, and shuddered.

"Slade!" he yelled into the darkness. No answer. "Slade! Are you there?" Nothing. *Dammit! Where the fuck was he?*

Backing out wasn't an option. He'd come too far, and the vegetation behind him was too thick. *Gotta keep moving.* The opening soon became too small to accommodate him on all fours, and he dropped to his belly, slithering through the slimy plant-ooze. Then, entering a turn to his left, it seemed that he could make out light up ahead. He squirmed faster, and pulled himself, hand over hand.

The tunnel abruptly dumped out into a small, dimly lit clearing, maybe twenty feet across, completely surrounded by vegetation like some organic womb. On the far side, Noah could see signs of habitation with a fire pit, a bed of leaves, some cans of food, cigarette packs, and several wrinkled magazines. Slade was nowhere in sight.

Glancing around the jungle enclosure, his body drenched with slime and sweat, Noah rose to all fours, then to his full height. As he took a step forward, his consciousness was suddenly dominated by a blinding light, a searing pain in the back of his skull, and he went down. Totally disoriented, he was only dimly aware of being dragged over damp loam and rotting vegetation before he lost consciousness entirely.

CHAPTER THIRTY-TWO

REEVES WAS CRANKY. He was stretched pretty thin, but there was no choice. He had to carry through at Kupuna, which meant he would reluctantly have to share a little more of the basic information with Helms.

"You've been doing a great job minding the store, Marcus, but I'm going to need a couple of other things nailed down."

The late afternoon sun reflected off the green hillside behind the general's office at Tripler. Reeves sat behind the desk, Helms in one of the two guest chairs in front of it.

"What did you have in mind, General?"

"For one thing, I'd like you to keep an eye on this U.S. Attorney, Pitts, over in Hilo."

"What can I do?"

"Well, we're going to have to get him some necessary evidence for the prosecution. I just don't have the time to follow up on that while I'm trying to keep things together at the compound."

"I'm afraid I don't understand."

The general struggled with his patience. "When Pitts called the other day, he said he didn't have enough evidence on causation, proof that Samson knew there would be killings when he continued the treatments."

"Understood. But how can I help with that?"

"Well, you're a pretty smart kid. You can certainly think of something."

"Like what?"

"How about Samson's report to me about the increasing violence of several of the men, and his concerns about an incident, possibly a murder, if the SSRIs were to be continued?"

Helms's look was questioning. "I don't remember anything like that. Does such a report exist, General?"

"Perhaps not yet, but it will in a few short hours, after I give you the wording. You will then prepare it, back-date it, and turn it over to Pitts, along with a few other odds and ends."

Now Helms eyed him doubtfully.

"I know it seems irregular, but I assure you, it is vitally necessary. Let me see if I can explain it." He leaned back in his chair.

Helms was unsure about this, but had no choice but to hear it. He searched for a comfortable position in his chair without success.

"Some years ago, some fellow researchers and I worked out, and perfected, a medication that actually cured battle fatigue. We called it Fuerontin." Reeves could discern no reaction. "It was a miracle, Marcus. During the Vietnam conflict, we were able to return affected soldiers to their units in record time. That was particularly critical in wars like the last few in which there was insufficient time to fully instruct all combat personnel so they could understand the threats, the importance behind what they were doing."

"But what does that have to do with Kupuna?" Helms asked.

"Good question. It goes like this. There were a few subjects in the study, very sympathetic cases, men who lacked the strength of character, the courage, to be successful soldiers. We tried to help them with larger doses of the medication because they were so severely affected by battle fatigue and depression. Unfortunately, they experienced some unpredicted side effects, a psychotic-like constellation of symptoms. Of course, we stopped the drug immediately when the complications were recognized, but the symptoms persisted. It was tragic. All of those men had to be hospitalized, then we put them together for ease in treatment."

Helms was nodding.

"Right," Reeves said. "Those are the men at Kupuna."

"And Samson?"

Reeves smiled, looked down, and straightened some papers on his desk. "Samson is the third psychiatrist over there, hired before I was transferred out here from Walter Reed. When I learned of his appointment, I hoped he would be competent to handle it, but he discontinued our regimen of treatment, MAO inhibitors and tricyclics, which had been so helpful in comforting those men. Samson said he thought he could reverse the effects of the Fuerontin with megadoses of SSRIs."

"So Samson wanted to try to cure the disorder?"

"Hell, did he think I hadn't tried? Of course I had! I'd tried everything, for years. But I knew there was no hope. There'd been tissue damage in the brain. I told him our objective should just be to make their last years more comfortable. Try to make them calm, less violent, keep them safe. It was really despicable what he was doing, stirring things up again. Causing so much more pain."

Helms was still stuck in the here and now. "But General, creating a report that doesn't exist?"

Reeves's glower was made more severe by the unruly, graying eyebrows. "He knew there would be deaths with the SSRIs! Everyone knew those drugs caused violent behavior in many patients. He told me he knew all about that. All we're doing in creating a report is making a record of something that actually occurred anyway." Reeves fixed on him menacingly for a few seconds, and then he smiled. "This is a report that he should have sent me in the first place. What he told me about those patients was a significant aspect of the medical record that should have been reduced to writing. He should have filled out the usual chart materials. That kind of documentation is critically important. You know that."

Reeves stopped. When he resumed, he said softly, "This is the only way we can get him out of there, Marcus. I've tried everything else."

"What about court martial for direct disobedience of orders?"

"We can't court martial him. He's not military. VA disciplinary action failed. And we have to be discreet. Anything that would call attention to the problem must be avoided. It's bound to be misinterpreted. Washington has been extremely concerned that our efforts with Fuerontin during the Vietnam conflict would be misconstrued if this all came to light. There would be those who would use our clinical trials as political ammunition. Blast us for being unsympathetic with men who were feeling the terrible effects of combat. You understand, don't you, Marcus? Ironically, exactly the opposite was true. We were trying to restore their confidence. Restore the innate strength that we knew they had. That's all any real soldier wants."

He studied Helms. "So my orders for you are containment. Only to remove the irritant, demonstrate that Samson is taking advantage of the plight of these tortured men to further his own career, but we have to do it with the least publicity possible. Then we go back to making these poor men comfortable as best we can. It's as simple as that. It's worthy. It's merciful, and you and I are going to get it accomplished. You understand?"

The phone rang. "Pardon me, Marcus," Reeves said, picking it up. "I have to take this."

The general frowned as he listened to the voice on the other end of the line, and then he said, "The desert?" He glanced up at Helms and cupped a hand over the phone. "Will you excuse me for a moment?"

Helms nodded and left the room, closing the door behind him as Reeves returned to the call. "Why the desert?" He listened to the explanation. "I see. Yes, I see. Okay, that's fine," he said. "But make sure it's permanent. We don't want any repercussions." He listened again. "Alright. I'm going to assume it's taken care of." Then, finally: "Good work." He hung up the outside line and clicked the intercom. "Send Captain Helms back in, will you?"

Helms resumed his chair, and Reeves began again.

"So, you're clear on my orders?"

"I'll do what I can, General."

"That's not good enough," Reeves snapped. "We have to be together on this. Our futures depend on it. We both go down in flames if we fail."

He let that sink in; then he stood, walked around, and sat on the corner of the desk. "I know what it takes for Black officers to succeed in this army, Marcus," Reeves said. "I've had a lot of Black patients who came to me because they felt the enormous pressures of the military. Their families were important to them, as yours is to you. I know that." The smile was sincere, understanding. "And I'm willing to give you some real good evaluations, recommend you for promotions. But promotions are for officers who see things through, complete the job."

He resumed his seat behind the desk. "Now, if things were to go south here, that is, if there were a full investigation, you know how these things are. Deals are made, and people like us become the bargaining chips."

Reeves looked down at his hands, eyebrows raised, nodding, trying to

assume a soothing visage as he let Helms reflect. He had known quite a
few of these guys. Helms would cave. He knew he was struggling right now
with that business about the effects on his family; the dangerous political
ramifications if this reached congressional levels. Not only would he be
thinking about demotion, loss of pay and benefits, loss of retirement, loss
of stature, but he would also be thinking about the humiliation to his
wife. Reeves looked up and smiled, but he didn't speak. The very essence
of Helms's service was the status and respect it bought him. He could not
bear the loss of it.

"I do know how these things are, General," Helms said.

Reeves nodded seriously. "Good. No cause for concern, Marcus, if we
do this right. Now let me spell it out for you."

* * *

Noah awakened, staring at the 1950s ceiling tiles above the bed in the
"guest" room. His wrists and ankles were bound to the bed frame. He was
aware of activity outside in the atrium, but he could not turn to look. He
caught only fragments of dialogue.

"Reeves just called—"

"—arriving right now."

"Trial starts tomorrow."

Through the haze of reassembling reality, Noah was almost certain
that he recognized Slade's voice. What did that mean? Head throbbing,
he rolled to the left as far as he could and peered out through the filmy
drapes. It *was* Slade! And a number of the patients, the Fallen Heroes.
Slade was addressing them furtively. Some kind of preparation was
underway.

Though his perceptions were jumbled, Noah struggled to understand.
His awareness faded in and out. From time to time he could almost make
out what was being said as the numbers of vets increased in the atrium.
With great effort, he tried to will his attention to solidify as he watched
the scene unfold through a gossamer filter.

At one point, it seemed like Reeves had entered the building, and
Slade was ushering him into the atrium. Noah could have sworn he saw

a number of the vets suddenly fall on Reeves, as if in slow motion. The general attempted to escape. Though it all seemed muffled, Reeves was definitely yelling, threatening. There were scoffs, accusations, promises he would "pay." Something about "VC justice."

Later he could see Slade striding in front of a bound Reeves, seated on the ground, a prisoner. Slade turned to the men, shouted something, pumped his fist in the air, to a guttural and rumbling, violently enthusiastic, response.

* * *

The three men moved with the precision of Special Forces operatives in a perfectly coordinated direct-action approach pattern, crawling toward the isolated structure in the darkness. Their faces blackened, they wore tattered green-jungle fatigues and hats which, though not optimal for camouflage on the barren lavascape of the Makua Valley that stretched between the Mauna Kea and Mauna Loa volcanoes, would nonetheless suffice. The target, the munitions depot, stood apart from the Quonset Hut village that constituted the Pohakuloa Army Training Area, roughly in the center of the Big Island.

After leaving the fourth member of their team with the jeep a quarter mile down the Saddle Road, an abbreviated highway which bisected the valley, they had split up, running in a crouched position over the jagged, long-cooled magma, until they reached a point a hundred feet from the objective. There, they dropped to the ground in the pre-arranged formation, and covered the last leg of the approach on their bellies as the driver silently brought the jeep forward.

One member of the squad stopped twenty-five yards south of the facility, posting as a sentry between the hut and the rest of the base. Reconnaissance had demonstrated that there was only one circulating guard, and he would not pass the munitions hut for another ten minutes. Only the single guard remained inside with whom to contend. The other two members of the Special Ops team continued north, then came around and advanced on the hut from the east, toward the front door. In the dim light, the terrain looked like the surface of the moon.

Arriving in position ten yards from the door, one of the two assault operatives crabbed around to the back. Once there, he scrambled noiselessly to the junction box, which was situated just under the right side of a wooden stoop that extended from the back door. He pulled a knife from the scabbard on his belt, and within seconds had the alarm system disabled, which he communicated to his squad members by hand signal. Then he stood and waited just outside the back door for phase three to begin.

On retrieving the signal, the team member out front approached the building and knocked on the door. Moments later, the guard, side-arm holstered, opened it with a smile, which made plain that he never expected to find himself face-to-face with an aging, Vietnam-era commando. Before he could make a sound, a strap was around his neck, and he went down hard on the back of his head and lay still. His attacker was instantly on him, ready to provide the blow that would afford the team the time it needed but, ascertaining that the guard was already unconscious, he moved swiftly to the next phase.

One of the assault operatives began opening and stacking boxes, verifying contents: M-16 rifles and cartons of twenty-round boxes of ammunition. The other team member began packing them out to the jeep. Within five minutes, they were within a carton each of completing the operation when there was a low whistle from the jeep driver that was relayed by the sentry. The two loaders looked up just as the lights on the night guard's humvie went on, its siren blaring as it approached. Immediately the guardhouse, about two hundred yards away, lit up, and the door opened. GIs began pouring out into the night.

The jeep powered forward as the commando sentry laid down a blanket of cover fire, backing toward the rendezvous point. The two loaders left the last two boxes and sprinted, crouching, to the jeep and jumped aboard just as the sentry piled in. The jeep careened into a wide skid, kicking up a mountain of lava dust and, with a grinding roar, fishtailed down Saddle Road toward Kupuna.

CHAPTER THIRTY-THREE

"CALL *UNITED STATES V. SAMSON.*"

Judge Asaki had finished his law and motion matters and moved on to the trial calendar. Samson's was the only case set for today.

"That's ready, Your Honor," Marvin Pitts answered.

Stephanie Kauna-Luke looked anxiously around to the back of the courtroom to see if, by some miracle, Noah might suddenly appear. Disappointed, she returned her attention to the judge.

"The defense has an application, Your Honor," she said. "Assistant Public Defender Stephanie Kauna-Luke appearing for Dr. Samson."

Asaki gazed down with the 'Perfect, right out of the box we're going to have a problem' look. "Very well, Ms. Kauna-Luke."

"Your Honor," she began. "As the Court may recall, lead counsel for Dr. Samson is Mr. Noah Shane from the mainland, who was admitted by Your Honor *pro haec vice* for that representation. Our office is assisting Mr. Shane."

"I recall, Ms. Kauna-Luke. Is there a problem?"

"No, Your Honor. Well, I mean, yes, Your Honor. Only that Mr. Shane is not here."

"That doesn't sound like a problem to me. What do you propose?"

She again looked around to the back of the courtroom. There were several members of the press, and a few onlookers, but no Noah. "He went up to the Veterans Affairs Medical Center at Kupuna several days ago, Your Honor, and has not returned. I've tried to reach him repeatedly by cell phone without success. I've also tried to reach the compound, but there is no answer there, either."

"Ah," was the harbinger of the never-ending judicial sarcasm that brothers and sisters of the bench sometimes mistook for wit. "That supplies us with a few additional facts, Ms. Kauna-Luke, but I still haven't heard the proposal I asked for."

"On behalf of Dr. Samson," Stephanie went on, "I would apply to the court for a continuance, inasmuch as lead counsel—counsel who had prepared to try this matter—is not available."

Sensing blood in the water, Pitts jumped up. "The prosecution objects, Your Honor. Today is the day set for-"

"Not yet, Mr. Pitts," the judge intoned, holding up a hand. "You'll have your chance." He pasted an exaggerated smile. "For now, I'm on top of it." He turned back to Stephanie. "Now then, Ms. Kauna-Luke, when will Mr. Shane be available?"

"I don't know, Your Honor."

"I see that your office is also of record. What about you trying the case? You are an experienced defense attorney."

"Yes, Your Honor, but I haven't prepared the case."

"Well, you said you have 'assisted.' What was that about?"

"Working with Mr. Shane in putting together the evidence and the trial testimony."

"Indeed. It sounds to me like you are well-briefed on the matter. We will go forward, and if Mr. Shane magically appears during the course of things, he may take center stage."

"Your Honor," Stephanie continued the protest. "This is charged as a capital case. Dr. Samson is entitled to his own attorney, the one who has prepared the case."

"We haven't gotten to the sentencing yet, Ms. Kauna-Luke. The ruling will be that defendant's application for a continuance of the trial is denied. The panel is assembled, and we will begin picking a jury at ten a.m." He turned to the prosecutor. "Does that suit your purposes, Mr. Pitts?"

Pitts gave an unctuous smile accentuated by a slight bow. "Most definitely, Your Honor."

Asaki rapped his gavel. "We will be in recess until ten o'clock."

"All rise," the bailiff announced as the judge left the bench. The gallery stood, most heading toward the exit doors. Samson wore a troubled expression as the guard approached to return him to the holding cell. "Okay doc," he said.

"Let me talk to him for a minute, will you, Jim?" Stephanie asked the marshal.

"Just for a minute, Steph," the marshal said. "I'll be over at the bailiff's desk, but I do want to get some coffee before we reconvene at ten o'clock."

"We won't be long," she said, then turned to Samson, who was apprehensive.

"I'm concerned, Stephanie," he said. "Kupuna may be a dangerous place at this point, particularly since Reeves has been there messing with the drugs. And not hearing from Noah, I don't like it."

"Yeah," she agreed. "Me neither. I was going to drive up there, but Asaki's jammed the case to trial."

"Is there any reason we shouldn't involve the Hilo police?" Samson asked her.

"Lord, I hate to get them into this whole thing."

"Why?"

"Just a public defender knee-jerk, I guess," Stephanie told him, but she obviously shared his concerns. "I guess I really don't have a better suggestion."

"What's your fear?"

"It's a very late free ride with no discovery. Suppose they find something incriminating? We never even find out about it at this point until it explodes in trial."

"But there's nothing to find," Samson protested.

"Sometimes when cops look too hard for the 'truth', it seems to just materialize, if you know what I mean. Ask O.J."

Samson considered it. "Alright. We'll wait and see if Noah turns up today. If not, we bring in the police, agreed?"

"Let's just hope nothing happens while we're fooling around trying to decide. I'd never forgive myself."

Samson hung his head. "Neither would I."

* * *

"Naw, man. The American flag goes on the right. This other thing with the snakes goes on the left," Coyote said.

He and Slade were making some adjustments to Samson's office. They had crafted poles from curtain rods for the flags that ordinarily hung from the flagpole out front, and stands for them by punching holes in overturned wastebaskets.

"Yeah, but whose right?" Slade wondered. "The judges' or the audience? And it's not a 'thing with the snakes'. Those snakes are the flag of the U.S. Army Medical Corps."

"So we put it on the judges' right."

Slade reacted angrily, eyes blazing, right one twitching. "We're gonna fuckin' get it right. I been waitin' a long time for this. Now check the manual again."

"You didn't think I was such an idiot when you asked me to be Chief Judge," Coyote snapped.

"So show me I was right for a change."

Coyote paged through a 1987 Edition of the U.S. Manual for Courts Martial. "Is this a capital case?" he asked.

"Fuckin' A, it's a capital case," was the machine gun response. "Does that matter to where the flag goes?"

"No, but there's supposed to be twelve judges if it's a capital case."

Slade was arranging the judges' chairs behind Samson's desk. "No way we're gonna get twelve judges in here. We're goin' with three. That way there won't be any ties in the voting."

Coyote continued to skim the manual. "Yeah, the American flag goes on the judges' right."

"Good. Those guys bust out the ordnance they brought in from Pohakuloa last night?"

"Barnes said they got it all unpacked. They're putting it in the mess hall."

"Good," Slade said. "We don't wanna be disturbed during the trial. Gonna take enough fire-power to make sure that doesn't happen." He rubbed his twitching eye with the back of his hand. When the chairs were positioned to his satisfaction, he turned back to Coyote. "They got the sandbags, trenches, and barbed wire in place on the perimeter?"

"Not totally, but I checked with Spic a while ago, and they're workin' on it."

"What about the check-point down the road?"

Even Coyote was beginning to notice that Slade was weirding out. He eyed him curiously. "Why do you think all the fire-power and security is such a big deal, Slade? We're out here in the middle of no-where, and we're not attracting attention."

"Good thing we're not counting on you for brains, man. We got Shane here as our guest, and he's supposed to start a trial down in Hilo—let's see"—he looked at his watch—"right about now. Don't you think someone, cops maybe, are gonna come looking for him sooner or later?"

Coyote pressed his lips together and nodded. "I guess."

"So let's beef up the perimeter with a total of six guards instead of four. Two radio-equipped sentries at the check-point exactly one mile down the road toward the highway. They'll come in that way first. Everyone else is in here with us. Guards'll have M-16s, and rotate every two hours to make sure they're fresh. That'll mean everyone gets to see a fair share of the trial. When the attack comes, everyone in here grabs a rifle and a bandelier of ammo clips and deploys to his post." The twitch was accelerating. "They on top of all that?"

"Hey, man." Coyote shrugged. "These guys are professionals. Give it a rest."

"They're gonna have to be. The first wave may be a handful of cops, but those guys got radios, and there'll be a regiment up here before long, and air power. No doubt before we get our conviction. Like I say, I didn't live through all this shit to see it go in the tank now."

"They're pros, Slade."

"Yeah. So bring me Shane."

Coyote bristled. "Who was your fuckin' lackey last week?"

Slade stared at him, eye dancing; then he turned angrily on his heels, struggling for control. "Okay, okay. Sorry," he said, mustering the monumental effort to paste a pseudo-smile. "If you'll bring Shane in, I'll brief him. That work for you? Thanks."

In a few minutes, Coyote returned with Noah at gunpoint, his hands bound behind him. Slade was still busy setting out materials on Samson's desk, which was now the "bench."

Noah was seething as Coyote sat him in a chair. He'd recovered mind and body for the most part and had been sitting in solitary in the guest suite, visited twice a day for meals.

"When do I get to find out what the hell this is all about?"

Slade turned to him. "Right now," he said as Coyote left the room.

Slade grabbed one of the folding chairs from the "gallery," and pulled it up next to where Noah was sitting on his hands.

"For starters," Noah said. "Any way you can bust me out of these shackles?"

"Not until we have full security in place. We can't be too careful."

"You're nuts, Slade. This is kidnapping."

"Well, I'm sorry about the inconvenience, but I'm afraid it was unavoidable."

"Yeah, and I'm sure there's a good reason for the bash on the head, and for the prison thing with bread and water."

"In fact, there was a good reason." Slade massaged his twitching face.

"Can you enlighten me?"

"You have been detained to participate in the Court Martial of General Harley Reeves."

"Of course," Noah said. "How silly of me. To participate in the Court Martial of General Reeves." Then he studied him in disbelief. *The nervous tic, rapid forced speech, deterioration of appearance, the delusional content, glazed eyes, intense affect. He'd seen the syndrome before. Either the guy had gone completely round the bend, or he was withdrawing from something cold turkey. Neither would be entirely reassuring, being trussed up here in the jungle with this wing-nut and all these other maniacs. But the worst of it was, they were most definitely serious.*

"Ahhhmm. . . just what did you have in mind as my participation in this Court Martial?"

Slade stared straight into his eyes, and Noah could feel the gravity. "You are here to defend General Reeves."

CHAPTER THIRTY-FOUR

"DEFEND HIM? DEFEND HIM against what?" Noah wasn't sure he'd heard it right.

"War crimes."

"War crimes? What the hell are you talking about?"

"Human experiments that have resulted in the deaths and insanity of these men." He gestured around to the several Fallen Heroes that were setting up the room. "Condemning them to a lifetime of subsistence at an animal level."

"How did he do that?"

"Just exactly the way you guessed. It started out as experiments on drugs for battle fatigue, and ended up with a bunch of symptoms bordering on psychosis, no return. Reeves knew that, but he continued the experiments, damning more and more of 'em to hell."

"And how do you know all this?"

"I suspected it for a long time, for all the reasons I told you. But then their memories started to come back."

"While Reeves was here?"

"Exactly."

"Didn't he know?"

"We let him think they stopped taking the meds, but I kept them up. I told them about the Court Martial—that when we had enough memory of what happened, we'd be able to get the bastard. Crimes against humanity. They don't have it all back yet, but we've got the treatment and the hypnosis, sending 'em on suicide missions. These guys were almost as hot for the Court Martial as me. Coyote, Garcia, Platz. They're the judges."

"So what defense did you have in mind?" Noah asked. "This sounds like some kind of railroad. Why not just turn him over to the military justice system?"

A sardonic smile spread amidst the twitching. "And take a chance on their getting it wrong? You fucking kiddin' me? He's a pretty powerful guy. We've waited way too long for this. He's a fucking army general, for chrissakes, Chief of fucking Psychiatry at Tripler. He goes deep with the brass in Washington. He'd never be indicted, much less convicted. This is the place it can happen. The only place. Right here."

"Then why the trial?" Noah asked. "If you're so sure about all this, why don't you just take the guy out?"

"Don't think I haven't dreamed about it. But that's too easy. This guy's going to get his day in court, then we're going to hang him." He ground his teeth. "I want him to know what's happening to him every fucking step of the way. I want him to have to look these heroic men in the eye, hear how they feel about forty years of hell, tell them what he fucking did to them. I want the fear of what's coming to churn in his guts."

Slade's whole body was jerking. He stood abruptly and turned his back. "In case you were wondering," he said, "I'm prosecuting counsel." When he turned around again, his face was contorted into a chilling grin. "You can bet this sadistic fuck is going to get what's coming to him."

"You?"

"Me."

"What's your stake in all this? Were you one of the Fallen Heroes?"

"Close. My older brother, Chris."

"Your brother?"

"All everything, not like me. Went to State to play for Woody Hayes. Phi Bate, the whole thing. For some idiotic reason, he and some other guys enlisted. After OCS, they sent him to Nam as a platoon leader. We heard from him a few times, then he disappeared."

Noah was fascinated by the Tourette-like gyrations, the insane eyes. "What happened to him?"

"Yeah. That's what we wanted to know. I left school in my junior year, enlisted, and followed him over as a supply sergeant. By the time I found him, he'd been through this research program. He wouldn't say anything about it, but they'd sent him to Special Ops School to become a fucking Green Beret. I couldn't figure it out. The easiest-going guy you'd ever want to meet. A fucking Green Beret. I didn't know him. He hardly paid

any attention to me. All he cared about was being out there in the game."
He was grinding his jaw. "Cam Ranh Bay, that's where it happened. Just
like you said. Makes my fucking blood boil. Reeves—"

Noah didn't know if he was finished or not. He let it drift for about a
minute, then said, "Jesus. Sounds rough." *A little boost would sometimes
jump-start his psychotic clients.*

It worked. Instantly, Slade picked it up again. "Not long after, Chris
was sent with two other Fallen Heroes into a company of entrenched
VC—to spring a downed pilot. None of them came back. They found
the plane later. The pilot was in it, killed in the crash. It was all for
nothing."

"How did you wind up here?" Noah asked.

"After the war, I stayed in, wanted to help vets who had mental
problems. That's how I ended up with Doc. We both came over to this
unit after Okinawa."

Noah was still not sure where he fit in. "So, what do you want from
me?" he asked.

"I don't know. I'm not going to tell you your business," Slade said. "But
I'd think you might cross-examine the witnesses. Isn't that the point of trials
in the first place? Maybe that sonofabitch wants to testify. Maybe he has
something to say." He leered ominously. "Like to fuckin' hear that."

"I can't imagine why he'd want to participate in this charade, or why
I would either."

Slade's twitching eyes narrowed instantly, and he became deadly
serious.

"Because he's facing the God. . . Damned. . . death penalty," he said.
"I would think that would be important to a dedicated public defender,
wouldn't it?" The eyes widened, becoming glazed again. "But if that's
not motivating enough for you, maybe this will be: As is the case in some
Middle Eastern cultures, his lawyer is facing the death penalty, too."

Once again Noah searched the animated face, probing for whether
he'd heard it right. *Could this be the Slade that was his father's right hand
for so many years? What had happened to him? He was clearly whacked,
but at the same time, quite obviously capable, and sporadically lucid. The
death penalty. Was this for real?*

"You're not serious," Noah whispered.

"But I am."

"You don't mean that you're going to kill us both if these—these—'judges' convict Reeves of war crimes?"

"That's exactly what I mean," Slade sneered.

Noah couldn't make it compute. *Slade's problem with Reeves was clear, but did it make sense that he had to get swept up in the dragnet? He studied the face for any sign that it was just a ploy to motivate him, that he'd back off in the end. But all there was was rage.*

"Why are you doing this?" Noah asked.

"The man murdered my brother. First he destroyed his mind, then he murdered him. It was all about his own greed, ego." His face came close to Noah's. "He's a fucking viper," he spat, then backed away. "He will be dealt with, and I'm the only one who can do it. God demands that there be justice."

"How is there justice in killing me?"

"The only way to ensure a fair trial, that you'll get after it." Then he smiled again, eyes gleaming. "But you're not alone," he said. His voice was deep, rumbling. "The angel of death hovers over us all."

Something awful was clearly channeling him. The man was doubtless round the bend but, however warped, there was also a highly honed intellect, and a definite mania that was fueling it.

"What do you mean?"

"I mean, it's only a matter of time until the outside sends in police, troops maybe. The Fallen Heroes won't be taken alive. They'll have their vengeance over this monster, and once they have that, the armies of the establishment will not be merciful."

Noah struggled to suppress his growing panic.

Slade went on. "Oh, yes. They will most certainly come for their 'beloved general.' You saw how the F.B.I. treated David Koresh and the Branch Davidians. They will come. But David Koresh didn't have the Fallen Heroes, did he. These men are all trained Special Forces killers." The twitching and blazing eyes punctuated and added affect. "No, Shane," he intoned. "You will not live through any attempted rescue. You will not live unless Reeves is acquitted of torture by the men he tortured."

Noah tried to hide the hyperventilation. *His only option was to stay alive as long as he could, to give the powers that be a chance to try to get him out. Surely he must have been missed already. Stephanie must have been trying to call. Hilo PD must be on the way.* He looked up at Slade.

"David Samson trusted you," he said. "My father trusted you."

"Your father would understand how much is at stake here."

"That may be," Noah responded. "But don't you see? You're taking me away from defending him. He's on trial down there for murder. He may never come back to these men if he goes down on those charges."

Slade's laugh exploded. "Now that's pretty funny, isn't it," he said. "You think you're the only one that can save him? I never fucking understood why he brought you over here anyway. We were dealing with this whole thing together. And we could have ridden it out if he'd gotten the Federal Public Defender like I told him. Those lawyers are local. They deal with the federal court, federal prosecutors, every day. But no. He had to have you—because you're his son." Slade scoffed and turned away, shaking his head. "After all I did for him."

He was pacing again, and then, twitching and jerking, he went on. "His PD is tough. I wanted him to use her in the first place." He waved a hand dismissively. "I don't think they're going to convict him, anyway. He didn't do shit. They'll figure it out. Besides, won't be anyone left up here for him to treat anyway." He ran a hand through his hair, then turned to Noah abruptly.

"Now why don't you go ahead and talk to the defendant?" He smiled. "See what the general has to say."

* * *

Reeves was sitting in an aged overstuffed chair in the corner, next to the bed, when Noah was shown in by Slade. Dressed in a blue denim shirt and jeans, Reeves was reading and did not look up. He appeared reasonably intact, clean shaven, well groomed. No overt marks or signs of abuse.

Slade locked the door behind them. This room, Samson's quarters in which Reeves had stayed after he assumed command of Kupuna, as well as the guest room, had been altered—boarded windows, external hasp locks—to serve as lockups.

Noah stood next to the door. "General Reeves, I'm Noah Shane," he said.

Now Reeves looked up. "Shane?" A frown. "Do I know you?"

"I don't believe we've met. I'm Dr. Samson's attorney, from the Bay Area, here to defend him."

Reeves assessed him visually. "Yeah? So?"

"Well, apart from the fact that we seem to be fellow prisoners here—"

"They're holding you, too? Why? What the hell is this about?"

"It's all pretty bizarre, General, but let me see if I can break down what I know."

Noah brought him up to date. Toward the end, Reeves stood and began pacing.

"Court Martial," he scoffed. "I assumed they would make up something about the experiments, but a Court Martial?" He shook his head.

"So what are you going to say when you testify?" Noah asked.

Reeves continued to pace. "That Fuerontin had all the promise of a wonder drug. That we were going to relieve suffering of countless GIs, return them to their units. That we could even head off disability at the first sign of depression." He looked up at Noah. "It would have alleviated the pain of thousands, given them back their self-respect, saved a fortune in medical and psych resources."

It was pretty convincing. "So what happened?"

"We set up profiles for the clinical trials. We conducted them pursuant to the strictest protocols. This is complex stuff. There were grant applications, reporting, strict screening, dose management—"

"But what happened to all those records, General? There have been significant efforts to find them, no success."

"I don't know. Where did you look?"

"I think all the medical record repositories were consulted."

"Well, experimental records are probably kept separately. I don't know if they would be maintained this long. We shut the studies down many years ago."

"Why did you shut them down?"

"The initial results were overwhelmingly positive, then when we found some cases of extreme battlefield depression that were resistant to treatment, I made the mistake of ordering increased dosages."

An air of contrition. That could be helpful. "So what happened?"

"The increased dosages apparently resulted in some kind of disruption of brain chemistry, maybe structural damage. We saw severe violent symptoms, paranoia, sociopathy. Only in a small percentage of cases, but we couldn't take the chance of further complications."

"Why not? Weren't you getting mostly good results?" *Were there some moral compunctions here? Maybe something to work with?*

Reeves didn't respond immediately. At last he said quietly, "The psychosis couldn't be reversed."

"So the Fallen Heroes are products of your experiments?"

"'Fallen Heroes'," he snorted.

"It's what Slade calls them. How do you account for the fact that many of them are decorated veterans?"

"After the changes began to take place, some distinguished themselves with unusual valor before they became disabled from psychosis. If only we could have sustained it—"

"Sustained what, General?"

Reeves dropped his eyes, conveying regret. "Sustained the program," he said. "I blame myself. I should have insisted upon more animal studies before we went to higher dosages. But there was the time pressure of a brutal war. The drugs were a powerful weapon." He stopped pacing and walked to the chair to sit down.

"That's why I warned Samson about high doses of SSRIs. I didn't want to compound the problem we had already created." He shrugged. "But he wouldn't listen."

The guy was good. Compelling story. Could it conceivably be true? It was consistent with the abstracts Jack had found in the archives. Now he just had to sell it to a jury of executioners.

CHAPTER THIRTY-FIVE

"HEY, STEPH, WHEN ARE you going to let me buy you one of those frou-frou drinks with the little umbrellas over at the Sleepy Tiki? I promise I become much sexier once your blood-alcohol level passes .10."

Pitts had geared up his standard smarmy hit on Stephanie in the hall outside Department Five as they waited with their carts and trial boxes for the law and motion calendar to conclude inside. She always lacked patience for the drivel, but this morning it was particularly irksome, given her state of mind after being ramrodded to trial by Judge Asaki and feeling her fears about Noah. Asaki had continued the jacked-up pace by driving the lawyers mercilessly through an abbreviated voir dire, and a jury had been selected by close of business the night before, in a murder case, no less. Stephanie was given scarcely enough time to get name, address, and prior jury experience, let alone get into the biases of each potential juror in any depth. She was extremely uncomfortable not knowing what she had on her jury. But then, Pitts didn't have any better handle on it than she had. Like it or not, this thing was going to start.

"You know what, Marvin, I'm sure that's true, but why not save yourself a buncha money and just hire yourself a hooker? I'd probably give you a heart attack, anyway."

"Damn good argument, counsel. You're gonna be a great trial lawyer someday."

The sexual harassment case closed, he moved on: "You know, I would have made you a plea offer by now if I had an inch of room. But like I told you before, I'm not calling the shots on this one."

"That's ok, Marvin. No offer would have been accepted. Samson's not guilty of anything, and you know it."

He still had the smile pasted when the marshal emerged from the courtroom and called them back. Five minutes later, they were all at the counsel table.

After the formal trial call, the court took up the motion for a gag order and press exclusion. Stephanie had expected that Noah was going to address that, and when she had to scramble to get ready for trial, she hadn't gotten up to speed on that "detail." Result? Though she took a couple of mighty swings, motion granted. After satisfying himself there were no other items of housekeeping, Judge Asaki directed the bailiff to bring in the jury.

"You may begin, Mr. Pitts," the judge said when all were assembled.

"Thank you, Your Honor." Pitts rose, buttoned his charcoal pinstripe jacket, smoothed his snow-white hair, and strode to the lectern in the well of the courtroom. After pouring himself a glass of water, he took off his watch and propped it in front of him. The twelve jurors and two alternates in the jury box fidgeted.

"Your Honor, counsel, ladies and gentlemen—" Pitts nodded to each in turn. "This is a case of premeditated double murder in which the defendant, the psychiatrist for both victims, knowingly permitted their brutal killings, making him as culpable for their deaths as if he had actually killed them with his own hands." He went on to describe the VA Medical Center at Kupuna and its unique compliment of patients, their history, and treatment over the years; Samson's coming to the compound and the advent of the megadoses of SSRIs. He explained how the dosages Samson employed were not approved by the FDA, nor the manufacturer, and were contrary to the explicit order of his superior officer that he desist.

He turned to Samson. "You may well ask, what accounts for the wholly unjustifiable conduct on the part of this defendant? I submit, ladies and gentlemen, that it was arrogance. Unbridled hubris. This was a man of deadly ambition who saw the chance for fame and fortune. Maybe he would get a prestigious journal article out of all of this, perhaps even an ego-gratifying chapter in a textbook. And who knows? That might be the entry to academia, the ivory tower of research. Is that motive enough? He'd paid his dues all those years, as a line psychiatrist in some pretty ugly venues. I suggest to you that he saw it as his turn to collect. Is that motive enough to launch on this misadventure, exploiting his patients? Men who trusted in him, subjecting them to this brutal treatment? That will be for you to decide." Samson cast a look at Stephanie, who took pains not to return it.

"Now, the defense will no doubt argue that these drugs cannot fairly be said to have caused the intensely violent state of mind in the patients who actually committed the homicides." Pitts dealt with the weakness in his case head-on before the defense had a chance to raise it, hopefully making Samson seem defensive when they brought it up. "We will call experts to explain to you the grave dangers associated with the drugs, antidepressants called SSRIs, dangers that can be particularly serious in large doses at which the effects of these drugs are unknown.

"We will also call General Harley Reeves, a distinguished and decorated medical officer and defendant's superior, Chief of Psychiatry at Tripler Army Medical Center in Honolulu, who will tell you how he cautioned the defendant about all this, even after the first death. We will demonstrate that Dr. Samson would not be reined in, even when his supply of medication was terminated by Veterans Affairs. At that point, he turned to the illicit drug market in Honolulu to purchase the death-dealing drugs from known felons and dealers." A sudden knot took hold in Samson's stomach. "And we will introduce written evidence, the defendant's own report, in fact, in which he clearly describes his knowledge of the risk of violence and murder." Samson shot a puzzled frown at Stephanie.

* * *

Coyote sat in the place of honor, between the other two judges, Mike Garcia and Sid Platz. Garcia, aka Spic, was a sixty-two-year-old Hispanic from Phoenix with thick, swept back black hair that was graying at the temples. This morning he was clean-shaven, wearing a crisp white shirt, open at the collar, and jeans.

Sid Platz, whom they called Schnoz, did not exactly fill the Semitic bill one might have expected given the name and nickname. He had thinning blond hair and a ruddy complexion, residual effects of repeated bouts with teenage acne. But the nose was definitely his distinguishing feature. Though not of epic proportion naturally, it took on the unique appearance as a consequence of being mashed and bent to the left, the product of multiple fractures. Schnoz also wore a white shirt, but he had garnered a Hawaiian flowered tie and khakis from Samson's closet to round out the ensemble.

Coyote had his usual well-pressed look and also had come up with a tie, a navy blue knit.

There was no counsel table. Noah and Reeves were now both unshackled in light of the placement of intense security. Slade had made it clear he would like nothing better than for one or both of them to make a run for it, having given the bailiff and guards orders to shoot to kill. The defendant and his counsel sat on one side of the first of three rows of gallery, with Slade on the other. All three were dressed neatly but informally, no ties. Twelve other Fallen Heroes occupied the remaining gallery chairs.

Outside, the compound was a fortified bunker. Vets with M-16s were everywhere. The arsenal of arms and munitions was assembled in the mess hall, now fully unpacked and ready for instant deployment when the expected attack occurred.

Coyote gaveled with a woodworker's mallet secured from the shop. "The Court Martial of General Harley Reeves for war crimes will come to order," he said. "Lieutenant Platz, will you read the charges?"

Schnoz started to stand, but Coyote motioned him to remain seated. He looked down at the paper in front of him and read solemnly: "General Harley Reeves, M.D., is charged with war crimes including murder, mayhem, human experimentation, and other atrocities. He severely altered the central nervous systems of more than one hundred and fifty men and kept them that way for thirty years for reasons of his own."

After an extended silence, during which Coyote was not sure if Schnoz had finished, Coyote said, "General Reeves, please stand."

Noah rose to his feet out of habit, but Reeves didn't move.

Coyote rapped the desk sharply with his gavel and barked, "Stand up!"

Reeves stood slowly, eyebrows drawn together, reflecting the storm that was raging behind them.

"Does the accused have any response to the charges?" Coyote demanded.

"This is a preposterous charade," Reeves said dismissively. "You are detaining a general officer in the United States Army, which will subject you to—"

"Silence!" Coyote bellowed. Reeves's eyes widened, and Slade bolted to his feet. On reflex, the bailiff took a step forward. Coyote raised a hand to restrain the bailiff and looked at Slade severely. Slade resumed his seat.

"You are a prisoner of this court, General Reeves," Coyote said sternly. "So long as you behave in a respectful manner, you will be permitted to remain here. But this Court Martial will proceed until it is completed with you here or not, and the consequences will be what they are. Do I make myself clear?"

Reeves stared at him defiantly.

"Now, General Reeves, I ask you again. Do you have any response to the charges?"

"I refuse to participate," Reeves said, wearing a sullen look.

"Very well. Then the court will enter a plea of not guilty on your behalf." Coyote moved on. "Mr. Slade, do you have any opening remarks?"

Slade was on his feet like a man who had mainlined too much caffeine. "I do, Your Honor."

"Please tell us what they are."

"Members of the Court," he began. "The prosecution will prove that General Harley Reeves is a Jekyll/Hyde monster, that he is guilty of all the charges against him. You all know the facts. Reeves engaged in experiments which turned soldiers into violent maniacs, all the men in this hospital, and many others. And he did it knowingly, for his own reasons. To make himself famous, and to make these men into psychotic killing machines.

"He didn't care that when the drugs were stopped, the Fallen Heroes couldn't be restored to their normal mental state. He knew about all that, yet he kept giving them the drugs. He gave them"—he turned and made a sweeping motion to the men behind him—"all of you, more and more drugs. It was all intentional, and we'll prove it. I won't say any more about that right now."

Slade went on, eyes fiery, speech pressured, loud, outlining the evidence like a driven man. There would be witnesses who had begun to recover their memories of the treatment, to different degrees, over the last six to eight months.

"Now, you might be suspicious of recovered memory," he blurted. "Probably you should be. I was. Except that these guys all have the same kind of memories, to which they will testify under oath. Also, we have a mole, deep within the Army Medical Corps, who helped us corroborate all the evidence."

Reeves glanced at Noah, his face drawn into a puzzled frown.

Slade saw the look and grinned at Reeves. "Yeah, that's right," he said. "We got you cold, Reeves. You'll see." He turned back to the judges. "By the time we're done with him, there's no way you'll be able to find him anything but guilty." Slade looked excitedly from Coyote, to Spic, to Schnoz, then abruptly sat down.

* * *

"Members of the jury," Judge Asaki declared, "the defense can choose to make an opening statement at the beginning of the case, reserve it until the prosecution completes its case, or waive the right to open entirely. Ms. Kauna-Luke, does the defense wish to make a statement at this time?"

Stephanie was not about to let the prosecution's allegations go unanswered and weigh on the jurors' minds throughout the government's case.

"Yes, Your Honor," she responded. "Thank you." She rose and strode to the lectern carrying a black trial binder which contained the roadmap of her case.

After she took a deep breath and slowly exhaled, she began. "Your Honor, ladies and gentlemen, counsel, Dr. David Samson is a compassionate, highly competent psychiatrist who cares deeply for his patients. The evidence will conclusively demonstrate that he would never consider taking any action that might conceivably cause injury to any one them. His motive was at all times to relieve the suffering of the men who were hospitalized at Kupuna. In fact, we will introduce his medical charts that will document the high standard of care that he provided, and the remarkable progress that was being made by his veteran patients.

"The prosecution wants you to believe that the drugs Dr. Samson was prescribing were mind-altering substances that turned these men into animals, and that he, for some reason, had this as an objective. Nothing could be further from the truth. You have been told that these drugs are called SSRIs, Selective Serotonin Reuptake Inhibitors. Perhaps some of you have heard of them. We will hear a lot more about them during the course of this trial. Some of you or members of your family may have taken them. In fact, they are some of the most commonly prescribed antidepressants in the world.

"Dr. Samson was trying new dosages to reverse a very serious, and resistant, aberrant mental condition. There is no evidence whatsoever that these drugs caused the men to be violent, or caused these killings. Let me say that again. *There is no evidence whatsoever in this case that the drugs Dr. Samson prescribed had anything to do with these deaths.* But don't take my word for it. We will bring a world-renowned psychopharmacologist, Dr. Martin Fells, professor of medicine at the University of Texas, who will give you the history of these drugs. He will testify that in their earliest form, SSRIs were suspected of causing violent reactions in a few patients. But that was many years ago. The drugs have since been refined and are no longer causing any significant deleterious side effects. And the prosecution very well knows that—"

Pitts rose to his feet calmly. "Your Honor," he said. "I hate to interrupt counsel's most"—sarcastic cough—"interesting remarks, but I must object on the ground that this has now become argument."

Asaki looked up, as if awaking from a distant reverie. "Ah yes, Ms. Kauna-Luke. Please confine your opening statement to what you anticipate the evidence will demonstrate. There will be plenty of time for argument later."

"Thank you, Your Honor," Stephanie said, and smiled. She had made her point and, having prodded Pitts to his feet, had the jury believing it had hurt him.

"The evidence that Your Honor mentions will show that the science relating to these medicines is now clear," she went on. "Years of study has elucidated their properties. Now, let me also say, that although the defendant in a criminal action does not have to testify, he may remain silent and force the prosecution to prove its case against him beyond any reasonable doubt, I promise you that Dr. Samson will in fact take the stand and tell you what his motivations, his expectations, and his intent were with regard to this therapy.

"The defense invites each of you to pay careful attention to the prosecution's case and to hold the U.S. Attorney to the promises he made in his opening statement. Make him prove to you each and every charge beyond any reasonable doubt. But do not formulate any premature conclusions, because we believe that after you have heard the defense witnesses, you will not have any basis to convict Dr. Samson. Thank you, ladies and gentlemen. We will talk again at the conclusion of the case."

* * *

"Mr. Shane," Coyote said. "Do you wish to make a statement to the Court?"

Noah stood hesitantly. "I do," he said. Half of him was consumed by the inanity of this scene. Here he was in a doctor's office turned courtroom, out in the deep jungle of Hawaii, the birds and creatures chirping and howling outside, with seriously disturbed mental patients presiding. The other half was petrified by the thought that never had so much been riding on his performance, and never would it again, if by some strange development he were to survive this. The first half wanted to burst into uproarious laughter, but the growing second half took every moment with total seriousness.

"Members of the Court," he began. "I know that each of you brings his own history to this moment of judgment. And those histories have been atrocious to be sure. Each of you has suffered immeasurably. But that does not make this man"—he pointed to Reeves—"guilty of the atrocities." Noah felt much better once he was on his feet. He was amazed to find himself able, at least for the moment, to shut out the pressure of whether he lived or died. The words and phrases came to him as they had so often.

"I am encouraged by the resolve that I see in this room, resolve that

has prompted this Court Martial as a means to ascertain the guilt or
innocence of General Reeves by due process of law before bringing
serious punishment to bear on him. After all, you could have chosen
simply to carry out the most extreme punishment. Some groups who
feel they have been wronged do that. You have not. This demonstrates
to me your core values and your strong commitment to the principles of
American democracy. . . ," he gestured toward the flag. *Gotta go to the
flag, no? These guys are soldiers, for Chrissakes. U.S. Army, for Chrissakes.*
". . . democracy that each and every one of you fought for, principles for
which your fellow soldiers died, principles to which you have dedicated
your lives. I ask you to remember the most important principle of our
democracy as it relates to a court of law, that the defendant is presumed
to be innocent until he is proven guilty beyond any reasonable doubt. I
ask only that you bear that in mind despite what, understandably, must
be your very strong feelings, feelings that have the potential to prejudice
your thinking in this case." All three judges were focused on him. He
turned to see that the men in the gallery were, as well.

"I believe the evidence will show that Dr. Reeves did his best,
as a physician and a scientist. He had a worthwhile dream: that men
confronted with the horrors of war who became depressed to the point
of disability, men who lost their self-confidence and self-respect, could
have those vital elements of their character restored to them. They could
become useful, efficient, self-reliant soldiers and citizens once again,
through the use of a medication he was trying to perfect. Was that not a
worthy goal? A patriotic goal?" He looked at each of them.

"But something went terribly wrong. Something he did not anticipate.
After chronic usage, the drug was found to cause pathological aggression,
and what's worse, that condition could not be reversed." Noah looked
back at Reeves, who was staring down at the floor. Noah hoped that,
despite his disgust for the process, he had now clearly come to understand
the seriousness of what was at stake here. There was little point in further
defiance.

"Like you, Dr. Reeves was horrified," Noah continued. "He will
take the stand, and will testify, even though he is not required to do
so. Another basic democratic principle is that a defendant cannot be

compelled to testify against himself in a criminal case. That's the Fifth Amendment and it means that Dr. Reeves doesn't have to get up there, but he wants you to know what happened. After all, you were involved — deeply involved. He will tell you that he raised the dosages in certain more resistant cases, that he has never forgiven himself for doing that before he performed additional animal studies to ascertain the effects, because it ultimately had devastating consequences. It was, ironically, his well-intentioned efforts to treat you effectively that resulted in his inability to reverse the effects."

There were a few soft groans and shifting feet. Slade shook his head. But mostly, the vets were listening.

"Dr. Reeves will also explain that the reason he continued to give you the drug was because he thought the failure of reversal could be corrected by behavioral therapy while continuing its use. He made some mistakes. He will admit that. Doctors are human. And the bigger the effort at healing, often the more profound the effects of the mistakes. But Dr. Reeves never intended any harm, only helpful medical care. That was his goal."

Noah breathed deeply. "Now we will begin," he told them. "All of us, to explore this story, to try to find out what really happened. Once again, I ask you to do your best, as we move through this process, to keep an open mind. Yes, you should listen to the case for the prosecution. We invite you to listen to their evidence because what we are all seeking here, after all, is the truth. But as you do so, please strive to refrain from judgment until you have heard from Dr. Reeves. And even though, for all the reasons you know so well, that may be the hardest thing you've ever been asked to do, I believe you will do it. I believe that because you are here, in this room, this courtroom. I believe that means you are fundamentally honorable and fair men."

CHAPTER THIRTY-SIX

"THE PROSECUTION MAY CALL its first witness."

"Thank you, Your Honor," Pitts said. "We will call Dr. Edith Anderson."

"Dr. Edith Anderson," the marshal droned.

A tall, slim woman with long brown hair streaked with gray was already on her feet. "Yes?"

"Please step forward and be sworn."

After the witness took the oath Pitts strode into the well and began his direct. First he established her credentials as Cornell educated, medical school at NYU, extensive practice and research in psychiatry, and her current professional activity as teaching at Johns Hopkins School of Medicine. Then he turned to the question at hand.

"Dr. Anderson, with your extensive personal experience, original research, and your knowledge of the medical literature, have you formulated an opinion with reasonable medical probability as to whether SSRI antidepressant drugs can cause violence in patients who take them?"

"I have."

"What is your opinion in that regard?"

"Both in my practice, and in the general population of psychiatrists according to the literature, there has been a substantial increase in violence, aggression, and suicidality among patients who have taken SSRIs."

"Just what are SSRIs, Doctor?"

"Selective Serotonin Reuptake Inhibitors are a class of antidepressant drugs that operate by blocking the reuptake of serotonin in certain synapses of the brain."

"What does that mean in English to us non-healer folk?" The jury response to the effort at downhome was minimal.

"Nerve impulses in the brain are conducted from place to place along neural tracts. As a part of our central nervous system functioning, the impulses are directed in different directions and with different degrees of force by switches, called synapses. Synapses work by secreting neurotransmitters, certain biochemicals whose release is stimulated by the arriving impulse, and these neurotransmitters cross a minute gap in order to activate a new impulse on the other side. One such neurotransmitter is serotonin, which is thought to stimulate feelings of well-being and happiness. Now, after the neurotransmitter is secreted, and the message is transmitted, the nerve cell wants to gobble up the remaining neurotransmitter, so it is out of the gap and no longer stimulating, getting ready for another impulse to arrive. That's called 'reuptake.'"

Pitts interrupted. "That's a lot to digest, Doctor. Let's come up for air for a moment." He walked to a covered blackboard adjacent to the jury box and raised the drape, revealing a diagram with little Xs and Os. He picked up a pointer and proceeded to backtrack, establishing the doctor's testimony with the diagram. When he had finished, he asked her, "So where do the SSRIs come in?"

"Well, as a very general proposition, the longer the neurotransmitter, here the serotonin, is in the synaptic gap, stimulating the receptors on the other side, the stronger the message received will be. Psychopharmocologists and neurobiologists believe that certain psychiatric disorders are caused by excessive stimulation of certain kinds of receptors by neurotransmitters, and other disorders are caused by inadequate stimulation. Things like depression, obsessive-compulsive behavior, bulimia, that kind of thing, are thought to be caused by inadequate stimulation by serotonin, insufficient stimulus, reducing feelings of well being."

"So?"

"So the genius in all of this is that some very smart scientists discovered a substance that will inhibit the mechanism by which the nerve cell gobbles up the serotonin, that is, inhibits its reuptake, thereby leaving it in the gap longer and increasing the stimulation, and decreasing the symptoms of depression."

"Very clever." Pitts smiled and looked at the jury in an effort to measure whether or not they were following. He put the pointer down and returned to the podium.

"Now, Doctor, when did these drugs go on the market for regular use?"

"In the early 1990s."

"And thereafter, did the literature begin to report some unfortunate side effects?"

"It did."

"What kinds of side effects were reported?"

"When the drugs began to receive widespread usage, there was a certain percentage of patients who were reported to experience excessive tendency to violence, aggression, and suicidality."

"When were those effects first reported?"

"Almost immediately."

"Was it known what was causing the side effects?"

"That is not well understood, but it would seem logical that if understimulation results in depression and cognitive slowing, and we try to increase the stimulation, that the right amount of stimulation may stabilize feelings of well-being, but overstimulation could cause too much activity resulting in violence and aggression. But it's a very complicated business."

"Were these isolated, anecdotal reports?"

"The literature was literally flooded with them. Lawsuits were filed, research was undertaken."

"So it would be fair to say that the tendency toward violence in patients taking SSRIs was a matter of common knowledge among psychiatrists since the early 1990s?"

"Unless a psychiatrist was brain dead, he or she would have been aware. These studies were definitely common knowledge in our field."

"Now, let's switch to another area, Doctor. Is the tendency toward violence when on these drugs, dose related?"

"I'm not sure what you mean."

"I'm wondering whether the likelihood of aggression in a patient increases, the higher the dose given."

"There really have been no clinical studies done on that subject."

"And why is that?"

"Because of the concerns about side effects, increasing the recommended doses with chronic treatment in a clinical setting is almost unknown."

"Well, would it be reasonable to assume that the effects would be more pronounced at higher dosages?"

Stephanie interrupted. "Objection, Your Honor. Calls for speculation. Lacks foundation. The doctor just testified that she knows of no such studies."

"Sustained," Asaki ruled.

"Is it a common principle of psychopharmacology that side effects of antidepressants are increased proportionally with the increase in the dose?"

"Same objection, Your Honor, and vague and ambiguous, overbroad," Stephanie interposed.

"I'll let her answer this one, Ms. Kauna-Luke," the judge said. "Goes to her general fund of knowledge. You can cross-examine on the matter if you wish. You may answer, Dr. Anderson."

"It is generally correct that drug effects increase with increased dosage."

"So if Dr. Samson was giving ten to twenty times the recommended clinical dosage of SSRIs to his patients, it is reasonable to assume that the violent effects of the drugs would have been compounded dramatically, is that fair?"

"Your Honor," Stephanie objected. "You have already sustained an objection to this question. It lacks foundation, calls for speculation, and is an incomplete hypothetical." This was the central issue, and Stephanie was not about to let Pitts get it by default.

"I'll withdraw it, Your Honor," Pitts said, having opened up his point, which he would return to later. He went on to the individual studies and the doctor's own experience with the drugs as bases for her opinions, building her credibility. She spoke with the authority of one who lectures on these subjects every day. Finally, Pitts returned to the counsel table. "Your witness," he said, and sat down.

* * *

"You jerks gonna give me a lunch break?" Jack griped. He was sweating profusely, his shirt soaked through. "I'm gonna be filing a grievance. Union doesn't like us to work through lunch."

It was nearly noon, and the high desert sun northeast of Victorville, southeast of Barstow—mid-Mojave Desert—was baking. One of the two operatives, about thirty-five, dark curly hair regulation-length, unshaven, sat smoking on a long Joshua log near the edge of the four-by-six pit that was now four feet deep. The other, closer to forty and completely bald, stood near the excavation. Both wore nondescript gray T-shirts, one in khakis and the other in jeans, both with sunglasses. Jack was in the pit up to his waist, digging.

"Shut the fuck up and dig, Gramps!" the bald one shouted, flicking his cigarette butt onto Jack's back. "I'm gettin' tired of your mouth."

Jack turned and shook the burning ember off, then looked up at them, beads of sweat rolling down his scarred face. He could make out little more than a blur through his good eye. His glasses had fallen off on the way out of his flat, and the men hadn't stopped to retrieve them. "You guys are damn short on management skills," he said.

Baldy stood and walked to the edge of the pit. "I want about one more foot out of there, then you're done," he said.

Jack studied him, wondering what "done" meant. He doubted this was going to end well. These guys had him locked in a dirt-floor shack a couple of miles away for two days while they consulted repeatedly on cell phones, though he couldn't make out what they were saying. No matter how he had approached it, he couldn't get much out of them, only epithets and threats. God only knew what all this was about, who they were, where they were from, what they wanted.

They'd had him cuffed the whole time, except for meals, until this morning. Bathroom breaks had been a special joy. But digging a hole this size wasn't about a latrine. He'd seen maniacs in his unit throw trenching tools at captured VC and make them dig graves, then shoot them and kick them in. He'd heard stories from escaped GIs that the VC had similar rituals. No. This definitely had a nasty ring to it.

After taking a few more bites with the shovel, Jack pitched it out of the ditch and dragged himself, crawling without his crutches, up the side as the sand collapsed into the hole around him. Baldy stood and took a step toward Jack, but Curly grabbed his arm.

"That's deep enough," Curly said.

Jack mopped a sleeve across his forehead after struggling to his feet. "So you gonna tell me what this is all about before you do me in?" he panted.

"Turn around, dickhead," Baldy ordered.

Jack turned unsteadily to face the pit. "It's the least you can do. Ain't gonna matter anyway."

The younger man came over behind Jack as Baldy picked up the shovel. "It's about your country getting tired of you poking your nose into a lot of things that don't concern you."

"My country?" Jack was puzzled. "You guys Feds?"

"Indirectly related to the Pentagon," Curly said.

"The fuck—" Jack muttered. "I'm a vet. I work with other vets. I can't think of any problem the Pentagon would have with that."

"I can!" Baldy grunted as he swung the shovel. The last thing Jack heard was a deafening ringing noise accompanied by a blinding flash as he pitched forward into the red-sand trench.

* * *

Stephanie walked to the lectern, her trial binder open to the section on cross-examination of Dr. Edith Anderson.

"Doctor," she began, "shortly after there were concerns about the SSRIs, the FDA did a full investigation, as far back as 1991, and found no connection between SSRIs and suicide and other violent behavior, isn't that true?"

"I wouldn't call it a 'full' investigation," Anderson answered.

"Well, if you want to quibble over words, let's just say there was an investigation, was there not?"

"There was."

"There were extensive hearings by the U.S. Food and Drug Administration, were there not?"

"Extensive? I don't know about—"

"There were hearings, weren't there?"

"It was a whitewash."

"Your Honor?" Stephanie appealed.

"Yes, Dr. Anderson," the judge interjected. "Just answer the question, please."

"There were hearings," the witness conceded.

"Many thousands of pages of transcripts of testimony?"

"Yes, there were transcripts."

"You've read them?"

"Not all of them."

"But you've seen some of them?"

"Yes."

"Because this is your field, isn't it, Doctor? This is of extreme interest to you in treating your patients? In teaching your students. So wouldn't you want to read everything you could get your hands on that debated these drugs?"

"I said I've seen them."

"My statement is accurate that there are thousands of pages of transcripts, isn't it?"

"Okay."

Stephanie would keep this up as long as the doctor was demonstrating she was an advocate, and was avoiding the question, which was seriously undermining her credibility.

"And at the end of those extensive hearings, the FDA concluded that there was no connection between violence and SSRIs, did it not?"

"They did not see all the—"

"Yes or no."

"You have to understand—"

"Your Honor?"

"Please answer yes or no, Doctor," the judge instructed.

Long silence, then an exasperated: "Yes."

"Thank you."

"Now, recent studies have shown that there is no increase in suicide or violence with the newer SSRIs such as Zoloft, correct?"

"But they haven't—"

"Your Honor?"

"Okay, yes, yes."

"Thank you." Stephanie picked up a transcript and opened it to a marked page. "Dr. Anderson, isn't it a fact that you have testified in eight civil lawsuits against the manufacturers of SSRIs?"

"I don't recall the exact number."

"Shall I read your testimony in *Flaherty v. Casey Pharmaceuticals?*"

"No, I think that is the right number."

"And in all eight you testified to the same opinions that you are advancing here today?"

"Well, it wasn't always—"

"Shall I read your testimony?"

"Alright, yes. I testified about dangerous side effects."

"And in return for that testimony, and your preparation for it, you were paid by the plaintiffs' attorneys handling those cases a total of 1,786,000 dollars and change?"

There was an audible gasp from the jury.

"I don't know the exact—"

Stephanie held up the transcript.

"I think it was something in that range."

"And you are being paid handsomely for your testimony here against Dr. Samson, aren't you?"

"Well, I don't know what you mean by—"

"Seven hundred and fifty per hour plus expenses, including first-class airfare and four-star hotel accommodations during your three weeks in the Islands to 'prepare and testify.' Isn't that what you called it in your bill?" Stephanie had the bill from expert witness discovery.

Another long silence. "I think that's right."

"Thank you, Doctor. It must be nice."

Before Stephanie was in her chair, Pitts was on his feet again.

"You agreed that the studies counsel asked you about did not demonstrate any relationship between SSRIs and violence. But did they involve dosages ten times the recommended clinical amount?" Pitts had not done his homework as well as Stephanie and Noah, or he would have brought out the newer studies that cast doubt on the older ones. By trying to distinguish the earlier studies and the FDA investigation based on dosage alone, he was, in essence, agreeing that they were correct at the dosages used.

"They most certainly did not. They involved the recommended dosages."

"Thank you."

"And besides," the doctor went on, "there are newer—"

"Objection," Stephanie stopped her instantly. "There's no question pending, Your Honor."

Asaki admonished her to "Just answer the questions you are asked, Dr. Anderson. Mr. Pitts doesn't need any help from you."

Before Pitts could find any further traction, Stephanie was back up. "But Dr. Anderson," she said, "—would you also agree that there is wide variation in efficacy of the drug and occurrence of side effects with SSRIs depending on the individual?"

"Yes."

"Meaning that most people experience no untoward side effects whatsoever?"

"That's true."

"And this class of drugs, for the vast majority of people for whom they are prescribed, is highly effective in relieving depression and anxiety without any side effects?"

"Yes."

"You prescribe them all the time in your own practice, do you not?"

"I do, but—"

"With excellent results?"

"Sometimes, but I—"

"You wouldn't prescribe them to your own patients, who are paying you for your services, if you didn't think they would be of benefit."

"I prescribe them."

"Thank you, Doctor. That's all."

Pitts tried to repair the damage, but got bollixed up in the dosages and half-lives of the drugs, flipping pages of the *Physicians Desk Reference,* a monumental tome containing all the labeling information on all the medications known to man. Finally, toward noon, he gave up, and Stephanie agreed that she had nothing further for the doctor either.

"Very well," the judge said. "Thank you, Dr. Anderson. You may be excused. We will be in recess until two o'clock this afternoon. I caution the jury not to discuss the case among themselves or with others until deliberations begin."

As Stephanie packed up, Samson's face showed deep concern. "That was a very nice job, counselor," he said. "But can we get with the Hilo PD now? We still haven't heard anything about Noah."

Stephanie glanced at her watch, then examined the incoming calls on her cell, which had been off during the morning session. "I'll check at the office over the noon recess," she said. "They may have heard something."

The jail guard arrived and put a hand on Samson's shoulder.

"Time to get some lunch, Doctor," he said.

Samson turned back to Stephanie. "If they haven't heard anything," he said, "we have to get the police involved. I know we said we'd wait, but that isn't going to work for me."

"Alright," Stephanie said. "I don't like it, either."

As they walked from the courtroom into the hall, Stephanie passed Pitts. "Hey, Marvin," she said. "Go get yourself one of those frou-frou drinks. Looks like you need one. And try one on your expert while you're at it. She definitely needs to loosen up."

CHAPTER THIRTY-SEVEN

"EVERYONE CAN BE SEATED," Coyote said. The twenty bodies crammed into the large office, but small courtroom, shuffled into their chairs.

"Okay, Sgt. Slade, you can call your first witness."

"The prosecution calls Wiley Matson."

It didn't dawn on Reeves or Noah until Coyote stood and moved to the witness chair. Then Noah was on his feet.

"Objection. The judge can't be a witness."

"Why not?" Slade said.

"He has to remain neutral. He's supposed to decide the case."

"So why can't he be neutral if he testifies?"

"If he testifies for the prosecution?" Noah argued.

"He's just going to recall some facts," Slade responded.

"But—"

Coyote was becoming impatient. "I'm going to rule that I can testify," he said. "Besides, the other two judges are witnesses, too."

"But—"

"That's all there is to it. Somebody hand me the Bible."

Slade started his direct. Pacing, sitting, standing, twitching, it was impossible for him to remain still. Occasionally he laughed inappropriately. He referred constantly to wrinkled notes on brittle, dried-out paper on a clipboard he'd probably been putting together for years. Except for the sporadic delays and the rapid-fire delivery, the examination was actually reasonably coherent.

"Lieutenant Matson, do you have any current memory of where you lived before your military service?"

"Some."

"Please tell the court what you recall."

"I lived in Philadelphia."

"Do you remember your parents?"

"I think I do."

"Describe them."

"My mother was a nurse. My father worked someplace where he wore a tie. A bank, I think."

"Did you have sisters or brothers?"

"No, I don't think so."

"Did you attend college?"

"Yes."

"Where?"

"Princeton, I think. These things are a little vague."

"We understand. Were you an athlete?"

"Varsity football."

"What position?"

"Running back. I think I had a scholarship."

"How did you do at Princeton?"

"Pretty well, I believe."

"What makes you think so?"

"I don't remember flunking out." Laughter from the gallery.

"What was your major?"

"I don't remember."

"What year did you graduate?"

"No clue." More laughter.

"Were you married?"

"I don't think so, but I remember a woman."

"Who?"

"Beautiful woman. Marguerite, or maybe it was Margie."

"You were in the military?"

"Army."

"Served in Vietnam?"

"Yes."

"What unit?"

"Ended up as Army Special Forces attached to the First Cavalry Division, Seventy-fifth Infantry Regiment."

"What was the highest rank you achieved?"

"First Lieutenant."

"Did you go to OCS?"

"Army ROTC. Got a second louie commission when I graduated college."

"What was your specialty training?"

"Originally supply. But when I got to Vietnam, I was reassigned to Cam Ranh Bay and sent to Army Special Ops School."

"How did that come about?"

"I don't know, really."

"Did you volunteer?"

"No, I was sent to the Army Hospital at Cam Ranh for some reason. That part gets kind of hazy."

"And your specialty in Special Forces?"

"Ordnance. Wiring and remote detonation."

"You say you were sent to Cam Ranh Bay for some kind of treatment. What do you recall about that?"

Noah's pen stopped scribbling. His eyes focused intently as he leaned forward.

"There were pills, and some kind of therapy."

"Therapy. Psychotherapy? Physical therapy? What?"

"Hypnosis of some kind."

"Do you remember anyone involved in this treatment you received?"

"Dr. Reeves, here in the front row. He was my doctor."

"He gave you the pills?"

"Yes."

"What were they?"

He shook his head. "I don't know."

"What did they look like?"

"Blue capsules."

"Did Dr. Reeves hypnotize you?"

"Yes."

"How many times?"

"Many. I don't know."

"More than ten times?"

"Oh, yeah. Way more."

"More than fifty times?"

"I don't know."

"What did he say to you during the hypnosis?"

"I don't remember that."

"How many pills were you taking?"

"Two in the morning, two at night."

"How many milligrams was each pill?"

"Give me a fucking break, Slade." More laughter.

"How long did you take the pills?"

"Months. Maybe more than a year."

"Did you feel any effects from them."

"I don't remember anything specific. But I was sent to Special Forces and did some pretty crazy stuff."

"Like what?"

"Like blowing people away, killing VC with my bare hands, killing civilians toward the end."

"Did that behavior surprise you?"

"At first. After a while, you got used to it. Hell, I even liked it sometimes." His face showed no emotion.

"Can you give us an example of a 'civilian' incident?"

They had clearly already talked it through. Coyote was ready. "Coming back from a forward reconnaissance one night, we encountered a company of VC, so we had to find cover in a small village, couple of huts. VC was nearby, and we had to take out a family of seven."

"Take out?"

"Right."

"You mean shoot them?"

"Couldn't. VC would've heard."

"So how did you —"

"We carry knives for things like that."

Slade paused to let that sink in. Noah grimaced and glanced at Reeves, who was emotionless. They'd have to discuss his demonstrating a little more concern.

"Think very carefully, Lieutenant Matson. Did you have any kind of depression or battle fatigue before you were sent to Cam Ranh Bay?"

"No."

"How can you be so sure?"

"I don't think I saw any action before that. Seems like I was reassigned as soon as we hit landfall."

"But you did see action after this treatment you received at Cam Ranh Bay?"

"You mean after the pills and hypnotism?"

"Yes."

"Pfff," he scoffed, and waved his hand.

"When they stopped giving you the pills, did you feel any changes?"

"Even before that I did."

"Like what?"

"I started getting real paranoid."

"How do you mean?"

"Hell, I don't know. Just felt like everyone wanted to kill me all the time. Things seemed different. I couldn't think very well. I'd see things—"

"So your behavior changed?"

The objection to this as a leading question reflexively formed on Noah's lips, but he saw the futility of objecting to a question when the judge was the witness.

"I did some things, I don't know."

"What?"

"I went off on some people. Gave the order to burn down a Gook village. Things like that."

"I see. Was that when you stopped taking the drug?"

"Well, first I went back to Dr. Reeves. He was still at Cam Ranh."

"And did you tell him about your symptoms?"

"Yeah. He said to quit the pills."

"What happened when you stopped the drug?"

"Nothing."

"No change in your thought process or behavior?"

"Not really."

"Did your superiors put you in the hospital?"

"That was the funny thing. They kept giving me assignments."

"Until when?"

"Don't know, really."

Slade turned his stubbled face to Noah, eyes glassy. "Your witness," he grunted.

Noah advanced slowly, without notes; he thought for a few moments before beginning. "Lieutenant Matson, your memory hasn't returned completely, has it?"

"No."

"There are gaps."

"Some."

"Lots?"

"Yeah."

"You've just been recovering your memory over the last few months, right?"

"Right."

"There are some things in your memory you're not sure about, right?"

"Like what?"

"Like whether you were married."

"Right. I'm not sure."

"And like how long you took the blue pills. You're not too sure about that either?"

"No."

"Like what unit you were in before you got transferred to Cam Ranh?"

"I don't remember."

"That period in Vietnam before Cam Ranh is pretty fuzzy, isn't it?"

"It is."

"So you can't really be certain whether you had any depression during that time, before you were sent to participate in the clinical trials of Fuerontin—the blue capsules—can you?"

"Wait a minute," Slade objected. "He didn't say that."

"I know he didn't, I'm just asking him now," Noah said.

"It's okay," Coyote responded. "I can answer. I don't think I was depressed before Cam Ranh."

"Were you aware that loss of memory is a symptom of depression?"

"No, I wasn't."

"Now, Lieutenant, you don't know what the purpose of these blue pills was, do you?"

"No."

"You don't know if they made you aggressive or not?"

"I wasn't that way before."

"Football is a pretty aggressive sport, isn't it?"

"I guess."

"And in fairness, you don't know what those blue pills were, or what they did, do you?"

"No, I guess not."

"And you don't know Dr. Reeves's purpose in giving them to you?"

"No."

"Never even talked to him about that?"

"No."

"And if he told you, you don't remember?"

"Right."

"You don't know whether he was trying to treat you for battle fatigue or not?"

"I never had battle fatigue."

"But you don't know whether Dr. Reeves thought you did, or not, or what he was thinking as to why he gave you the drug, do you?"

Coyote thought about it. "I guess not," he said.

"Thank you, Lieutenant. Thank you for your candor and honesty."

CHAPTER THIRTY-EIGHT

"WE'RE GONNA KEEP GOING," Coyote ruled.

It was almost 8:00 p.m., and they'd been "in session" all day, breaking twice for sandwiches for half an hour. Garcia and Platz had testified. Though not giving carbon copies of Coyote's testimony, they had established essentially the same facts. Both were excelling college graduates and athletes who had gone to Vietnam and been immersed in some unknown kind of clinical trials, then had been reassigned to Special Forces and, after training, saw major action.

When asked about his tendency for violence after the Reeves treatment, Spic testified about an experience while attached to a division aviation group—S-3 sections in northern I Corps—training the RVN, Republic of Vietnam, troops. Their section was operating the group tactical operations center twenty-four hours a day, seven days a week. One night, he was off duty in his hooch, smoking a joint that had been painted with opium. He was pretty loaded and dozed off for some unknown time, then heard noise outside. Waking in a totally paranoid stupor, he peered out through the sandbags and saw movement along the nearby road. Despite the efforts of his hoochmates to restrain him, he grabbed his M16 and bolted into the night. Arriving at the road, he set his rifle on fully automatic and mowed down a line of humanity. He described the screaming and shrieking, which had had no effect on him whatsoever. When it was over, he sprinted into the jungle and collapsed. In the morning he awoke in the bush, and started back to the hooch. When he reached the place where the confrontation had occurred the night before, he found an extended family of Vietnamese dead on the road, eight bodies ranging from an elderly grandfather to three children under ten. Slade took him through the gore, the effects of automatic fire on the family members—the visible internal organs and various wounds, the positioning of the bodies, the crawl marks that demonstrated several had temporarily survived the massacre of their family members—and established that he had felt no emotion or remorse at all.

By now, Noah had spoken to Reeves about trying to show some degree of emotion, at least act the part of the compassionate psychiatrist that Noah was trying to sell him as. So as Spic laid out the grisly details, Reeves buried his face in his hands toward the end of the account.

Platz's story was similar. In 1969, he had been assigned to a training mission with the Ninth Infantry Division, which had been deployed from Ft. Riley, Kansas to Vietnam in 1966. Their responsibility was the rich bottomland of the Mekong Delta. When the monsoon season came, they were up to their asses in leeches, mosquitos, and rats. The rats tried to occupy the high ground simultaneously with the humans. Although he could survive the snakes and leeches, Platz found himself loathing the rats more and more. At one point, after he had been on Fuerontin for nearly a year and a half, he ordered the RVN sergeant under his command to bring in civilians from a local village and instruct them to clear the rats from their encampment. One night, after the job had reportedly been completed, Platz awoke to gnawing on his neck and ear. He grabbed a handful of the biggest rat he had ever seen, a foot long, which screeched and bit him. Totally overwhelmed by blinding rage, he staggered, bellowing, into the camp where he found the RVN sergeant and pumped a full M-16 clip into him, then pitched his body into the river. No, he had no remorse. No, he had thought little of the incident until recently.

Noah had difficulty believing what he was hearing. *Jesus. That drug was some kind of potent poison. From successful college kids, these guys had been turned into serial killers. What if they hadn't been in combat?* He sucked it up and cross-examined both witnesses, establishing only that neither had a clear understanding of Reeves's involvement from his personal knowledge. In light of the horrific nature of their stories, he thought it better not to get into anything that would allow them to get back into any part of the inflammatory testimony.

Slade told the Court he had two more witnesses planned, Barnes and Mitchell. When he called Barnes, Noah asked when the court planned to adjourn.

"We want to finish this thing as soon as possible," Coyote said. "We're going to be disturbed at some point." He turned to Reeves. "We'll get it done no matter what, but it'll be easier if it's not while we're holding off a battalion. We'll finish with Barnes and Mitchell tonight. Call Captain Barnes."

Ron Barnes was a tall, lanky, gray-haired man with an unkempt salt-and-pepper beard. His dress was disheveled VA issue. A little younger than the others, he was in his late fifties. He ambled to the witness stand, picked up the Bible, and repeated the oath, then identified himself, as he had seen the others do.

Slade formulated the first question. "Captain Barnes," he said, "you heard the others testify?"

"Yes, sir."

"Did you hear their testimony about their pre-service histories?"

"Yes, sir."

"And did you have—"

Suddenly, repeated burps of automatic rifle fire erupted outside. They all were on their feet simultaneously. Within seconds, the radio from the forward sentries down the road beeped. The bailiff answered and announced that Hilo PD was challenging the check point. No adrenalin could be perceived in the room other than that of Noah and Reeves. Of course, Slade was wired as usual. By the time Noah realized what was happening, the bush vets were moving briskly into the mess hall armory where, one by one, they obtained automatic weapons and munitions; then each assumed a pre-assigned function as intermittent automatic weapon bursts were heard outside. No rush, no panic, no conversation.

After leading Noah and Reeves to their rooms, Slade locked them down. Noah went to the basin and splashed water on his face. Outside, the firefight continued for an additional few minutes. He could hear automatic ordnance intermingled with single-action weapons. There was movement and conversation in the front offices. Then abruptly all was quiet again, the entire episode consuming less than five minutes. *He clearly wasn't going to get search-and-rescued tonight.*

Noah went to the bed and stretched out. Within seconds he was up and pacing. *How the hell had he fallen so far down this rabbit hole?*

It was almost ten o'clock when Slade returned. Noah was still pacing when he unlocked the door.

"What happened?" Noah asked.

"As predicted," he said. "Hilo PD."

"Was anybody hurt?"

"Not that I could see. I briefed these guys that we don't need World War Three here if we can avoid it. That'd only complicate things. They'd bring in air support and all the rest, and then we'd never get this trial finished."

Noah still didn't have a clear picture. "So what did the cops—"

"They demanded entry to the compound, and our guys refused. Cops don't do well with refuse, so they tried to bust in. We gave 'em a little preview of coming attractions with the M-16s, and they backed out. No big thing."

"But it will be," Noah said.

"Yeah," Slade agreed. "It will be."

"When do you think we'll hear from them again?"

"Well, they're out there calling in more fire-power right now, no doubt. Depends who they call, and how insistent those folks're going to be."

"Who do you think will respond?"

"My guess is National Guard. That's who hangs out at Pohakuloa. They're the closest, and they've got a fair amount more beef than the Hilo PD. But with the automatic weaponry we've got, and our guys using them, they'll never know what hit 'em. I mean, these guys are good." He smiled proudly, like a coach gloating over his crack defensive line.

They sat in silence for almost a minute, and then Noah said, "Why don't we call this thing off, Slade, while we still can? It's going to be annihilation."

When Slade looked up at him, Noah knew immediately there was no hope of that. The masseter muscles in his jaw were flexing rhythmically, his face a mask of hatred. "It's gonna happen, Shane," he whispered, and strode to the door. Then he looked back. "No matter what they do." He slammed the door and locked it behind him.

Noah couldn't sleep. His thoughts were a jumble of all the ways this thing could possibly play out. Every so often, he would imagine a role for himself in the struggle, what he could do, how he could do it. The ending was always the same: zero. His only thought was to prolong the trial as much as he could to give the authorities a chance for a serious move. *But what could he ask? What could he say? Was there anything these guys would believe that was in any way exculpatory? And if the verdict was guilty—hell, if? No, when the verdict was guilty. Then what? Appeal to a higher court? A higher power?*

He was exhausted, unsure how long he could stand the tension. His thoughts raced, and when things seemed almost to get away from him, that he was beginning to fragment, he found himself groping for a calming image, and he finally found one, always the same one. He would remember how Kate looked that last night, how she had insisted he go back to the Islands, do what was best for him and his father, even if it meant they couldn't be together. The thought of her steadied him, slowed him, and he would return to the present mobilized—until the next time. Thirty hours and counting. If only he could sleep.

* * *

He was standing in the well of an enormous courtroom, the walls of which were high and dark. In front of him, the bench stretched far above. He could not see the judge who was lost in the gloom that surrounded him. In fact, he could not see anyone, but he knew it was a courtroom, and he was the defendant. Consumed by fear, he was trying to make some kind of cogent argument on his own behalf, but he didn't know what to say. Still, he kept talking, trying to find a thread of passionate logic. Every so often, he would feel he had it, but when he spoke, it made no sense. He knew it was vitally important that he be understood, and as he realized the futility of it, his fear grew. He became increasingly aware that the judge was murmuring something critical. He struggled to make it out, peering and straining into the darkness.

Out of the murkiness, the judge's face was taking shape, a large, terrifying, unshaven face, etched with grime, its mocking smile missing teeth. The wretched filthy overcoat. Who? It was familiar, but he couldn't place it. Then suddenly, he knew.

"*Colonel,*" *he shouted.* "*Colonel Maxwell.*"

The whispering voice from above became louder and louder. Consumed with dread, he strained to hear.

"*The laaast daaay—*"

There were explosions, gunfire, distant at first, then ever closer. He stood there in the huge darkened courtroom, utterly vulnerable, unable to run, unable to stop it. The explosions came closer and closer. It was deafening. "*No—*" *he said, and then he screamed it,* "NOOOOOOOOO!"

* * *

All hell was breaking loose in the compound. Incoming mortar shells landed in front of the building, then one in the atrium, each with a deafening *WHUUUUUUMPH!* that seemed to suck the air out of everything. The explosions were punctuated by staccato automatic rifle fire.

Noah's eyes opened. He struggled for reality, his dream cogwheeling with events outside. Bounding from his bed, he ran to the window, searching the spaces between the boarded slats into the darkness of the atrium. *WHUUUUMPH!*, another mortar shell landed. He ducked and crawled back to the bed, gasping. Footsteps and voices in the offices up front and elsewhere in the building rose above the din of battle. On impulse, he shook the door. Nothing.

Panicked, he struggled into his pants in the dark. All he could do was pace as the incoming shells landed and gunfire continued. He could not tell if anything had struck the building, nor if anyone had been hit. The automatic fire became more and more intense. Utterly helpless, he held his ears and tried to focus on the face, Kate's face, framed by the loosely flowing brown hair, that beautiful smile that he loved, her voice repeating that this would all soon be over.

Gradually, the explosions slowed. The burps of automatic weapons became more intermittent, and finally stopped. He returned to the window. Through the cracks in the boarding, he could see the destruction in the atrium through the predawn dusk. He judged that two, maybe three shells had landed. Several jagged craters yawned where beautiful palms and ferns had stood, smoke still rising from the mutilated ground. Footsteps were moving briskly down the covered outdoor walkway. Suddenly the door unlocked. Noah flipped on the lights as Slade burst into the room.

"Morning," he said, grinning. "Pretty exciting wake-up call, no?"

"What's happening?" Noah demanded.

"It's the Guard. They thought they'd just overpower us with some mortars and a head butt at the front checkpoint. But we laid down a giant sheet of continuous fire all the way across the jungle, both sides of the checkpoint out there, and they backed off to reconnoiter. Exactly the play we had called in the huddle. My guess is they're phoning in for FBI reinforcements as we speak."

"This is crazy," Noah gasped. We're all going to fucking die!"

Slade's eyes ignited. "There's beauty in death," he sneered. "Maybe you'll be a hero. Now get yourself together. The trial's going to reconvene a little earlier than planned."

CHAPTER THIRTY-NINE

It was 6:00 A.M. in the visiting room of the EH Detention Facility in Hilo, and Samson knew immediately that something was wrong, because there was a pot of coffee on the table when they brought him in. Next to it, Stephanie sat dressed in jeans and a sweatshirt, flanked by two men.

"David," she said, "this is Deputy Chief Kimo Holomua, Hilo Police, and this is Major Simon Barton of the Hawaiian National Guard."

The room with the multiple gray visiting tables was empty except for the four of them. Samson's reaction was pure reflex.

"Is Noah okay?" The usually hooded eyes now burned with sharp concern.

"We have no reason to believe that he's not, Dr. Samson," Holomua told him. "But in all honesty, we don't know."

"What happened?" Samson demanded. Do you know where he is?"

The Deputy Chief was dressed in his usual khakis and aloha shirt. He was a large, heavy man in the Polynesian body habitus, with a currently severe visage, although the laugh lines made him seem likable. Major Barton was more serious. A tall man in his mid-forties, he wore dark green jungle camouflage fatigues. His wire-rimmed pilot's glasses covered chronically narrowed eyes, making him look more like an intolerant school teacher than a military commander.

"We believe he's at Kupuna," Holomua said. "But we can't confirm that under the circumstances."

"The circumstances?"

"Yes, Doctor. That's what brings us here." It was Major Barton who spoke this time, also looking unsettlingly grave. "Let me start at the beginning."

"Please," Samson said.

Barton described round one of the efforts to secure Noah's release. He explained that when fired upon, police took a defensive position behind their patrol car and briefly returned fire. One suffered a leg wound and was evacuated as reinforcements were called in. In light of the automatic weapons inside, the decision was made to invoke the Interisland Police Agency Alert, bring in the National Guard, and notify the FBI in Honolulu.

Samson put both elbows on the table and buried his face in his hands. Stephanie listened apprehensively.

"We brought up a light infantry company from the base at Pohakuloa," Barton said. "It's some twenty miles from Kupuna in the Makua Valley—"

"I know the place," Samson said impatiently.

"After deploying our assets, we called upon the occupants of the compound to lay down their weapons and come out, or we were going to open fire. We could tell they were well-armed and entrenched. Once again, they refused to submit, so we began tactical fire with small arms and some mortars."

Samson's head snapped up, his eyes squinting in a deep frown. "What in God's name were you thinking?" he exploded. "Weren't there other options? They have hostages, for Christ's sake. Was anyone injured inside?"

Barton paused, allowing Samson to gather himself. "There really were no options, Dr. Samson. If you don't move with dispatch on these matters, they deteriorate rapidly."

"They deteriorate rapidly when you open fire on mental patients, don't they?"

"Doctor—" Barton said.

"Was anyone injured inside?"

"We don't know. We haven't been granted entry. Fortunately, none of the National Guard people were wounded, yet. Only the one Hilo officer, and he's going to be all right."

"God-dammit!" Samson slapped an open hand on the table.

Holomua instinctively shifted his weight in Samson's direction.

"Look, Dr. Samson," Barton said, his voice measured. "I'm not here to argue protocols of engagement with you. I know this is upsetting to you, but let's just focus on where we are now."

Samson glared but said nothing. The enormity of his harebrained notion of bringing Noah to the Islands for his own selfish reasons, only to get him killed, was boring in on him.

"We didn't come here to simply report the status up there to you."

"Then what?"

"We agree that there is little to be gained from a full-scale frontal attack on the compound. These 'patients,' as you call them, seem to be highly trained and skilled in combat operations."

"They were all Special Forces and decorated war heroes in Vietnam," Samson said. "And by the way, they've been living a pretty marginal life for a lot of years, and they're probably feeling like they have very little to lose right now."

Barton and Holomua shared a look. "Ms. Kauna-Luke conveyed something like that," Holomua said. "How many of them are there up there?"

"Twenty-six. What did you have in mind?" Samson asked.

"We understand from Ms. Kauna-Luke that you have some influence with these men."

"Let me go up there," Samson said abruptly.

"Yeah, that's what we were thinking. Is she right that you have some —"

"Of course, I'm their therapist. And they're not only highly trained combatants, they suffer from a psychotic-like syndrome which is characterized in large measure by aggressive and violent tendencies."

Barton and Holomua glanced at each other again. Barton shook his head slowly.

"I'm not overstating this," Samson went on. "We were treating the condition and making significant progress until I was arrested, but I'm not sure what the hell has happened since I've been gone."

"It was our thinking that although we can't seem to gain entry without starting World War Three," Barton told him, "perhaps they might let you in."

"I'm sure they would," Samson said. He had to get up there. His fear for Noah was overpowering, but he also feared for Slade and the Fallen Heroes. He suddenly looked at Stephanie. "What about the trial?" he asked.

"I'll wait 'til you're gone and renew the application to continue. Asaki can't deny it with you off on an emergency mission at the request of the Hilo Police and the National Guard. He'll be forced to at least trail the case while you're gone." She looked at Holomalu. "I'll get declarations from these guys that you're needed up there." He nodded.

Samson turned back to Barton. "When do we leave?" he asked.

"As soon as we can. With what we seem to be up against here, we're gonna have to alert an airborne unit to bring in some Apache helicopter support, just in case."

"We'll get on the paperwork with Ms. Kauna-Luke and the logistics of getting you out of here," Holomalu said. "Probably'll require you to be OR'd." He stood and moved toward the door. "I'll get it in the works."

CHAPTER FORTY

"Call General Harley Reeves," Slade droned.

The court had been in session since six o'clock, and it was now nearly nine o'clock. They had completed the testimony of the remaining Fallen Heroes, and it was time for Reeves. He took the Bible and, after being ordered, he uttered the oath. Two days of trial, two prolonged pitched firefights with automatic weapons, and no sleep had left him pretty shaky.

Noah thought about objecting to the prosecution calling the defendant as part of its case, privilege against self-incrimination and all, but he knew there was no way he could talk them out of putting Reeves up there and pitching boulders at him. He'd gone over the issues and prepared him for direct, but now it was to be Slade asking the questions first. God willing, the General would have his testimony down pretty well and be able to withstand the twitching, blitzing onslaught. The toughest part of the case for Noah was always the cross-examination of his client, when he was out there on his own and there was nothing to be done to help him. That was why he almost never put his client on the stand. But on the few occasions when there was some special reason to call him, there was nothing for it but to smile and give the impression that whatever the idiot was saying wasn't hurting the case.

Noah's heart rate doubled as Slade approached the witness, eyes narrowed. Everyone in the room knew this was what he had been waiting for.

First he drew out Reeves's story about the whole thing being a well-intentioned experiment and clinical trial gone bad. Slade repeatedly returned to Reeves's purposes and objectives, and each time, the general repeated the mantra that it was all about a cure for battle fatigue, an effort to relieve the suffering of combat soldiers and restore them to their duties. He had no idea that it would bring about all this suffering. He never would have gone forward if he had.

Slade asked what he thought about the fact that each of the men denied having battle fatigue. They just didn't remember, Reeves told him. Depression plays tricks on our memories. If only he had the records, he could show them. What about Reeves's continuing to bring new men into the program and increasing the doses, after he knew that the effects of Fuerontin could not be reversed? Reeves protested that he never knew that. He thought the effects were simply difficult to undo. He never let himself believe the result was some permanent psychotic syndrome. For better or worse, he continued to have faith in the program. He swore it. There were even a few tears.

"So, Dr. Reeves," Slade asked again. "Your testimony on God's oath is that you never intended for these men"—he gestured around the room—"to develop this hyperaggressive condition."

"Never," Reeves said.

"You never intended for them to turn into sociopathic killing—"

The chirp of the radio from the advance checkpoint interrupted. Everything stopped as the bailiff picked it up. After listening a while, he announced: "Dr. Samson is at the checkpoint."

"Dr. Samson?" Coyote echoed.

Slade was grinning wildly. "Bring him in," he said, beaming, and then added seriously: "But make sure they understand, no cops, no military."

There was a buzz of conversation, and within minutes, Samson walked up the steps. The room fell silent as he moved through the men toward the front; then he turned back to take in his patients and the trappings of the Court Martial.

"Good morning," he said.

"Good morning, Doctor," Slade answered.

"Grayson," Samson said, and then, without hesitating: "you've stopped taking your medication."

"I don't need it now, Doc."

"Maybe," he said to Slade with his gazed fixed on Reeves. "I presume I will find out what this is all about?"

"I presume you will," Slade answered.

Before Samson could begin any kind of plea for restraint that might destabilize things, Noah thought it best to fill him in.

"I would ask the court for a brief recess," Noah said. "To—to talk to my father."

Coyote hesitated. "Be brief," he instructed.

"How are you doing, Sal?" Samson asked the bailiff as he took them back into Noah's room. "Looks like there's a lot going down."

"There is, Doc," the bailiff said. "Long overdue."

"Good," Samson responded. "That's good."

The bailiff locked them in, and Samson turned to Noah.

"Are you all right?" he asked.

"For now," Noah answered.

"I think I can guess what this is all about," he said. "They've recovered some of the memory of their treatment, haven't they? Fascinating that they would think of going to a Court Martial. Shows very high functioning. The SSRIs have apparently stabilized them enough to get it together."

"Slade said he wanted to have Reeves live through this whole thing—contemplate what was going to happen to him every step of the way."

"Figures. Did he tell you about his brother?"

"Yeah. Why didn't you tell me all that?"

"I'm sorry, Noah. I only told you what I thought you needed to know."

"Where have I heard that before? How did you get up here? What's going on with the trial down in Hilo?"

"I guess I'm temporarily released on my own recognizance. The Hilo PD and the Guard wanted me to come up here to see if I could talk them into some kind of resolution before there's any more bloodshed."

"More bloodshed?"

"One of the Hilo PD patrolmen was hit. Not serious."

"I don't think there's much chance of talking Slade down. He's pretty serious, and pretty gorked. Not a good combination."

"What did you mean when you said 'for now'? That you're okay 'for now'?"

"Whoever said 'First kill all the lawyers,' Slade must be a big fan. He says he's going to kill me along with Reeves, unless Reeves is acquitted of war crimes."

Samson's face was frozen, but when he spoke, the fear was suppressed. "I really don't think he'll go that far," he said. "I've known Grayson a long time."

"Well, he's pretty nuts right now."

"Yeah. He's bipolar."

"Bipolar?"

"His first overt episode was after his brother died. It was pretty well-controlled on Lemotrigine and Lithium, but he's stopped taking it. That accounts for the mania you see. He desperately wants the high-powered buzz this is giving him. Probably isn't sleeping, either."

"Then let's get him to take the damn drugs, I mean, he's dangerous."

"No doubt, but I don't think it would be consistent with his character to harm you. You're not part of his obsession with Reeves. I think his plan is just to motivate you to go along with this Court Martial."

"It's working."

Noah studied him. *This guy's living on the edge, playing the percentages, betting things'll come out like he thinks with the stakes about as high as they could be. Jesus. He's lived with the same ticking bomb I'm dealing with now all these years. He could've been killed at any moment.*

"Where are they in the Court Martial right now?" Samson wanted to know.

"Reeves is on the stand."

"What has he said?"

Noah told him about the general's defense of a misguided experiment.

"It wouldn't be good for him to testify any further," Samson responded. "I'm going to try to talk to Slade and hopefully end this."

"Why?"

"Trust me."

"More 'need to know' basis?"

"I guess so."

"Even if I knew what you were talking about, with Slade on this crazed vendetta, there's no way in hell you could prevent him from completing his cross of Reeves. Might make things worse if you lined up against him."

"Don't worry. I won't go after it right away. I'll pick my—"

Before Samson could finish, the bailiff unlocked the door, entered, and returned them to the courtroom.

* * *

With Reeves settled in the witness chair, Slade resumed his examination.

"Your adjutant is Captain Marcus Helms, right?"

"It is."

"Good man?"

"Yes. In my experience, men of his background may not always be trustworthy. But Marcus is."

Slade smiled. That had to please the three Fallen Heroes who were African-American, including Coyote. "Is he honest?"

"Yes. That's what I said." Reeves answered, groping to anticipate where this was going. "Very honest."

Slade handed him a document. "So when he signed this affidavit under penalty of perjury saying that the attached Memorandum Report was a correct copy of what you submitted to the Pentagon on April 14, 1986, that would naturally be a true statement, right?"

Reeves studied it. His breathing quickened. How in the name of God? What was Helms doing to him? He paged through the document, his hand trembling.

"I, I don't know. I submit a lot of documents to Washington. I'm a department head. I—"

"I get that. Just take your time. Tell us if you remember it."

Reeves again fumbled with the papers. "I don't remember this," he said. "Like I said, I transmit a lot of reports."

"Seems to be an epidemic of memory problems around here, huh, Doctor?" Slade was rewarded with a chorus of laughter. "Why don't we just go through it together."

Reeves forced himself to look back down at the document, as if hoping it might disappear if he ignored it.

"It would seem to be a 142-page report of these experiments on battle fatigue and the complications that occurred," Slade observed. "It's called Project Q407, isn't it?"

"That's what it says."

"Did you prepare this report? It looks like you signed it."

"No," Reeves retorted. "I mean, I don't remember—doing so."

Noah leaned forward. *What in the hell?*

Slade resumed. "Let me just see if I can hit a few of the highlights for you, Dr. Reeves. It seems that the whole thing started out as an effort to develop Fuerontin as an antidepressant for battle fatigue, am I right?"

"I—I already told you that."

"What is a paradoxical effect, Doctor?"

"The drug acts in a different way than expected."

"Right. Says here that it was discovered that in larger doses over long periods of time, Fuerontin had a 'paradoxical effect.' Tell us exactly what you meant by that."

"I don't—know."

There was no doubt in Noah's mind. *Jack was right. This was no accident. Christ, now what? It was all there. What could he do to stop this freight train?*

"I think you do. It says 'larger doses had the effect of creating massive aggression, violent tendencies, particularly in subjects with high muscle bulk and/or high concentrations of quick twitch fibers.' What does that mean in English?"

"I said I don't know."

"It means it acts more strongly on athletes, doesn't it?"

"No, I, not necessarily, it—"

Noah began to see it all. *It was the jocks, and the bright students he wanted.*

"So when you found out this drug made athletes superaggressive, you gathered all the athletes you could, particularly those with good grades, leaders in their colleges, or in the military, and sent them to Special Ops school. Then you turned them into supermen, soldier superheroes, didn't you. And you hypnotized them so they would never remember. Isn't *that* the truth, Doctor Reeves?!"

Poised to stand, to object, to raise some kind of hell, Noah was on total alert, but he didn't move. *No way to keep it out. Too late anyway.*

The general dropped his gaze to the floor.

"Well?" Slade shouted. "Isn't it?"

Reeves slowly looked up. "It could have been the greatest boon the fighting man had ever seen," he murmured.

"What? A boon? Is that what you said?" Slade jumped on it and blasted out the machine gun questions. "But instead, after a while it destroyed a critical part of their nervous system, didn't it? The place in the brain that controls aggression. These men went crazy didn't they? And you couldn't get them back, because there was damage to the brain. Isn't that the real story, Doctor Frankenstein? It's all here." He threw the report onto the desk.

"No, I—"

"And you didn't even try to stop the madness when you found out about it, did you."

"Yes, I did. I tried to—"

"The truth is—you kept recruiting more and more subjects into Q407, even *after* you knew all about the stuff?"

Reeves stared at him in silence.

Noah just sat there, slowly shaking his head. *Judas Priest. How can there be doctors like this?*

"And it gets worse, doesn't it, General? Like you allowed these guys to be sent into impossible situations, suicide missions, Rambo shootouts, which you knew they would accept because of their drug-induced passion for combat, for killing soldiers, civilians, children. RIGHT, DOCTOR REEVES?" He was within a foot of the witness, shouting relentlessly.

Now Noah lurched to his feet. "Your Honor!" he protested. "I object to the intimidation of this witness. I ask that Mr. Slade be admonished to let the witness tell his story."

"Back off, Slade," Coyote instructed. "There'll be plenty of time for the victory dance."

"Isn't that what this whole project was about, Doctor?" Slade repeated. "Taking geniuses with their whole lives ahead of them and turning them into military monsters? Wasn't that your beautiful dream?"

No response.

"Sure it was. And you sent Christopher Slade and three members of his team to get chopped up. In a sector occupied by three entrenched VC infantry companies. Sent them to radio reconnaissance information back to Special Ops command, knowing there was no way they could ever get out alive." The tears were streaming down Slade's face. "You let them be cut to pieces. DIDN'T YOU, YOU DIRTY BASTARD!"

"No," Reeves murmured. "I had nothing to do with—"

Noah stood again but Coyote intervened before he could object.

"Okay, okay," Coyote admonished. "Let him answer the question. What's the answer, General?"

"I didn't—" Reeves whispered. "I only gave the medicine. I didn't order anyone—"

Slade backed off slowly, sneering. "Ohhhh, perfect." It was long, low, and sarcastic. "You were only giving the medicine. You were the doctor. You were only following orders. Where have we heard that before, Doctor? And you know as well as I do that it's BULL-SHIT! Bull-shit for the Nazis, and bull-shit for you. You invented this whole process. It's precisely why you developed the 'experiment.' You killed good people, just as if you killed them yourself. These men"—he motioned around to the Fallen Heroes—"were your weapons, and your victims." He turned his back, shaking his head. "But they were also your patients, Doctor, and you ruined their lives!"

"Wait a minute," Noah remonstrated. "Is there a question, or are we just making speeches?"

"No," Reeves interjected before Coyote could rule. "I'm a a psychiatrist. My job is to help."

"Do you remember Chris Slade, Doctor?"

Reeves stared at him. "No."

"You don't even remember." Slade's eyes were blazing. "Probably too many of them to remember just one. Says here there were two hundred and eighty-six in all. Is that right?"

Reeves said nothing.

"And of two hundred and eighty-six men, only thirty-eight survived the war?"

Nothing.

"And you, Doctor. You recommended that they be sent here, to this backwater compound in the jungle of Hawaii to bury the truth—a truth that might cast you and your precious fucking monster pills in a bad light."

Slade finally paused, walked back to his chair, and shuffled through some papers, then returned to the desk and picked up the Memorandum Report.

"Who knew about the Fallen Heroes other than you?"

Noah objected again. He knew it was futile, but it was instinct. "Objection. Calls for speculation, no foundation, irrelevant."

Coyote didn't rule. He was waiting for the answer.

"Who knew, General?" Slade reiterated. "Who else was privy to this evil nightmare?"

Noah let it go. Hopeless.

"Very few," he said. "It was top secret."

"Not anymore, so please share with us—"

"My boss—several others at the Pentagon—and—and my co-investigator."

"Your co-investigator." Slade approached Reeves again, frowning. "Who else knew about all this? Who was this co-investigator?"

In the long silence, no one moved. Reeves's answer was definite. Without looking up, he said softly: "Dr. David Samson."

CHAPTER FORTY-ONE

DOWN THE KUPUNA ROAD, a safe distance from the check point, the major networks and the cable news, CNN, Fox, BBC, had assembled, talking heads all speaking feverishly against the backdrop of National Guard helicopters, various military vehicles, personnel, and hastily erected olive-drab operations tents. In studios around the world, engineers moved slides, threw switches, and created tape for later telecast and splicing into editorials and video news magazines. The vultures were assembled, awaiting the second coming of Waco.

Inside the compound, there was absolute silence. David Samson sat in the witness chair, wearing a look of resignation. Five feet from him, Noah sat riveted, struggling with the revelation. *So this was what he had meant when he said it wouldn't be good if Reeves's testimony continued. Slade had done it. He had proven that Reeves was the war criminal he had claimed. But worse, David was somehow involved. How? How could he have been responsible for transforming these promising college athletes into drug-crazed Rambos? Impossible!*

All eyes focused on Samson. The room was now packed with all the Fallen Heroes that were not essential to the defense of the compound. They sat on chairs, pillows, floor, anywhere.

Slade began the questioning slowly, establishing that Samson was in Vietnam and had worked as a co-investigator with Reeves on Project Q407. Samson said that he was first led to believe that the project simply involved clinical trials for Fuerontin, a so-called 'wonder drug' that he understood would be effective in relief of battle fatigue in the patient population with which he was working. Then Slade got to the crux of it.

"Did you ever find out that Fuerontin was turning GIs into violent Rambo-like soldiers?"

"I did."

"How did you find out?"

"While Dr. Reeves was away in Japan, I was asked to cover his clinic patients in his absence. I recognized one man from the Fuerontin trials, a decorated hero, who was experiencing psychotic symptoms, delusions, impaired thinking, loose associations, fears, panic. It looked like schizophrenia in some ways, but there did not seem to be any hallucinations, or other hallmarks of psychosis. I went to the chart to get his recent history and saw that these changes had come about gradually and that Dr. Reeves had suspected the Fuerontin. The patient's chart also mentioned that there had been other cases, and when I looked further, I found those charts. It shocked me that all these men had been participants in the Fuerontin trials. All had been outstanding soldiers, most had been decorated."

"Did you speak to Dr. Reeves about this discovery?"

"Of course. When he returned, I confronted him."

"What did he say?"

"He said I had no business looking at his charts."

"What did you tell him?"

"I told him he had to discontinue the drugs immediately. He said he already had."

"And?"

"I asked him why the patients were continuing to show symptoms if he had discontinued the medication."

"Go on—"

"He said that it appeared the syndrome was irreversible, that he suspected some Amygdaloid destruction, actual destruction of brain tissue."

"What was your reaction?"

"I was devastated. I asked him if he was continuing Fuerontin with any patients. He said he was, because he was hopeful that it would only affect a small percentage in this deleterious way. I told him we had to stop all the drugs at once and hospitalize the soldiers that had shown the lingering, negative effects."

"Did he agree to that?"

"Not at first, but finally he said we would stop all the drugs, put the patients in treatment, but he ordered me not to reveal a word about these findings to anyone."

"Did he threaten you?"

Samson sighed. "He said he would ruin my career."

"How?"

"He said I was a co-investigator, that I would be seen as having known all about the complications. We would go down together. I would be dishonorably discharged, and would never work in another hospital."

"Did you agree not to say anything?"

He hesitated, looking at Noah. Seconds went by as he struggled with the intolerable burden. He looked down and shook his head. Finally, he spoke. "Yes," he said quietly, and swallowed hard. "Psychiatry was my life. I was weak." Dampness was welling up in the corners of his eyes. "I am ashamed of my cowardice."

Noah's breathing intensified as he chewed his lip.

"What did you do then?"

"Shortly thereafter, I was transferred to the Army Hospital at Okinawa. I always suspected that Reeves had something to do with my transfer." He looked at Reeves, seated several rows back to the side of the room. He did not meet Samson's eyes.

"What happened to the Fallen Heroes?"

"I tried to find out, but I never could. They seemed to have vanished."

"And you still said nothing to the authorities?"

He shook his head again. "No. I never did."

"When did you next hear something about these vets?"

"After the war, at Okinawa, a nurse came through who had worked with us at Cam Ranh. She had stayed in Vietnam after I was transferred. She told me the men had been quarantined together."

"What was her name?"

"I would rather not say. I dated her for a while, and she told me that the whole project had been sealed and labeled top secret, that she faced court martial if anyone found out she told me. Besides, she's dead now and identifying her would serve no purpose."

"Did she reveal anything else?"

"She confirmed that Reeves had not stopped the drug, that many men had been sent back into battle, on terrible missions, when it was known they had extremely aggressive tendencies, psychosis. Many were killed. A few survived."

"So what did you do?"

"I felt unbearable guilt. Perhaps if I'd spoken out, many of those men might be alive. Now it was too late for them. I was tortured by it, actually clinically depressed for over a year. Then I made up my mind to find them."

"Find who?"

"These men"—Samson looked around the room—"The Fallen Heroes."

"Why?"

"I was obsessed with them."

"What do you mean?"

"If I could find them, I was going to give everything I had to focusing on their treatment, try to undo some of what had been done." He looked at Noah, then lifted his glasses and wiped his eyes. Noah looked away, struggling for composure, his throat constricted. *What could he have done? What should he have done? He groped for what he would have done in the same situation.*

"And you did you find them, eventually?"

Samson took a deep breath. "First, I called Reeves, who was by then at Walter Reed."

"And?"

"And he lied to me. Said he had no idea what happened to the men." Samson's voice gained volume as he looked over at Reeves. "He absolutely stonewalled me."

"Then how did you find them?"

"I spoke to a VA psychiatrist at a meeting on depression in Honolulu, while I was still stationed at Okinawa. He told me there was a position available at a VA compound in a remote area of the Big Island, working with a group of depressed Vietnam vets. I immediately suspected."

"What did you do?"

"I applied for the job. I resigned my commission and went to work for the VA. They hired me to take over Kupuna eight years ago. I guess no one else would come here."

"And that's when you hired me?"

"Yes, I knew your brother, Chris. He was one of the soldiers in the Q407 Project. I knew you had a special interest in these men, as I did."

"What happened to Reeves?"

"I assume he stayed in Washington until he came to Hawaii. I had already begun treatment with the men, and he immediately launched a vendetta to get me out of Kupuna."

"Did you ever absolutely confirm that the men at Kupuna were in fact the Fallen Heroes?"

"I knew. I think I knew it from the beginning. I tried to trace their histories, but there were no records. Then, when the men on SSRIs began to recover memories, it became clear. Reeves threatened me, had the VA bring disciplinary action about the drugs, then the Federal criminal prosecution. God knows what else."

"What do you mean?"

"Well, there were the missing records, and Bustamente's death. You and I always suspected—"

"Did Reeves say Washington was calling the shots?"

"He always said that, but it was pretty clear he was certainly a moving force."

"Even believing like you did, you still said nothing? Nothing to me, nothing to anyone to bring this so-called healer to just—"

Before Slade completed the sentence, his face exploded. The blast was deafening. Instinctively, Noah dropped to the floor, as the room erupted in chaos. His ears rang with an all-consuming, high-pitched reverberation shutting out all sound. In the blur of stampeding figures, Noah saw Sal, the bailiff, his weapon drawn. Two more shots and Sal fell, then two more. Screams came from somewhere behind him: "Nobody move! Nobody move!" Another shot, then: "Nobody fucking move!" Gradually the tumult subsided.

Noah pulled himself to his knees and looked down to see that he was spattered with blood and brain tissue. Taking several steps backward, Reeves panned the Glock nine millimeter automatic around the room. Reaching into the open file drawer next to him, he grabbed an extra fifteen-round clip. Samson took the opportunity to lunge from the witness chair and put a finger on Sal's carotid to check for a pulse. Reeves jerked the Glock toward him, then leaned down and snatched Sal's .45 Colt revolver and stuffed it in his belt.

"Outside," Reeves commanded, yanking Samson up by his shirt. "You too," he shouted at Noah, motioning with the Glock. One of the vets bolted forward from Reeves's right, grabbing for his arm. Reeves whirled and squeezed off another round. A stain of red bloomed on the man's chest, and he fell. Others moved in behind to block Reeves's retreat. The general snaked an arm around Samson's neck and jammed the Glock to his temple.

"Everybody back," he growled, and the Fallen Heroes backed away to give him room. Reeves wrenched Samson down the front steps and pulled him toward the parked vehicles as Noah followed. Continuing to press the automatic to Samson's head, Reeves crushed him up against the drivers side of the jeep.

"Get in," he shouted, then he brandished the sidearm toward the group of Fallen Heroes that was pressing forward on the stairs. "Stay back!" he warned, and pointed the pistol back at Samson. Reeves looked over his shoulder at Noah and barked, "Get in the back, now!"

Samson climbed into the vehicle and under the wheel. Noah threw a leg over the tailgate and squeezed into the back. Holding the Glock in both hands, trained on Samson, Reeves backed around the rear of the jeep and slid in on the passenger side.

"The keys are in it," Reeves yelled, veins bulging on his neck, as he again jabbed the pistol into the side of Samson's head. "Get us out of here!"

Samson started the jeep, ground it into reverse, backed it around the other vehicles parked in front of the compound, then swung it out onto the Kupuna Road. "Now what?" he asked.

"Khe Sanh," Reeves ordered. "Get us to Khe Sanh!"

Samson bounced the jeep down the muddy road, away from the compound and toward the barracks. When they had gone a few hundred yards Samson, eyes on the road in front and battling the wheel, said, "This isn't going to work, Harley—"

"Shut up!" Reeves snarled.

"It's madness—" Samson rejoined, glancing over at him.

Eyes glazed, Reeves swirled toward the back seat and pressed the Glock into Noah's forehead. "God—dammit! One more fucking word, and I'll take him out right here!" Noah froze. Samson stepped on the gas and the jeep surged forward. They jerked over the ruts and potholes, and Reeves turned back to the front and again pointed the automatic at Samson.

After ten minutes of lurching and rocking, the jeep entered the clearing at Khe Sanh, and Samson pulled up in front of the barracks. Before the vehicle had stopped moving, Reeves was out, running around the vehicle to the driver's side with the Glock aimed at Samson.

"Get out!" he shouted.

Samson and Noah slowly emerged, watching him.

It wasn't fast enough for Reeves. Face etched with rage, he squeezed off a round over Noah's head. "Inside! Move!" he screamed.

Noah and Samson both ducked instinctively when the Glock discharged, then both ran toward the barracks. Noah took the stairs to the front door two at a time, followed by Samson at gun point.

They stopped just inside the door, Reeves breathing hard. "Who would have believed this!" he spat, repeatedly checking outside.

"It's all out in the open now, right, Harley?" Samson said. "Quite a relief for me; how about you?"

"Shut the fuck up!"

"It's over!" Samson told him. "You can't get out of here. Those guys back there have already reached a verdict, and the troops out front will know you just killed three men. You can't keep doing this, running from this thing forever."

Reeves leveled the gun at Samson. "I can live with the rest of those whack-jobs surviving," he said, still panting. "Once they're off the drugs, they'll be back where they were. Nobody'll believe a word they say. But you, and Shane"—he glared at Noah—"that's a different story."

Noah cast a glance toward the back door, groping for possible escape routes. Reeves saw it and snapped the Glock toward him.

"Not a chance, Shane," he said. "You know I can't let you out of here. You're going to become two more casualties of the war, taken out by the Fallen Heroes." He looked back at Samson, squinting. "You pitiful asshole. You were willing to sacrifice the most important discovery in the history of warfare for a few lucid years for these lunatics. What a monumental waste."

"No, Harley—" Samson said.

Noah knew what Samson was up to. Keep him talking. Noah's eyes strayed again to the back door, then the front, the adrenalin pumping.

"You have to give it up," Samson told him. "They have the report back there. It's finished."

Reeves reached into the inside pocket of his fatigue jacket and extracted a thick document.

"You mean this?" he said. "I don't think so."

"But Helms has the original," Samson rejoined.

"I've taken care of Helms. I didn't know when I left to come back here that he'd given up the memo, but I knew I'd told him too much. So I hooked a little IED to his starter motor. He's done by now. And by the way," he said, turning to Noah. "Your friend Jack Donohue had a fatal mishap too, in return for his curiosity. So no one has to know anything about the Fallen Heroes."

Noah struggled to understand. *Wait. What did he say about Jack? What does he mean? They can't have—"*You bastard!" Noah rasped from deep in his gut.

Reeves took a step forward. "Stand against the wall. Both of you!" He took a position in front of them, a one-man firing squad. Raising the blue-black automatic with both hands, he stretched it out in front of him.

"Sorry about this, David," he said.

Reeves turned five degrees to his right and stuck the Glock in Noah's face.

"You will witness what can be accomplished with fortitude," he sneered.

Noah's fingers twitched, his eyes darting to his father, to Reeves, and back, his mind desperately grasping for something, anything, that could end the insanity.

A shot reverberated throughout the jungle canyon. The mongooses, frogs, and jungle birds ceased their chatter, and an abrupt silence settled over everything.

PART THREE

REDEMPTION

"Seeking to forget makes exile all the longer; the secret of redemption
lies in remembrance."

—Richard von Weizsaecker

CHAPTER FORTY-TWO

THE SUZUKI ROLLED TO a stop adjacent to the National Guard operations tent. Stephanie jumped from the bike, kicked the stand down, and pulled her helmet off as she jogged toward the entrance. Shaking her hair loose, she ducked inside.

"Major Barton," she said breathlessly when she noticed him standing over a communication tech. The Major turned.

"Ms. Kauna-Luke."

"I got up here as soon as I could. What's happened?"

"Okay, let's step outside. I'll try to fill you in."

Outside, the Major guided her to an area behind the tent where they were alone. "Dr. Samson went in right after we got here. Things were quiet until about thirty minutes ago, when there were definitely shots fired in the compound."

"Oh God. What was it?"

"No way of knowing. We're about a quarter mile from the buildings here. Our advance people are still over a hundred yards away. I've got no clue if anyone was hit. There's been no call-out made. We've tried to call in, but they're not answering."

"Anything since then?"

"After the shots, a jeep left the area of the main hospital building for some unknown destination. It's not clear how many occupants there may have been in the vehicle. I deployed my people into a containment position on the perimeter along with the FBI and the Hilo PD. We're going to hold in that position for the moment."

"What do you make of the gunfire?"

"Can't say much. We're guessing it was a sidearm. There doesn't seem to be anything happening now, no imminent threat at this time, so we've decided to wait to give Dr. Samson some more time to do his thing. No telling what would happen if we moved prematurely, brought in helicopter support."

"How long will you wait?"

"I don't want to guess, but if we hear further gunfire, or if nothing is resolved within a reasonable time, we'll be forced to move in."

"You mind if I hang around?" she pleaded. "I gotta know what's happening."

"Sure," Barton said. "Come on inside. We'll follow this thing together."

* * *

Diving over the fallen body of his father, Noah grabbed Reeves with both hands by the front of his shirt and head-butted him mid-forehead three times, each thrust punctuated by a grunt. "You mother—fucking—sonofabitch!"

Reeves was the larger man, but Noah was the younger, quicker, and more agile. He had Reeves by the right wrist, and slammed it on the concrete floor. The Glock slid, spinning toward the back door, and Noah lunged after it. Reeves pulled himself up groggily and went for the .45 in his belt, but Noah got to the Glock first. He snatched it, rolled, and fired at Reeves who was diving for the door, still struggling with the Colt. Noah scrambled to his feet and fired again, but Reeves was already outside.

Arriving at the doorway, Noah was just in time to see Reeves disappear around the end of the building. He sprinted after him and, reaching the corner of the barracks, saw Reeves already thrashing into the jungle. Noah took a step to follow, then stopped. Turning, he rushed back to Samson, who had taken the Glock slug in his right chest as he dove in front of Noah just as Reeves squeezed the trigger.

Kneeling over him, Noah could see that his father's lungs were filling with blood. His breathing was labored, accompanied by gurgling blood streaming in pulsatile gushes from his mouth. He looked up at Noah with the heavy-lidded eyes and coughed, expelling more blood.

Seized with a sense of utter helplessness, Noah began to pull Samson across the floor. His mind went to the jeep, how fast he could get him back to Kupuna. But then what? It must be miles to any medical facility. Wait—there had to be a medic with the National Guard unit.

"We gotta get you out of here," he said, on the verge of panic.

"No. . ." Samson's voice was barely a whisper interposed with gurgling gasps. "I'm sorry. . ."

Noah pulled on him again. "We have to-"

"Stop. . ." Samson murmured. "Let me. . ."

Barely able to hear him, Noah leaned down, cradling his head, his ear close to Samson's lips.

"Let me. . ."

Noah pulled back, studying the calm eyes, and the full comprehension set in. "Don't talk," he said.

"Have to. . ."

Noah leaned down again, his cheek softly brushing Samson's as he strained to hear.

"Now you know—why I didn't come—" Samson struggled.

As he rocked gently back and forth, Noah's tears were flowing freely.

"I was—so ashamed," Samson gasped. "I had to make it right."

"It's gonna be okay," Noah said. "We'll make it right together."

"Together..." Samson whispered.

Holding his father's head next to his, weeping silently, Noah waited for the rest to come, but there was nothing more.

* * *

It seemed an eternity that Noah remained there, embracing his father, emotion overwhelming him. Gradually the image of Reeves crowded out everything. Noah stood, the dried fluids from Slade on his clothes now mixed with his father's warm damp blood. He left the barracks, passing around the building, and into the jungle at the point where he had seen Reeves disappear. A few feet into the bush, he stumbled onto a trail and broke into a determined run, muscles taught, Glock in hand, fueled by rage. He scanned the thick jungle on both sides of path as he ran.

Rounding a curve, he thought he sensed movement up ahead, almost out of sight, and quickened his pace. Then he could see it, something on the ground, blocking the trail. Soon he could make out the body of a man, lying on his back. He slowed, readying the automatic. When he was close enough to see the open eyes, the protruding tongue, the blood-saturated blue shirt, he realized it was Reeves.

What the—? He squatted next to the body and ripped open the shirt to reveal a four-inch gash in Reeves's left chest just below the nipple. There was no pulse. *A knife wound, but how?* He was suddenly conscious of a presence behind him. He lept to his feet and wheeled to see the enormous figure of Ferguson, hands at his sides, staring at him with wild eyes, ten feet away. The giant's glance went to the body on the trail, then back to Noah. In Ferguson's right hand was the jagged-edge combat knife. A slight smile curled his lips, as if proud of the trophy kill.

Noah dove out of the trail and into the adjacent bush just as the massive man lunged. Scrambling to his feet, Noah held the Glock in front of him with both hands, its barrel leveled at Ferguson, who was rising slowly a few feet away. Noah steadied the automatic, struggling for a way to end this without shooting. He knew Ferguson was crazed, rocking from one foot to the other, emitting indecipherable grunts. In an instant the giant hurtled forward, and Noah reflexively squeezed off two rounds. As the psychotic vet went down, Noah could already see that one of the slugs had entered his face, just below the left eye.

* * *

"He's a tough old fart who's taken a lot worse hammerings along the way than the one he got yesterday."

The young, white-coated attending physician on the med-surg ward at Loma Linda University Hospital was talking in the hall to two heavily-tanned teenagers in cutoffs, T-shirts, and ball caps. One T-shirt touted the health benefits of cannabis.

"But he's lucky you guys came along when you did. If he'd lost any more blood, the old cat woulda run out of lives."

"Me and James just wanted to come down and check in on him, see if he made it—y'know?"

"Well, the official diagnosis is occipital skull fracture and cerebral concussion. Sounds impressive, but there apparently wasn't any bleeding into his brain. We ought to have him out of here in a few days. He'll be down for awhile, though. You want to talk to him?"

"Yeah."

"What's your name? I'll tell him you're here."

"I'm Snake. This is James."

The doctor went inside and emerged soon after.

"You guys can go in, but don't stay too long. He's still a little scrambled."

Jack was smiling as the two boys entered the room. Both of them winced when they saw his face.

"Nah," Jack chortled, pointing to his scarred face and vacant eye. "This wasn't part of my weekend in the desert. Goes back to another fun vacation I had a long time ago."

"They told us you're gonna be okay," Snake offered.

"So they say, that is if you can't die of a headache. What were you guys doin' out in no man's land?"

"Buggyin'," James answered. "We hang out there all the time."

"Damn good thing for me. Where you from?"

"Apple Valley," James said. "What were you doin' way out there? And how'd you hurt yourself?" He nodded to the facial scars.

"Cut m'self shaving," Jack said. "What'd you guys come all the way down here for?"

"Just to check you out, I guess," James said. "You didn't look too good when they loaded you on the chopper."

There was an awkward silence, then Jack said, "Listen, you guys into birds?"

They looked at each other. "Not really—" Snake answered.

"There's an incredible bird lives out there on your desert. Gambel's Quail, it's called. Been found from below sea level in Death Valley up to six thousand feet. It can take horrendous heat, dehydration, predators. Total survivor. Mojave Indians used to believe it brought good luck."

"So?" James wasn't following.

"So you guys're my Gambel's Quail. Hangin' out there in the desert. Hell, I'll gamble on you any time."

"Right," James scoffed.

"If you'll write down your addresses, I'll send you a coupla full-color portraits of that bird."

"Whatta we want those for?"

"Remind you of the day you pulled this old warthog up outta the sand." Jack propped himself up and looked at one, then the other, a bit more seriously. "You guys need to think about it. It's a once-in-a-lifetime thing to save someone's bacon." Then he smiled again. "Those same Indians I was tellin' you about say that you save someone, you're responsible for 'em for life."

"Sure," Snake sneered.

"Don't laugh, boys," Jack said. "I'm gonna hold you to it. And like you see, sometimes takes a lotta trouble keepin' old Jack alive."

* * *

"How long do you think it's been now, Major?" Stephanie couldn't stand it. She was about ready to mount up and ride into the compound herself.

Barton looked up from the monitor screen. He was standing behind the reconnaissance tech, who was manning a closed-circuit TV hookup that trained a telescopic lens down the Kupuna Road toward the checkpoint.

"Not long," he said. "I know this is tough on you." His voice was even, calming. "But we're going to have to wait it out. The FBI people, Hilo PD. We're all together on this."

Stephanie knew this had Waco and Ruby Ridge written all over it and that no one wanted to sign on to that, but she wasn't about to sacrifice Noah to some political do-right. God knew what was happening in there. It was going to be too late. "Dammit, Major, we have to do something," she said. "Things aren't going to get better if we sit here on our hands. They're only going to get worse."

At that moment, the reconnaissance tech leaned closer to the screen, squinting. "Major—" he said.

Barton looked back toward the monitor. He frowned and strained to make out what the tech was looking at. Stephanie rushed over and looked around the young man's shoulder as he jacked up the telescopic magnification. "There's definitely movement," the recon tech said, pointing with his pencil to a shadow beyond the checkpoint. Stephanie leaned in, straining, but could see nothing.

Barton grabbed the phone that lay next to the monitor. He crushed the lever activating the line. "Lieutenant!"

"I see it," came the response.

"Take alpha and charlie and get down there!"

"I'm on it, sir."

On the monitor, they could see guardsmen scurrying toward the road and shouting as they took up positions, waving press and onlookers back. Suddenly Stephanie saw what they were focused on. Now she could clearly see the movement, too. As she stared, the image slowly came into view. A line of men was walking slowly up the road, single file. Stephanie shrieked as she made out the unmistakable face of the man in the lead. It was Noah, carrying a white flag, followed by Coyote, Spic, Schnoz, and the rest of the Fallen Heroes.

CHAPTER FORTY-THREE

NOAH POINTED HIS FORK at the magnificent meal before him. "Anybody who can cook like this has a gift," he raved. "Amazing that you manage to hide it so well."

They sat over dinner on the deck outside Stephanie's flat, with Kane under the table between them. It was Noah's last night in Hilo, and they were celebrating: life, love, survival, the sunset, everything.

A warm evening tradewind nestled ashore. Noah wore the wild Hawaiian trunks he had purchased for his surfing adventure, and a white tank top. Stephanie's evening dress was a blue and black flowered sarong with a yellow orchid over her ear, acknowledging the importance of the occasion.

"Hey," she said. "Can't have just anybody know my delicious secrets. Might wanna marry me." She winked, then topped off his wine-glass. "So what are we gonna drink to?" she asked.

He thought a moment and raised his Chardonnay. "To Mondo Kane," he toasted. "Who lucked into a slice of the good life with a beautiful Hawaiian princess." Noah dug his toes into the Mastiff's fur. The huge head rose as the tail thumped.

It was ten days since the events at Kupuna, and all of it was still raw for Noah. Stephanie had been close, supportive, and had showed an encouraging sense of humor that kept his spirits up and his emotions grounded. She'd let him readjust at his own pace while he hung around for the initial stages of the Federal and State investigations.

Tonight the banter went on into the night. It seemed like neither was at a loss for words. Inevitably, things came back to the blue elephant in the room.

"How's the Feds' inquiry going?" he asked. "You get any sense of what's going to happen to the Fallen Heroes?"

"Marvin the pervert tells me there's not much interest in any kind of prosecution. Consensus is that the Fallen Heroes were pretty much victims of the whole thing. Everyone close to it in Washington's running for cover, claiming they never knew anything about Q407, or any cover-up." She took another sip of wine.

"Also, nobody wants to touch a prosecution that might be defended with the allegation that there was premature action by police and National Guard out at Kupuna. Gotta avoid the committee hearing hot seats that bubbled out of Waco and Ruby Ridge."

Noah took the last bite of grilled fish and savored it. "Good to hear," he said. "When do you think there'll be final findings filed?"

"The report won't come out for months, but we can be thankful about the best news," she said.

"What's that? he said, chewing slowly.

"The U.S. Attorney officially withdrawing the charges against your father."

He looked up at her. "Yeah," he agreed. "We got that much goin' already. I don't know what we would have done otherwise."

"Y'know?" she said, nodding at him. "I think Pitts may have had a hand in that."

"Nah," he frowned. "That guy'd never do anything right."

"Probably less out of goodness of his heart, than not wanting to lose some major case in an election year." She grinned. Her toes found his under the table.

"Maybe."

She went back to her plate. After a long silence, she said, "So, you gonna leave me tomorrow."

"I guess." He popped a slice of papaya into his mouth. "Back to my practice in Oakland."

"What kinda practice?"

Noah gazed out at the ocean. "Same, I suppose. I really haven't given it much thought."

"The psych cases?"

"Probably, if there's still a job for me."

"What's so great? Thought you said they were all homeless misfits."

"Yeah, well, there may have been some detective work in it I was missing. Take the guys up at Kupuna. They're pretty much homeless types, but it turns out they were all in college, headed for bright futures. See, they all start from someplace, and all that's not visible from the outside. I'm beginning to think I like the idea of giving guys like that a chance to make something good happen." Her expression was blank. "So," he said. "I'm getting too serious."

"Definitely," she countered. "You talk to your friend Jack since Kapuna?"

"Jesus." Noah looked up from his plate, canting his head to the side with a contorted grimace. "I feel terrible about that," he said.

"What's to feel so terrible? He's okay."

"I just keep thinking it was me who got him into this whole thing in the first place."

"It was your dad got you into it, but that's okay too, right? Needed gettin' into."

Noah smiled, taking her point.

"What did you and Jack talk about?" she asked.

"About how much it hurt to lose my father before we got all our baggage straightened out. That I felt like now it would all be with me forever."

She put a gentle hand on his. "And the guru said?"

"He said that things will fall into place. He told me I was lucky to have had the time with him that I did, found out who he was. He said we had a lot together in that short time."

She stared, then finally shrugged. "Yeah," she said. "That's what I woulda said, too." She got up and busied herself clearing dishes. "You want some coconut brandy? Make you crazy wild Casanova."

"Think I'll just stick with the wine."

"So, Noah," she said from the kitchen. "This Kate chick you so nuts about, you call her too since Kupuna?"

"Matter of fact, I did. Several times."

She returned to the table with her brandy and a touch of disappointment. "You gonna marry her?"

Noah heard himself say: "Maybe." It scared him a little, maybe more than a little.

"She must be some kinda goddess if this Aloha Island Fantasy can't compete."

By nine-thirty it was dark, but still warm, the ocean breeze wafting up from the water. Thanks to Stephanie, the Mai Tais, and the wine, Noah was finally escaping the reality. "What about a walk on the beach?" he suggested.

"Great. I'll bring the brandy."

They wandered the two blocks to the ocean, and along the white sand toward Hilo. A handful of surfers still paddled in the water beyond the point. They wandered through grass-covered Bayfront Park. In the dark, the huge Banyans with their dropping branch-roots looked like aliens gobbling up local life-forms. Lilting strains of steel guitars from a seaside bar drifted out over the incoming tide as they meandered through Liliuokalani Gardens and out toward Coconut Island. Stephanie took his hand.

When they reached the point, the high-tide waves were crashing ashore and washing far up on the sand. The breeze was warm and pleasant.

Stephanie tugged on his arm. "Let's go walk in the water," she said.

They splashed in ankle-deep foam as the breakers rolled in and receded. Stephanie pulled her sarong up to her well-proportioned thighs, then ran up on a dune and sat. She dragged Noah down next to her and he stretched out on his back, gazing up at the expanse of moonless sky, dotted with a billion stars, the glow of the Milky Way bifurcating the heavens. Her perfumed scent and the warmth of her body next to him were intoxicating. Now and again a shooting star flashed across above them.

She took his hand, insinuating her fingers between his; then she lightly squeezed. "I'm going to miss this, Noah," she said.

"Yeah, me too."

"It's been great with you here. Wish it would go on forever."

"I know. Like I said, a guy could get used to this."

"If you thought you could, I know Kane and I could get used to you, too. And that's a pretty strong statement for him, 'cause he's one fickle dog. Not like me."

He reached over and lightly pinched her thigh. "Right," he said. "You're just a one-man woman."

She punched him in the shoulder—hard—then jumped to her feet and sprinted for the surf with him right behind her. After several strides, he dove at her heels and pulled her down. They rolled over each other in the soft sand as she shrieked and pounded his chest. He came to rest on his back with her on top of him, looking down into his eyes, her long hair framing her playful grin. After a long moment like that, she said: "Never noticed how much your eyes are like your father's." His smirk melted. "Kinda sexy," she sighed. "Half mast." He stared a bit longer, then he drew her head down and kissed her.

Back at the flat, Noah brushed his teeth, then, clad in his shorts, he stopped by Stephanie's room to say goodnight. Once again she had adopted the island sex goddess pose—her full, smooth breasts mostly visible above the deep-brown Hawaiian-print duvet that almost covered her. *She had this down to a science.* Lying next to her, Kane lifted his head lazily when Noah appeared, flapping his tail several times on the bed.

Just as before, her dark, sleepy eyes looked him up and down. "You still one pretty man," she murmured.

He took a few steps into the room.

"Come on over with me and Kane. We can celebrate our last night together."

Remembering the fragrance and the feel of her, superimposed on the enticing vision before him, he struggled mightily. *Was he letting this amazing woman get away? She was something, for sure. But what about those too-many island guys who had succumbed to the same logic, probably in this very room?*

He reached out and tugged at her toes through the coverlet. "I gotta be nuts to turn it down," he said softly. "But I think I'm going to say goodnight—and thanks." He backed slowly out of the room as her eyes followed him, her face scrunching into a pout, but she didn't press it. Just before he disappeared, the corners of her mouth curled ever so slightly.

"I check with you again some day, okay?"

Smiling, Noah nodded. "Do that," he said.

Next morning, after coffee, Noah grabbed his bags and descended to the street to wait for his cab to the airport. Stephanie donned her leathers and retrieved the Suzuki from the garage, off to an early court appearance. After guiding the bike onto Lehua, she slowed as she passed him, stretching out a gloved fist, braking the big machine to a stop. "Aloha, pretty man," she said over the purr of the engine. Noah extended his own fist and bumped hers. They shared a smile as she goosed the Suzuki a couple of times, then loudly powered down Lehua toward Waianuenue, the jet black mane whipping from under her helmet.

CHAPTER FORTY-FOUR

THE LARGE TV SUSPENDED from the ceiling in the passenger lounge of Oakland International Airport was blaring as Noah emerged from the jetway, proceeding toward the concourse. The reference to "Fallen Heroes" caught his attention, and he wandered over.

"PBS News Magazine also discussed the Fallen Heroes with Brigadier General Walter Helman, a physician and Deputy Chief of the Army Medical Corps. Like the others, we asked him about Washington's views on this group of unique Vietnam veterans."

"Well, as I think you are aware, Margot, we have a vigorous high-level investigation ongoing into how all this came about and who may have been involved. We're looking into both the conduct of the original program, and the fact that it wasn't brought to light for over thirty-five years since the end of the Vietnam conflict in April 1975. It goes without saying that our Medical Corps, and the entire Department of the Army, believe that these kinds of experiments are totally unacceptable."

The balding general, in his mid-fifties, appeared in his dress greens with a blinding array of ribbons and a glittering single star on each epaulette.

"What are the preliminary conclusions that are emerging from your investigation?"

"The fact that we have been unable to locate any military personnel who were aware of Project Q407 leads us to the hypothesis that General Harley Reeves may have been acting alone. Obviously, our investigation is continuing."

"What is currently being done for the Fallen Heroes? The victims of Project Q407?"

"The Department of the Army and Veterans Affairs are collaborating in an all-out effort to bring these men home and return their lives to them. Of course, we cannot restore the thirty-plus years that they have lost, but we are informed that the treatment regimen devised by the late VA physician, Dr. David Samson, is an effective one, and it is therefore being continued. The Pentagon is hopeful that the remaining eighteen men will soon be released from the hospital and be able to return to normal, or near-normal, lives."

"What VA benefits will they be eligible for when they arrive home and complete their treatment?"

"It's my understanding they're already back here on the mainland, being hospitalized at the Veterans Affairs Medical Center in San Francisco under the care of Dr. William Siegel—an army expert in PTSD and other post-war psychological conditions. They will receive full military pensions, with back pay for the time missed. You can probably imagine that thirty-five years' lost pay will represent a considerable sum for these men. Those who want to work will be given training and placed in jobs in the private sector, or as civilian employees of the military, if need be."

Noah picked up his bag and continued down the concourse. He was passing a lounge several gates down when he glanced at its hanging TV, where the CNN piece was still playing. He saw his own face filling the screen as he was being interviewed, and paused again.

"We have been trying to ascertain whether any Pentagon personnel were aware of the facts surrounding Project Q407. To whom was this memo that you salvaged addressed?"

"It was originally sent to a Colonel Bart Hendricks of the Army Medical Corps," Noah heard himself say.

"Colonel Hendricks. Has he been contacted about the contents of the memo?"

"Colonel Hendricks apparently passed away."

"Then, was it possible to authenticate it?"

"I am informed that a Captain Marcus Helms, General Reeves's adjutant, was able to affirm its genuineness. It was Captain Helms who apparently retrieved it from the files of the Army Medical Corps."

"We were told that there may have been a recent attempt on Captain Helms's life. A car bomb?"

"Yes. Fortunately, Captain Helms was not present at the time of the explosion, although a motorpool maintenance man was seriously injured."

Noah moved on again, down the concourse to the stairs, and into the main terminal. He was still a hundred yards from the security gate when he saw her, and his smile was immediate and irrepressible.

She spotted him at about the same time, and their eyes met and held. He stopped about ten feet before he got there, still beyond the cordon, and stood a moment, staring. *Her hair seemed longer, down onto her shoulders, but how could that be? He hadn't been gone that long.* The gray-green eyes were flashing as she nodded the knowing smile he loved so much.

"Long time," he said.

"One month, nine days"—Kate glanced at her watch—"fourteen hours and—"

"Seems like a year," he responded, as he took the last three strides, dropped his bags, and embraced her. She threw her arms around his neck, and he kissed her, then held her close. Neither spoke. Finally, he pulled back and looked at her again.

"What?" She smiled, her eyes damp.

"Just taking a mental picture," he said. "I want to remember this."

"I might not let you forget," she said, laughing.

He threw the backpack over his shoulder and picked up the bag, then stretched an arm around her waist as they started for the car.

"So," he said. "How's by you?"

"I'm good. Don't need to ask how you've been. I've seen nothing but your face on the news the last two weeks."

"Don't you like me being a famous guy?"

"Works for a while," she said. "But let's not get into the tabloids."

"I don't know. Kind of appeals to me. Maybe they'll say I'm thick with Jennifer Aniston."

"Nah. She's not your type."

"Really? So what's my type?"

She smiled up at him. "Something more on the professional side, maybe?"

"I don't know," he scoffed. "Never went much for the pros."

The repartee continued as they reached the car. She handed him the keys to her Honda Civic, and he unlocked it. As he slid behind the wheel, he studied her again. *God, he'd missed her.*

"How's Sandy?" he asked as they pulled out onto Highway 80, heading for the Bay Bridge and San Francisco beyond.

"Why don't you ask him yourself? I told him we'd stop by the Oarhouse later. You up for that?"

"Uh—sure," he said, then added: "I just want to drop off my bags first."

"Right."

The door to the 'suite' was hardly closed before they were tearing at each other's clothes. The lovemaking was passionate, desperate. She kissed him hungrily, nibbled on him, pulled his hair, and sobbed through round one. Round two was gentler, softer, consumed more with longings than release.

When it was over, they lay still, wrapped in each other, glowing.

"You can't know how many times I've thought about this," he said.

"Me too." She disentangled herself and lay next to him on her back. "Noah."

Uh oh, here it comes. "Yes."

"Remember we said we were going to talk when—"

"I remember."

"Well, you're back."

He propped his head on an elbow and looked down at her. *The serious part. No way out.* "So," he said, "let's talk. Tell me what you think."

"No, Noah. I know exactly what I think, but I can't speak for you."

"What do you mean?"

"Just that, it was always you who were unsure, who backed away. So, now, I guess I need to hear from you first."

He looked at her for a few moments longer, then rolled over on his back again. *Hmmm. Time for Plan B.* "Okay," he shrugged. "I want us to be together."

"Meaning?"

"Meaning I want us to be—committed to each other, exclusively."

"Do you see that going anywhere?"

Jesus! What was he? A goddam ventriloquist's dummy? She pulls the little string and he says what she wants, if he could only figure out what that was. "I hope so."

He lay back and gazed up into the dark recesses above. Again, she didn't speak. *God. What was she thinking? No matter how long he lived, this would never be easy.*

"Kate," he started again. "There were a lot of heavy things that happened out there. I found my father and lost him, all in a few weeks. I discovered what his life had been, and found out a lot about myself. I mean, I was nearly killed, I saw him die, I killed someone. It shakes you right down to where you live."

He turned back to her and, in the dim light from the street outside, he fixed on the lovely gray-green eyes.

"But, through all of it, at the worst times I found out one thing was a constant for me." Her eyes were riveted, expectant. "It was you, Kate."

Tears welled up and spilled down her cheeks.

He took her chin between his thumb and forefinger and smiled. "Now, is that what you meant?"

She nodded several times quickly, but could not speak.

CHAPTER FORTY-FIVE

THE RASPY DRAWL OF a whisper came from his right, accompanied by the waft of a distinctive cologne. "Noah Shane. Man. Been followin' your career in the press. Too good for us courthouse hacks now, I guess."

It was late afternoon in Department 17 of Oakland Superior, and the 270 calendar was winding up. After some serious negotiations, Noah had been put back on his old job with the commitment calendar, at least temporarily. This afternoon, he had run out of cases early and had wandered over to the main courthouse, and upstairs to Department 17 where Kate was doing her thing, thinking to drive home with her in Captain America.

Noah turned to the impeccably dressed lawyer who had slid in on his right. The handsome smile was charming. The hand grappled Noah's in the slappy shake of the hood.

"Fill," Noah whispered with a grin, altogether pleased to see his former mentor.

"How you been, my brother?"

"Got my head above water, I guess. What brings you down to the deadbeat dads?"

"Former client ran afoul o' marriage and family support rules. Stopped in to check if he's on calendar tomorrow before I call it a day. So I'm hearin' you and Kate are an item these days."

Fillmore cast an eye toward the well where Kate was back-pedaling as usual, mid-pitch on behalf of the wretch on the witness stand.

"We been pretty tight the last six months," Noah told him in a muted murmur. He looked up at the bailiff, who was eyeing them and mouthing to keep it down.

"Hey," Fillmore said. "How 'bout I check on my case with this surly bailiff, then you and I duck downstairs for a libation? You can break down the marriage plans for me."

"Let's do it. Chow Ming Ling over on Franklin work for you? I'll leave Kate a note to join us when she's through."

"Deal. Meet you in the hall."

They sat in the back of the darkened Chinese restaurant, drinking white wine out of jam jars. Fried won-ton was in the works. It was 4:45, and they were the only ones in the place. "Never thought I'd see you get down to buyin' the license, man. You were my hero out there ever since I dropped out of the race. Figured you for the Hebrew Wilt Chamberlain. Workin' on the big two thousand."

Noah chuckled. "So, how's your practice?"

"Busy, man. Which is good, of course. But I'm going to have to do something about it."

"Meaning?"

"Meaning I've had a couple of big verdicts over on the civil side, so those are paying the rent. But it's increased the flow of referrals."

"Not a bad thing," Noah observed.

"Yeah, well. . . My mama used to say 'Too much of a good thing is still too much.' The referrals are gonna dry up if I can't service them. And shit, man, I could blow a statute. Then what?"

"What are the options?"

The waiter in a white jacket brought the fried won-tons.

"They're few." Fill drew out one of the Chinese raviolis and crunched. "You want a job?"

"Sure. Mind if I start tomorrow? Got some plans for tonight."

"No, I'm serious, bro. Last time I talked to you, you were needing a ticket out of the grinder, to my view."

Noah looked at him doubtfully, trying to separate the straight stuff from the seamless line of BS.

"Hear me out," Fill said, munching. "You got three, maybe four, years in? Had some high-profile cases, even got yourself a little ink of late. All helps the image. Couldn't be a better time to trade on that shit." He looked up and took another swallow from the jam jar. "I got more than I can handle of stuff you could step right into. I think it's time you took that leap I been tellin' you about."

Noah considered it. "Jesus, Fill, I guess I never really thought about it that seriously."

"Thought about what?" The female voice came from behind Noah.

"Ah," Fill said. "Enter the lovely lady lawyer, right on cue. Move over, you clod, and let her sit. Jar of the brutal white, Kate?"

She slid in next to Noah.

"Well, I think I've just been offered a job," Noah told her, looking at Fill.

"Not a job. A partnership. I'm offering to make this brother rich."

"What are you guys talking about?" Kate had to catch up. She extended a couple of plum-painted nails and delicately selected a won-ton.

Motioning the waiter for another glass of wine, Fill said, "It'd be a bit of a change you coming over to civil, but if you can try a case, you can try a case. I got a couple of major injury complaints screaming for someone to file 'em. I advance you something to live on while you're moving those suckers to the point where they pay off, then we share the contingency fees. You pay back the advance; the rest goes to overhead and a little sauce for the rainmaker from the hood. In a year or so, we go to a full split of the whole magillah. What do you say?"

Noah was still gaping. "You *are* serious." he said.

Fill turned to him. "Dead serious," he said.

Noah looked at Kate. Her finger was circling the rim of her jam jar-wineglass, just the hint of a smile.

"Well, of course I'm interested—" Noah said.

"So we have a deal?" Fill pressed him.

"Umm—just let me try it on till tomorrow. See how it feels in the overall scheme."

"A wise choice. Proving precisely why you're the right guy." He nodded toward Kate. "She's knows I'm makin' sense." He glanced at his watch. "Oh, shit, I'm supposed to meet Dolores for dinner." He grabbed another sip of wine, then stuck out a hand. "Call me in the morning. I'd really like this to work, man."

Noah nodded, as he glided through the complicated hood-shake. "Thanks."

Fill stopped for a word with the waiter as he left, slipping him a few bills and pointing back to Noah and Kate.

"He doesn't waste any time, does he?" Kate said as they watched him leave.

"So what do you think?"

"Sensational is what I think."

He reflected for a moment. "The only thing that hangs me up is that I finally like what I'm doing."

"Devil's Advocate, right?"

"You know it's not."

"Seems to me you don't owe the PD a thing. If it weren't for all that publicity you got, they never would've taken you back."

"It's not about owing, these guys I represent have become important to me, especially the vets."

"Excuse me, sir," the waiter said, putting down a bottle of Far Niente Cabernet Sauvignon and two glasses. "Compliments of Mr. Parks. He said to say it'll help you think."

"Be nice to get used to this stuff," Noah mused as the waiter opened it.

"Maybe you can do both," Kate said suddenly.

"Do what?"

"Vets and civil. Veteran's Defense Groups. You know, non-profits that provide legal services to indigent vets. You could work with Fill *and* volunteer with one of the NPs."

"Wait, non-profits? That give legal services to vets?"

"I think I've seen them appearing in my department. I don't know why it didn't occur to me before."

"Jack should know something about that, maybe."

She smiled, nodding, and raised her glass. "Parks and Shane," she said.

CHAPTER FORTY-SIX

NOAH AND JACK WERE lounging in the counseling chairs, ruminating after one of Jack's patented steak feasts.

"So what happened with that outfit I referred you to up in the Bay Area?" Jack asked.

"VA Legal Alliance. I've been in court with them one day a week for the last month. Guess you saved me again."

"Seems like a trend." Jack chortled.

"Doubt there's anything I can do for myself."

Jack shook his head. "You do have a knack for beating yourself up, Boyo."

"Come by it honestly," Noah said. "It's in the Talmud, y'know. 'Thou shalt smite thyself morning and evening.'" Then he added. "Speaking of 'smitings,' I still feel awful about dragging you into that Reeves thing and getting you a spade in the back of the head for your trouble."

"Hey, that kind of *tsuris* keeps an old soldier young. So keep your damn guilt-ridden Hebraic DNA to yourself."

After a moment of musing, Noah said, "Kate's flying in in the morning; how about we get her over here for a drink? Time you met her."

"Here? Man, you really are bringing her home to meet the family."

"You don't know the half of it. We're having dinner with my mother tomorrow night."

Jack's good eye twinkled behind the aviator glasses. "Now this is serious, not only bringing her to old Jack, but dinner with Mom? I thought you'd burned that particular bridge."

"Thought I'd give it another try."

"Wait a minute, another try is a Mother's Day card. Bringing your girl home's a whole different dimension. What brought you around?"

"David filled me in on some facts about her I didn't know. Turned out she had more going for her than I thought."

"Like what?"

"Like she had this lifelong dream of being a teacher. Times were tough after she got out of school, had me. But she was half-way through the credentialing program when Shane left the country, leaving her precious little. She clerked nights at a drug-store, even quit school a few times to work full time and lay aside a few bucks. Then her father got sick, and the house of cards came down. David was sending her a few bucks for me, but she was trying to send something home to her father, and what with the rent, the student loans, and this five-year-old that had gotten used to eating—"

He paused and looked over at Jack, suddenly conscious of going on at length. Jack was intent on the story.

"Yeah? And?"

"And she'd had this studio in little Santa Monica, not far from here, but she had to let it go. We lived with friends, but her father was in a nursing home that Medicare mostly didn't cover. Finally it all came unraveled, and she decided to pitch it in and marry the guy she'd been seeing. Wouldn't have been my choice, but the way she saw it, she didn't have options." He shook his head. "I don't think she ever got over it."

"Did she ever get back to teaching?"

"For a while, but when they moved uptown, the new husband didn't want her to work."

"She went for that?"

"Like I say, she didn't see a lot of options. It's made her a pretty angry woman."

Jack nodded slowly, eyebrows raised, extending his lower lip. "Apparently your old man isn't the only one who got his image changed."

* * *

Noah groped through half-sleep for his cell, which was chiming in the dark on the end table next to the couch. He picked it up and peered at the screen. 3:10 a.m.

"Hello?"

"Is this Noah Shane?"

"Yeah." Noah sat up, trying to shake out the cobwebs.

"This is Dr. Harold Johnson. Intensive Care Unit at San Francisco General Hospital. We have a patient here, a Lisa Sanders, who asked that I call you."

"Lisa. My God, what happened?" Now he was wide awake, feeling for the light.

"She's had some significant medical problems, Mr. Shane. She's asking for you."

"I thought she was in Minnesota."

"She apparently was, until recently. She tells me she just returned to the Bay Area with her daughter."

"Maggie. Is Maggie all right?"

"Yes," the doctor told him. "She's staying with friends."

"What's happened to Lisa? Was there an accident?"

"No accident. There's been some severe hemorrhaging, and she's developed a very significant blood disorder. It's called disseminated intravascular coagulation. We have her in intensive care."

"It's serious?"

The doctor hesitated a beat. "Very," he said quietly. "I would say that if you want to see her, it would be important for you to come right away."

"You're not saying—"

"I'm afraid I am, Mr. Shane. This is most definitely life-threatening."

"Good God. She's not even thirty."

"My suggestion would be that you get here as soon as you can."

* * *

It was almost 8:00 a.m. when Noah arrived at the hospital. He was directed by the desk nurse to meet Dr. Johnson upstairs at ICU. The doctor was walking forward with a hand outstretched as Noah emerged from the elevator. Dressed in a white lab coat over surgical greens, he was about Noah's age, much younger than Noah had expected.

"Mr. Shane?" he asked.

"Doctor."

He stuck out a hand. "Harold Johnson. Glad you could get here so quickly."

"How is she?"

"Unfortunately, she's deteriorated some since we spoke."

"Can I see her?"

"Absolutely." The doctor led him toward stainless-steel doors.

"Jesus," Noah said as they walked together. "How could this be happening?"

"She delivered a baby boy about twelve hours ago. It was a very difficult delivery. The placenta was blocking the birth canal. We did what we could, but she was bleeding before she got here. We ultimately had to do an emergency C-section. She lost a great deal of blood, and has gone steadily downhill since."

Noah was trying to follow. "Baby?" he gaped.

"Yes. She was almost full-term."

Johnson led Noah into the open ward that was playing a symphony of beeping and flashing monitors. Noah struggled for control as he passed the beds containing human shells clinging to life. Then he saw her. It seemed that a living face could not be that devoid of color, like a painted Japanese geisha. Strung with lines and tubes, she seemed so much smaller. Lisa opened her eyes as he approached.

"Noah," she murmured.

He put a hand on her arm, then leaned down and kissed her forehead. It was damp and cold.

"I had to see you," she said, struggling to speak.

"I'm glad you called," he said. "I want to be here and help you and Maggie any way I can."

She stared at him through several labored breaths. Finally, she said, "I don't think you understand."

"Understand what?"

"The baby."

"The baby?"

"Yes," she said. "He's yours."

He was still breathing. But in that moment, standing motionless in the strobing half-light, everything had changed. His mind was racing to catch up and process what she had just said. As his thoughts gained some semblance of traction, for an instant it occurred to him to ask how she knew, but he didn't have to. She knew.

She was whispering again. At first, he was not aware of her efforts to speak, but then it jerked him back from the depths of his near-fugue state.

"I planned not to tell you," she was saying, "to just stay in Minnesota." She gasped for a couple of deep breaths. "Oh, Noah," she whispered, attempting a smile.

He took her hand and squeezed, utterly devoid of any idea of what to say.

"I wanted this baby so much—" She stopped again to gather her strength. "My father died, and there was no one left back there. . . " she rasped, "so I. . . decided to come back—and now this."

"Try not to talk, Lees," Noah said. He took her hand in both of his.

"I've been told. . . I lost too much blood—"

"Shhhh, you're going to be fine."

"No, Noah. I know I don't have much time. I saw Maggie, but I didn't want her to be here at the end. I didn't know what else to do, so I had them call you."

"It's good you did," he said. His thoughts went back to his father's last moments. He could feel the heat of the tears welling up and wanted to dry them so she wouldn't see, but he dared not let go of her for fear she would drift away.

"I know it's not the best time for you," she whispered, "but I have to ask you..."

"What?"

"The Goldmans said they'd take Maggie, and the baby. . . . But Maggie loves you so much. Will you look in on them? Make sure they're all right?" She stopped and fought to smile again.

There wasn't an instant's hesitation. "No chance," he blurted.

Her half-smile faded. "What?"

"I'll take them both." He tightened his grip on her hand, an expression of resolve. "I won't have it any other way."

Lisa's eyes became moist, and she nodded feebly. "We would have been good together," she whispered.

"Yeah."

"He's a beautiful boy, Noah. . . They brought him in to show me. He has all that black hair of yours."

"Shhhh—"

"His name is Eric."

"Eric?"

"For my father..."

He pondered it. "Eric Shane," he said softly.

Suddenly Noah was startled by the blare of a horn on one of the monitors. In seconds, nurses were at the bedside dealing with the urgency of life and death. One grabbed him and pulled him away. His eyes met Lisa's. In later times, when he recalled that moment, he was convinced her look had been one of serenity.

CHAPTER FORTY-SEVEN

"IT DOESN'T CHANGE MY feeling for you, Kate. Nothing can change that."

At almost 7:00 p.m., an exhausted Noah stood in front of the massive windows of the neonatal nursery at San Francisco General. A tearful Kate stood next to him. This was not her finest hour.

Earlier, Noah had been to the Goldmans to see Maggie, and had spent most of the day with her. She was devastated by the news of her mother's death. He didn't want to rob her of her grief with so many changes all at once, but he did want to reassure her. In an effort to comfort her as best he could, he told her that she and her baby brother were going to live with him now, and that in his heart, she had always been his little girl. She threw herself into his arms and sobbed endlessly.

Late in the day, Noah didn't want to leave her, but he explained he had to go back to the hospital to make arrangements for things, and would return before she knew it. Then he called Kate and asked her to meet him at San Francisco General. He would explain when she got there.

They met in the lobby, and he told her about his relationship with Lisa. Most of it wasn't anything she hadn't known. He and Lisa had been friends for years. He had been fond of her. No, he was never in love with her, but she was important to him, and he treasured Maggie. There had only been the one time he slept with her. Kate had doubts, but he swore to it. He had known nothing of the pregnancy until that morning.

Then he told her that he was taking the two children. And that's when the tears began, slowly at first. He tried to hold her, but she pulled away. She said she wanted to see the baby, so they went up to the nursery. Now they stood there together, alone, in silence, consumed by the empty-full feeling that comes with crisis. The urgency, then the sudden tranquility, alternating between being tossed by the overpowering force of it, and drifting in the eye of the storm.

They stared, each of them contemplating the dark, curly-haired life in the plastic bassinet in the second row, third from the end, arms and legs jerking and wriggling randomly, oblivious to the members of his new found species who stood several feet away, struggling mightily with his future, his sudden being. "Sanders" had been crossed out on the little card with the blue stork on it, and "Shane" had been written in.

Kate was weeping quietly, sniffling every so often. Then she stopped. As a door opened and closed down the hall, they could hear the cacophony of squeaky cries from behind the soundproof, reinforced glass, then silence again. An obstetrical resident passed behind them, her white coat rustling as she walked.

"How could you do this, Noah?" Kate challenged him quietly. "After everything we said. We're supposedly serious about each other. Why didn't you talk to me before agreeing to all this?"

He didn't look at her. "I didn't 'agree to it,' Kate. It was my idea."

"But, why?"

The answer came immediately, as though he'd been thinking the words before she asked. "Because there was no other way."

"How could you? How could you not talk to me?" she repeated, the weeping beginning again.

"It wouldn't have made any difference. Some things are just not up for discussion." They both continued to stare into the nursery.

"Eric is my child," he said. "And so is Maggie, in a very real way. I hope you can understand that." That's when he looked over at her. He wanted to reach for her, but he knew it was better to let her find her way in her own time. "I really want us to work this out," he whispered.

Kate was absorbed, utterly transfixed by the crinkled little face, the perfectly round head, the diminutive nose, the familiar tight black curls. Other onlookers came and went, chatting, giggling, tapping on the glass, making silly faces and idiotic noises. After what seemed like an eternity, her soundless weeping slowed. Still focused on the curls, she sighed, and silently reached for Noah's hand.

He took it without looking at her. Another minute went by as they stood there. Still staring, he murmured, "Eric Samson."

Now Kate glanced over at him for the first time. "Nice," she said, her voice cracking just slightly. "Eric Samson Shane."

"No," he said, fixed on his son. "Eric—David—Samson."

EPILOGUE

"FILL SAID HE LIKED Parks and Shane better."

It was a clear, crisp fall afternoon. Kate and Noah sat on a bench at the San Francisco Zoo, watching the blond eight-year-old push her three-month-old, olive-skinned, brother in his stroller. The baby cooed contentedly, looking up at her, underlining the striking contrast.

"I know," Kate said. "He told me that, too."

"He said there was something less Jewish about Shane."

"Less Jewish?"

"Than Samson. He asked me how I'd like it if he changed his name to Washington."

"What did you say?"

"I told him Fillmore N. Washington sounds more like an intersection than a lawyer."

They came to a bench and sat.

"I don't know," Kate said. "I think Parks and Samson definitely has a ring to it."

"Kaaaate," Maggie called.

"Yes, Sweetie."

"Can I give Eric his bottle?"

"Sure, honey. Come on up and sit next to us. I've got it in the bag here."

When Maggie was situated, Kate handed her the baby, then the bottle. Maggie slipped the nipple deftly into her little brother's mouth, and he instantly began sucking hungrily.

"You're going to be a great mommy, you know that?" Kate told her.

"Being a mommy's fun." Maggie smiled.

Kate glanced at Noah. "Yeah," she said.

"Listen, squirt," Noah said. "Can you cover Eric's lunch duty for a couple minutes? Kate and I are going to take a little walk down to the elephant yard."

"Sure," Maggie said. "We saw a baby elephant in the pen. The mother was blowing water on it. It reminded me of Eric."

"Hey. Lighten up—" Noah pinched her and she squealed. "His nose isn't that big yet." He took Kate's hand, and they wandered off down the path.

"I love seeing you all together," he said.

"I love being with them," she said. "Who wouldn't? They're wonderful kids."

"I've been wanting to talk to you about that."

"About what?"

"Maggie loves you, and Eric does, too. God knows I do. I'd like to tie things up a little tighter between us."

Her head turned slowly, incredulous, morphing into frown-smile. "'Tie things up'? God, Noah. All these years of dreaming since my childhood. The romance books. All the magazines, the fantasies, the movies. I guess I never thought I'd hear it put quite so poetically."

"Easy now, I worked hard on this." He started walking again. "I know this has all been rough for you. It kind of descended on both of us, so I just didn't want to rush you."

"Damned decent of you," she muttered.

He snatched a glance and was relieved to see her half-smiling. They sauntered past another bench. He led her over to it. After a beat, he began again.

"I guess I was just thinking how wonderful you've been, not only with me, but with the kids these last three months. I couldn't have managed without you."

"Okay."

"And I know I've got to find a new place. We're all over each other at the Larkin and, well, you're having to come over all the time—"

"So?"

"So, I—I was just wondering how big a place I should be looking for."

"What are you suggesting, Noah?"

"You know what I'm saying."

"If you're saying what I think you are, about something permanent, then I need time to come to terms with all this." She closed her eyes. "It was pretty mind-blowing when this instant family was just dropped in my lap. Kind of a game changer. A whole new set of rules."

She paused. He didn't interrupt.

"I mean. . . " she looked over at him, struggling. "These kids aren't mine, you know. . . ?"

"I know. . . "

"I mean. . . " she looked down at her feet. ". . . just how much of a saint am I?" She breathed in and out slowly. "God. I just don't know. . . I've thought a lot, but. . . " She went silent. At least a full minute passed. There were distant sounds from unidentifiable zoo animals. The slight breeze played at her hair, blowing wispy tendrils around her cheeks.

Then she abruptly straightened. "Alright," she said with quiet firmness. "How about I give up the place on Hayes? We do this thing together for a while, then we'll see." She looked at him with an inquiring expression. "I have to make sure we really are together. You know what I mean?"

"I can understand that. But the most important thing to me is that you love me, and that you love them." He nodded back to where Maggie was mothering her little brother.

Kate inclined her head and frowned a little. "You know that."

"Then the rest will work itself out."

* * *

All staff members of the Department of Psychiatry at Tripler who were not on vital duty were gathered in the Grand Rounds auditorium by order of Colonel Arthur Roman, the new Chief of Psychiatry and acting Chief of Psychiatry for Veterans Affairs, Hawaii.

Colonel Roman, a tall man with an angular face and an aquiline nose, stood at the podium, wearing round, tortoise-shell glasses and a rather unfriendly, all-business, expression. Due to his height, his white lab coat seemed a bit short, almost like he was wearing someone else's. Head down, he was looking out over his glasses at the sea of faces, forcing a smile as he wrapped up his remarks.

He looked down at the dais in front of him, and up again. "I want to express my appreciation to Major Marcus Helms," he said. "For all he has done in making me feel welcome in the last few months since my arrival from Walter Reed." He looked over at Helms, who sat to his left at the head table. Helms was beaming. "Major Helms has attended to my every need. He and his wife, Sharon, have gone the extra mile to make Judy and me feel at home."

His attention returned to his notes. "As you all probably know from the scuttlebutt, we have devised some new clinical schedules and treatment protocols for the Department. I understand that these may seem complicated at first, but I believe that in the long run, they will make all your jobs much easier." He glanced at his watch. "I have a conference call in a few minutes, so I am going to turn the meeting over to Major Helms to brief you on the new schedules and protocols. Thank you for your attention. Major Helms?"

Helms rose, walked to the podium and, smiling broadly, shook hands with his superior officer. "Thank you, Colonel," he said. "And again, welcome aboard."

Roman left the auditorium and walked down the empty hall, turned right, and then into the office that bore his newly painted name on the door, formerly Reeves's office. The suite was empty, the office staff being at the meeting. He sat at his desk and looked over a memo in front of him, making a mark or two. The phone rang and he picked it up.

"Colonel Roman. Yes, Mr. Secretary, I was just reading it over."

As he listened, Roman swiveled his chair 180 degrees to the window behind him and leaned back to take in the view of the mountains. The discussion focused on the memo that occupied front and center, the only item on his desk. Then the conversation wound toward a close.

"Yes, sir," Roman said. "I think we can make it happen on that timetable. Yes, sir. I'll call you next week, after we sort out the scheduling. Indeed I will, Mr. Secretary. Goodbye."

He replaced the receiver and turned back to the memo, pen in hand. The words TOP SECRET were emblazoned across it in twenty-point red type. He scanned it once more to make sure it was perfect, then initialed it at the bottom to acknowledge his having read and approved it.

TOP SECRET

U.S. ARMY MEDICAL CORPS
MEMORANDUM

To: Colonel Arthur Roman
From: Assistant Secretary of the Army
RE: Clinical Trials of QM 437
Date: August 10, 2013

This will confirm our recent conversations concerning the clinical trials for QM 473, to be performed at the Army Hospitals at Tripler, Guam, and Okinawa. As you are aware, QM 473, formerly known as Fuerontin, will have similar actions, and mechanism of action, as before. That is, it will enhance courage and valorous behavior in ordinary personnel, but it is expected to be more effective at lower dosages. The purpose of the clinical trials is in part to confirm to the extent possible that reversibility is maximized by the new preparation, and that side effects will be minimized.

You are hereby ordered to ensure that QM 473 is ready for use in the field by January 1, 2014 with the specially selected subjects of the 101st Airborne Division. After preliminary treatment, subjects will be sent to the John F. Kennedy Special Warfare Center and School at Fort Bragg, North Carolina and, upon completion of that curriculum and training, be immediately deployed for service in the Afghanistan theater under the initial supervision of the 101st Airborne Command.

Please keep this office closely informed.

Date: August 10, 2013
/s/   Arnold C. Wiggen
Assistant Secretary of the Army

ACKNOWLEDGMENTS

As a newcomer to this landscape, I have many to thank.

It was my lifelong friend and mentor, Steve Cannell, who encouraged me to write about my imaginings in the first place. Steve was the consummate writer. More than forty network TV shows, eighteen bestselling novels, a studio to run, and still time to mentor his old pal. It was over cocktails and fresh seafood on the beach in Formentera, Spain, that we hatched the idea of Noah Shane. Truly a night to remember. Larger than life, Steve left us way too soon, and I miss him a lot.

I was fortunate to have the help of Sheldon Siegel, also a bestselling novelist, and an excellent lawyer I might add. I've read all his books, and I love his style. He was kind enough to read my early work, and he encouraged me immeasurably.

Thanks to my agent, Mitchell Waters at Curtis Brown, who stayed with me through a lot of years and many efforts. Wayne Williams lent me his great eye in the early editing, and Scott Heim lent me his at the end. Greg Mortimer's expertise helped make a complex process doable. Thanks also to those who provided helpful input after reading the manuscript, especially Vince McLorg, Dinty Moore, and Terry Tillman. Special thanks to my son, Bo, an excellent writer in his own right, who supplied so many inventive images, along with his invaluable ideas in stitching them together.

More than anything, though, it was the unrelenting, quiet patience and support of my sweet wife Marilyn that never let me quit.